I0603920

The Art of Cheating Episodes: S1E6

Ménages

EXTENDED AUTHOR'S CUT EDITION

HoLLyRod

COPYRIGHT

The Art of Cheating Episodes is a short-story work of fiction inspired by real events. Certain names, places, dialogue, characterizations, and incidents have been altered for purposes of dramatization and to protect the privacy and livelihood of all referenced or involved.

Ménages
'Extended Author's Cut Edition'
Copyright © 2022 by Angela Marie Publishing, LLC

Ménages
Copyright © 2017 by Angela Marie Publishing, LLC

Originally Published by M.O.B.A.N. Entertainment, LLC in 2015 via
www.HoLLyRods.com

Published for e-book/print under **Lurodica Stories** *from* **Angela Marie Publishing, LLC**

All rights reserved. No portion of this work may be reproduced in any form without written permission and consent from the publisher and/or author.
www.angelamariepublishing.com

ISBN: 978-0-9987197-6-4 (PRINT EDITION)
ASIN: B09VTKQK5K (KINDLE EDITION)

April 2012

The sharp lightning bolts flash first, before the loud thunder booms snap me outta my blurred memories.

I'm still staring at my bright phone screen, suddenly remembering to blink and breathe again. The sound of my heart thumping in my chest eventually starts to blend in with the rain and hail smacking against my fogged-up windshield. Any other time, I'a be flipping out about the mere possibility of hail damage to *My Precious*. But right now, I'm just stuck – frozen in time and space on the side of the highway.

I'm disappointed in myself. For real, doe. Cuz how could I forget about that true pivotal moment in my belligerent history? How could I block out such a defining point of no return in my overall journey like that? Is this what Dr. Julie meant when she said I got 'intentionally selective memory'? Did I block this shit out on purpose? What else have I rewritten in my mind about my past?

For all these years, I've told myself that the first time I heard the full-blown *voice* of my inner **beast**, it was with *Sassy* and that attempted ménage. But if that was true, then how did I recognize it with such clarity? How was I immediately so familiar with his voice and not confused when he spoke with so much ease that 'first' night?

"You getting old, nigga – like I just said. This is why you still need me."

He knows I ain't tryna admit it, but maybe the **beast** is right – yet again. At the same time though, this is why reflection is so fukcin' important. The real takeaway in this moment…is that it's all finally coming back to me now.

Like…really coming back.

I've felt the presence of my inner, darker spirit prolly from the moment I started getting erections as a horny teenager. In the beginning, like I said, it was just a bunch of vulgar thoughts from sexual frustration. Thoughts that I felt guilty for having at a young age…thoughts that I ain't think I should even be having in the first place. The thoughts then transitioned to quiet whispers in my head, and I eventually developed the habit of talking to myself, having side conversations either in my mind or out loud (if I was alone).

But back then, it was my *own* voice. And I mean, for real – I ain't never really think it was weird to be having conversations with myself. Talking yourself through or outta certain kinds of situations seemed normal for a teenager. In my case, however, most of those early voice of reason conversations centered heavily around getting my freak on.

See, before I lost my virginity, I was already obsessed with the idea of having lots of sex. I mean, I was watching soft porn before high school and then my freshman year I discovered my *Uncle Mike's* X-rated stash. With so much pent-up anticipation, my first piece of pussy was like a crackhead's first piece of rock – an unexplainable high that I was immediately addicted to.

It seemed like the more activity I got…the more my hunger grew. And let's be clear – in those early days, the opportunities to fukc came fewer and far less in between. But, like I said before, what Pops told me about the *Son's Curse* was real. As crazy as it still sounds, females were indeed always naturally drawn to me from as early as I could remember. It was just a matter of finally learning how to actually get myself *in* those positions of opportunity, and once I *did* – that's what gave birth to those self-talks in the beginning.

It's wild when I think about how simple shit was back then. But it's even crazier to think about how quickly things escalated in my sexual journey. Within what seemed like a heartbeat, I went from being a virgin who thought I'd never even get pussy – to a playboy chasing the fantasy of ménages and group sex. Then, before I could barely take a deep breath in that lifestyle, I was full-blown ***pimping*** – selling the same lustful fantasies that I used to chase like a fiend.

For nearly every step along the way, the whispers from my inner **beast** were front and center, trying to help me maintain control.

Yeah, man…it was always about me being in control. I can see that now.

In moments where I was in control the least…the **beast** energy grew stronger. Like when *Tianna* had me tied up getting tortured – that was my breaking point and I just felt completely helpless in that moment. So that was really the first time my **beast** *truly* broke out the cage…the first time I was turned into a real animal.

In the blink of an eye, my dominant and aggressive spirit had been unleashed. Suddenly I was more bold and vulgar than I ever knew I could be, with mannish energy and personality that I had never seen before. Hearing the separate voice of my alter-ego was downright scary at first. I remember trying to tune it out. I remember trying to act like it wuttin' there.

But once I decided to get back with KeLLy that following spring, I just couldn't hide this newfound side of myself. I tried everything I could think of to shake it off. I even stopped fukcin' wit Cookie for a while – thinking that my main side chick somehow gave the beast more power. That ain't help calm down my aggression in bed with Kells though, and it wuttin' long before she regularly questioned me about my new habits.

Naturally, she always had a bunch of insecure questions about where I had picked up this more demanding energy, and the conversation switched to accusations about Cookie every damn time. That shit used to piss me the fukc off – but what was I gon' tell her? That the shit ain't have nuttin' to do with Cookie and my beast was let loose when I was fukcin' wit some kinky chick named Tianna that I met off the internet? A bitch that me and the homie Tre ran a game on? Was I supposed to tell my girl how I lost control after I let Tee tie me up and pour candle wax on my chest?

Yeah right.

I already made the mistake of telling on myself to KeLLy about my side affair with Cookie – wuttin' no way I was gon' spill the beans to her about Tianna and the beast. Hell, I ain't know how to spill the beans even if I *was* willing to. I was still tryna figure out what the fukc happened myself.

"Man, how 'bout you figure out how to get back on the fukcin' road, nigga? We wasting time again."

"Shut up, nigga! It's only 4:04 – it's literally been two fukcin' minutes!" I mumbled, glancing at the top left corner of my phone.

"Yeah, and Sug prolly in Saint Louis by now, nigga! Quit fukcin' around!"

"Man, chill out — she ain't that far ahead of us, not in no two minutes, nigga. I'm just gathering my thoughts, damn."

"Nigga, you been doing nat all damn night! And the longer we sitting here bullshitting — the bigger dat head-start get! Come on, Holly — for real, doe."

"Aight, bro! I'm coming! Damn! Lemme just pop another pill and I 'a be ready," I start reaching in the backseat, fumbling around for my duffle bag.

"Man, just hurry the fukc up, bro. You stalling."

I know I said I was gon' stop popping these x-pills. And to give myself credit, I ain't took a pill to the head in damn near a year before this weekend with Sug. But shit, maybe I am addicted to these muhfukcaz like I'm addicted to the chase. Cuz once I was in the same room with *Skip* (the pill man) again this weekend — I had to keep a few to myself for old times' sake. I used to despise the very thought of getting high off pills — mainly because of how *Sashé* picked up the habit in those few weeks before she walked out on me.

"Yeah, yeah — nigga you was in a dark space when Shay left and you started poppin' yadadas! Ok — we get it! How many times you gon' bring dat shit up, nigga? Damn!"

"Man, why you doing me like that, cuzz?"

"Nigga! Cuz you keep going around in fukcin' circles! Is this shit about Sashé, Sug, or Kelly?!? Which one, nigga? I need you to make yo mind up."

"It's about all 3 'a dem, nigga! It's all connected!"

"Yeah and I'll be glad when you figure out HOW then — if that's the case."

"Man, nigga I know you see it, too! You know there's a point to all of this!"

"It's just hard to make a long story short, huh?"

"Exactly, nigga!"

"Man, HoLLy...gone and pop yo pill so we can get back on the road, nigga. I'm not 'finna do this with you right now."

"You always talking like you in control or some shit!"

"You always talking like I ain't, nigga!"

The thunder roared loudly, interrupting my thoughts and forcing me into another still trance. I gripped the bag of pills tightly in my numb right hand, but I couldn't feel the plastic. I hated having inner conflict like this — the imminent back and forth seemed to be never ending.

"Man, you got me fukced up, cuzz!" I bite my lip. *"I'm 'bout to tune yo ass out, for real this time, nigga!"*

"Yeah yeah...you tried that many a time before, lil nigga. We both know how that worked out."

"Man, whatever! Fukc you, nigga!"

"Fukc wit me, nigga! And when you done trying — get yo punk ass back on the road so we can catch Sug, bitch ass nigga."

Biting my lip in frustration, I reluctantly switch my hazard lights to the left turn signal as I open the plastic bag of ecstasy pills. I do need to get back on this road, so I'm not gon' try to prove my alter ego wrong this time.

"You got it, big dawg," I mumbled, putting my seatbelt back on. *"We can debate about this shit later."*

The time now reads **4:07am**. My eyes still feel just as heavy as they did a couple of hours ago and I can't remember the last time I slept. This whole weekend in KC been nonstop, all gas/no brakes. I can feel my body starting to crash, but this pill should at least help keep me up for the rest of the morning. Lord knows I'ma need the extra energy tank.

I'm just outside of Columbia, MO now and if I truck it, I can prolly reach the Lou close to 5:30. That's still later than I originally planned, though, so I can only hope that's still enough time to catch this bitch. Again, the fact that she don't know I'm only 45 minutes behind her should work in my favor, but I still need to hurry up, like the *beast* keeps reminding me.

"Let's go then, nigga!"

"I'm ready! But damn, can a nigga get his mind right, nigga?! Get off my dick!"

"Nah, nigga, cuz you keep thinking you gon' come to some profound conclusion with this shit, HoLLy! It ain't that fukcin' deep!"

"It is that deep, nigga! All this shit is related — I keep tryna tell yo ass, bro!"

"Man, you ain't talmbout shit, HoLLy. You just bouncing from wall-to-wall like a sloppy drunk!"

"Dawg, it's all coming full circle now, though — if yo ass just pay attention!"

"Nah, I'm paying attention — you the one been confused, muthafucka!"

"How, bro?"

"Cuz we already been over dis shit, bro! It's all about the side chick factor! Nuttin' else! I told yo ass just connect the dots about Carmen! Carmen is like a repeat of Cookie, nigga! If Carmen ain't tip you off about Sug like Cookie did about Kells — we woulda never saw this shit coming!"

"Nah, man…it's deeper than that, bro!"

"It ain't though, HoLLy! It's really just that simple!"

"Yeah, but what do that even mean then, bro? The Son's Curse showed me that Warrensburg sign déjà vü for **what**, then? Like for what **purpose**? That's what I'm saying. It's more to it than that."

"So, again, I'm asking — what else? What else have you connected after all this time, HoLLy? Answer me that! We been on this road damn near two hours, flashing back to irrelevant shit, my nigga. Break it down to me one more time then, louder for the beast in the back."

"Man, bro," I shake my head, swallowing one of the green Hulk pills. "You tryna be funny."

"Nah, I'm for real. Help me with the puzzle pieces, famo. Talk to me like I'm slow and stupid."

"Man, go to hell, bro!"

"I'm serious! Walk me through it again, HoLLy. So we can figure it out together."

"Ok, well for one — we saw the pics from Sug's diary, so we know she plotting."

"Right. That's why we pulled over — to look at the pics again."

"Exactly."

"And what did she say in the screenshots? Go 'head and read 'em again."

"Yeah, I'm pulling 'em up now. Carmen sent like five of dem muhfukcaz. Hold on."

"So, what did they say, HoLLy?"

"I said 'hold on' — nigga lemme pull dis shit up, nigga!"

"Aww, I thought you was 'HoLLy Digital' — what's really going on?!"

"Aight, so in the first one — she talking about running off with my half of the money we been saving, how she gon' make me let my guard down so I never see it coming."

"Nah — read 'em verbatim, nigga!"

"For what, nigga?! You just said niggaz ain't got time for all'at! We gotta get back on the road, remember?"

"So, you on some hoe shit now, nigga? Get out yo feelings!"

"Nah — that's what you keep saying, bitch ass nigga!"

"You know we need to hurry up, so don't be a lil bitch about it! I'm just tryna make sure you ain't pull over for no reason. I'm just tryna have yo back, dawg."

"See, now you mocking me."

"Nah, real shit, brodie. You ain't gotta read 'em verbatim, it's cool. So what else did the screenshots say, HoLLy? You can read and drive — just don't drop the phone again."

I ignored his pettiness and pulled back out onto the road with caution, *"Then she start talking about how the Italian been helping her put together her exit plan. She calls her plan* **Operation Anew.***"*

"And you don't think Lorenzo is the Italian?"

"I ain't decided yet. I mean, yeah — you know I thought it was him at first, but…"

"But Carmen pointed out that Sug ain't say his name."

"Right. Exactly. And when I first read that shit, I automatically was thinking that Sug gotta be snaking me cuz of the Silent Promise."

"The Silent Promise to Sashé. You still think tonight is our karma for that?"

"Well, no. I mean, at first I did. But then I saw the Warrensburg sign."

"The déjà vü."

"The déjà vü. That's when I peeped the Son's Curse tryna remind me of something deeper."

"And that made you start thinking about KeLLy."

"Yeah, nigga. The shit was obvious. The highway, the sign, the emotions — you can't tell me tonight don't feel like a replay of KeLLy's Revenge, bruh."

"But for what PURPOSE, HoLLy? So, now you think the Curse is saying tonight is karma for Kells…instead of for how we did Shay with the Silent Promise, right?"

"I mean — it just made me start thinking about everything again. Like everything that we did with KeLLy, leading up to Sashé and then the Promise. Cuz why was I even being reminded of Kells and that night? That was years ago."

"Ok — dig that. But see, that's why I said it's just on some 'side chick appreciation' shit, though. Cookie tipped you off to KeLLy's Revenge and you hopped on the highway. This time, tonight, Carmen tipped you off to Sug's plot…and you hopped on the highway again, like before. Case solved."

"Man, nah. A déjà vü means I **missed** something. A key point…a lesson…SOMETHING."

"See, man, here you go."

"For real, dawg. You know it work like dat. I gotta retrace **everything**. How I got addicted to sex, how I started with this cheating shit, how I got turned on to the Dom life, how you got so strong…"

"You on dat bullshit, HoLLy…"

"Am I the rebirth of Grandpa Jerry? Was Pops wrong about me getting into music? I just got some many questions now."

"You doing it again, dawg…"

"Cuz how the fukc did I end up **here** again? It's like a pattern at this point. KeLLy hurt my pride and I started chasing ménages…leading me to Sashé and the music. Shay left me in the cold…and next thing you know, I'm helping Sug sell pussy! It's like I take it a step further…every time. Like, I always gotta find a way to feel like I got the upper hand again. Knowing all the dirt I've done, instead of just charging it to the game and taking a 'L' when I get burnt — I always got you in my ear, pushing the limit."

"So, now you back to blaming me for everything again..."

"Man, see dat's what I'm saying — I'm not just blaming you for everything, bro. I'm saying — one thing always led to another. And if I can get to the root of all this shit — I can figure out what the Curse is really warning me about. If I'm completely in tune with my reality...I can figure out the best way to stop Sug."

"Nigga, we already figured out how we gon' stop Sug! We gon' make this bitch bleed for crossing us!"

"But what if it's a better way? If we follow through with this shit — you know it ain't no turning back."

"It already ain't no turning back, HoLLy. Ain't no better way. Just get out yo own head and let this shit play out like it's supposed to."

"Man...nah, bro. That's what you always be on."

"Cuz it's true, nigga! Everything always plays out the way it's supposed to."

"Until it don't, nigga!"

"Man, you telling me you ain't enjoyed this ride we been on, nigga? You telling me you regret going after yo biggest fantasy?"

"I didn't say dat, bro. I'm saying I missed something!"

"If anything, you missing the most important point in all of this, HoLLy! You needed a girl like Sashé in yo life when Kells broke our trust. Chasing the ménages was prolly the best thing that coulda happened to you."

"Man, what?! What the fukc you mean, bro? You on some bullshit!"

"*Think about it. If Shay don't lead you to the threesomes, then we never woulda met George and Carol. Remember them, loverboy? Think about all the money opportunities they put us on to — shit, even the party just this weekend! Come on, HoLLy — you know I ain't lying.*"

"*The swinger couple, nigga?!?*"

"*Bingo! The MONEY couple, nigga! Tha fuke?!*"

"*Aww, nigga — whatever! All money ain't good money, fool. Obviously. That's what I mean. The shit was less complex before the money chasing, and you know dat.*"

"*Man, please! So you 'ont remember the night we met George and Carol?*"

"*Man, stop playing — you know I do.*"

"*Everything leading up to the night we met them was complex, nigga.*"

I slowly drifted off in a starry gaze once more, recalling, "*Not the way I remember it.*"

"*Then how do you remember it, HoLLyRod?*" the beast snapped with sheer sarcasm, before posing yet another distraction of a challenge. "*You got the floor again, go 'head. Take us back to when HoLLy met swingers...*"

I turned my nose up in confusing disapproval, irritated at the beast's mention of the older white swinger couple. I been trying my best not to even think about them tonight. But, whether he knew it or not, the full story of how I met *George and Carol* — the nightclub owners and event planners who hosted *OG Marshall's* party this past weekend – was more than worthy of a flashback…

*   *   *   *   *

…to be continued in TAOC Episodes S1E6

*Have you ever seen a picture or a portrait —
full of beautiful color and intricate detail, so
complex and deep, and exploding with pure
artistry???? Give it but a glance and you'll never
appreciate the true brilliance behind it.
Yet…stare at it for too long….and you'll
become consumed by its mystique and engrossed
to near obsession.*

Cheating is a work of art.

This…
*…is the masterpiece that I've always liked to
call…*

The Art of Cheating

1

It's almost time to start heading out. But a few moments ago, something strange came over me and I got lost in an unexplainable trance. So, I'm standing in the bathroom mirror now – reminiscing about my ***ménages***...

"It's crazy how the tables can turn so fast," I mutter under my breath, slightly shaking my head as my memories start to wander into the not-so-distant past…

*   *   *   *   *

September 2005

When KeLLy and I finally broke it off for the last time…it was awkward.

We grew apart. Things just…changed. The both of us were holding on to what we had and refusing to let go. You know how Usher said, *'let it burn'?* That shit is much easier said than done.

KeLLy was my heart and soul…and for a while we were the best of friends, even with all the creeping I was doing on the side. Late in our relationship…the cheating had become my next addiction after being hooked on sex.

Being unfaithful turned into a nasty habit I just couldn't seem to break. Relapsing with ***Sassy*** had lasting effects and awakened something in me I thought I successfully caged away. But I had gotten so used to the idea of having hoes on the side and having what I deemed as necessary fun, that I reached a point where it felt like it had *no negative effects* on my relationship at home with Kells.

I know that's hard to believe, but lemme try to explain.

See, the night of **KeLLy's Revenge** was profound for me. I mean – I know I keep going back to it, but that night was so profound in the sense that Kells gave me actual *reasons* why she was getting her creep on. Those words she said that night never left my head, and I took real heed to 'em:

"I love the way you used to treat me…"

"You used to make me feel like nothing else mattered."

"It's not the same, Rodney, it ain't been the same all semester. You used to leave me little love notes all over the place…all the time – that used to just make my day!"

"The poems you used to write me. How you would surprise me with dinner…surprise deliveries. Every other day, every other week…you used to make me feel so special, Rodney."

"When's the last time you gave me a massage? Or a foot rub?"

"You know how I feel about you, Rodney! How I break my fukcing neck and back to make sure you happy and taken care of!"

*"…you know I like to feel special, appreciated. And you know better than anybody how to make me feel like that…you **know** me, Rodney. So why don't you? Why let me feel unappreciated lately? You ever stop to think about **why** I would be doing all this?"*

All'at shit she yelled at me that night made perfect sense. It was essentially one of the first rules to keep in mind in **The Art of Cheating** – YOU HAVE TO TAKE CARE OF HOME.

With KeLLy, because of my unbreakable habit, I lost touch with home and got sloppy. And honestly, it woulda been the same with any *other* habit if it wuttin' *cheating*. Think of your worst habit, or group of habits for that matter. If you ever find yaself at the point where yo habits are causing stress and drama at home, it's time to get a better hold on ya habits. It's that simple.

KeLLy and I got back together a few weeks after shit hit the fan with *the HooKup* and *Tianna*. That Tianna situation sparked two things in me – the initial uncaging of my sexual **beast**…and the guilt that came along with it. The guilt that *should* have come along with it all…all along.

That guilt was my key to becoming a better man at home for KeLLy, and it made me take her back. But it also made me confess about my affair with Cookie. I broke a cardinal rule in *The Art of Cheating* when I confessed – I gave myself up when I ain't have to.

Or *did* I have to?

See, even back then, I still had so many questions, which meant I was still learning lessons. But the *guilt???* That guilt was a *muthafukca*…a whole other new monster to deal with. At any rate, I told KeLLy about Cookie to *even the playing field*, and we vowed to start over 'fresh' and move forward.

I liked to think I curved the guilt by covering up my cheating like never before and making better decisions more in tune with *The Art*. I put Cookie on ignore status. A major move, considering that she was my *main side chick* for so long. But my relationship with Cookie was also the only side fling I had with *longevity*, and those are always the ones that pose the most risk. Cookie and I had a strong sexual relationship before then, but we had been involved on the side for so long that we had grown on each other in *nonsexual* ways. This was always dangerous. So, in an effort to cut down and try to be a better man for KeLLy at home, I cut Cookie off completely.

Now when I cut Cookie off, not only did I give up my most trusted side bitch, but I also gave up my #1 ranked partner on my *fukc-count* list. Cookie was a natural sex animal, a real nympho in every sense of the word. Our sexual chemistry was always crazy…and she fukced me better than anyone before or even after her at this point in 2005, including KeLLy. Yet and still, before I fukced Tianna, *my* sexual *beast* hadn't been fully released.

Tianna was the bounce-back bitch during my break from Kells…and she helped unleash the inner *beast* I never knew existed before. But I quickly found out that the *beast* would be much more of a problem to deal with than my guilty conscience.

For maybe the first time in a *reeeeally* long time, I was getting to know myself better sexually and learning just who this new monster was raging inside of me.

That sexual *beast* is the topic of *tonight's episode.*

And tonight, we have much to break down. This episode is more than just an episode, this is like a true season finale. Tonight, we dive deep. Deep into the origins of the *beast* that drew me away from my KeLLy…and deep into the story of the woman who helped train, feed, and nurture that *beast.*

Let's formally call her *Sashé.*

Sashé (or Shay as I call her most times) became a problem for me almost instantly from the night we met, despite the fact I had been doing so good with my new strategy at home with KeLLy. With no Cookie or Tianna to distract me, after the relapse with Sassy a few months prior to meeting Shay, my cheating habits had finally turned responsibly minimal.

But, like I said, things with Shay happened so quickly and differently that I never even had a chance to prepare for the many twists and turns that ultimately came along.

So, picture me now – at the point where I done started to manage my cheating in a way that was lowkey healthy for my relationship at home. No more complaints from KeLLy about lack of romance. The couple of times after Sassy that I *did* step out, I stepped back *in* even stronger. I set boundaries and rules for myself. If I made a bitch cum outside my home, I made KeLLy cum *twice* and she got gifts and poems shortly thereafter. KeLLy was my Queen, and all these other random side hoes were just my supplemental entertainment. If KeLLy and I got into a fight, I would take my frustrations out on some side pussy, and come back to Kells with apologies, taking the blame for our argument regardless of fault.

Cheating had become therapeutic, and I was taking full advantage of the system like a regular at the veteran's hospital. It was a challenge, but I lived for that shit back then. That rush, the pressure of finding the perfect balance and not getting caught, it's when I was at my best. Even with all the new experiences that *2005* brought – switching to a higher paid job, helping launch the *DymeWear* clothing line with my line brother, *Shabba*, and jumping into music now that the homie *Jaz* had a building to run his studio out of – I still managed to keep a fairly good hold on all the intriguing extra opportunities.

And then there was Sashé…

Man.

It's hard to find the words to even describe Sashé, that's another thing holding me up in getting on with this story. To truly paint the picture of Shay with words is mind-boggling to say the least.

No…for real.

She was…

…so innocent and youthful in the face, but glowing. Beaming with both mischief and curiosity. She was lighter than KeLLy – which was easy since Kells was the darkest chick I'd ever fukced with. And dark was *my type*. But Sashé was more peanut-butter brown…and I mean, I've fukced with chicks of all colors and shades, but strangely Sashé's shade seemed new to me at the time, at least in how I was drawn to it. It's some weird shit – but there's this certain automatic level of attraction I have for a chick if her skin is dark. Sashé was nowhere near KeLLy's darkness…yet I was equally as attracted to Sashé's complexion. Was it that *'glow'?* Hard to tell, but it was something.

Sashé was fukcing gorgeous, even by her skin tone alone.

Her body was perfect for modeling…and she'd already made a name for herself with some viral internet shots, but I ain't think she was no video vixen or bullshit influencer material. This girl was made for magazines. Not tall like the runway models, Shay was only 5'6" and maybe 120 lbs. Most of it was in her *tits*…the bitch was carrying 36 DDDs on a small frame. She reminded me of Roger Rabbit's bitch the way she stood. She was one of few chicks I couldn't compare to a porn star right off – they ain't have no hoes this pretty in porn. She was like a Melyssa Ford, or a Esther Baxter.

Yeah *Esther*…that's *really* who she reminded me of – that cleavage and them big ass eyes. Sashé was so fukcing stacked, bruh.

Her ass was average – nothing like KeLLy's fatty or Cookie's wagon. But Shay ain't need that thicky-thick hood look that I was used to. In fact, Sashé was the complete *opposite* of hood. This girl was as bubbly as it gets – but her squareness surprisingly drew me in just the same. She talked like a white girl and didn't wear weave. I mean, even Kells wore micros sometimes…but Sashé wouldn't even do *that*. She was quite different from what I was used to before…just in general. Sashé was…*different*.

And she caught me at the right time.

Shortly after we met (and I'm talking maybe a week at best after I met Sashé) KeLLy and I had a huge fight during *another* huge fight I was having with my nigga *Tre*. Crazy shit – but in the end, Kells and I took a turn for the worse…and the eventual end.

Now at the time, after the fight or whatever…we stayed together – Kells and I. But shit wuttin' the same. We kept fighting for days on end. All of a sudden, things were all being thrown out on the table between us…and buried feelings were finally coming out.

"I don't know what the hell you could be talking about when you say that, Rodney!" she yelled at my comment about the *3 F's Formula*. "So, now I only keep you *fed* and *focused*? You a damned lie if you tryna say I ain't been keeping you *fukced*, boy! I been kissing you more and everything, so don't even go there!"

I shook my head, "Ok yeah, I'll give you that. But that's not what I'm talking about!"

Kells' face turned up, "Well, what the hell you talking abou…"

"I'm talking about the *other* shit I been trying to do, too!" I cut her off mid-sentence. "Shit…you won't even let me call you a *'bitch'* when we fukcing!"

"You know how I feel about that word!" she snapped back. "What's wrong with having sex without you disrespecting me?!?!"

"It's not about me disrespecting you…it's about letting loose and throwing it all out the window when we in that moment!" I ranted in frustration. "I'm not saying it in a disrespectful way…you just don't fukcing get it!"

"Well, maybe I *don't* get it," she agreed with sarcasm. "That's how niggaz talk to *'hoes'* when they get fukced – you got me messed up!"

"But you not my hoe, though," I pointed out.

"So, why you wanna talk to me like one?" her voice was filled with anger. "Why you wanna treat me like a porn star or some shit? Who the hell was you fukcing when we was broke up that got you on all this kinky, crazy shit?"

I rolled my eyes, "Maaaaan…kinky, crazy shit like *what* KeLLy? Is it *really* too much to ask? Who else am I 'sposed to express myself with sexually if it ain't you?"

"Ok, but I'm saying!!! You wanna call me a *'bitch,'* you wanna choke me out! I let you pull my hair…but then you wanna go overboard!!! You fukcing *bit* me that night! You start getting on this rough shit and I'm just supposed to adjust?? You ain't used to do it to me like that, Rodney…"

"Whatever, man."

"Yeah, so now it's just *'whatever'*? No – eff that! I'm asking a question. You saying I'm supposed to just *change* what *I'm* into…to fit what *you* wanna experiment with?? Is *that* what you saying??"

"No," I paused to think. "I mean…man, I don't know. Am I supposed to keep my fantasies to myself?"

"No – but I mean, come on now, Rodney! You wanna bring another bitch in! Like what the fukc?!?! I'm not gay…I don't even like girls! So am I 'sposed to just say *'oh ok – sure, I'll be gay for you'*?? Can I bring another *nigga* in???"

"Don't fukcing play with me," I bit my lip, snarling. "And that ain't even what you into…so you just trying to be funny."

"Ok, whatever," she smacked her lips at me. "But that's my point!"

"So, what *is* yo point?!?!" I wondered. "Just like how you ain't never had yo toes sucked – and now I'm doing *that* – why can't you try something new just to please me???"

"Cuz I don't like girls," KeLLy reiterated. "That's different! You being extra!!"

"But it's for me!" I shot back. "What if she just messed with me? Like – you don't have to touch her."

"What fun is that for you??? What's the point?" she shook her head. "Plus, no…cuz I'ma get mad if she all up on you. No. I can't do it…I just can't."

"But you ain't got nuttin' to be jealous of…you my *girl*," I lowered my voice, speaking more gently. "I'm going home with you. I'll be all up on you the whole time, too, babe."

"Yeah, but you don't know that," she cried out. "How am I supposed to know how you gon' act if it went down? What if you like her better than me? I mean, who are we even talking about here?"

*   *   *   *   *

2

I paused for a split second, kind of surprised at what she asked. But I knew not to get my hopes up. I've been here before.

"Nobody…we just talking," I replied carefully.

"I mean…is that the way you had sex with *'her'*?"

"With who, KeLLy?"

Of course, I knew who she meant before I asked. Ever since I told KeLLy about Cookie…anytime we fought, she brought her ass up. See, I *thought* I was doing the right thing by coming clean and being honest about my main side chick. Now it was starting to become the biggest headache and mistake I had made thus far.

Telling Kells about Cookie gave my girl a *'villain'* to fall back on. It was the perfect, convenient thing to bring up whenever shit got too heated. And I was becoming more and more frustrated with it.

"Man, I know you ain't talking about Cookie again!" I sighed, lowering my head.

"Answer the question, Rodney," she demanded. "Is that who you missing now?? *If* you really stopped talking to her, like you said."

I turned my nose up, "Ugh! I'm not fukcin' talking to Cookie anymore, dude!"

"Ok…sooo is that what it was like with her?" she kept pressing the issue.

"No," I confirmed, telling the truth. "She don't like girls, either. I don't know why you always bringing her up!!!"

"Because you *cheated* on me with her, Rodney! She obviously was doing something that I wasn't."

"What makes you so sure??"

"You said yourself that she knew how to 'fukc' you the right wa – "

"KeLLy," I cut her off again. "Dude! This ain't about her…or what she did that you don't do."

"Well, that's how I feel," she admitted. "I feel like if I don't do that *hoe shit*…you just gon' go back to her. And that's not fair."

"Man, but you ain't got no reason to feel that way. You only tripping off her because I *told* you what was happening. I shouldn't 'a even told you dat shit!"

"Don't say that to me, Rodney."

"I'm for real, man! I wish I never told you dat shit! I shoulda just kept it to myself so I wouldn't have to hear this shit every time!!!"

KeLLy frowned, "That's not fair to me, though. You can't get mad because I feel some sort of way about what you did! I can't help how it makes me feel, Rodney! That's not fair and you know it!"

"Yea, but you wanna make everything about *her*…and that's not fair either, Kells," I countered. "I told you about the shit so we can move on from it."

"Well, excuse me for having feelings about it. If you ask me, that's *exactly* who this is about!"

"Yea, but it's *not*, though. Not even a little bit. You just don't get it."

And so we fought on and on…and just like that, it'd always end with Cookie and nothing got resolved. It was starting to turn into quite the boring routine…and I had grown extra tired of it. The **beast** in me was thirsting to be set loose to play freely once again…and KeLLy just wasn't having it.

I was emotionally as detached from Cookie as I had ever been, but yet Kells couldn't help but to keep giving her energy and relevance…and that was becoming mentally draining. I mean, deep down, I *wanted* KeLLy to be everything – and be dedicated to doing whatever to satisfy me. After Sassy, I felt like involving Kells in my fantasies instead of cheating was the right move. I wanted her to *want* to be my only source of pleasure. And have my back the same way I would have hers.

I woulda never got involved with a fight between KeLLy and one of her friends like she did with me and Tre. And never in a million fukcing years would I take her *friend's* side…like she did me. *In front of Tre.*

It felt like Kells and I didn't see eye-to-eye anymore on each other's positions in our union. Things were beyond fragile.

*   *   *   *   *

Sashé became the perfect getaway during this time. She was everything that KeLLy wasn't. Whereas Kells had a snappy, sassy attitude that could go from 0 to 100 in a split second…Sashé was carefree and just happy to be alive. Her face was always lit up. And Shay was wide open while KeLLy was more reserved and conservative in her womanhood. She was much younger than both Kells *and* Cookie…and her youthful spirit was her strength. No matter what was going on, whenever I talked to Sashé or was in her presence, she was in a good mood.

No, wait.

She was always in a *great* fukcing mood…nothing could get her down or make her upset. Her aura…just being around her quickly became addictive. The crazy part was, I wasn't fukcing her at first.

Not *at first*. When she initially came into the picture, it was mostly talking through text messaging and nothing more.

Shay was in her junior year in the Burg…which almost made it another déjà vü type situation now that KeLLy was back in the Burg again finishing her last semester. In fact, *Cookie* was in her last semester, too, down there now, although we hadn't talked in a while. No matter how you sliced it up – the block was hot. My main chick KeLLy was in the Burg, and across town was Sashé…a new side chick of sorts – who I was having a nonsexual relationship with on the low.

This is where *The Art of Cheating* started to consume me. I was breaking all types of rules with Sashé, spending more time with her than Kells. I was making impromptu trips to the Burg to be with Shay and sneaking out of the city without paying KeLLy a visit. I would talk to Sashé all day – from early morning to late night, and then every once in a while, one of us would convince the other to get on the highway. Being with her in the beginning was so intoxicating.

I was thoroughly infatuated with everything about her – the way she smelled, her soft-spoken/sweet voice, shoulder-length hair, her youthful spirit, her humble nature. Even crazier, though, she was just as mesmerized by me.

When I spoke, Shay hung on to my every word and didn't interrupt or rush me to finish my thoughts. It was like she *had* to hear what I had to say. She wanted to know everything about me, she seemed honestly interested in who I was and didn't look down on me for anything I saw as negative about myself before. Sashé just didn't operate like that – she always saw the light in things. Maybe it was because KeLLy knew me so much more and things were so fresh with Sashé, but there was never a dull moment with her, never any awkwardness.

And we weren't *fukcing*. Not technically. Like I said, we talked quite often through texting…but our physical interactions were few and far in between.

I started to catch some serious feelings for Sashé after talking for a couple of months, and it was all based on nonsexual interactions and conversation. I mean sure, we talked about sex –A LOT. But while Sashé had an open mind and curious appetite…she wasn't very active at all, having only been with 3 others before me.

Shay also had a boyfriend who was going to school miles away down south, and they only saw each other maybe four times a year. When I met her, she hadn't had sex in almost six months. And she took her boyfriend's virginity, so the sex was pretty basic. She was attracted to my age and experience, but hesitant to go there with me right away…still shy about her own limited experiences. In spite of all'at, Sashé thought about sex quite often, and fantasized about bringing all of her sexual fantasies to life someday.

She made it clear after so long that she wanted to live those fantasies out with *me*. Every one of them.

And there were plenty of them to go around. Like for instance, Sashé had never done a 69. She was new to giving head in general…she had only done her boyfriend, *Keith*, before. But he was just as brand new to giving face himself. Sashé longed for a man who just loved eating pussy and was good at it.

That hot text conversation in mid-November changed everything…

*   *   *   *   *

November 2005

ME: "So u saying u never had good head…at all?"

SASHÉ: "No, I didn't say that. My ex-boyfriend was pretty good at it. But he didn't do it long enough, and plus he only lasted 2 min when we had sex anyway. I'll pass lol…"

ME: "Oh wow! That sucks! See, I actually like doing it…it turns me on to please so 2 min isn't nearly long enough for me."

SASHÉ: "Well he ate it for longer than 2 min, but he couldn't last longer before he came. Pissed. Me. Off."

ME: "I know what you meant. That too though. I told you I can last a while."

SASHÉ: "Yeah u did. Which is crazy...I've never seen that. Boys don't have endurance like u claim u do."

ME: "Kegals...I told you..."

SASHÉ: "Lol right. But I mean...who does that? Boys I know don't even know what the heck that crap means!"

ME: "Lol! Well I'm not like other boys."

SASHÉ: "Maybe we shall see. One day."

ME: "I gave you a sample...remember?"

SASHÉ: "Oh my gosh – don't remind me! And see?!? Even though it wasn't for that long, I've never came that fast! I didn't even think boys could eat pussy like that...I wish you had more time lol."

ME: "Lol so that wasn't long enough to give an accurate rating? And what u mean 'boys can't *eat it that good"? You talk like you've sampled both or something..."*

There was a long pause in between replies to this last text sent. I felt like she was throwing me hints about her and another chick…but I couldn't be sure. This was late 2005, and even though I had close calls with *Sassy* and *Kitty* earlier that year…I still had yet to cross that river into the world of **ménages**. Again, this story takes place before it was common practice and cool for chicks to be into each other…and they most definitely wuttin' out in the open about it yet.

Still…this remained my biggest fantasy at the time. After Tianna uncaged my sexual **beast** the year before, my level of nasty had changed. KeLLy could see it…we were fighting about that amongst the many other things. And as nasty and kinky as Tianna was, she was still strictly-dickly. As was Cookie…and KeLLy *damn sure* wuttin' having it.

The closest I had come to a threesome was the shit with Sassy…and remember – she disappeared after her dude found out about us. Kitty was in St. Louis and our fling was all but over anyway, at least on the ménage tip. But coming that close with them two had my mind spinning about the possibilities. And if this chick Sashé was into chicks…this couldn't get any better.

I fumbled with my phone…as Shay took longer than three minutes to reply.

ME: "U there???"

SASHÉ: "Yes…"

ME: "???"

SASHÉ: "No comment."

ME: "Wait. What?! No f' that – you gotta tell me! What does that mean?!?!"

SASHÉ: "Oh no buddy…you're not gonna get me to text about that. I've never even talked to anybody about this!"

ME: "U can talk to me!"

SASHÉ: "Not through text. Is she around?"

ME: "She's not far…"

SASHÉ: "Well you're just gonna have to wait then Mr!"

*   *   *   *   *

The wait was well worth it.

Later that night, when KeLLy wasn't around me…I talked to Sashé about the time she got drunk and had lesbian sex with one of her BFF's from high school – *Kourtney.*

Kourtney was the ying to Sashé's yang…in every way. While Sashé was more of a valley girl and suburban, Kourtney was more hood and full of swag. Sashé had the tits…Kourtney was thick and more like Kells. In fact, Kourt was the same *complexion* as KeLLy and had the fat ass cheeks to go along with it. Sashé was the binge drinker who had never smoked weed…Kourtney was a smoker and could roll blunts with the best of 'em.

Ying and yang.

Kourtney was openly bisexual now that they were older…but back in high school it was only a rumor. Her and Sashé had been close friends since they were 15.

So, Shay tells me that one night during her senior year, they were at a house party with some other friends doing some classic underage drinking. Kourtney and Sashé ended up falling asleep in the same bed in a room upstairs. Kourtney wakes up to use the restroom and runs into another one of their other friends, this white girl from Russia named *Kristina*.

Kris was still up partying and doing rounds around the house with a camcorder. She ends up following Kourtney back in the room where Sashé was sleeping and thought to get some classic footage of Sashé sleeping with her mouth open. Kourtney had a better idea.

Camera still rolling…Kourtney starts fondling Sashé's huge tits through her t-shirt…squeezing and grabbing tightly, trying to wake Shay up. When that doesn't work…Kourtney goes the extra mile and starts to pull Shay's volleyball shorts and panties down her legs…exposing her bare pussy for the camera. Sashé is still completely outta commission…drunk as fukc off multiple shots of Vodka, so she still doesn't wake up.

Her pussy is small and tight…but her lips are juicy and she's always wet. She'd told me about her always-moist pussy the first night we met…and this night many years before was no different. With just a slight adjustment of her lips, Kourtney displayed Sashé's juices running rampant on camera…and it was *then* that she couldn't resist. She started licking and sucking Shay's wetness up on camera…giving Kris the best freak-show of her life.

This of course wakes Sashé up abruptly…but Kourtney is experienced, and it feels so damn good that Shay immediately throws her head back and opens her legs up more so Kourtney can really go to work. She tells me that she ends up cummin' for the first time ever…and that no orgasm after that night has been that intense.

"Damn," I was breathing hard into the phone, full of lust. "So, where is the tape at? I wanna see dat shit!!!"

Shay giggled gently, "I honestly have no idea what happened to that tape. I only watched it once. Crazy."

"Hell yeah, dat's crazy! I'd pay good money to see that muhfukca! For real!" I licked my lips.

"I bet you would," she replied seductively. "Mr. Nasty Man."

"Aye, you can't blame me! That's just a big fantasy for me…something I never really thought chicks were into, ya know?" I tried to explain the excitement.

"I mean, that's the only time it's happened…for me anyway," she clarified. "I mean, Kourt is open about her bi-ness now. Girls are more open down in Atlanta."

"Yeah, that's what I heard. Damn man…when she coming home???"

"I don't know, that's a good question. Either Thanksgiving or Christmas break though, I'm sure. I haven't seen her all year."

"Well, you need to see when she's coming home," I casually demanded.

"Why? You wanna meet my best friend??? Don't be getting any ideas, Mister."

"Whaaaat? I'm just saying…ain't nuttin' wrong with us all hanging out…right???" I asked with a grin.

"Hmmmm," Shay let her mind wander. "I don't care, really. I'll text her when we hang up if you want."

"Really???" I was shocked she agreed.

"Uhm…yeah…really," she sounded surprised that I was so shocked, but I could tell our minds were in the same place. She then whispered softly after a brief pause, with her tone full of mischief, "Why not???"

*   *   *   *   *

3

I hung up the phone with Sashé with the biggest grin on my face, one of those *'up-to-no-good, evil-villain'* joints.

Thanksgiving was only two weeks from then. If I could pull this shit off…

Exactly *what* I was pulling off, though, was still up in the air. So far, I hadn't had the best luck when it came to ménages…and in the back of my mind I was almost thinking that it wasn't meant to ever happen for me. Maybe I was chasing a lifestyle that didn't exist in the real world; maybe these porn reenactments were just dreams that would never come true. I'm already putting way too much energy behind making it happen, as it is.

I mean, it's almost becoming the only thing that instantly stimulates me – the whole idea of me with two chicks. And in my lustful thoughts, it's all gotta go a certain way for my fantasy to be fulfilled.

Like for one, the two chicks gotta *both* be eager to suck and fukc me. That's just a given. Ain't no point in the ménage if I'm not fukcing. I guess I could settle for only hitting one of the chicks, but then it's like a B-list ménage and I'm looking for top shelf.

It's gotta be all-out…a free-for-all. And that means that the females gotta also be freaking *each other*…they both gotta love pussy the same way I do if this is gonna play out right. Can't have no pillow princess, scared-to-taste-the-rainbow type bitch…ain't no fun in that. KeLLy was right about that part. I wuttin' tryna settle for a half-ass fukc session. I needed this shit to be epic.

So, I'm lost in my thoughts now – so disengaged that I don't notice KeLLy is back from the store and in the kitchen. I'd been on the phone with Sashé the last thirty or forty minutes, in my bedroom on the other side of the apartment.

Now that Kells had moved out and back to the Burg, I was living with Tre on some bachelor shit. I knew KeLLy moving out was a bad idea and I tried to talk her out of it that summer, but she fought for it. She needed to finish one more semester and Tre needed a new spot. The space between us would be good, she said – maybe we moved back in together too fast after the breakup. Plus, even though we moved to a two-bedroom and Tre would only be there for 8 or 9 months, she didn't wanna be living with me and one of my friends. Kells loved Tre to death, but she felt like she'd be *in the way* if she stayed.

I didn't agree with any of that bullshit. I thought it would be a major step backwards any way you sliced it up…and I was almost offended she wanted to move out after I asked her to move in with me. Not to mention the last thing I needed was to not be under the same roof with Kelly. Especially not with *Tre*…even though we weren't getting along as well, this nigga was still my longtime running mate when it came to this *Art of Cheating* shit.

Not a good idea.

Sure, she was home every weekend…but KeLLy and I started spending less time with each other the moment she moved her shit out. And sure, I had cut down on my habits substantially…but I still had my moments. Let's face it, I never woulda pulled off the shit with Sassy, Kitty, or even Tianna if KeLLy was still my live-in. A nigga like me can't handle the pressure of long distance. Now that I got this cheating shit mastered, I need obstacles and barriers to keep me restrained. Then there was the fact that I was now doing commercials and fashion shows for DymeWear, around all these fukcing models!!! And I can't forget about all the eye candy down at *64111 Studio* hanging around while I created art n'shit.

KeLLy moving out was major.

But she's here now at my apartment *tonight*…and in the kitchen moving shit around. I had no clue how long she had been here, since she came in without speaking. And I couldn't tell if she still had an attitude about some fight we had earlier that week, or just an attitude in general.

KeLLy had mood swings like a muhfukca…this was no secret. Once upon a time, I would push through and try to change her moods for the better…brighten up her day. Nowadays, I'm simply tired of being her punching bag.

What's the point? She ain't never gon' get over Cookie anyway…so it's best to just stay outta her face when she obviously don't wanna be bothered with me.

Yea, she just gon' end up snapping out about some bullshit anyway!!

I walked out of the bedroom and into the living room. KeLLy was in the kitchen at the microwave, warming up something.

"Did you bring me something to eat?" I wanted to know.

"I texted you and asked if you were hungry, you didn't reply," she replied dryly.

"So, you just ain't bring me nothing?!?!" my face cringed. "Why you ain't call?"

KeLLy's voice remained low and nonchalant, "I did. It just rang and went to voicemail. You were on the phone."

I sighed in frustration, "Man, I'm not understanding how you ain't just bring me something!!"

"I'm not understanding why you didn't answer the phone…so I guess I can understand you not understanding something," she snapped back with pettiness.

"Man, I'll be back, KeLLy," I threw my hands up. "You on dat bullshit!!!"

"No I'm not, I called you."

"You wrong."

I slammed the door behind me and had my phone out within seconds, dialing my brother from another mother – *Vondell*. If I was gon' deal with Kells' attitude for the rest of the night, I needed some *GG* and Dell knew where it was at. I could talk to *Dell* about my sexcapades, too – we grew up next door to each other in the projects and went back to virgin days.

Since I was the oldest, I was the first outta the project crew to start fukcing – but that never stopped Dell and *Kam* from trying to compete and keep up with me. As a matter of fact, we were all chasing some of the same bitches from the hood back in the early 90s and Dell was holding on to the crown after he banged *the twins*. Not at the same time, but still, this nigga fukced *twin sisters*.

I knew my nigga would appreciate the work I was putting in now with trying to get this ménage popping, so we got a good laugh in before I pulled up on him.

"Where you at now, cuzz?" he asked me.

"I'm getting off on Truman now, bro," I told him before going back to the threesome convo. "Nigga, you telling me you don't remember dat shit with Nae-Nae and her one little cousin??? I can't remember the lil chick's name, cuzz, but I know you remember this shit I'm talking about, bro!"

Dell paused for a split second, "Nah, bro. Man, I mean – I remember *Nae-Nae*, cuzz! You used to be fukcing her on the porch n'shit, nigga! I remember *dat* shit!!!"

"Yeah, nigga," I chuckled. "You don't remember I was telling you about her and her cousin, though?!?!"

Dell laughed harder, "Nigga, I remember you thinking you was slick and fukcing Nae on the porch, bro. You wouldn't admit dat shit then either, nigga. I know I remember *dat part.*"

I was still chuckling, "Yeah, nigga, *whatever!* But nah…I'm talking 'bout that one time they had me down by the office building, bro. In the bushes."

"Nigga I do *not* remember you telling me about that one, cuzz…"

*   *   *   *   *

July 1996

Nae-Nae was the chick I lost my virginity to, on Grandma's front patio. I always denied it if anyone asked, cuz she was a straight up *rat*. She was also a dark-skinned young freak, though, and as a young teenager I could never resist. Anytime she got me in a corner by myself, she was always lowering her eyes and voice, grabbing for my dick. When we could get a quickie off, she let me put it in, anytime, anywhere – condom or not.

It was always a quickie, anyway; I never lasted longer than three minutes with Nae-Nae. It was most definitely embarrassing, and I always tried to play it off – hurrying to get dressed *'before we got caught'*. Nae-Nae wasn't fooled for long though and started making side comments about my *two-minute-man* status, but it never bothered me. I could care less because in the end, I was still getting pussy.

Then, one night during the summer before my senior year in high school, Nae-Nae was spending the night at one of her cousin's spot.

See, we all lived in the projects, and most of us – including me and Nae-Nae – lived with our grandmothers. Those of us project kids who *didn't* live with Grandma – still had Grandma nearby, and in some cases just a few buildings down. Some Grandmas were stricter than others…and Nae-Nae had one of those big mamas that stayed on her head, watched her every move, and made sure she was in before dark. *Grandma Dottie* was less strict with me…I rarely got in trouble. So, it wasn't uncommon for *me* to be out late…but for Nae-Nae it was almost unheard of.

This night in particular, she was staying up the hill over her cousins' crib…and they were all out late with the rest of the project kids.

This usually meant one thing in the projects: playing *hide-and-go-get-it*.

Somehow, I ended up on the far side of the office building in the middle of *Parker Square* with Nae-Nae and her younger cousin. I can't remember the lil girl's name, so let's just call her *Lil Mama*.

So, Lil Mama was a few months younger than Nae-Nae…and much more of a looker in the face. She had an older sister who was gon' be the future version of Nae-Nae's grandma…and if big sis knew Lil Mama was off in the cut right now with me, she would wake the whole hood up.

Her older brother was my age…but one of them hands-off type niggas with his two sisters, so naturally I was more worried about *Big Sister* than *Big Brother* catching us. But at the moment, she was nowhere to be seen…and Nae-Nae and Lil Mama had me backed against the wall of the building, behind some bushes.

Nae-Nae was staring me in the eyes, smiling.

"What the fukc you smiling about?" I raised my eyebrow.

"Ain't nowhere for you to go," she smirked. "And ain't nobody over here."

She reached down at my shorts…and I immediately slapped her hand away, debating with myself in my head.

*We can't be doing this shit in front of Lil Mama like this…she be done told somebody and then everybody gon' know I been smashing Nae-Nae. Can't have that. Plus…it's her cousin…her **little** cousin at that. Nae-Nae is barely 16 so Lil Mama gotta be too young!!!*

"Stop that," Nae-Nae smacked her lips. "What you scared of? She not gon' say nothing."

I glanced at Lil Mama standing closely to the right of her cousin, and I noticed that she had her eyes locked on my crotch, not budging. I frowned my face up in confusion and looked back at Nae-Nae, who'd taken a step closer to me. Her right leg was pressed up against mine and she pulled my shirt up, putting her hand down my shorts. Her hands felt warm with sweat against my stiffness.

"Man…what are you *doing???*"

"What does it look like I'm doing?" Nae-Nae rolled her eyes. "Undo yo belt. Pull it out."

"Nah, man," I refused.

"She wanna see it," she tried to reason with me.

"WHO?!?!" I exclaimed.

Lil Mama stepped towards me; her eyes still locked as Nae-Nae took her hand away. The younger cousin then started unbuckling my belt with a sneaky look on her face…loosening my jean shorts. Instinctively, I took a step back. Not to move away…but to *help* her pull my belt loose.

I can't believe this shit is happening…whatever is happening!!!

But then, that quick, I remembered we was all *outside.* Sure, we was in the cut by the office building, but we was *outside* just the same.

"Nah…hold up," I stopped. "I ain't taking my shorts off, dude."

"Why not??" Nae-Nae whined. "Ain't nobody even over he – "

"Nah, fukc that," I cut her off. "Nope."

"Let me just see it," Lil Mama chimed in.

"Let her touch it," Nae-Nae pressured me, biting her lip.

I froze up and Nae-Nae pulled my shorts away from my waist as Lil Mama reached in my boxers. Her hand was smaller…and softer. She started squeezing my dick like a pump. She was looking down the whole time, trying to get a peek at it from the streetlight haze.

I'm stuck…speechless. And my dick is throbbing uncontrollably. I've never felt it jump so much.

Nae-Nae glances at her cousin, "See?"

"Hmmmm…yeah," Lil Mama had both hands down my shorts now. "It's a lot of hair."

Nae-Nae stepped in closer and they kept whispering to each other.

Fuuuuuuck!!! They both so close now!!!

I couldn't even comprehend what they was saying at the time; it wuttin' 'til later that I replayed all the dialogue to myself.

But anyway, Lil Mama was playing with my dick…with a much lighter grip than Nae-Nae ever touched me with. It felt good as fukc. Nae-Nae had her face in mine, breathing hard…hands on my shoulders.

"Noooo," she shook her head. "Remember what else I was telling you??"

Lil Mama kept stroking, running her other hand through my pubic hairs, "Ohhhh! Uhmmm…I don't know yet."

"Watch. Keep going," Nae-Nae instructed her.

Without warning, Nae-Nae then stepped backwards and put *her* hand down my shorts…grabbing the base of my dick as Lil Mama squeezed the head. Before I could blink, Lil Mama leaned in on her toes, head tilted back. Then she started kissing me – wet and sloppy, wetting my face up.

My dick felt like it was gon' explode. Nae-Nae started rubbing my ball sack gently. It tickled like a muhfukca…and when I flinched, Lil Mama squeezed my dick and kissed me harder.

The hair on the back of my neck rose and I let out a soft groan, "Hmmmm."

"Just watch…girl," Nae-Nae kept whispering to Lil Mama. "Watch."

"Watch what?" I asked hastily, breathing hard.

"You'll see," she traced a finger under my sack.

"I don't know," Lil Mama pleaded. "He woulda done it by now."

What the fukc are these bitches talking about?

"This is the longest it ever took," Nae-Nae sounded disappointed, but borderline the 'good' kind of letdown.

"Ooooo…it's *hard*, though," Lil Mama held her tongue out. "It really is."

Nae-Nae was staring me in the eye as she took her hand out briefly to lick her palm. She quickly got back at it and both of 'em were stroking me in my shorts now. I tugged on Nae-Nae's shorts, and she stepped closer so I could start fingering her. Her pussy was wetter than I'd ever felt it…and it made me start humping to my hand job.

"How come you never lasted this long before?" she wondered.

"Yeah, cuz I don't see what you talking about, Nae," Lil Mama said softly.

"What you talking about?"

"Don't play dumb," Nae-Nae snapped. "You know you can't keep it up for five minutes, Rodney!"

"Fukc you," I grunted in embarrassment. "I can't tell."

"*I* can't tell," Lil Mama echoed me.

"Nah, I don't know what's going on, Nae-Nae admitted. "But this ain't how it be."

"Just shut up," I told her, feeling the cum build up.

"You feel it jumping???" Lil Mama's eyes got big.

"You shut up," Nae-Nae barked back at me. "I bet I know what it is."

"What is it???" I lowered my voice, digging my finger in her tightness.

"Damn," Lil Mama gripped harder in amazement.

"I bet if we do it, you can't keep it up," Nae-Nae kept pressing. "I *know* you can't."

"I bet I *can*. Come on," I said it with no hesitation…but my confidence in the situation was nothing less than shook.

I knew I had never lasted more than a few minutes in some coochie – Nae-Nae was right. I just couldn't get past the fact that these two chicks were jacking me off at the same time. I wanted to fukc so bad…and given the opportunity, I'd do whatever right now. Or go down trying.

"No. Not that," Nae-Nae shook her head.

"Well, *what*, then???" my knees buckled. Lil Mama was kissing on my neck now as she touched me.

"What else can we do???" Nae-Nae stared me in eyes.

"Hmmmm," I moaned, throwing my head back.

"Huh, Rodney??" Nae-Nae's lips brushed against mine.

"Y'all…can…shit," I panted. "Come on…suck it."

Lil Mama gasped in shock, "Do what??"

"Y'all heard me," I said firmly. *"Suck it."*

*   *   *   *   *

Nae-Nae just looked at me like I was crazy. Of course, this was '96…no dicks were getting sucked back then…at least not in this scenario. I had never had dome before — seeing that shit in pornos back then was the closest I was gon' get. I was lucky to be lucky enough to have two chicks just freaking me down. Asking for head was a bit overboard, but it was worth a try. Worse they can do is say *'no'* – right?"

As it turned out, though…I was just left to *assume* the answer was *'no'*.

As Nae-Nae stared at me in shock…Lil Mama's older sister came running from up the hill, screaming and looking for her. She couldn't see us where we was in the shadows, but they both scooted away from me in unison — Nae-Nae running off in one direction and Lil Mama in the other — leaving me with a hard dick, blue balls, and an imagination running wild and rampant.

Damn…what if they was gon' do it???"

*   *   *   *   *

That impromptu freak session in the bushes coulda been so much more under the right circumstances. The fact that they was cousins threw a wrench in the whole deal. No way could cousins get down with each other — that's just…*weird.*

But the idea of having multiple chicks touching me sexually gave me one helluva rush. Even though I ain't fukc, I was feeling on top of the world after that incident. I mean, I had already did it to Nae-Nae, and who knows – if we was alone *inside* somewhere instead of outside in the bushes, I mighta fukced Lil Mama, too. She was definitely down for the cause…and Nae-Nae obviously wanted to show her some things through me.

I was just so caught off guard…I mean, I ain't even have a condom on me. And I had been telling myself after the last time I fukced Nae that I was gon' start strapping up – can't be having no babies out here. Next time – if there was a next time – I needed to be prepared and ready for whatever. I vowed to start carrying condoms with me after that, at all times.

But the other thing that kept fukcing with me was the way Nae-Nae was telling her cousin that *I bust quick*. It felt different hearing her tell another female that, instead of the usual subliminal jokes in my presence. I mean, it was *true*…soon as I stuck it in, I would be damn near ready to cum. That potential ménage in the bushes wouldn't 'a been much to talk about if it did go down that night. I needed to step my game up…somehow figure out how to last longer.

I found myself obsessed with it after that…researching and reading everything about sex I could get my hands on. I learned masturbation exercises, like edging and kegals, and made it a daily habit to practice holding that nut to increase my staying power.

*　　*　　*　　*　　*

42

November 2005

The results would pay off over the next few years…and now that this shit with Sashé had fallen in my lap – all these memories was coming back to me, building the anticipation with a newfound rage.

I ain't that same muhfukcin' trigger happy lil nigga in the bushes anymore…and it's been a long time coming.

Literally.

I mean, let's keep in mind – I ain't even fukced Sashé yet and I'm already thinking ménages. Truth is – I hadn't fukced anyone but KeLLy since *August*, the month before I met Shay.

*The thought of getting some new pussy is exhilarating enough. The thought of **two** slices of new pussy is still fukcing unbelievable!!!*

*   *   *   *   *

Thanksgiving didn't work out after all, though, since Kourtney *didn't* come home from Atlanta. It was prolly a good thing. I spent most of the holiday with Kells and besides – Sashé's boyfriend, *Keith,* was in town on break from Oklahoma anyway. It woulda been tough to be ubiquitous that weekend, a necessary skill in *The Art of Cheating.*

Still…opportunity always presents itself.

The day after Thanksgiving was Black Friday. This meant one thing in KeLLy's family – *SHOPPING DAY.* All the females in the family, young and old alike, met up annually around 4am to strategize and plot the full day of chasing bargains across the town…and that meant that I would have some free time to get away.

Sashé had a small window to creep with me as well…since her parents and grandparents went out of town for the holiday, and Keith was with his family for most of the early part of Friday. We decided to meet at Shay's parents, to get a quickie in.

Yes. A *quickie.*

Oh wait, I'm skipping around! Lemme catch y'all up.

I'd *finally* had sex with Sashé the week *before* Thanksgiving…and we both were seriously feenin' for another round. Our sexual chemistry was *amazing*…even with her inexperience, the whole atmosphere was intense. She was eager – eager, anxious, and willing to enjoy every inch, every moment between us. She was the perfect level of submissive, giving me complete control and dominance in the bed…responding to my words and body language without hesitation. Sashé ain't need a ton of experience to compete with the best of 'em…the vibe of her hormones carried her the whole way. She knew what felt good to her and how to be reciprocal…just how the **beast** liked it. The shit was crazy.

We'd had many foreplay sessions before that first night…long, and freaky ones. Just the sight of her naked body would make any nigga weak in the knees…there's no way you can keep ya tongue to yaself. So, the couple of times before we went all the way, I had gotten to know her curves and contours – how her skin felt in certain places, and where she responded to my touch. Her pussy was so *small.* She kept it waxed and smooth. And I mean, this little kitty was *smooooooth.* It looked virtually untouched…but her clit was hella fat and poked out right at you. And fukc. It was…*TIGHT.*

I mean *so tight*…you couldn't fit your index finger in halfway without it clenching up. Sashé might've had the tightest pussy I'd ever been inside…and like I said before…it stayed wet. *Super wet*…all the time. She was always ready to fukc…and you would never even know it from how she acted otherwise. I mean, just looking at her in the face, them big ass eyes screamed innocence and naivety. But if you managed to get your hands on it…get your face down in front of her bare pussy…you quickly found out she was an ocean of nymph heaven.

Tight…wet…sweet pussy. I should call her **Sweet P**…

So anyway – after we get the quickie in at her parents, the conversation turns wild again as we get dressed.

"Are you sure he won't be able to tell?" Sashé asked with a look of concern. "I'm pretty sure he's gonna wanna have sex later."

"Look…I'm sure," I reassured her. "Yo pussy is too tight…it's gon' take more than a couple of times to open you up. He won't know the difference…ain't no way."

"But like, how do you know???" she frowned, staring at me with them Esther Baxter eyes as she fixed her hair in the mirror hanging on the far side of the dining room. "It definitely feels less tight after that, Daddy."

I fukcing loved how she called me *Daddy*. I mean, of course…she wuttin' the first to call me that. But when *Sashé* said it – she really sounded like she *meant* that shit.

"I just know," I responded calmly. "And I mean…if you really scared, just tell him you got a new dildo."

"He'll know I'm fibbing because he knows I only like vibrators," her jaw dropped. "Oh my God – he's gonna know!"

I turned around to walk towards her, straightening the collar of my plaid Nautica shirt. Stepping in close from behind, I wrapped my arms around her waist and pulled her in closely. She was shivering in front of me.

"Calm down, Shay. He's not gonna find out. I promise."

"But how can you promise me that? I'm so not good at lying. I've never done anything like this."

"That's fine," I said with confidence. "It's cool. Really. Just follow my lead…we can figure out what to say to him."

Shay was still having anxiety, "But like, what if I screw up? He already thinks I'm fukcing the Ques since my roomie's always kicking it with them! I just know he's gonna be paying extra attention to how tight it feels. Oh my God, Daddy…we shoulda waited 'til after I saw him!"

"I know…I'm sorry. It's so gooood, though. I couldn't wait. I want some more *now*."

"Hmmm," she moaned. "Me, too."

I reached upwards and grabbed her left breast…staring at her in the mirror. Even through her bra and blouse…her nipples are poking out.

"I can't believe her tits are so big…even bigger than Tianna's!!!" the *beast* screamed in my head.

"Come on, then," I gave her that look.

"I can't, Daddy," she stopped me. "I really, *really* want to, but…"

"I understand. We gotta go, anyway."

"But I'm gonna be a nervous wreck!" Shay kept whining. "You have to help me, Daddy."

"I got you," I promised. "I told you I'ma help you figure out what to say."

"No, Daddy! You have to tell me everything!"

"What you mean? Tell you everything??"

"Yes," she pouted. "I'm gonna need you to tell me everything you know about *cheating*. I *cannot* get caught. I don't know what I would do."

"Wow. You talk like I'm some expert or something."

"You *are*, Daddy!" she reiterated matter-of-factly. "Tell me everything you know…help me be good at this. I'm serious."

"Ok," I smiled before getting serious. "Ok. I hear you. I got you. First…you gotta remember the story you gon' tell like it's a movie."

"Right," she smiled as she remembered our lessons.

"So, where were you today?"

"Oh, he's not gonna ask about today," she told me. "He doesn't expect me to be here. He knows my parents aren't at home."

"Right…but where does he *think* you at?" I posed an important question. "Just in case he *does* ask…you gotta spit that shit out like clockwork."

"Right…right," she nodded in agreement. "Ok. I'm in Lee's Summit at my aunt's. With my little brothers."

"What if he asks your brothers about it?"

"He like never talks to my little brothers," she explained. "They're too young."

"But what if he *does?* Where yo brothers think you at right now?"

"I don't know," she cried out. "I just told them I had to make a run."

"You gotta get all'at shit on point," I coached her. "No holes…no loose ends."

"Oh, wow…see? I didn't think of it like that," she hung her head. "See, Daddy…that's why I need you in my life."

I let out a light chuckle, "Ok, so let's go over this again. What time did you leave ya aunt's?"

*   *   *   *   *

The next few weeks were pivotal between Sashé and I. She was a fast learner and paid close attention to details. It was fairly easy to help her cheat on Keith…he was too far away to catch her up like that. I taught her how to focus on the small details to a story…how to make everything connect and make sense. If you had the right type of alibi…you never got questioned about it.

Since we mostly talked through text – I came up with a *code question and answer* for when we made contact, a different set than the one I used with Cookie, but identical concepts just the same. In fact, most of the techniques that I had perfected over the years cheating with Cookie…they all came in handy during this time with Sashé.

The irony.

Lowkey…and before I really tripped off it, Sashé was slowly, but surely becoming what Cookie used to be for me. Something *bigger* even.

I had cut my main side chick off because of our longevity. And the last two times I cheated on Kells before Sashé was with randoms – one of them being a bridesmaid from my nigga Jaz's *wedding party* that summer and the other one was a little freak I met on a road trip to Saint Louis. Quick flings with no strings attached…that was my theme.

But even back when Cookie was my main side bitch…I still had other hoes here and there. Now that Sashé was the only one I was cheating with…she's the *only* other one.

This was new territory for me.

But not because the desire to fukc other chicks had suddenly gone away. No, that wasn't it at all. If anything, those urges were now more present than a nigga could ever hope to imagine.

Things with Sashé were just…different.

And Kourtney was most definitely coming home for Christmas...

If I could...somehow...pull this shit off…

*   *   *   *   *

5

December 2005

It all happened so fast. We went from a shaky summer…to a rocksteady fall. And by winter – the air between us was chilling and ice cold.

Neither one of us wanted to say it. We had been too strong for too long…it wuttin' supposed to end like this. She was being insecure; I was being selfish. I wanted her to get over my mistakes…she wanted me to make her feel irreplaceable again. I didn't know how. She didn't know why.

It all just happened so fast.

And I couldn't bring myself to just breaking things off with KeLLy for good. She wouldn't let me finish the words whenever the fight got too heated. Kells felt giving up was not an option, since we had already promised to give things another shot for the long haul.

It's like my future don't seem so clear anymore now, though.

I was tired of dealing with Kells' attitude…tired of her stressing about school and bills.

*She just had to go back to finish up…but **why**?*

Yeah, she already had the teaching job! She shoulda just stayed at home with you, bro!

All it's doing is putting her under more pressure anyway! I feel like she changed, not me!

Not to mention she so self-conscious about her weight now, tripping off Tre making fun of her cooking!

Tre is a fukcin' asshole – I don't understand why KeLLy let him get to her!

Suddenly Kells was all unsure about herself…where she had always been confident before. I missed that cockiness…that sass. And Kells wuttin' soft by no means…she sholl was quick to turn her sadness into rage with the swiftness to snap on *me*.

We just argue so much now...and always at the wrong fukcing times!!!

*   *   *   *   *

September 2005

Let's backtrack again for a second:

So maybe two weeks after I met Shay back in September, one of my aunts was found dead in an alley in St. Louis. Everybody knows how family oriented I am, so it came as no surprise to KeLLy when I took off work to make plans to be at the funeral. She also knew how hard deaths in my family get for me, so she insisted on riding along with me for support. The only problem was my sister, *Ronnie*, went half on the rental car...and was riding along as well.

Now we won't get into *who* my sister is here, that'll come later in the story. What's important to note is the fact that KeLLy and Ronnie barely got along...and for good reasons.

My family was tough for any woman to deal with, and Ronnie was the hardest wall to break by default. Though they never had an all-out brawl in the middle of the floor – I always found myself in the middle of Kells and Ronnie fighting, struggling to keep the peace.

The trip to St. Louis was better than expected, but the morning of the funeral turned all bad, as me and Ronnie got into a big fight on some brother-sister bullshit right before we all left *Grandma Flo's* in the limo. The shit wuttin' even related to KeLLy in any way, but because Ronnie was so pissed at me, she threw Kells a slew of idle threats throughout the services and on the ride back to Grandma's house from the church, just to keep getting under my skin.

Long story short – shit got physical with me and Ronnie, guns were drawn, and Ronnie got left in St. Louis at the end of the long day.

The ride back to KC is where things got heated with me and KeLLy, alone in the car for a long four hours. All the feelings and emotions were spewed out into the air...built-up tension and opinions about each other's families showed up in the form of harsh words and sarcasm. On one hand, I could understand KeLLy's frustration with Ronnie and some of the realities about my family. I mean, like I said – dealing with my roots was a difficult feat for any woman I've come across, and one of the reasons I rarely let anyone close.

But on the heavier other hand...the fact that Kells had been around for over four years now had raised my *expectations* for my main girl, especially during my time of grieving. I didn't necessarily need a lecture or reminder about how grimy my family was, or how thugged-out shit typically was. I was well aware of how disrespectful and inconsiderate my people could be – I was raised in the same environment and inherited plenty of bad habits of my own along the way.

Already an emotional wreck, I really just needed KeLLy's support, even when she simply needed mine. You damn right – I was upset and furious with Ronnie for being on the bullshit she was on with me – even more furious for her taking it out on KeLLy. Kells *had* to *know* that...but yet she was in the car coming down on me for continuing to deal with and put up with my folks how I did. Ronnie had lived with KeLLy and I for a brief period last year and there was still plenty of bad blood between them over silly female mess.

I felt like both of them was continuously trying to turn me against the other and my aunt Stephanie's funeral was just the absolute wrong place to keep that shit going. Especially when the initial argument with me and Ronnie had zero to do with Kells.

Why couldn't KeLLy just eat that shit and not add to the drama?!? Just have my back and shut the fukc up! I'm tired of dealing with this shit...all of it!!!

Man, fukc all'at, HoLLy! Sashé is like our vacation – our getaway from reality.

Yeah, but now it's to the point where I don't wanna even go home!

I'm thinking about bailing. I'm coming up with all the reasons why I should go...making excuses for myself.

Man, it's a no-brainer, bruh! This shit been a wrap!

I should tell Kelly exactly how I feel…I owe her that much, at least.

Still…it was so hard to just have the conversation.

Every time I tried, I couldn't just…*tell* her.

"I just think we need some time apart," I tried once again, nearly whispering through the phone.

"Again, Rodney?" Kells was shocked and full of disapproval. "How is that the answer? We tried that before. No, I don't like that idea."

"Yeah, we tried that, and we got back together, too," I reminded her. "But whatever…I don't know if that's the answer or not. I don't even know if an answer exists."

"What's that supposed to mean, Rodney?"

"Nothing. Just what I said."

Kells sighed, "You giving up."

"I didn't say that, KeLLy," I shook my head, already sick of this conversation.

"Ok, but *are* you??? Giving up on us?"

"We need time apart."

"Answer me. Is it somebody else?" she wanted answers. "Are you talking to Cookie again?"

"No, I'm not talking to Cookie again, KeLLy," I rolled my eyes, thankful she couldn't see my expression.

"So, you haven't talked to her?"

"I have. I ain't say that."

"Wow. So, when did this start?"

"But not like that," I tried to make myself clear. "It's not Cookie. That's not what it is. At all."

"Then what is it, Rodney? What happened to all'at *'fight through it'* stuff you was talking? You said we wouldn't quit. You said that, Rodney!"

"I'm not quitting! I know…I know what I said. I just really think we need time apart. It's not getting no better."

"But are you really trying, Rodney???" she challenged.

"Can you say *you* are, KeLLy?" I shot back.

"I think we both could do better. I just don't think time apart is gon' help. I feel like I'm losing you…and it's frustrating. I don't know what we need to do…but I just don't see how time apart is gon' change something."

"I don't know what else to do either. I do know that we can't stay away from each other's throats. I'm tired of fighting, man. I'm tired of the attitudes. Like…we not even fukcin' *friends* right now."

"So, why can't we work back to that point??" Kells suggested.

"That's why I'm saying we need time."

"But now, though?" she asked in disbelief. "Why now?"

"What you mean, Kells?"

"I mean, I have all this stuff going on with school. Like, the timing is just fukced up" she explained herself. "Why can't we wait 'til after graduation? Can you at least wait 'til after I walk??"

"What happened to you walking next week?" this was news to me.

"I have to take one more class part-time in the spring," she admitted. "At least give me until then, babe. Things will get better. I don't see why they wouldn't."

"Nah, man," I started shaking my head again. "I don't know about that."

"See? You really are done with me," her voice was full of sadness.

"I'm trying not to be."

Kells kept venting, "It's like —you tell me I'm the one changed but then, look at *you*. You not even tryna give us a chance. You claim it's not about somebody else. Then, what is it? Is it this music stuff you doing with Ricky and Jaz at the studio now? You still mad about what happened after the funeral in St. Louis?? What is it? How are you not giving up when you won't even talk to me?"

I turned my lip up, giving the phone a dirty look, "I told you what it was, KeLLy! We just need some time! I'm not putting the blame on you…I think we *both* need to reevaluate some shit. You still not over Cookie. When you get insecure about her…it makes me ask myself *'well, why am I not insecure about **him**'?* I'll never know for sure if you fukced dude or not! That goes both ways!"

"But I told you I didn't!" she sounded offended. "And you said yourself…*you cheated on me with her more than once*, Rodney! How do you just expect me to get over that?!?! I'm a woman…that shit hurts! Then you say you *regret even telling me??* Well, damn – how am I supposed to even trust you after all of that? How do you expect me to just move on?"

"I don't," I sighed. "I don't even know why I thought we could move forward in the first place. That's what I'm saying…we need to take a break."

"I mean, so what is this?!?! We take a "break'…and that mean you single again? You can just fukc whoever you want and run wild?!?! That's what this is about, Rodney?"

"No, KeLLy! I mean…"

"You mean what? Rodney. I know you. If you say we taking a break…then you feel like you free to do whatever the hell you wanna do!"

I shook my head yet again, "I'm saying that's not why I wanna take a break, though."

"Whatever," she mumbled sharply.

"See? Now you got a attitude. That's what I'm talking about. You won't admit it…but you don't even like me no more, Kells. You might love me…I know you love me. But you don't believe in me like you used to KeLLy….you don't believe in us. And you can't stand me for real. It's evident."

"I don't like the person you being right now. You not being fair. After everything we been through…you are not being fair. You telling me that after all the shit I've done for you – fed you, washed ya clothes, took you back and forth to work when you didn't have a car? Gave you the keys to my car and let you pick me up from work! I was going in an hour early just so you could have the car!"

I immediately got defensive, "Oh, now you wanna throw that in my fa – "

"No, I'm not doing that," she interrupted. "You listen to me. I'm asking a question. I did all'at shit…held us down when you first graduated and couldn't find a job. Cooked for you and all ya little cousins when wuttin' nobody thinking about food down there at *Aunt Betty's* but me. On top of all'at – you *cheated* on me and broke up with me. I stayed around…you said you needed time then.

"Ok. We've been fighting a lot lately…and not getting along. It's fukced up. But now you need time *again*? And after all of *that*…you telling me you can't wait 'til I *graduate???*"

My throat was dry…and I just sat holding the phone in silence. I didn't really know what to say. But I needed to get off the phone soon. I had been sitting outside of Sashé's apartment in my car for almost forty-five minutes. It was cold in the Burg tonight…mid 30's.

"Hello?!?!" Kells cried out at the still air between us.

"I'm still here," my voice was nearly a whisper.

"No words??? You telling me you can't wait 'til I walk across that stage? Christmas is coming up in what – three weeks? What am I supposed to tell my family?!"

"I'm going back to St. Louis for Christmas anyway," I quickly reminded her. "I won't even be in town."

"Ok, but you don't think everyone is gon' eventually notice that you're not around all of a sudden? What am I supposed to tell them?" she asked a second time, this time with more frustration. "You said part of the problem before was that *'all our family always knew when we had drama'.* We needed to keep our shit in house – you said – *'put on a unified front at all times'!!* Ok – but *now* what? You wanna just take this break right now? What do I tell them???"

"Tell 'em I'm in St Louis."

"You know what I mean!" she snapped. "Do I tell my family we broke up...or what? Why can't we wait 'til I graduate?? Four more months, Rodney?"

"That's longer than four months," I tried to deflect.

"Ok – *five!* We been together going on four years and I can't get a few more months??? I'm not even saying *'don't break up with me'* or *'let's stay together'* at this point. I'm just asking you not to *leave* me right now…just not now is all I'm saying."

"KeLLy," I frowned at the thought. "I don't know, man."

"I'm almost done, Rodney," she kept pleading her case. "You know how hard it is for me and school right now. You *know* I don't wanna be down here. You don't even come down here to see me anymore. I'm almost done. I need you to get through this. Just…not…*now.* You making me feel like I'm begging."

"I don't want you to beg, though. I'm not looking for that if that's what you thinking."

"Hell, I might as well be! And you still haven't said *'yes'!* You want me to beg – I know you, Rodney."

"KeLLy. I'm not asking you to beg. I'm just asking for some time. If it's meant for us to be together…we will be in the end, regardless. That's all I'm saying…like – it's at the point where we don't even have fun with each other anymore. You don't wanna admit it, but this shit is all over the place, KeLLy. We need to miss each other again…we need to learn how to be friends again. Time. That's all I'm asking for. Time."

"Do you still love me, Rodney?" she asked suddenly, stopping me in my tracks.

"Don't ask me that."

"Do you? Answer me."

"I…man," I froze up, feeling trapped. "Yeah. I love you, KeLLy."

"Ok. And you *hear* me telling you – *I need you.*"

"I'm not gon' disappear, Kells," I said with reassurance. "I'm still here. We just need a break. Breathing room. Let me breathe."

"And you promise you not just trying to leave me??"

"KeLLy."

"You can't blame me for being unsure, Rodney. This is hard for me."

"It's hard for me too, KeLLy," I truthfully admitted.

"You not acting like it," she sniffled in my ear.

"Well, it is. You making it harder," I told her, wishing I didn't have to hear her crying right now.

"*I'm* making it harder?!?!" she yelled, her voice switching to pure rage. "How can you say that?!?!"

"KeLLy," I paused. "I gotta go."

"How can you say that, Rodney?" she repeated the question.

"I'ma talk to you later, KeLLy. I have to go."

"Are you gonna call me back?"

"I have to go," I said again, emotionless. "I'll call you back, KeLLy. Let me go right now."

As fukced up as it was…I had to get off the phone right at that moment. I couldn't keep Sashé waiting any longer; I'd been sitting outside her apartment far too long.

The chronic had kicked in…my eyes were too slanted and low for tears. The guilty conscious was weakened at the moment. And thinking about Shay's sweet pussy had the other monster in me ready to take back over.

I had to go.

*   *   *   *   *

The next morning, I woke up around 6:30am so I could get back on the road to KC and get ready for work. Plus, it was early enough that I knew KeLLy would still be sleep and at home.

Early mornings are the best time to sneak out of the Burg – the whole campus is usually hungover from the night before. Sashé and KeLLy's apartments were both on the east side of campus…but Sashé stayed further south. I had learned long ago that the back road to the highway was the best way to avoid any unwanted sightings. I could hit Business 50 and be back on the highway in the blink of an eye.

Still, on this morning, I called KeLLy when I got in the car…just to make sure she was still sleep.

Last night that guilt was barely there. Now…I can feel it creeping back. I can hear her in my head again…urging me not to give up.

It's starting to hit me.

But not enough for you to give her what she wants and stay.

Nah. I'm in too deep. I mean, I love KeLLy....I really do.

Right! So, if anything, you're more concerned now than ever…to not get caught.

*And I've been here before. This is how I learned **The Art** in the first place.*

If Kells finds out the shit I'm on with Shay now, in the middle of our rocky road, it'll devastate her. Whether this is really the end for us or not, I have to stay focused. I can't let her see me sweat.

She can never find out the whole story, bruh.

I got you, Rod. For real, this time. This time — we got this.

*   *   *   *   *

My trip back from St Louis the day after Christmas was filled with anticipation and eagerness. I remember

being hyped up about the *NFL* – the *Broncos* had clinched
the *AFC West* and secured the #2 seed with one more
game left in the season.

I had finally found a water bong that I liked in the
Lou and couldn't wait to get home to try it out. It was
coming up on a year since I had decided to stop drinking
for a while….by now I was completely immersed in the
herbal life. NYE 2004 was the last time I had taken a
drink. Well…technically.

I went from January '05 to sometime in August
without drinking any hard liquor – and then I had that big
fight with KeLLy in Oklahoma during Jaz's wedding
weekend. She didn't know it, but I had a drink that night
when I left the room for a little while. Double shot of gin
and pineapple juice – just one. I was pissed off that night
and we were fighting about some dumb ass random text
message she received about me. That made me relapse
over the weekend – with both the liquor *and* the cheating.

And just like with the cheating, I tried to be more
responsible with the drinking. So, after that wedding trip, I
started drinking strictly beer again – and Kells knew that
much. But what she didn't know about was how Sashé
had me thinking about hard liquor again. Me and GG had
gotten real close over this last year, but Sashé…she was a
drinker.

Since I had been kicking it with Shay on the
low…she had convinced me to take a shot or two here
and there. She had a bi-racial chick named *Tasha* for a
roommate and these little bitches loved to get white-girl
wasted in the Burg. Shay felt like sex was wilder when she
was drunk…and I felt like it was better with weed. I
hadn't been drunk in almost a year…but I promised Sashé
that I would get drunk with her if she got high with me
for the first time.

She decided that we would do just *that* when Kourtney came to hang out with us…the day before New Year's Eve 2005.

If I could pull this shit off…

*　　　*　　　*　　　*　　　*

December 30th fell on a Friday, and I had the spot to myself that night. I can't remember where Tre was. I just remember him not being around.

The stage was all set. I had a fifth of *Seagram's Gin*, two big cans of pineapple-orange juice, and a small bottle of *Sunny D*. Not to mention a half ounce of the finest mid-grade GG I could find. I was ready to get fukced up again…and bring in the new year the right way.

I was deep off in my own pre-party cloud of smoke when Sashé called me. I put her on speaker so I ain't have to put the blunt down.

"Hello," I answered, mid-puff.

"Hellloooo…Daddy? Are you home? Is that youuu?" She was obviously tipsy.

"It's me, baby," I confirmed calmly. "Are you drunk?"

"I am fuuuuuucked up! Oh my God, you can tell?!?!?!" she gasped. "Kourtneeeey??? *He can telllll!*"

"Where y'all at? Are you driving???"

"Hell no!" she replied quickly. "We're almoss dere, Daddy. Ok??"

"Ok," my lungs were full of smoke. "Are you aight?"

"Yeah. I think," she gulped. "Are you ok, Daddy?"

She sounds so vulnerably sexy. My dick is jumping. I hear Kourtney screaming something in the background but can't make out what she's saying.

"I'm ok," I grinned. "Hurry up and get to me."

"Ok…ok…"

"Ok, bye," I started to end the call.

"No, wait!" she cried out. "Yeah! That's right! I had something to ask you…to *tell* you when I called. What waas it Dad…oh, right, right. Kourt said she's gonna pair you when we get there."

I looked down at the phone confused, "Kourtney said she's gonna do what???"

"She's gonna pair with you…huh?" she mumbled something away from the phone. "Ooooohh…no…she said *'match'!* She's gonna match you."

"Oh, ok," I tried to hold back my laughter. "Right. Ok, that's cool. I'm at home. Come on."

"There was something else," she said, voice drifting off.

"Ok?" my eyebrow raised in anticipation.

"I can't remember Daddy," she admitted, sounding flustered. "What was I gonna saaaaay??"

"I don't know, baby!" I stood up to walk to the window. "You're drunk!"

Shay busted out laughing hysterically, "Oh my God, I ammmm!!! Yikesss! We took shots of Patron earlier! And I don't know how the hell Kourt is not drunk. I have no ideeea!"

"Is that y'all pulling in the lot??"

"You see us?!?! He sees us, girl! Are you looking out the window? Can you see me?"

"I can't see in the car, lil baby," I licked my lips, full of eagerness. "But yea, I see y'all. Here I come, I'm 'bout to meet y'all downstairs."

*　　*　　*　　*　　*

6

So I'm on the far-right end of the couch and Kourtney is sitting next to me…with Shay on the other end.

We drank for about a half hour as Kourtney and I rolled up Swishers. The girl had skills…she finished twisting up well before I did. Then again, I took my time as I broke the GG down…paying attention to the girls. How they interacted, their chemistry.

They were really close.

Sashé was a naturally friendly person; this I had already figured out. But there was something noticeably different in how she interacted with Kourtney versus her roommate in the Burg, *Tasha*. When Kourtney spoke, Sashé looked at her as attentively as she did when *I* spoke. There was pure admiration in the air between the two of them.

They were both tipsy before they walked in – you could see it in Kourtney's hazel eyes the same as Sashé's big browns. When talking to each other…they were mutually giggly and white-girl dingy – hugging up as they shared laughs about silly shit.

When Kourtney talked to me, however, the hood came out. She was witty and sharp-tongued.

"Damn, nigga! You still ain't done rolling that blunt? Shay, you forgot to tell me he was slow."

"Oooooh…we got jokes, though?"

"He's just taking his time," Shay came to my defense.

"I'm just saying," Kourtney sucked her teeth.

"*I'm* just saying – you babysitting that cup, though," I looked down at her barely touched drink.

"Oh, you ain't saying nothing but a word!" she sat up towards the wooden table in front of us, swooped her red cup up and took it down in one motion.

Shay playfully helped her tilt the cup back with her head, grinning ear to ear. Kourt gulped it all and looked me in the eye with a raised brow…sucking her teeth once again. She wore her hair in a short bob to her ears and didn't flinch as Shay started curling strands around her pinky finger.

"But I *did* tell you he was cute," Shay whispered, biting her bottom lip.

"Yes, you did tell me that," Kourtney kept her eyes on me. "And he is. This nigga think he *too* cute, though."

"How? What I do?" I asked, playing innocent.

"Mmmm hmmm," Kourtney stared me down, sizing me up. "I know your type."

"Oh, for real? What's my type?"

"You one of them schoolboy – hood ass niggas," she replied with a smirk. "Think you fly n'shit."

Sashé tilted her head to get a good look at me, "That's riiiiight, baby! See? She's good."

"See…look at that nigga, girl!!!" Kourt blurted out, getting louder. "Licking his lips n'shit like that!! You ain't gotta wet the blunt up like that!"

"What you mean?? Can't roll it dry," I licked the Swisher again slowly.

"Mmmm hmm…you just like using that tongue! You a freak, nigga too!" her eyes lowered, focusing on my mouth.

"He *is* a freak. Yes," Shay whispered in agreement. She was loving this exchange, nearly drooling as she stared at the side of Kourt's chocolate face.

Kourtney licked her lips at me in jest…and I looked away smiling. Reaching for the lighter, I noticed that my red cup was still full…though it felt like I had taken more than just a couple of sips. I ain't know whether to slow my pace down or speed the fukc up.

Man, I don't know, Rod – but it's hot as a muthafukca in here right now, nigga!

The **beast** wuttin' lying. I was known to keep the heat on blast at the crib – me and Tre were forever going back and forth about it. Especially when I was expecting female company…but I mean, duh! That's the oldest trick in the book.

Tonight, my plan was sho-nuff backfiring, though.

When the girls pulled up, I was in my usual home attire of gym shorts and a wife-beater. But Sashé had other plans for me – she wanted to show me off to Kourt. So the first thing she asks me to do was put some clothes on and get real *'HoLLyRod'* for my guests.

A half hour and a club outfit later, Kourtney and Sashé were sitting cool and comfortably…while I was the one sweating in my socks.

Just stay cool, yo. This is first time we've been alone with two chicks – with a real chance at the ménage!

Stay cool? How, nigga? The thought alone was already more than enough to break a sweat – but you got the heat on 80 and we sitting here looking crazy in a damn V-neck sweater!

I know, man. I know. Just let it play it out, though.

Ain't that about a bitch!

"Girl, you can't be having me up in here with no freak," Kourtney tells Shay. "I got rid of all my freaks in KC, I told you."

"I knowww!!! But I haven't seen you in forever, babes! FOR-EV-ER!!!" Shay was obsessed with *'The Sandlot'* movie…especially when she was drunk.

She catches me looking at her and bites her lip before she faces Kourtney again. They were holding hands now, close enough to kiss. It made me freeze up…anxious to see what happens next.

Kourtney licked her tongue out at Shay's lips…and they both burst out laughing. This caused me to snap back to life, and I grabbed my cup off the table, lighter still in hand. It's ice cold against my lips…momentarily cooling me off.

I can't keep these fukcin' clothes on much longer, though…

I'm wearing a burgundy *Polo* sweater with a red button-down underneath, blue jeans, and slip-on *Steve Maddens*. Nothing too fancy…but then again, it's so *'HoLLy'*, just the way Shay liked me. Luckily my *HoLLy Shades* had long moved from my face to the V-neck of my sweater, though. At least I could see clearly through the heatwave.

"Bitch, when you gonna come visit me in Atlanta??" Kourtney asked her friend casually.

I let them keep talking and start to pull my sweater over my head…carefully so I don't fukc up my wave pattern.

"I don't knowwwww," Shay responds, full of energy and excitement. "Maybe next year for my twenty-first?!?!"

"Girl, yes!!!" Kourtney matches Shay's energy. "Then we can celebrate together!!!"

"Yes! Oh my God, baby, can we go?!?!" this girl is super excited right now…and looking at me, waiting on my answer.

I think she's starting to forget that she has a boyfriend down at Langston University…which is far as fukc, but still. She's talking to me like I'm her man. Like seriously as if she's disregarding this nigga. I guess now that I think about it, it's very much the same way I'm starting to fade KeLLy out over the last few months. I mean, this whole affair is crazy belligerent. For the both of us.

Yeah, this is real life HoLLy BeLLigerence.

But I can't get enough of this Sashé chick!

How could you, nigga? She's all fun…all the fukcing time.

No holds barred!!! And she ain't held me back or slowed me down one time since we've met.

Hell yeah! I mean, by now, a bitch woulda at least made a comment or been offended by our smart ass, rude mouth!

*Who you telling?? KeLLy gets mad if I even **cuss** in public!!!*

But Sashé just let me be me…cheering me on like the ultimate groupie. She was seriously on my jock, 100% engulfed in me. Laughed at my every joke…and I ain't that damn funny. She was in love with the way I dressed, the raspy sound of my voice. I've known this chick three months and not once has she had a bitchy attitude with me. Which was crazy, because I was used to KeLLy being mad about whatever and taking it out on me.

Don't get me wrong – Sashé was still human. I'd seen her slightly angered or annoyed about shit since we met. But her face and tone of voice switched up just as quickly when she turned my way…like I just made her 'tude go away instantly.

This was new territory for me…

Not the groupie-style way that Shay was on my tip; nah, I was used to that. Just not from *my girl.* Your #1 is programmed to be the opposite of the groupie…she ain't the one to be all on ya nut sack just because. No – she gon' tell you like it is; she ain't with all that *fan* shit.

Being a Nupe, I definitely had my taste of fans chasing after me for my status. KeLLy came from that pool that didn't wanna be looked at as my *'groupie'*…and after damn near four years of tasting humble pie at home with her – now I'm jones'n for the way Shay feeds me more of myself.

Sashé got me thinking I'm the shit at a time when KeLLy thinks I ain't.

I mean…when was the last time Kells made you feel like you could do no wrong?

Yeah, why can't my girl be my main cheerleader?

Why can't Kells be on our jock like Sashé is?!?!?!

I mean, look at this shit – we only been fukcing for about a month, ain't had many sessions at all…and she's already bringing me different bitches!

She's already willing to give us anything we ask for…

"You wanna go outta town with me?" I asked her. "What about your man?"

"What about him?! We're probably not gonna even be together then," she decided on the spot. "I'm sure we won't. So, what about him?"

"Yo, what about that blunt, my nigga?" Kourtney impatiently interrupted. I almost forgot I was holding it.

"No, wait!" Shay yelled suddenly. "Can we try the bong first???"

I also almost forgot this was Shay's first time smoking. KeLLy wouldn't dare smoke with me. She thought it was gross and unladylike. Right now, though, I think it's sexy as fukc what I'm witnessing.

Kourtney is showing Shay how to take a pull from my water bong. Well, at least *trying to*. The clean hit of smoke hit Kourtney's chest a little too hard so she's really struggling to catch her breath and stop Shay from laughing so hard.

"See???" I smiled with satisfaction. "Tryna be cute n'shit!!!"

Kourtney tried to talk shit through the coughs and managed to flip me off. I undid the rest of the buttons on my shirt and started walking towards the thermostat. It felt like the smoke in the room was making it hotter.

Out the corner of my eye, once I got to the wall, I noticed Shay coming out of her shirt…sports bra looking like it was gon' rip apart. Before I could blink, Kourtney followed suit – but she was standing up peeling her jeans off. Within a split second, she had her green boy shorts exposed…chocolate ass cheeks hanging everywhere.

"*Now* I'm tryna be cute, shawty," she lowered her eyes at me. "What you know 'bout it??"

Both me and Shay were staring in awe. Kourtney had some big legs, and an even bigger ass. Up top she was small – maybe a B-cup…barely. Reminded me of Cookie's missing cleavage. But Cookie was *petite* with ass. Kourtney was *healthy*…with wide child-bearing hips to go with the ass. And dark.

KeLLy-dark.

I'm lowkey missing the fukc outta my ex-side bitch and main girl. But right now I'm in a room full of my cravings.

"Daaaaamn…like that?" my jaw dropped.

Kourtney laughed, "No, but for real, dude. It's hot in here!!!"

"I turned the heat down," I shrugged.

"Hey, it's okay!" Shay threw her hands in the air. "Get naked, it's New Year's! Well…almost. Or whatever. Yeah."

We all laughed for a second. But I wuttin' opposed to bringing in the new year early with a bang.

That's some serious talk right there, nigga.

Real shit! Let's get muthafukcin' naked!!!

This shit is really about to happen, the wait is over!!!

It felt like Nae-Nae and Lil Mama all over again for a nigga. Two chicks ready to get down…*déjà vü.*

This time I was ready. I had Sunny D in my system…and was popping Ginseng pills all day. Got a good stretch workout in and let off that first nut before they pulled up. Condoms under my mattress, under the couch pillows, in my gym shorts.

My gym shorts. That's all I need. I'm ready.

"Yea," I smiled devilishly. "Let's get naked then!!!" I then took my cup to the head and finished it off.

Time to get this party started.

I walked towards Kourtney, who was still standing in front of Shay, squeezing her own ass.

"Bitch, you know you can't get naked right now anyway!" Kourt yelled at Shay. "Stop playing!!!"

Huh? How come she can't?

"Oh, yeah," Shay sounded disappointed. "Dang it!"

Wait. What is she talking abo…

"What you mean?" my eyes got wide, giving Shay a look of confusion. "What you talking about?"

"Remember?" she frowned. "I told you, Daddy!"

Bitch you ain't told me shit!!!

"Told me what?"

Kourtney started laughing and turned around to face me. She then put her hands on my shoulders and poked her ass out at Shay.

"What's so funny?" I demanded to know.

Not again!!!

"Girl, that's what you called to tell him in the car!!!" Kourtney reminded her friend, still laughing.

"*And I forgoooooot!!!*" Shay's reply was loud and dingy, she thought it was funny as fukc. "Oh my god – that's hilarious!!!"

I don't see shit funny!!

"No threesome for you," Kourtney shook her head at me, in a tisk-tisk manner.

"Mother Nature, Daddy," Sashé added, apologetically.

Wow! Just wow!!!

Not again, Rod!!!!!

And just like that, the party was over.

*   *   *   *   *

Well, not exactly. We kept kicking it, got high and drunk as fukc, and kept our clothes on. Kourtney even put her jeans back on so I *'wouldn't feel teased'*.

That shit ain't work. I had been anticipating this shit all day…just like before. It's always something.

After all this…here we are shit outta luck again!

Maybe it ain't meant for me to have this ménage!!! What if I'm supposed to just stick to the normal shit? I ain't cut out for this type of disappointment — not when I'm drunk and horny like this!

You know I usually say, 'don't sweat it'. But this is for real that bullshit, bruh!

Of course, Sashé and Kourtney were optimistic and in great spirits about the whole ordeal. They just insisted that next time Kourt was in town, we could try again. Shay was really, really, really wanting to explore her bisexuality; she wanted the best of both worlds. She was sure about that. But shit – when was Kourtney coming back? They couldn't answer that with anything but more laughter.

Then shortly after 1 in the morning, Kourtney was ready to leave, and we said our goodbyes.

The worse part of the way this night ended was me not getting no pussy *at all.* I mean, no freaking, no head, no nothing. We just hung out and drank and talked shit.

I mean, I guess that's what we get for expecting something, right?

80

Man, my dick is too hard for this shit right now, though!

I gotta do something. I had gotten used to having pussy at my disposal whenever I wanted it. But I ain't talked to Cookie in forever and now I'm all but done with KeLLy.

But I wonder what she's doing right now, though.

For real. I wonder if she'll answer my text...

*　　　*　　　*　　　*　　　*

7

Cookie...or...KeLLy?

I wanna text them *both*.

Kells is somewhere in KC, I'm sure…and not too far. And I know that even though it's late, there's a good chance she'd be willing to come through, despite all the drama we got going at the moment.

Nah, cuz that's just gon' open shit back up! We'll be right back where we ended with her all over again.

Yeah, but then again…that's where I'm at anyway!!! I mean, I'm sitting here with a erection just going to waste, thinking about my old bitches! This some bullshit!

Cookie is in the Burg…I think. She mighta went home to St. Louis for the holiday, though. I know she graduated a few weeks ago, we talked about it. She really wanted me to make it to the ceremony and I told her I thought it was best we stayed away…*blah blah blah*. But now…I'm thinking about how nice it would be to just palm her ass again…how awesome it would be to watch her throw it back at me.

Then, at the same time, I don't wanna fukc up what I got going on with *Sashé*. And if Cookie found out about Sashé…she might try to confront her. If she found out I stopped fukcing with her *and* Kells…Cookie be done threw salt on my whole opportunity at a ménage.

The whole thought process is selfish in itself…but I can only be me. I ain't been this drunk in a while…since I kicked it with Kells' fam last New Year's. I most definitely ain't been this drunk with no pussy around. Not ever.

My dick feels like it's gon' burst open!!!

Dammit, Rod!!!

I know it's almost 2 in the morning but I've gotta get somebody over here to take care of this shit, bro. I can't take it no more!!!

I'm not sure if this is the first drunk text I've ever sent…but it's the first one I can remember.

ME: "I want u so fukcin' bad right now…"

It's simple and classic…desperate and pathetic.

Waiting on a reply to a drunk text is the worst. It seemed like everything was in slow motion. But the reply to the *missing reply* was even *more* pathetic than the original text. After 7 minutes that seemed like twice the time, I sent her another.

ME: "???"

I laid there in my bed, alone in my apartment, burping with a bad case of drunken hiccups, waiting on a response. My dick was throbbing in my shorts now and suddenly being gripped by my left hand outta nowhere. Human nature would soon take over…

*   *   *   *   *

I halfway woke up some time later to my phone vibrating with texts. There was drool all over the side of my face from the puddle on the pillow. Since I was half sleep…I wiped my face off and grabbed my phone, covering it with my slobber. But even if I *was* fully coherent, I wouldn't have cared after reading the replies.

She bit the bait…and all I had to do was tell her Tre wasn't home for her to be on her way. She was missing it, too. It's hard to just…*let go*. We agreed that it should be no-strings attached. After everything that happened, no one needed to know that she was willing to get it in one last time on some grand finale shit.

For me that was even better. A reasonable downgrade from Plan A – and it kept my chances with Shay safe since we was keeping it on the hush.

Hormones always keep *The Art of Cheating* moving.

My first ménage didn't happen after all that night…but it did put me in a deeper state of mind within the realm of possibilities. If I played my cards right with Sashé…if I could pull this shit off...

Maybe...

Just maybe...

…I could satisfy the hunger of my inner *beast* more than just temporarily…

*   *   *   *   *

January 2006

But then...my new year started off shitty and fukced up.

First, my Honda died on me, on the highway heading in to work. I had put over 200,000 miles on *Annie Mae*...riding that shit 'til the wheels literally stopped turning. The stress and frustration with buying a new car was heavy – and it was even harder now that KeLLy and I were separated. I don't give a fukc who you are or what shit you talk with ya homeboys...it ain't nuttin' like having the support of a strong woman when you down and out.

I most definitely felt the ramifications of my actions when *Annie Mae* died....and I felt even more guilt considering all the extra miles I had been recently putting on my car driving down to see Sashé. We were getting closer...but I was nowhere *near* the level with Sashé that I was with KeLLy when all this shit happened. I knew that instantly when I felt uncomfortable even talking to Shay about my real-life problems n'shit.

The car I chose after *Annie Mae* was in the *Dodge* family...an olive green *Intrepid* with lower miles. Nicknaming her was a no-brainer. I called her *Keisha*, one for her color...and two because she was truly a bounce-back bitch after *Annie Mae*.

We all got that rebound chick after losing the one we loved. And Keisha seemed like the appropriate handle; it was as common as freaks that went by that name. It would be hard to get over Annie Mae, but I felt like Keisha was in perfect enough shape to help me move on. I paid for her outright – and drove her off the lot like a boss.

But then *she* died on me a month later. The sour lemon taste left in my mouth was hella bitter. Bank account was empty, funds depleted after replacing my car, and no warranty or dealer ties. I was all the way THEW.

My worst start to a New Year ever. And it took me into deep thought. It felt like **karma**, if karma was a real thing. But even more than that, it felt like the *Son's Curse* teaching me a lesson. Obviously, I had done something to deserve all this shit hitting me at once – and of course, I took it as a sign that I was being punished for leaving Kells. I mean…the symbolism was crystal clear for me – especially when I thought about all of the wild fantasies I was trying to live out with my real-life rebound chick, Shay. I started to believe it served me right.

This made me fall back from Shay for a little while – giving her the cold shoulder for a few weeks, as I locked myself in my room and focused on just writing music. But then that put me right the fukc back where I was the night Kourtney and Shay left me drunk with blue balls. Alone again.

It was during this time that I finally thought about the fact that since I'd lost my virginity to *Nae-Nae* all those years ago in *Parker Square*, I've never truly been alone or single. I've always had a chick I could call or fall back on; never truly been in a drought.

Man…this journey is a muhfukca…

A drought is simply *un-HoLLy-like*…so even though I'm in shutdown mode with anybody close to me, I still found time to get on some frustration-fukcing mode missions.

I started calling up all the old random chicks I could get in contact with. Hopping on *MySpace* meeting new freaks, finding chicks on *Yahoo* all over the world to have sex chats with. I basically fell back into the old me: before

Sashé and before KeLLy – with no ties and more lies.
Getting multiple pieces of pussy almost always makes a
nigga feel normal again and fukcing chicks with absolutely
no emotional connection was still the same old rush. I was
in a full-blown relapse now, on an adrenaline high from
the ménage chase.

But every morning I woke up became a new reality
check for me. I was without a car, with no money or plan.
I had some help with my frat brother *Shabba*, who lived
nearby in Raytown and offered to take me back and forth
to work until I figured things out. That was huge. But like
I said, otherwise I had no plan. I knew it was gon' take me
months to save up enough for a new engine or car. I had
spent all I had on Keisha's ass.

Meanwhile, Sashé eventually started to get tired of
me avoiding her and demanded to know what I was going
through that had me shutting her out all of a sudden. So I
told her the deal…expressing how real life just hit me
hard, how the timing was so fukced up. It was a crazy
conversation for her…because she'd never dealt with stuff
like this, and she couldn't imagine something stealing her
joy like that.

In a way, this situation that I was in *was* in fact
stealing her joy…because it was taking me away from her
at the moment. She started telling me how much she
missed talking to me, how I always made her day
complete. She tells me she just really wants me back in her
world – no matter what it would take. All of this was
healthy for my beyond overweight ego…but it really did
little to make my real problems go away.

Then Sashé tells me she's gon' give me the funds to
get a new engine…and won't take no for an answer. She
had some money saved up and said I could just pay her
back whenever I got it. I was hesitant and reluctant as ever

with this offer. I mean, it was crazy that she was even considering it. But regardless of how much I resisted, she refused to let me decline…and insisted that I take it.

"No, like seriously…you're gonna accept my help," she sounded like her mind was made up. "That's what people do…they help the people they care about."

"Yeah, but I can't take that from you," I shook my head at the phone. "It's just not right."

"How come it's not, Rodney? You act like we just started talking or something! We've been doing this almost five months, you know? That's almost half a year! Please…don't even try it."

"Yeah, but," I was shocked at her persistence. I don't think I've ever heard her speak so firmly. "Still. I mean – what about *Keith*?"

"Oh wow…you love to bring him up," she sighed.

"I mean…that's ya boyfriend!"

"And?!?!?" she cried out with irritation. "Ok, first of all…he doesn't even need the help – his parent have money and he's an only child. So even if this was going on with him, he wouldn't even ask me for help. He doesn't need my help."

"Well, but I'm not asking either," I calmly pointed out.

"Yeah, but *you* need it," she shot back quickly. "And secondly…me and Keith are not gonna be together that much longer anyway."

"See, you keep saying that," I started rubbing my closed eyes, not liking where this appeared to be headed.

"Because it's *true!!!* I told you that! You make me see and think about things I never thought about with relationships and I just don't wanna be with him anymore. This long distance isn't helping. I mean, he's just so immature compared to you."

"But you know I'm not tryna break y'all up."

"Yeah, yeah — *'the rules of cheating',*" she mocked me. "You've told me a hundred times now. But, so what? You're *not* breaking us up — this is *my* choice. I just have to figure out the right time to have that talk with him. Even if you and I don't end up together or whatever…I still know that he is not the one I wanna be with now. So, it's not you *directly* breaking us up. Just like I'm not making you break up with KeLLy."

"I can't really say if it's you or not," I admitted to both her and myself. "I know you got a big part in it. Especially when you do stuff like *this.*"

"Well, that's fine…I don't see anything wrong in that," she shrugged. "And I don't see anything wrong with me loaning you this money to get your car fixed, either. It's a loan agreement. People do that in this country all the time! Where else are you gonna get the money from?"

"I don't know," I hung my head. "I'm tryna figure it out."

"Well, it's figured out," she countered with haste. "You just need to figure out what time I should come to the city to give it to you."

I let out a long sigh, "You're serious huh?"

"Yes. You have to see me sooner or later. You are *not* getting rid of me that easily. I'm not done with you, Mister."

"You say dat like you got plans for me," I chuckled. "I don't know how to take that."

"That is *exactly* how you should take that! We have unfinished business," she replied with sass. "So, when are you free for me to come up today?"

She's normally not this aggressive…but she's taking command to get what she wants. I think I kinda like that shit.

"Uhm…I don't know," I thought about it. "I get off work at 9 and it takes me and Shabba about a half hour to get back to my spot."

"Oh, that's perfect!" she said excitedly. "So, tell your bruh that he doesn't have to pick you up tonight and I'll see you at 9. I'll make you enchiladas."

"Wait…what? You gon' cook?" my eyebrow raised in shock. Shay never cooked for me before.

"Yes, silly! I have to learn sooner or later, like you said – right? The *3-F Formula*…remember?"

I smiled hard, "Damn. Yeah. That's right. *The 3 Fs* you gotta 'keep' a man…in order to keep him."

"Fed. Fukced. And Focused. It's time to master those other two. This is as good a time as any."

"Damn, Shay…see look at you," I shook my head again. "It's like you forget you already got a man."

"No," she disagreed innocently. "I'm just learning my lessons from *Daddy*."

Dammit I loved when she called me that. It always made her convo take a turn in the right direction.

"Don't start calling me that," I teased.

"Daddy?" she asked, playing confused. "But…you're Daddy."

I bit my lip, "And why am I Daddy?"

"Cuz I'm your *'bitch'*," she responded submissively. "I'm Daddy's bitch…"

"Maaaan," I started drooling. "You just say all the right things, huh?"

"I just want my Daddy back, Daddy."

"Good girl. I'm here, baby."

"Good. So, I'll see you tonight?" she asked with eagerness.

"Hmmm…I don't know," I hesitated playfully. "You got me thinking now. You talmbout *'we got unfinished business'* and *'you got plans'* n'shit. I don't know what all I'm signing up for here."

"Oh, please – whatever!" she snapped back. "You know you want what I have planned, boy."

"Say it," I commanded her.

"What do you wanna hear me say? That I want you to fukc me while I fukc my friend? Is that what you wanna hear, Daddy?"

"Is that all you want?"

She paused, "Hmmm. No. I want you to eat me while you fukc her, too. I wanna see you hit it from behind when I'm playing with myself. I want us both to make you cum, Daddy."

My dick started throbbing. Shay really knew how to talk to me; she handled her sub role naturally.

"Fuuuuuuuck, man!" I groaned in agony. "When is Kourt coming back to KC, man?!?!"

"I don't know. Spring break, I think. I mean – that's the soonest."

I pouted like a brat, "Man, that's so long from now."

"Yeah. I know," Shay agreed, just as disappointed. "But, I mean…what else can we do? It's not like we have anybody else that's down, babe."

"Man, it's gotta be somebody else you know that'll do that shit. All them damn chicks you hang with down on campus!"

"Hmmm," she thought about it. "No, I don't know, Daddy. I mean…the only one I would even feel comfortable with is my roomie Tasha – *maybe*. But I don't even think she's into girls like that. What about all the chicks you used to mess around with? You haven't talked to Cookie or any of ya old girls?? You know more females than me, Daddy."

I paused, as my heart skipped a beat.

Stay cool, Rod!

"Uhm...nope. Haven't talked to her. And Cookie is strictly dickly anyway – I know she's not down. We got a better chance with Tasha. I don't know any bi chicks."

"I don't know. I mean, I really don't think she likes girls," she reiterated. "I know she'll fukc *you*...she told me she wanted to. But there's no way I'm sharing you if I can't do her, too – and she knows *that*. So, if she liked girls...she woulda told me by now, right?"

"I mean...not necessarily. Maybe you should just outright ask her. Ask her if she's down for the ménage," I suggested with a smirk.

"I don't know," Shay contemplated. "I really wanna wait on Kourt."

I licked my lips, envisioning all'at thick chocolate, "I know but...maaaaaan. That's like three months from now!"

"Right. Ok. I'll ask her. For you, Daddy," she whispered softly.

"You will?? It's for you, too, though. For us."

"I like the sound of that. *Us*."

I couldn't help but laugh, "Oh, here you gooooo."

"It has a nice ring to it...you have to admit. We're good together," she declared confidently.

"Yeah, but we bad together, too," I reminded her. "We stay doing bad shit."

"But *'everything that's supposed to be bad…make me feel so good'*," Shay started reciting that *Kanye* track *'Addiction'*, the song we loved to get high together listening to. It was almost like our theme song. It described our situationship almost to a tee.

I chimed in immediately with the next line from the song, "*…Everything they told me not to is exactly what I would'…*"

"'*…man, I tried to stop now…I tried the best I could, but'…*"

"'*…you make me smiiiiile….*'" I sang off-key, grinning big.

"You make me smile, too, Daddy," she ended with the ultimate touch of sexiness. "I'll see you later, baby."

*   *   *   *   *

February 2006

In the weeks that followed, I started straightening up my acts of cheating again, and Sashé and I got our mojo back. Even though again – *technically* I wuttin' cheating on Shay because she wuttin' my girl…I still considered it cheating in a weird way because I hid the shit from her like she was. At any rate…once she helped me out with my car and showed me how much she was rocking with a nigga…I lost some of those sneaky urges again. Sashé's sex was off the chain…and the anticipation of the ménage life was enough to keep me sexually loyal to her.

It still took me a minute to find a used engine that was suitable for Keisha, however. Something about the VIN of my particular *Intrepid* model determined the type of specific engine to be used…and I was still without a ride in the search. Shabba and Shay held me down, though…him making sure I got to work, and her taking every chance she could to drive to KC from the Burg to take me home. This routine surprisingly never got old…and we all thugged it out for a little while.

But the shit was stressful as hell, I can't even bullshit about it. This was something I couldn't even bring to my closest family, not even Dell or Ronnie. To be clear, I mean – Ronnie and I hadn't spoke for over four months now; the longest I had ever gone without talking to my sister.

Dell and Ronnie had become super close after I left for college and were even tighter now after Dell's brother *Lloyd* was killed last fall. So, I couldn't even holla at Dell right now if I wanted to...with me and Ronnie into it. In fact, things were so shaky between Ronnie and I at this point that I was nervous about her even knowing where I stay. When project kids are fighting, things get grimy as hell –something only few would understand.

*   *   *   *   *

April 2006

So, I moved to a new spot out in Overland Park, KS that was much closer to my job, and that took some of the load off of Shabba's commute now that I could almost walk to work. Sashé held me down the rest of the time until my car was done with repairs.

The night Keisha was finally up and running was cause for a celebration. Shabba and I got a bunch of other Nupes to have a Brotherhood session at *Buffalo Wild Wings* so we could hang out and make toasts. It was also my line's 7-year anniversary, so Nupes were ready to be out. As I was getting ready for the night of bonding and breaking bread…I get a call from Sashé, asking for a favor.

"Uh oh. I don't like how that sounds," my eyebrow raised in its signature motion.

"Why you say that, Daddy???" Shay giggled. "You don't even know what I'ma ask!"

"Ok. What is it, lil baby?"

Shay's voice lit up, "Ok, well…it's two things, actually."

"I'm listening," I prepared to brace myself. You never knew what Sashé would come up with next.

"Ok, so, me and the girls wanna get drunk tonight; we want to come up to the city. The rest of the girls are already up there still from Spring Break."

I squinted, "Ok…who you coming to the city with – you talmbout *Tasha?*"

"Yea, duh…my roommate. We just all wanna hang out before we go back from break, and Tasha is back from the Lou a few days early."

"O…k. Whatchu need from me? You know I'm on my way to Brotherhood in an hour or so."

"Right. Well…but you know none of us are '21', Daddy."

"Ohhhh," a lightbulb went off in my head. "Right. The usual. You need me to buy y'all some liquor."

"Yes…of course," Shay confirmed. "That's the first favor."

"And the other one??"

"Ok, well," she paused for a split second. "When we get to the city – we don't have anywhere to get drunk at!"

"And you wanna…"

"We wanna know if we can hang at your place while you're at Brotherhood with the Nupes!!! We promise we won't get too crazy or anything."

"Oh, wow," I looked up at the living room ceiling. "Uhm…so who all we talking about here?"

"It's me and Tash, and then Angie and Maria. So just us 4," she explained excitedly.

"Hmmm. I don't know," I thought about the scenario. "I mean, it's cool…but…"

"But what, Daddy??" she cut me off. "Pleeeeease??"

"I mean, I would do it…but I got my little cousin *Rico* staying at my spot this weekend. He's here now."

"Oh, that's fine! We're just gonna be there partying and doing drunk girl stuff…we won't be in his way,

Daddy. He's just gonna play PlayStation all night like he always does anyway."

"Yeah, but you know that fool still a virgin and be getting nervous around girls," I reminded her.

"Leave Lil Rico alone!" she whined. "He's only 17!"

"Aye I was fukcing before 17!" I shot back. "And that nigga's birthday ain't for a couple of months, but still. All I'm saying is…he might not be able to handle all y'all college chicks over here like that."

Lil Rico looks up from his video game at me, face screwed up, "Aye, forget you, cuzz! I can handle whatever!"

Sashé started screaming frantically into the phone, "See?! He can handle whatever; he got this! Say yes, Daddy! I'll do anything!"

"Anything like what?" I bit my lip.

"You name it."

Hmmm. I could use this to my advantage. It'd be all good if I wasn't on my way to hang with the Nupes tonight…but I can't miss this meet for the world. And Lil Rico staying over for the weekend was already a stretch. I rarely left that lil nigga alone; he was still at that age where he could get reckless. Rico was a good kid, though. He reminded me of myself minus all the womanizing.

Wait, Rod! I got an idea…

"Ok," I smiled at my thoughts. "I'll let y'all crash. On one condition."

"Name it, Daddy!" Shay repeated anxiously.

"Ok, I'ma have to get y'all liquor and be gone before y'all make it from the Burg," I started explaining. "So, text me what y'all want and I'll let y'all party over here while I'm gone. But…y'all gotta all do something for me."

"What, Daddy? You want us to have a ménage?!?! Are you still upset that Kourtney didn't come home for Spring Break?"

"No…I ain't even say all'at. I mean…she's coming home for the summer, right?"

"She's coming for a hot second before she goes to summer session," Shay clarified.

"Right. No. I'm not mad about that. What I'm asking has nothing to do with me…actually."

"Well, what do you want, Daddy?" she urged me to spit it out.

"Y'all can crash at my spot," I told her. "But since y'all gonna be here with my little cousin, I want y'all to *freak him down*."

"What?!?!" Lil Rico yelled at me.

"Shut up, lil nigga!" I barked back, grinning.

"Wait…what, Daddy?" Shay gasped, her voice going up a notch. "You want us to freak *Lil Rico* down??!?! Seriously???"

"Dead serious. This nigga need to start preparing anyway…ain't no way he ain't fukcing yet!"

"Leave him alone!" Shay came to Rico's defense again.

"No, for real," I wasn't joking. "I want y'all to freak him down, show him the ropes a little. Tease him. Fukc with him."

Shay started cracking up, "Oh my God, Daddy! You are craaaazy!"

"So, is it a deal?" I asked for confirmation.

"Hold on, Daddy," she pauses for a second and I hear her talking to Tasha in the background. Lil Rico is sitting there frozen, staring up at me…in shock at how I'm talking this up.

"I'm just saying," I smiled at my cousin. "Not too much to ask."

Sashé comes back after a couple of seconds, "Hmmm. Ok. Deal! Tasha is down…and I know the other girls will do whatever."

"You serious???" I was actually shocked. "You know what I'm asking?"

"Yes. I got you, Daddy."

"So, what time are y'all coming?" I bit my lip.

"We're leaving here shortly, and Angie and Maria are near you in O.P.," she told me. "So, we should be at your place in the next hour and a half maybe?"

"Ok. Well, lemme hurry up so I can go get y'all liquor. Text me what y'all want. Rico 'a be here when y'all pull up."

"Ok, Daddy," her voice was filled with happiness. "Tell Lil Rico tonight it's his lucky night!"

"Ok, I will," I laughed as I ended the call. When I hung up…Lil Rico just kept staring at me with his mouth wide open.

"Bro, what the fukc, man?" he cried out in confusion.

"Shut up, punk," I snapped at him firmly. "Come on and ride with me to the store real quick. Tonight might get crazy."

*   *   *   *   *

8

I got back from Brotherhood close to 2 in the morning – maybe around a quarter 'til or so. I remember because when I got home, Lil Rico and Sashé were sitting on the couch, eyes glued to the tv, waiting on *'BET Uncut'* to come on. The scenery was crazy when I walked in the door. You could definitely tell that they had a night of wild drunken fun.

Lil Rico was on the far end closest to the front door, his tall and lanky body stretched out with his legs and feet to the floor. Rico was tall as fukc now…about a half foot taller than myself, so I kicked him in the foot to make some room for me.

"Quit playing!" he shouted, his voice cracking.

"Move, nigga!" I snarled. "What the fukc going on in here?"

"Hey, Daddy," Shay smiled. She tries to stand up to gimme love and makes it about halfway before I have to catch her in my arms. Her eyes are low…glowing red. She's got on a halter top and volleyball shorts…and I could tell her legs were oiled up.

Pulling her close enough to give her forehead a kiss…I reached under her right cheek to rub her thigh. She grabbed the back of my neck and got closer, grinding up against me with her hips.

"I'm drunk, baby," she mumbled in my ear. "We're all drunk. Every-bodeeee."

"I see."

Shay's friend, *Angie*, was curled up on the other end of the couch, in a deep sleep. She was snoring softly, but loud enough where you could hear it. And I hate snoring.

Angie was the anomaly of Shay's crew…on the heavier side. Other than that, she was cool – a young redbone with some long wavy hair. I'd never seen her with weave, either. In fact, I never saw *any* of these hoes wearing weave. She had some perky, huge ass tits…big girl, 46E tits.

And she wuttin' shy about flashing. Anytime Angie was at Shay and Tasha's when I was around, she was always pulling a tit out on muhfukcaz. She was bigger than my style…but I mean, we've all fukced a bigger girl. I can admit I've had my fair share. And Angie had some gorgeous toes and a foot tattoo – so I'd definitely fukc.

I've always gauged the way I talk to a chick based on whether or not I would fukc her if it came down to it. All of Shay's campus crew was fukcable…and she never minded me flirting. It was quite normal for everyone in the room to be doing some serious flirting and shit talking at any given moment. The whole crew was pretty open.

In fact, I was almost sure that at least Angie was getting ran through by the Ques back on the yard…and more than likely, *Maria*, too. I was on the fence about whether Tasha was a Que *set-out*, too…as far as she had shown she was more of a Nupe fan. Two of my bruhs had already fukced…but I hadn't spent enough time with her to really tell if she was just a groupie in general. Whatever the case…*Tasha* was the one I wanted to fukc *the most* out of Shay's campus crew.

Tasha was slimmer than Sashé…she didn't really have a curvy shape. Her ass was average; her tits in the A-cup fam. She, too, was a light bright complexioned chick…mixed with a black dad and Italian mom. Her hair was long as fukc – that shit always looked wet like she was fresh out the shower; curly and thick. Her face and smile were the source of her appeal…she had some ghost-white ass teeth and the perfect jawbone structure – very photogenic. She was youthful in the face like Sashé, but a bit more hardened. Her only flaw was the bit of acne on her cheeks, but it kinda worked for her. She had a good attitude, on the carefree side like Shay.

Tasha was at the computer desk in the open office area next to the bedroom…chair spun around to see who was coming in the apartment. She was smiling as usual, in a crop top and *Hello Kitty* pajama pants with pink footsies on. She never had her feet out indoors…which was weird cuz I was sure I'd seen her walking outside to the car barefoot before. A brain fukc, but like I said…she was mixed with Italian.

Once Tasha noticed it was me, she stood up and waved, then started stretching her petite torso, "Hey, Rod."

"Where is Maria?" I wondered, scanning the front room again.

"She's fuuuucked up, baby," Sashé told me. "Passed out."

"Passed out where? What the fukc are y'all watching?" I looked at the tv screen as Shay fell out of my arms and crashed back on the couch in between Lil Rico and curled-up Angie. Her focus switched back to the tv as I stepped away and towards the kitchen a few feet from the computer. Me and Tasha brushed shoulders as I walked past.

She looks at Sashé, "Uhmmm. Should we tell him?"

"Tell me what??"

"Tell him what??" Shay echoed. "How horny we are???"

Whoa.

I stopped in mid-motion at the bar in the kitchen…my face screwed up. Lil Rico starts laughing hard.

"No, girl!" Tasha yelped. "I'm talking about 'Ria passed out in his bed!"

"Well, you just told him! Duh! But he's gonna be nice to her tonight," Shay looked my way and smiled.

"Wait…hold up! What the hell is going on here?" I wasn't yelling, but I was hyped up and drunk too.

I'd had a great time with the Nupes that night and took several rounds to the head. We kicked it hard celebrating our cross-date anniversary…and my year was finally starting to get back on the right track. The whole time I was at *Buffalo Wild Wings* I was thinking about what was happening at my spot…and the after-party I was missing.

"Everybody's drunk, Rod," Tasha explained. "We've been getting it in. Like seriously. Maria passed out in your bed after we got out the shower."

"So, she's in my room right now?" my eyes widened. "In my bed? After *'y'all'* got out the shower? Like together?"

Lil Rico chimed in excitedly, slurring his words, "Yeeaa cuzz!!! They like…all took a shower togethaa, bro. No lie."

"Yes, we did," Sashé cosigned with a devilish smirk.

There were red cups everywhere. I started wondering if it was more than just the few of them here partying. I mean, I counted at least *eight* cups, scattered around from the kitchen bar to the office desk and throughout the living room.

"Are you drunk, bro?" I gave Rico a stern glance.

This little nigga (tall ass, little nigga) better not be drunk!

His mama would kill me if she found this shit out, for sure. Rico was my great cousin and I had been assigned his mentor at a family reunion over 10 years ago. He was getting ready to start his junior year in high school and being the youngest of five was tough when you were the only boy. I was determined to break this nigga in before he graduated…but I still had to pace it and keep it clean. Lil Rico had four older sisters and a half-Mexican mama who was super overprotective about him.

Then again…maybe drinking was a *good* thing for young Rico. It might loosen him up. He was always so stiff and uptight around females…trained since birth to be tamed. I'd made some progress over the years…grooming him during periodic weekend visits and summer hangouts. But my little cousin still had a long way to go if he was going to live up to his bloodline's legacy. One day I might have to live vicariously through this nigga.

"Uhm…no," he mumbled in response. "Well, wait. Man, I promise, cuzz, it wuttin' my fault. The…they made me doo it!"

Sashé stepped in between us, "Doesn't it just feel so awwwesum?? And we freaked him like you said, Daddy."

"Y'all did???" my face lit up like a proud parent.

"Well…more like *they* did," Shay bit her bottom lip. "I didn't do too much."

Lil Rico kept rambling, stumbling over his words, "Cuzz, I can't buleeve youuu wasss for real! I thought you was lying 'til…'til they really knocked on the doooor!"

Tasha laughed, "Yea…his ass looked all nervous n'shit when we came in! Like spooked!"

"Cause…y'all gotta understand," Lil Rico's voice got louder, "This duuude always playing wit me! Who would buleeve that for real??"

"So, what happened, yo???" I was ready for the juicy recap.

"He blew it…that's what happened, Daddy!" Shay shook her head.

"Yes. And now we're up and horny and stuff," Tasha had a look of disappointment and frustration written all over her face.

"Yeah, I've been up waiting on you and Tasha's ass is at the computer – looking at porn, all hot and bothered," Shay added.

"Wait…you was watching porn???" I looked at Tasha, staring her up and down.

"No comment," she replied.

"Yeah, bro," Lil Rico told on her. "Sh…she been over there on the compooter forrr like 30 minutes, man."

"Bro, so are you still a virgin???" I skipped to the important question.

"He is most definitely still a virgin," Shay confirmed with the quickness.

"No…wait…wa…big cousin!!!" Lil Rico started blushing and stuttering. "Le…lemme tell him!"

"It would be safe to say that you blew it, Little Rico!" Tasha teased him. "But we still love you!!!"

"I think Maria might hate him right now," Shay grinned harder.

"Whoa…hold up!" I leaned forward on the kitchen counter, trying to figure out where this was going. "Y'all gotta tell me what happened!"

*   *   *   *   *

The three of them start telling me how it went down, each of them chiming in to give their own accounts as the story developed.

Rico was caught off guard…not taking my advice seriously before I left and thinking I was just fukcing with him – talking shit again. When I dropped him back off at the crib with the liquor…he was just happy to have my spot to himself. He immediately ran to my computer to watch some porn…and let off a nice one that almost put him down for the count. Now feeling hella relieved, he then starts playing PS2, planning on falling asleep before long. Well before long, there's a knock at the door and he finds Shay and her crew outside, waiting for him to let them in.

Sashé and the girls come in anxious and live…with bags full of juice and plastic cups. They all give Rico a hug as they enter eager and very friendly. Rico can't believe this shit.

Sashé knows her way around the new spot and so her and Tasha head to the kitchen to start making drinks. They quickly located the gin and vodka in the freezer and wasted no time getting the party started.

Angie was first to break the ice, introducing herself to Rico by standing in front of the tv and blocking his view.

"Hey! What are you doing?!?" he barked at her, immediately aggravated.

"What does it look like I'm doing?" Angie shot back. We're here now. The game is over."

Then Tasha yelled from the kitchen, "Yes, you just had a bunch of bad bitches walk in! We like attention!"

"Little Rico, you have to party with us," Shay demanded. "Rodney said so."

Rico was standing up now, towering over Angie…trying to move her to the side. He couldn't budge her, though, and she smiled as she stuck her chest out, rubbing her cleavage against him.

Lil Rico puts some bass in his voice, trying to be stern, "I don't give a freak what Rodney said, he's not here right now!" The girls all burst out laughing and Rico turns red with frustration, following up with, "Wha…what's so dang funny???"

"You can curse around us, Rico," Sashé told him.

Then Maria chimed in, "Yeah, you can say *'fukc'.*"

Angie put her hand on Rico's chest, "And *'shit'.*"

"And *'damn',*" Tasha joined in.

"And *'BITCHES'!!!*" Shay kept teasing.

"It's a celebration, bitches!!!!!" Tasha screamed at the top of her lungs.

The girls then all started singing loudly as Angie stood on her tiptoes with her mouth close to Rico's chin. She puts her arms around him and grabs his ass…catching my cousin off guard and causing him to back away.

"Stop playing!!!" he warned her bashfully.

"Hey, *'no being shy',* Rico!!!" Shay gave a warning of her own.

"Yes, because we are just getting started," Tasha smacked her lips.

"Shit…we ain't even started yet, papi," Maria admitted, her voice full of plotting.

"Started what???" Lil Rico was confused.

Shay ignored his question and started fussing at Maria, "Hey, can we get these shots going? What are you waiting on, chica?? Open the vodka!!!"

Maria stood still, staring Rico down, "My bad, damn. This nigga is kinda sexy, yo. Look how tall he is!"

"Yo…hold on! Getting started with what?" Lil Rico asked again. "Wha…what the heck are y'all up to?"

"Do we have shot glasses???" Tasha wondered, not paying him no mind.

"Nope – damn, bitch! Why didn't we think about that at the store??" Angie hung her head.

"Rod has one I think," Shay told her crew. "Look up in that cabinet."

Rico's questions continued to get ignored and the girls gathered in the kitchen, putting ice in cups. All he could do was stand there in shock while they worked. Maria asked him to put some music on and kept her eyes on him as he walked to the computer desk.

He sat down to start searching through my library, when Maria came to stand next to him, "Put on something crunk, papi."

"Ok, what y'all wanna hear?" he asked, trying to be accommodating.

"Play that *'Ms. New Booty'!*" Maria blurted, before asking him, "How tall are you?"

"6' 4"," he answered quickly, almost robotically.

Maria started rubbing his shoulders as he froze up in the chair, "Hmmm. What size shoe you wear???"

Before he could answer, they got interrupted by Angie approaching Rico from the other side…shot glass in hand, "You have to take the first shot."

Rico's eyes opened wide, "Wait! No! I don't drink. I'm not old enough."

The girls all reply at the same time, in unison, "None of us are!!!"

*   *   *   *   *

I'm still standing at the counter bar in the kitchen, cleaning the bowl out on *Big Bertha*, my 4-hose genie-styled base hookah, "Did y'all smoke, too?"

"Angie and Shay were using that thing," Tasha informed me.

"I...I didn't smoke, cuzz. Swear to God," Rico spoke up quickly.

"What *did* you do, nigga?" I cut my eyes at him. "You really ain't fukc??"

"Baby!" Shay tried to stop me.

"What? I'm just saying, dude" I shook my head at him. "I wish I had a big cousin that let me spend the night at his crib with a bunch of drunk college chicks when I was his age. Ain't no way!!!"

"Ooooo…what you tryna say, Rod???" Tasha lowered her eyes at me.

"I'm just saying…what the fukc happened? I woulda sealed the deal!!"

"You would, baby??" Sashé asked, walking into the kitchen towards me. She can't stay away from me for too long. She loves to be up under me, following behind my every step. The fact that I don't mind is – again – *new territory for me.*

"Hell yeah, I would," I replied full of confidence, turning to greet her with a wet kiss, one she was already expecting with her tongue out. As we pulled away…I see Tasha staring at me behind Shay. She's biting her lip…and she hesitates before she looks away.

Damn, I wanna fukc her so fukcing bad.

Me, too, nigga! Like, right fukcin' now!

I had pressed Sashé to see if Tasha was down for a ménage more times that I could count. It didn't come off as thirsty – this was back when thirst was encouraged between humans.

But then again…this is also back before the social media era – it wuttin' as easy to be connected or exposed to so many others across the world yet. We talkin' *MySpace* era. Shit's come a long way since *MySpace,* from where I'm telling this story. And the shit that I'm on right now is only common for those select few who stayed ahead of the times…even if by accident.

Even when it's by accident, it's still by design.

And it's been a long time coming. I was now in a situation with Sashé where we could openly talk to each other about fantasies and desires…about urges and taboo thoughts. She says that I'm the most pleasure she's had from a man ever. And not that she's had many…but she's had enough to know that I'm her perfect match sexually. But there were things that she knew a female could give her that I couldn't…and she was as anxious to explore those things as I was to participate in the festivities. She wanted to include me every step of the way…the thought of it put her in a horny frenzy every time.

As far as Tasha was concerned, though…Sashé told me that she could tell her roomie wuttin' completely down for the ménage. At first Shay would drop subtle hints, but the more I pressed…the more upfront the inquiries got. Tasha was definitely attracted to me…as was the case with most of the crew. Sashé eventually concluded that her roomie would fukc me…*and maybe*…just maybe, even her, too. But not together. She's more convinced that Tash would give me the pussy, but not so sure that she would be down to eat Shay's snatch. And Sashé ain't okay with that, per se. Even though Shay also dreamt of watching me fukc, she wanted the full deal.

So, all in all, she's told me that Tasha is *off limits*.

And I wuttin' digging Maria or Angie as much. I mean, I'd fukc Angie's big ass on the late night by myself, perhaps – but she didn't get me excited when I thought about her being the third party in my fantasy. Then, Maria had a fukced-up attitude. That Mexican blood brought out the worst in her. We had conflict and words before…and while she was sexy in her own feisty way….she wuttin' the type that I would fukc with all the extra that came along with it. Then, on top of that, the bitch had a nice shade of a mustache that she refused to acknowledge…and I was past that point of looking the other way just for the sake of some pussy.

But as far as lil cousin Rico, the same didn't apply to him. The potential of the circumstance I placed him in was space-age type shit…a long way from the Nae-Nae/Lil Mama days before his time.

I can't believe he ain't close the deal!!

Of course, I knew that Sashé wuttin' gon' fukc him; she was just there to lead the way. But Angie, Tasha, and Maria??? Shiiiiit…this nigga shoulda at least fukced *one* of these drunken hot girls.

Without even hearing the rest of the story…I was already feeling some type of way. But once they broke down the rest of the night to a nigga, my disappointment went over the edge.

"Well…he came close," Tasha admitted.

"Yeah. I mean…we know Maria was gonna fukc him," Shay chimed in. "Hell, we all know that. She said she wanted to."

"What the fukc, man?!?!?! Why didn't he?" I looked at Rico. "Why didn't you, cuzz??"

Tasha laughed before adding, "Technical difficulties."

"Couldn't get it up, cuzz," Lil Rico confessed, embarrassed.

WHAT?!?!?!?!?!

"You lying!!!!!!" I screamed, seconds away from losing my marbles.

Lil Rico started stuttering again, "No…no…only cu…cuz I had watched some porn before they came! I ain't think you was for real, anyway! Man…I just fukced up, cuzz. I wuttin' ready."

I shook my head frantically, "Woooow!!! How can you not be ready for some shit like this, dude!?!? What happened? Like bro…tell me what happened. Every detail."

"Hey, I still say he had a pretty good night for a virgin. And he did have a lot to drink! Give him a break, Rod," Tasha pleaded with me.

"Yeah, boo…quit being so mean," Shay said softly. "It was his first time drinking."

I rolled my eyes, "I'm not being mean."

"You are," Shay disagreed.

"Ok. Ok," I sighed. "Just tell me the rest of the story."

"Cuzz, they just caught me off guard, bro," Lil Rico explained himself. "First, they all in the kitchen just standing around whispering. Then we start taking shots. Then, next thing you know, they just all looked up and attacked me!"

*　　*　　*　　*　　*

Maria most definitely had the hots for Lil Rico. She couldn't stop talking to him once the music and shots starting flowing. At 5'3", she was the shortest in the campus crew, and instantly intrigued by his height. From what Shay and Tash tell me…the girls all decided before they got there that they were gonna just jump right in to teasing Lil Rico. But Maria took it the extra mile without warning.

She led the charge right after they all had taken a bunch of shots from the liter sized *McCormick Vodka* bottle. Rico says he was standing up by the computer, with his back to the side door that leads to the outside balcony. Maria walks up on him with this look on her face like she wanted to bite him…and he just froze up. Before he could stop her, she had her hand down his sweats…reaching for his limp meat.

"Whoa…what are you – watch out!!" Lil Rico cried out desperately.

Maria kept reaching, "Hold on, just lemme see how – "

"No!" he interrupted her mid-sentence. "Are you serious – "

"I'm serious…be still!" Maria snapped back as she made contact with his member. "Shiiiiit!!!!"

"Yo…stop!" Rico whined in agony.

He pulled away from her, taking a step backwards and bumping against the door. Maria's hand came out of his pants…but she was still reaching and grabbing at him. As he tried to straighten himself up, he realized that he was now surrounded by the crew. Angie and Tasha were on either side of him, grabbing his arms while he twisted and turned. Sashé was standing behind Maria, eagerly awaiting her report.

"That muthafukca felt *big,* y'all" Maria's mouth was wide open. "I couldn't grab it for real, he move too fast with his skinny ass."

"Stop fighting us Rico!!!" Angie commanded.

"We're not gonna bite," Tasha told him, trying to calm him down.

"Well, Angie might," Maria confessed.

"Hey, I like that rough shit!" Angie said with no shame.

Maria wasn't ready to give up, "Hold his arms down, y'all! Lemme pull it out."

Lil Rico kept squirming, "Yo y'all, for real…stop playing! Let me go! Sa…Sashé, make them stop!"

Shay wasn't trying to hear it, "Stop being like that, Rico! Pull it out. We wanna see it."

"Yeah, we might like it," Tasha whispered to him.

"For real, papi," Maria followed suit, softening up her voice.

Rico found himself letting his guard down. I mean, it's hard to stay tough when you cornered by a gang of bitches being adamant about seeing your manhood. All they needed was that small window of opportunity. Before he blinked again, Sashé grabbed the left side of his jogging pants and helped Maria pull them down to his knees.

The answer to their questions hit Maria in the head as she stood back up straight.

"Oh, he's not wearing underwear!" Tasha blurted out.

"DAMN!" Angie stared in disbelief.

"Ay, Papi!!" Maria held her tongue out.

Shay gasped, "Oh my God – it's *huge!!!*"

"Yes, it is," Tasha reached down at Rico's crotch. "I wanna touch – damn, it don't even feel hard yet!"

"Cuz this nigga still soft!" Angie yelled. "Oh, hell nah…I can't even try it!!!"

Sashé stood still, still staring at Rico's girth, "Oh my God…don't tell your cousin I said that!"

"This is crazy, yo," Lil Rico was still in just as much shock as the rest of the room.

"How old is this nigga?!" Maria wanted to know. "How old are you, papi? Ain't you like 16 or 17?"

"He's gonna be a junior next year," Shay told her.

Tasha shook her head again, "This don't make no sense! Touch it, y'all."

"I'm scared to," Angie threw her hands up.

Maria, on the other hand, was more than willing, "Help me get it hard. Fukc that. I wanna see it when it's hard!"

Sashé looked away and started walking towards the kitchen, "I need another shot."

"Me too," Angie followed behind her. "Wow."

Shay and Angie walked back in the kitchen while Tasha and Maria stayed with Rico, giving his limp-biscuit a hand job. He stood very still…looking down at their hands all over his dick. He couldn't believe this shit was happening.

"Ca…can I have another drink?" he asked nervously.

"You gon' get hard for us??" Maria whispered, not taking her eyes off her new play toy.

"Come on, Rico. Stop being shy," Tasha encouraged him, anxious to see how much bigger it got when engorged.

"This nigga ain't used to this type shit!" Maria shouted. "You ain't never had a bitch play with ya dick, boy?"

"You're a virgin, right?" Tasha asked in the sweetest voice.

"Ye…yeah," Lil Rico could barely speak.

"Girl, but it's *two* of us, too," Tasha continued, trying to give him the benefit of the doubt.

"It's *four* of y'all!!!" Lil Rico corrected her shyly.

"This nigga need to lose his virginity," Maria decided in that moment. "He need to learn how to work this thing."

"See, it feel like it's growing now," Tasha bit her lip. "Damn. He probably gonna scare girls away with this."

Sashé yelled from the kitchen in agreement, "He most definitely will scare a girl away with that!"

"Bitch, ain't no way he putting that in me…it ain't even hard yet!" Angie had her mind made up on wanting no parts of it. "Y'all can have it!!!"

"Shit, can I have it? I ain't scared," Maria looked him in the eye. "You scared, Rico???"

He started nervously stammering yet again, "No…no I'm not sca...scared."

"Why won't you get hard for us?" Tasha asked, getting impatient.

"He nervous," Maria said with lustful empathy.

"This *is* his first time," Shay reminded her friends. "Help him relax."

"Relax, Rico. Just go with the flow," Tasha changed her voice back to the soft tone.

Rico tried to relax…but the blood just wouldn't flow. Too many shots of vodka, perhaps? Not if you let Rico tell it. He believed the problem was that he jacked off before they came over and now he didn't have any more gas left. Tasha says she thinks that shoulda made him even *more* ready to go…especially after her and 'Ria took it a step further.

"You wanna see some pussy?" Maria asked abruptly, full of boldness.

"Hell yeahh!" Rico slurred with innocence.

"Tash, show him ya coochie, girl," Maria slyly suggested.

Tasha was giggling, as she kept stroking Rico softly, "You show him yours!"

"I am," Maria responded quickly. "But yours all pretty n'shit. And I ain't even shaved."

Angie yelled from the kitchen, "Bitch, you never shave!!"

"Yes, I do – don't do me!!!" Maria shot back in her own defense. "I'm just hairier than y'all bitches!"

"Wolf pussy!" Tasha let her have it.

"Papi, you gonna let them talk to me like that?" Maria asked Lil Rico, her tone full of flirty energy.

Lil Rico gathered up his courage, "Ay…aye y'all leave my girl alone."

"That's ya *girl* now, Rico?" Shay smiled, pouring another shot.

"See, I was gonna show you, too," Tasha shook her head in letdown.

"No wait…wait," Rico changed his mind swiftly. "I'm just playing!"

"Oh, for real, Papi???" Maria tightened her grip on his semi-hard dick. "It's like that?"

"Oh crap," Lil Rico hung his head in defeat.

Tasha laughed again, "We're just teasing, Rico –
chill. We need him to wake up. Here…gimme your hand."

She takes Rico's left hand and puts it down her
stretch pants and on her pussy. It was soft, wet, and
completely shaved.

Shaved pussies were becoming the new thing…as
we transitioned from the hairy bush in the 90s to the
trimmed and groomed look of the 2000's. Now that we're
in the new millennium, girls cut it all off and niggaz don't
know how to be happier. With nothing to hold the juices
back…it's always wetter with a bare pussy.

Tasha pulls her pants down to her upper hips so he
could get a look at what he was rubbing on. The boyish
grin on his face was classic. This nigga had no idea how
lucky he was.

But before he could stick a finger in, Tasha pulled
away, tugging at her pants, "Nah…that's gonna get
something started."

"Aww, man," Lil Rico whined.

"Shit, we already started something," Maria pointed
out. "Here…help me take this shirt off."

Maria stepped back and started pulling her shirt over
her head…her plump 34D's nearly coming out her bra in
the process. Rico stood there, unable to move or provide
the requested assistance. He'd never seen titties in the
flesh before.

Tasha then took a step in her direction to help 'Ria
get the shirt off, "Girl, he don't know what to do. You
want the bra off, too?"

"Yeah," Maria confirmed. "Come here, Rico."

They guided him to the computer desk chair and made him take a seat. The music was blasting out the speakers, now playing *Lean Wit It, Rock Wit It*.

His dick was still out…still soft. Maria stood in front of him, putting her breasts in his face as Tasha started stroking his shaft again. Angie and Sashé watched from the kitchen as they sipped from red cups.

"Touch em, papi," Maria instructed. "Girls like for you to play with their titties."

"Hell yes. We love that shit," Shay chimed in, grabbing her own boobs.

Rico started fondling 'Ria's tits… with no regard for how sensitive they were. He was overly anxious and unfamiliar…but she ain't care. She wanted to bone this nigga…and she was turned on at the opportunity to teach. After a couple of minutes of squeezing…she leaned in and put them in his face, "Suck em, papi."

Tasha lets his dick go and moves to the side as Maria straddles Rico…reaching down for his dick.

"Lemme get out y'all way," Tasha let out a deep breath. "Got me getting horny n'shit. I need a drink."

*   *   *   *   *

I'm choking on the hookah now as they finish the story. I'm pissed – beyond ready to make Lil Rico sleep outside on the balcony tonight. Apparently not much happened after he got slobber on 'Ria's tits and sucked her nipples *the 'right way'*. He still couldn't wake his mans up.

"Bro…and you ain't fukc her?!?!?" I couldn't believe what I was hearing.

"Man…you gotta understand – I like never been in no shit like that before!" Rico's face was begging for mercy.

"Man, fukc that!"

"Next time he just can't get so drunk," Shay came to his defense again.

"It might not be a next time," I complained. "You gotta take advantage of shit like that!"

Tasha halfway agreed, "Yeah, 'Ria was mad! She all hot-n-bothered. She got in the shower first."

"Yeah, and I think she got mad when we got in with her cause she was in there playing with it," Sashé snitched on her homegirl.

Tasha's eyes lit up, "Yeah, I was thinking the same thing!!!"

I just kept looking at Lil Rico, "Bro, you let them get in the shower together???"

"I mean, cause we all got horny from that shit," Tasha kept venting. "And it sucks being horny when you don't have anyone to fukc you at the end of the night…"

Lil Rico frowned, "Maaaaan…I can't believe this shit!!!"

"Well, I'm glad you're home now, Daddy," Shay smiled at me. "I'm ready to lay down, anyway."

"Me, too," Tasha smiled at us both.

"Where errbody supposed to sleep at???" I looked around the apartment, trying to do another head count.

Tasha gave me a quick glance…then looked away when I returned it, "I'm sleeping in the bed with y'all. Angie already hogging the big couch."

"But ain't Maria in there?" I looked at the closed bedroom door. "We all can't fit in that bed – it's only full-size."

"I can sleep on the floor, cuzz," Lil Rico offered, giving up the smaller couch to Tasha.

"Yeah, but I'm not sleeping on that little couch," Tasha shook her head. "Matter fact, I'm going to lay down now. I don't know what y'all gon' do."

"Tash!!" Shay stopped her. "Wait…I'm coming, too. So, how is this gonna work???"

"Calm down, y'all," I said smoothly. "If we all sleep really close to each other…we can make it work." I saw Rico shaking his head out the corner of my eye and I shot him a quick wink.

"So, we're all gonna squeeze in ya bed, Rod?" Tasha thought about it. "That'll be a tight fit."

"Well, whatever," Shay was done talking it over. "I'm going to the room."

"Ok, me too," Tasha headed towards the room. "I'm tired."

"Ok. Lemme hop in the shower real quick. Y'all better leave some room for me," I started unbuckling my belt.

"Daddy…you know we will," Shay whispered, following Tasha. "Hurry up and come to bed."

*   *   *   *   *

9

My bathroom ran the length of the apartment – with a way in from the living room, and another entry door from the bedroom. The washer and dryer were in a closet across from the sink and huge wall mirror…and the shower had a see-through glass door. I liked my showers steamy and hot…so I let the water run for about ten minutes with the doors closed.

Now Lil Rico and I are in the living room, alone, with Angie knocked out on the couch. Her snoring is louder now.

"Bro, I don't know how you gonna sleep with that lawn mower in here," I chuckled.

"Man, fukc that, cuzz!" Rico snapped, keeping his voice down. "You 'bout to go in there and sleep with all those chicks?!?!"

My chuckle quickly turned into deep laughter, "Yeah, we just bout to go to sleep, cuzz."

"Bullshit!" Lil Rico wasn't having it. "They trying to fukc! The…they been tryna get freaky all night."

"This nigga cussing n'shit! Yeah, nigga…and you blew it!"

"No…no, for real, cuzz…I was trying!" he insisted. "You don't understand how crazy it is to just be around all these girls like that! Shit like this only happens in the movies! How can you not be nervous?!?!"

"Yeah, nigga…you can't drop the ball on shit like this, dude!" I barked back, in teacher mode. "See, I did some shit like that when I was around your age and didn't seal the deal, either. But I ain't have nobody to show me the ropes, nigga! You disappoint me."

"Man, no…I promise. Te…tell 'em to come back tomorrow or something, I'll be ready."

"Bro, they might not come back. Not on no shit like *this!!!*"

Lil Rico hung his head in defeat again, "Well, yeah…and 'specially after you get in there with them. I se…I see what you saying."

"Nah, but cuzz, for real…I can't fukc her friends. She already told me," I explained, trying to downplay the situation. "Not unless they fukc *her*, too. I'm just bout to go to sleep."

"Yeah, whatever," Rico wasn't convinced. "Well, sleep out here den and lemme sleep in there with them."

My eyebrow raised as I gave him a *yeah right'* look, "Nah, fukc that. I ain't no fool, lil nigga…"

*   *   *   *   *

Maybe I was, though.

When I got out the shower, I quickly realized how small my bed was…standing there for a second at the sight of three chicks in it. Maria was on the end, her feet just a few feet away from where I stood by the bathroom door. She was laying on her side, on top of the covers, her back to the edge of the bed. Tasha's ass poked out next to Maria, under the sheets curled up with Sashé – who was facing Tasha.

There was literally no room. We would have to lay on top of each other, if not packed airtight.

"We left some room for you, Daddy," Shay looked up at me with her big, innocent eyes.

I walked around to the other side of the bed, boxer briefs and wife-beater hugging me. I had to be careful since it was so dark in the room – other than the moonlight through my window, there was no light. And there were clothes and shoes everywhere. This was turning into one helluva co-ed sleepover.

"Y'all not hot???" I stretched, trying to cool off.

"Heck no! We're in our panties," Tasha mumbled. "It's cold."

"It's nowhere to lay," I shook my head.

"Sure, there is…right here," Shay scoots closer to Tasha, crawling into her embrace…which frees up a little more room on the edge of the bed. There's now about enough room equal to the length of my hand.

"See, man, y'all playing," I stood still in disbelief.

"We're not…get in this bed with us, *Daddy*," Tasha said playfully.

"Hey!" Sashé quickly snapped at her friend in disapproval.

"Oh, you're the only one who can call him *'Daddy'*?" Tasha smiled in the darkness.

"Baby, tell her you're just my *'daddy'*," Shay started whining.

I sat down next to Shay's ass…which was cuddled up under the covers and in between Tasha's long legs. I almost sat on Tash's foot…and she playfully kicked me when I got settled. I was barely on the mattress…even as they both scooted closer to Maria.

"She knows, boo. She just fukcing wit you," I caressed her face. "Like y'all fukcing with me about this bed."

"Just lay down, baby," Shay replied gently. "Don't be shy."

"Yeah, don't pull a *'Rico'* on us," Tasha took her chance to be petty.

"Oh, never that," I smirked at her. "Let me up under the cover."

Sashé flips on her back…and pulls the brown and black comforter down to her waist. Both her and Tasha's nipples are so hard…my dick starts growing before I can get under the sheets. Tasha notices it too, because she bites her lip again…moving close against Maria to make room. Maria is knocked out…barely budging, although it looks like she can fall out the bed at any moment.

I wouldn't care anyway, in all honesty.

So, now I'm in the bed, legs wrapped around Sashé's…Tasha's legs tangled with ours. They're both freezing. Sashé pulls even closer to Tasha but at the same time pokes her ass out at me…feeling around for my hardness. I lift my head up and move Shay's hair out of the way, looking at Tasha. She's up in Shay's face and smiling hard. I can see and feel their hands moving around under the sheets…rubbing on each other's goosebumps.

"Dang, y'all cold for real?" I asked them in my bedroom voice.

"Warm us up, Daddy," Shay whispered.

"How y'all want me to do that?"

"I'm sure you can think of something, Mr. Kappa Man," Tasha lowered her eyes at me.

"Baby!" Shay exclaimed excitedly, trying to turn her head around at me, "You're like that Nupe in the infamous painting! With all the bitches in ya bed!!!"

"You silly," I reached around with my left hand for Sashé's left breast…which was resting against Tasha's right nipple, smothering her chest.

Shay's breasts were so soft and plump. These were definitely some of the biggest tits I've ever had…right up there with Tianna's. Tasha wuttin' as blessed, but she had some long, firm nipples. When I grabbed Shay's, my finger brushed against Tasha's hard nipple…and she scooted closer.

So, now I'm palming Shay's tit from behind…and rubbing my fingers and knuckles against Tasha's nipple. Shay has my left leg and Tasha's right leg clamped up under hers.…and she lifts her left leg up as my squeezing gets harder. Her pussy is always wet…but I can tell she's lifting her leg up because it's throbbing…and begging for some attention.

"You're pulling the cover off me, Shay," Tasha shuddered.

"Oh, my bad," Shay whispered. "Hmmm. You feel warm, though."

"My feet are cold," Tasha told her.

"You got yo feet out??" I was shocked, realizing I've rarely ever see Tasha's toes.

"Shay said you don't like socks in your bed."

"He doesn't," Shay confirmed.

"She's right. She knows me," I pulled her closer.

"Hmmm," Shay let out another soft moan.

My left hand is now on the inside of Shay's thigh…fingers moving toward her crotch. Just before I make contact, Tash moves in closer to us…rubbing her pussy on my hand through her panties. All I feel is warmth and anticipation….and the jumping in my briefs. I move my body closer…and now my back is on the edge of the bed with maybe about an inch to spare.

Heavy breathing is the only sound that fills the air.

As soon as I rub two fingers on Shay's lips through her underwear…she grinds into 'em, moving her hips in a circular motion, knocking both me and Tasha backwards. We both grab on Shay's waist to stay in bed and remain balanced.

"Dang, Shay," Tasha braced herself.

Sashé doesn't respond. Instead, she flips over on her back again and then turns to face me. She wraps her legs around me, as I scoot in closer and reach around her body to grab Tasha's waist and pull *her* in closer, sandwiching Shay. I smell the liquor on her breath as she comes in for a kiss and we start slobbing each other down, real sloppy and wet. Shay reaches for my dick. As we continue to kiss, I feel Tasha rubbing on Shay's arms…until she gets to mine. Once she touches me…she then rubs her hand up my arm and to my shoulder, squeezing my muscle and digging her nails in me.

She wants me. And dammit, I want her ass, too.

But Shay and I have talked about this scenario before and like I said, she told me explicitly that Tasha is off limits because she not down to fukc Shay, too. Or is she?

Like, dude…come on now. They in dey panties, in bed together…and feeling each other up!

I mighta played *Mr. Cool* with my little cousin Rico, but hell, I ain't never seen or been around no chicks like this my damn self…and this has all the right ingredients for a ménage.

Then again…everybody is drunk! This could all be something they'll regret in the morning!

Bro, you might as well take full advantage while you can, Rod! Shit like this may only come around twice in a lifetime.

The *beast* is absolutely right. So, as Shay was squeezing my dick and sucking my tongue, I reached for Tasha's nipples. She moved close, as I expected, and I started pinching 'em softly with two fingers…going back and forth as she gyrated.

I feel Tasha's right hand reaching around…it's found my waist. She starts to reach down lower…and finds that Shay is already playing with what she wants. Tasha quickly moves her hand back up…and now she's running her nails down the side of my body. This shit makes me moan…and Shay starts kissing me harder.

My dick is so hard. Sashé is fingering her pussy with one hand and jacking me off with the other. We're all breathing hard…and it's heating up.

I wanna do more than play with Tasha's nipples, though. She's got her eyes closed now and licking her lips…biting her bottom one as I pinch-massage her.

How can I take this further?

As if Sashé could read my thoughts or sense what I was thinking…she suddenly pulled away from my lip lock and turned over on her back again.

"Ok…wait," she shifted around, whispering to me. "Here…move over a little."

"Like this?" I scooted towards her.

"No…like…hold on…*this*," Shay motioned for me to lay more on my back. "It's hot."

She tossed the covers down to our knees, but most of Tasha's legs were still covered. Maria was still sound asleep on top of the covers next to Tasha. Shay was right…it *was* getting a little warm.

"Yea, it is," Tasha agreed.

Sashé then sat up…fanning herself. Her roommate lifted her head up, resting her chin in her hand…elbow on the pillow. I could see the both of them clearly in the dark now; Tasha's bright skin made her highly visible. Shay's silhouette was just as clear; both girls were much lighter than what I was used to.

When I reached for Sashé's shirt to try to help her out of it…she threw her left leg across mine and spun her body around, her other leg quickly following suit. She then got up out the bed without any other warning.

What the fuke is she doing?

Tasha and I were now facing each other…the look on her face suggested we were having the same thought.

"Where you going, boo?" I looked up to my left.

"I'll be back. My head is spinning," she walked off.

As soon as Shay shut the bathroom door behind her, me and Tasha started going at it. We hopped towards each other, and she grabbed the back of my head…pushing it into her chest. My tongue was trying to find its way under her shirt, running across her neck and top part of her left breast. She helped me out, stretching and pulling the collar down…exposing her small, but round tit. She held it up for me to suck…and I took her nipple in my teeth before trying to swallow her breast whole.

She moaned lowly in my ear and stuck her tongue in it. This drove me crazy…so I jerked my head backwards, and she cuffs it from the back and brings me in for a kiss.

And Tasha can *kiss*.

Kissing is my biggest turn-on if you haven't figured that out already….and this kiss from Shay's roomie on this night really took me to that place. My dick was throbbing in my briefs now; it almost hurts cuz now my **wooD** has no breathing room. Tasha must've known this somehow because she reached up under my drawls and grabbed my dick with her bare hand.

Her grip was AMAZING.

I mean…she's got the perfect touch, the right amount of everything. She's grabbing and stroking my shit like it's precious – squeezing and releasing, pumping and jerking. I ain't even realize I was humping and thrusting until she pulled up for air…looking me in the face as she jacked me.

"It's so haaard," she whispered quietly.

I don't respond verbally. Instead, I grabbed her ass with my left hand and pulled her petite body towards me…reaching under her panties to feel her bare skin. Her ass was soft…the little bit she was working with. She kicked her leg out across mine and I felt her feet on my calf muscles before she started playing footsie. Her skin was soft as well…just like Sashé's. It's amazing how Shay's friends all complimented each other…like they were all made to be enjoyed together.

But Sashé is still in the bathroom. And this ain't considered 'playing together', right? Is this cheating? It feels like it.

But it also feels so damn good, Rod…as cheating normally does for us. Don't overthink it, nigga. Just let it play out.

He's right again. Cuz Tasha's warm body feels equally as good as cheating ever did. I've got my right hand on her waist as her body weight rests on top of it…and now I'm twisting my left arm and wrist to go under her panties from the front. I knew from Lil Rico's story that she had a completely bare pussy…I was more than anxious to see for myself.

These younger chicks are a different breed! The shaved-pussy movement is real out here in '06 and I ain't touched enough bare kitties in my time.

Nigga! Who you telling?

Tasha's pussy was fatter than Shay's – only slightly, though. Remember, Shay had an extra-large clit with the hood that poked out…Tasha's largeness was in the lips. But the wetness was nearly identical. She was so fukcing wet that you could hear it splash just from me tapping it. Soon as she felt my touch, she grinded into my fingers, flicking her tongue in my mouth. I responded by sucking her tongue as she moaned softly.

She started to turn her hips with my pussy rubbing…and then quickly took her hand off my dick. She then pulled her panties down…so I lifted my right leg up towards my body, still on the bed, to use my foot to help her get the panties towards her ankles. She let them rest there…kicking her right leg free and draping it back over me. Without a pause, she grabbed my left hand and guided it back to her pussy…pushing my index finger inside….and then reached back in my briefs to grab my dick.

Her breathing was getting harder…louder. Her twisting and squirming getting more aggressive.

If we keep moving…we might wake Maria.

"I want you," Tasha whispered seductively. "I want you inside of me."

"Hmmmm…how bad??" I moaned.

"*Real* bad, Rod," she squirmed. "Hmmmm…fukc! *So* bad."

"You so bad," I panted in her face.

"*You* so baddd," she groaned, twisting her body with the pace of my fingering. "Psssst…hmmm…you so damn bad, boy."

"I wanna fukc you."

"I *want* you to fukc me," she replied quickly, staring into my eager eyes.

"Right now???"

"Yeah," she bit her lip. "You got a condom???"

So, by now y'all know my style; y'all know how I get down. I stay ready. And this is my home – my domain and my territory.

It was rigged like a hunting trap…as usual. My spot was made for panty-dropping from the moment you stepped through the front door. The bedroom, of course, was the kill zone. Everything from the lighting to the mirrors on every wall to the color of my bedspread to the smell goods all over was meant to seduce. I had oil plug-ins and scented candles everywhere…and whenever I changed my bedsheets, I sprinkled baby powder on the mattress and pillows before I put the sheets down. Bitches love fresh fragrances.

As a tactic against drama in *The Art of Cheating*, I also sprayed my sheets and pillowcases with female body spray. *Strawberry Mist* was my favorite, but any fragrance could work – that part ain't matter. The goal was to make sure ya bed always smelled like a female so you never got questioned about perfume or shit like that. Bitches were always wearing some perfume or body spray, so if you creeping and you ain't got time to change the sheets…trust me, this works. That *Strawberry Mist* will either eliminate whatever she's wearing altogether or it'll give off a blend that's the perfect nose trick for chicks.

As long as every chick that entered the *Kumfort Zone* knew I just liked my sheets powder fresh…it was foolproof. Good aromas and fresh sheets make a chick feel comfortable…and like I've said before, that's more than half the battle of the panty drop.

I also had a nightstand cabinet full of emergency items. Warming Oil/Lube, edibles, *Carmex*, mints, wet wipes, and condoms. I normally kept condoms all over my spot…like I said, y'all know my style. But in these last few months since Shay had slipped into that main spot…the condoms disappeared with us.

She still wuttin' my *'girl'* – I mean, the girl's boyfriend Keith still thought she was in Missouri being faithful. Nonetheless, I was the only one Shay had fukced since Thanksgiving of last year and she'd taken KeLLy's place as my bareback girl. Where I woulda normally had hats in random places all over, including under my mattress, now I only kept a couple in my nightstand cabinet on some *just-in-case* shit. And Sashé knew and was fully aware of that stash. She suggested I keep a few for whenever we fulfilled our ménage fantasy.

My first thought when Tasha asked for a condom was how far I'd have to reach if I was gon' grab one. Now don't get me wrong, the nightstand was right next to the bed, on the same side I was lying on the edge of. But…it's still a further distance than if they was under my *mattress,* like before. Plus…reaching for the cabinet was a lot less discreet than the *under-the-mattress* trick. I could reach under the mattress and have a condom in hand before a chick even realized it before. Now I gotta roll over and reach a little further.

"Ok…hold on," I told her.

My *beast* had taken over me. I wanted this chick so bad right now…I wuttin' thinking about nothing else. I done forgot that Tasha was Sashé's roommate…and that she told me that I couldn't fukc her. I wuttin' giving a damn about the fact that Sashé was cool with me fukcing another chick as long as that chick fukced her, too. I ain't even care at the moment that Sashé was right in the other room and could walk in at any second. I wuttin' thinking about what she'd do if she did catch us…what I might lose in the end.

So, I take my hand away from Tasha's wet pussy. She lifts up to let my other hand loose…and I rolled over on my left side to reach down for the nightstand cabinet…my back now to Tasha, who was still laying on her side. I could feel her pulling the sheets back up to cover her legs as I fumbled around in the darkness, knocking the *KY Oil* over while I looked for the condom. Tasha's rubbing my back as I search…and our legs are still intertwined under the cover.

"Damn, where that shit at???" I mumbled in frustration.

The sound of the bathroom door swung open on the other side of the room behind me…as if it heard my whisper of a question. The person on the other side of the door most definitely heard me, though…that was evident in her response and reaction.

"Where is *what* shit at? What are you guys doing???"

* * * * *

10

I freeze up.

Heart skips a beat.

But I ain't new to *this* part of the game.

I've been here before.

"I'm tryna find some *Carmex*," I casually played it off, smooth as ever.

Sashé's footsteps sounded off as she stormed toward the other side of the bed. I was still facing the nightstand, trying desperately now to find the tube of lip therapy before Shay walked around. I felt Tasha shift behind me as her roommate reached the middle of the room.

"Carmex???" Shay sounded perplexed.

As she stepped on the other side of the bed where I was hanging off…by the grace of the *cheat gawds* I found the tube of *Carmex* I wuttin' looking for.

"I think I have some in my purse, boo," she offered plainly.

"No, I got it, babe. Are you ok??? You was in there for a minute."

She plopped down on the edge of the bed where I sat before…scooting me in closer to Tasha, who was just lying there still. Straight…and motionless. But still breathing hard.

"Yeah, I was trying to make myself puke but nothing came up," Shay explained. "I felt like I was gonna pass out from a heat wave. Y'all not hot?!?!"

"Maybe a little," Tasha replied, halfway nervously. "Now I am."

"I can go turn the air up," I offered, looking for a way outta this jam. "I'm not that hot."

"No…it's fine. I'm fine. I'll just lay on the covers. Scoot over, Daddy."

"You know it ain't no room for real," I reminded her.

"Well, make some!" Shay settled in next to us. "Scoot over!"

Whew!!!! That was a close one.

Almost too close.

So, now I'm sandwiched *in between* Tasha and Sashé…in a weird instance of trading places. Tasha almost instantly lifted her legs up to tangle up with mine…so I'm lying on my back, right leg locked with Tasha, left leg on Shay. The both of them turned on their side to snuggle up and lay on my chest…almost simultaneously.

I coulda died and went to heaven right then. Like…this shit was unbelievable. I'm lying in bed with two chicks on either side; a dyme to an arm – straight *I Am Legend* shit.

I mean, technically, I was in bed with *three* of 'em – and most likely coulda been banging all *four* of dey ass had I been here all night. And at this point…I'm really starting to believe in myself. I belong here. This is what life is supposed to be like for a nigga like me…the writing is on the wall and the key is in my hand.

Now, figuring out how the key works and exactly what doors it opens up is a whole other task. I've never been down *this* particular road…and my tour guide, Sashé, is following *my* lead, in all actuality.

Sure, she's leading me to the water, but how I drink it and how I share it is all on me.

And truthfully speaking…I'm not sure how to make all these dots connect. It's here I realized that in all my years of experience in *The Art of Cheating*, outta all of my episodes…I had no case law or rules or strategies when it came to *multiple chicks at once*.

This is all new territory for me.

All we can do is go with the flow. Let it play out, Rod.

Going with the flow is always risky, especially when you horny and being controlled by the **beast**.

It's the **beast** in me that waits about six minutes and then turns slightly to my right side towards Tasha. That same **beast** used my right hand to grab Tasha's right hand…which was resting on my stomach. The **beast** put her hand on my dick because my hoLLyWooD misses her touch. The **beast** is selfishly selfless…as my left arm wraps around Sashé's left thigh, pulling her closer to me so I can grip her ass cheeks. Shay kisses the *beast* on his neck and I feel the sensations down to my ankles.

The *beast* is more dangerous than you can imagine; born and raised in *The Art*. He can sense that Shay has no clue that my right hand is now on her roommate's bare crotch…or that she doesn't realize Tasha's panties are still at her ankles. The *beast* pays complete attention to Tasha's vibe – her willingness and determination to keep quiet. She knows Sashé wouldn't approve, yet she's tugging and pulling on the *beast's* dick…staying still otherwise, even as the *beast* rubs her clit with his two middle fingers.

Slowly. Silently.

Well…not so silent. Tasha's pussy is dripping wet. You can hear it if you paying attention. If you know the nature of this *beast* that has been unleashed…if you know what to expect from this monster that's been rebirthed, then you would recognize the faint sounds of interrupted wetness under the sheet.

But *no one*…not Sashé…not Tasha…not even *myself* was familiar with the *beast* being in command like this. The small splashes blended in with my fountain on top of the tv. Sounds of water sprinkling was of the norm in my domain… and it all worked in the *beast's* favor.

Heavy breathing filled the air in the room. But the *beast* knew that Sashé's heavy breathing stemmed from fatigue. She was almost out for the count, with the same type of breathing that Maria had on the other side of the bed. Tasha's panting was filled with lust…the pleasure from my fingers undeniable. She knew my dick was in hands that were just as good at what they do…as she ran her fingers up and down my balls, palm rubbing my shaft.

Sashé is half sleep now…she still doesn't realize any of this is going on with Tasha. I'm screaming at the *beast* silently in my head…telling him how belligerent this is and how he's gon' fukc up everything, but he ain't listening. He kept fingering Tasha with zero fukcs to give…still caressing Shay's ass with his other hand and being as bold as he could be.

Boldness rubs off in situations such as this…as Tasha suddenly shifted her body again, lifting her head up to look me in the eye. After a quick glance at Shay's closed eyes, Tasha then stuck her tongue in my mouth again and started kissing me with more passion than before.

My dick jumped in her hand…and she responded with a firm and tight squeeze.

I let out a low moan. But it was more like a *groan*, which was even worse. I immediately realized my mistake as Sashé abruptly lifted her head up.

Tasha's face fell on mine…and the split second and a half felt like an eternity. But nonetheless, after a second or so…Sashé laid her head back down. In fact, she turned her body completely to the *other* side…with her back to me, ass poking me in my left thigh.

Now remember…it wuttin' that much room on the edge of the bed she was on. So, her knees was hanging off the side…but I'm still holding on to her waist with my left arm. The *beast* must've been contagious, though – because within the next instance, Tasha was sitting up *again*, pulling the covers back and exposing my **wooD**. Now that Sashé had turned to the other side…Tasha was jacking my dick under my boxers with no regard, out in the open and with a tighter grip.

The **beast** takes my left arm away from Shay and turns closer to Tasha…grabbing her pussy lips with my left hand. She started kissing on my neck and licking my nipples underneath my wife-beater, whispering, "Don't stop."

Even if I wanted to stop now…the **beast** was in full command. I started humping and thrusting, meeting her hand strokes as I dug into her pussy with my fingers.

The more I gained momentum to hump…..the more I kept pushing Shay closer to the edge of the bed, which at this point literally had just inches to spare.

And then…it happened.

Sashé suddenly hops up.

MY HEART STOPPED BEATING…

Tasha fell limp to my chest, her hand on my stomach. The covers were pulled back…but my throbbing **wooD** was now reduced to a bulge in my boxer briefs.

MY EYES ARE CLOSED. I LAY STILL.

I can't tell what Shay is doing, but she's definitely moving and shifting around. Her body weight was nearly off the bed now. Not completely…I could tell she was still there. But her legs were now gone away from mine…no longer was she lying down.

"Baby?" she whispered, sitting up with her back to my left thigh.

I LAID STILL. SILENT.

"Oh my god…it's so hot," Shay mumbled frustratedly. "Baby."

I could feel her nudging my left shoulder…but the *beast* tells me to remain still and not say a word.

"Baby, wake up," she mushed me a couple more times before she stood up and walked off again towards the bathroom and eventually stepped into the walk-in closet.

Tasha grabbed my dick again in the darkness. I laid still as the *beast* stuck my middle finger in her pussy further…pressing hard against her g-spot. Her loud moaning refused to be muffled.

Bro, you gon' get me caught!

Just let it play out, Rod.

Sashé came storming back towards my side of the bed…mumbling something neither the *beast* nor I could make out.

I slightly turned on my back again, away from Tasha. As I cracked my eyes…I could see that Shay done went to the closet to get another comforter. She walked to the side of the bed with the cover wrapped around her shoulders as I watched her throughout the mirrors scattered across my walls.

And then, she laid on the side of the bed – ON THE FLOOR.

What the…???

I felt Shay toss the cover on the bed over me as she curled up on the floor…so it's like we was sharing it. The *beast* now knew it wuttin' no way that Sashé could know what's going on…so, without hesitation, he hopped right back to it.

Actually…*Tasha's **beast*** does so before mine. As soon as the cover fell on top of me – she grabbed my hand and put it back on her pussy. We started masturbating each other again…with the bed now free to ourselves. Maria ain't even a concern no more. And the ***beast*** ain't even thinking about a *ménage*…he's just thinking about conquering at this point.

I started to push her head downwards…giving her that universal *head-hint*. The ***beast*** wants some dome.

"Come on," I whispered, breathing on her face.

Tasha shook her head at me in disagreement, "Uhhh uhnn…get a condom. *You* come on."

She's on the same page as the ***beast***…albeit a different sentence.

But me – I'm still fighting through the drunken urges…still thinking about the end result of all of this.

I can't let the ***beast*** fukc up my chances at my fantasy…not like this. I mean, Shay was on the floor now for crying out loud!!!

What kinda *HoLLy-BeLLigerence* would I have to be on to fukc her roommate while she laid on the floor because of lack of room in the bed?

Wuttin' I supposed to get out the bed instead? And shouldn't it be me laying on the floor now instead of her?

Why was I *still* fingering Tasha and thrusting into her soft hands like I ain't give a fukc about getting caught?

Why did I have my tongue out…swapping spit with Tasha like this wuttin' the greediest shit ever???"

How did I lose control of the situation like this?

The questions kept flowing…but the answers were unclear. The small moments of cloudiness were all the *beast* needed as I found myself turning over to my left side again…reaching for the nightstand cabinet.

SLOWLY. CAREFULLY.

Sashé was breathing hard, which she only did when she was sound asleep. Still…this whole scene was risky as fukc. We was sharing a comforter now….so every movement I made moved her half of the cover. I gotta be like a ninja or spider with my motion at this point.

The rush was making my dick harder in Tasha's hand…and she responded with a tighter grip and even more passionate grind against my fingers.

Sashé let out a deep breath. I start to silently yell at the *beast* that *'she knows everything'*; that *'the jig is up'*. The *beast* ain't listening…he just continues to shift to the side to reach for the cabinet door.

How the door is supposed to get opened and searched through without hitting Shay in the head in beyond me. Like…for real – ain't no way.

But like I've said a hunnid times: *one of these days, I've gotta stop thinking with my dick.* It seemed like the *beast* only thought with my dick, though. So again – tonight wouldn't be that night.

As I my hand reached the door handle, the shift of my body weight caused the cover to fall off me…*and on Sashé.*

Even that ain't stop me. Or is it still the **beast** in control??? Either way…I finally managed to get my hand around the cabinet door handle…pulling at it slowly.

Tasha's pussy was gripping my fingers now. She matched my poking with the perfect rhythmic strokes, and it was making my dick swell up.

HER PUSSY THROBS…

…MY DICK JUMPS…

I've almost got the door open…

Momentarily…that guilt factor showed up, making me release the door and reach to the floor for Sashé.

She gotta know this ain't my fault; she gotta know I want her to be a part of this…

But the guilt factor was no match for the **beast**. Momentarily meant just that.

…I keep reaching…

Tasha keeps stroking. Gripping hard…pulling away…

…my fingers keep digging…she's squeezing 'em with force and anticipation now…

And then…*it happened…*

The first squirt was powerful…strong enough that she had to turn her head away to avoid the impact. My thick stream landed on Tasha's left shoulder. The drops that followed hit my chest and finished up on her arm and hand. She kept jerking and tugging away…stopping me dead in my tracks toward the nightstand stash.

With every spurt, my hopes and expectations skeeted out…putting me no more closer to a ménage than I was back in the bushes with Nae-Nae and Lil Mama. No luckier than I was in my attempts with Sassy and Kitty. No different than I was the night with Kourtney and Sashé. And making me no better than shy Lil Rico was earlier tonight.

With every drop…I BLEW IT.

*　　　*　　　*　　　*　　　*

The next morning…the *beast* had disappeared, giving that guilt factor the time to shine again.

Maria was up and moving around first…promptly trying to wake Tasha and Sashé up as soon as she realized where she was, "Y'all get up! Shay, what the fukc you on the floor for?!?! I swear…what kinda nigga is you?!"

I shrugged at her, used to her taking shots at me by now, "I hear you, trick."

"Fukc you, nigga!" she shot back. "Come on, y'all…let's go. Take me home."

"Y'all…it's too early," Tasha yawned, trying to prevent me and Maria from verbally sparring.

"Come on, Shay," Maria rolled her eyes. "Get up!"

I reached down and started nudging Shay…but she quickly pushed me away within a split second.

"I'm up, ok?" she snapped. "Just let me be for a second, ok?"

"My bad, boo," I treaded carefully.

"Right," Shay mumbled under her morning breath.

They all started moving around and gathering their clothes up while I stayed in bed. Shay didn't look my way once…until she walked back in the bedroom through the bathroom after the crew was all in the front room waiting at the door.

She then leaned in to kiss me on the cheek, telling me dryly, "We'll talk later, Mister."

*   *   *   *   *

11

Every nigga hates getting that text or hearing those words, *'We need to talk.'* Nothing good ever comes out of it. Soon as the words register…you know you done fukced up.

But after that wild night with Lil Rico and Shay's crew…I knew I had to prepare myself for one helluva 'morning-after' talk. What's worse – I ain't hear from Sashé *all day*, so I could only speculate on the night's events and wonder what all she knew.

Did she hear me and Tasha? Was she aware the whole time? I mean, if so…why she ain't join or try to initiate the ménage? Was she testing my loyalty…trying to see how far I would go?

I was never good at these type of tests…not when it came to pussy. This lifestyle Sashé was leading me to was a lot to handle for a nigga…and not even my *Pops* could give me advice on chicks who dig chicks. He tells me in all his stories, he's never had a chick bring him chicks. To Pops…that was some *pimps-n-hoes* type shit.

I mean, damn…is it?

This shit is hard to process. You would think it's a no brainer – if Sashé is down to let me bang another chick as long as she's involved…why can't I just accept that for what it's worth and not be on some sneaky shit? I guess now that I think about it, it's just hard to break old habits.

Cheating is what I'm used to…but am I now at the point where I gotta do it just to feel *normal?*

Is it even technically cheating? Me and Shay ain't together…not *officially*. She still with Keith! *Right???*

That's still a tricky train of thought, too, though, with what I believe to be true regarding *The Art.* Cheating is considered to be *anything I wouldn't do or say in front of her*…whether she was my girl or not. Whatever her title was, Shay was *technically* now my main chick. And like any others…I had to make her at least *think* she was the only one.

I'd been doing so good, too. The sneaking around was at an all-time low. I had to admit my urges to cheat were a lot lower than they'd been before I was rocking with Shay.

Why the fukc can't I tame this damn **beast**??? Is the **beast** truly empowered by *taboo sex acts*…or was his real hunger the *cheating?* Whatever it was…I needed to get a hold on it and fast. I was way too fukcing close to a ménage now and I'd be a fool to let this opportunity slip away.

Anyway, after most of the day had passed and I hadn't heard from Shay…I then started wondering if Tasha had told her what happened – in the event that Shay *somehow* didn't hear us. I had never had a conversation with Tasha outside of hanging out with her and Sashé.

Sure, last night we was on the same page about being sneaky, but all'at coulda changed once the bitch sobered up and her guilty conscience regained the upper hand.

Then again…if she really wanted to fukc me…she wuttin' gon' tell on herself. I had enough experience with chicks in general to know this much, and although Tasha wuttin' down for the *ménage*…it was crystal-clear that she would take the male half of this duo without question.

*　　*　　*　　*　　*

So, I'm sitting at my computer that night when she finally calls me. I can tell by her voice on the other end that whatever it is…it's serious.

"So, what are you doing?" she asked as I tried to read her energy.

"Nothing, just at my computer," I gulped. "Writing."

"Do you wanna talk later??" she offered, still concealing her mood.

"No, we can talk now," I was ready to face the music.

"Are you sure?"

"I'm sure," I tried to convince myself. "I mean…do you not wanna talk?"

"No…I do," she replied quickly. "We need to."

"Ok," I braced myself. "So wassup?"

"Well," she started before drifting off.

"Well???"

"Do you have something you wanna tell me?" she gave me a chance to come clean.

Shit.

Don't panic, Rod. Never let her see ya sweat...

"Uhm," I raised my eyebrow, suddenly super nervous about where this was going.

"Don't hold back."

"I mean," I thought about it for a second. "No."

"No?" she sounded shocked. "You *sure?*"

"I mean, yeah. I'm sure," I sighed. "Should I? Do you got something to tell *me?*"

"I do, actually," she admitted.

Hmm. Well, this should be interesting.

"I'm listening," I sat up, giving her my undivided attention.

"Ok. Are you sitting??" she paused, stalling.

"Just tell me, Shay."

"Ok. It's a lot," she warned.

"I got time," I replied nonchalantly.

"Ok. First – I broke up with Keith."

"You what?!?!?" my jaw dropped.

"You heard me. I broke up with my boyfriend."

"When? What happened?"

"Well, we got into it when I got back from the *Ozarks* Wednesday" she started explaining. "I told him I didn't wanna be with him anymore and we broke up Friday."

"Wow," I was taken aback. I definitely wasn't expecting this. "I mean, so what...y'all got into it about the Ozarks trip??"

Sashé and the girls had returned from a spring break trip at the *Lake of the Ozarks* some days ago. They had split the cost of a condo with a few of the *Ques* from campus and apparently had a wild vacation. Before she left...I was teasing her about her going out there and cheating on me, but it was just jokes. Shay was cautious about anything she did potentially getting back to Keith and so the likelihood of her getting fukced on that trip was pretty slim to none.

Not that I woulda been hurt or fukced up about it. I told her that if she wanted to get wild she could and should. You only young once – I'd told her. But she insisted that she wuttin' gon' fukc nobody. And so, when she got back, that was my only question about the trip. She told me she ain't have sex with none of them niggaz, so I never asked anything else.

"Well, kinda," Shay continued. "Sooooo...I kinda...told him...that I cheated on him."

You did what, bitch?!?!?!?

"Wait a minute...you did what?!?!"

"Just hear me out, Daddy. Don't get mad yet," she urged. "My guilt got the best of me…and I've been doing a lot of thinking since the trip."

I started panicking, "I mean, so why did you tell him you cheated?!? What if it gets back to KeLLy?!?! Man – dude! KeLLy is gon' kill me if she finds out I cheated on her with you! If she finds out about you *period*! I told you that! She might *kill* you!"

"Rodney," she stopped me. "Chill. Relax. KeLLy isn't going to kill anyone…nothing is going to get back to her. This isn't even about us."

"What the hell does dat mean??"

"Well, it *is*. But it *isn't,*" she corrected herself. "Just let me explain. Let me tell you what happened."

"Fine. Ok. I'm all ears," I shook my head.

"Ok, well you know we went to the Ozarks on Friday when class let out," she started the recap. "I pretty much didn't talk to him the whole time I was there."

"Ok…you ain't talk to me, either," I was confused by her bringing that up. "Reception sucks down there for the most part, anyway."

"Yeah, but you and I *agreed* that we weren't gonna talk until I got back. Keith isn't so hands-free. So…he kept trying to get in touch with me."

"And he got mad cuz he couldn't," I guessed, trying to decipher what happened.

"Yes!" she exclaimed. "Like, he really got *mad!* All he kept saying was that he knew I was down there in the

Ozarks getting ran through and how all of my friends are hoes. And so, I got mad and I just told him I cheated on him. I couldn't take the way he was talking to me."

"So, you told him about me?!?!" I felt a lump in my throat.

"Uhmmm. No."

"Huh?" now I was really confused. "Then, what the fukc did you tell him?!?!"

"Well, that's what I'm trying to talk to you about. Some things happened in the *Ozarks*."

I didn't like how that sounded, "Ok…so, you lied to me then."

"I didn't lie to you," she disagreed. "You never *asked* me about the trip."

"I asked you if you had sex."

"Right. You asked me if I had *sex*, but that was *all* you asked me," she pointed out. "I didn't lie…I don't lie to you, Daddy. Let me explain."

Ok, she had me there. Sashé was quickly becoming another one of my progenies…the same as Cookie before her. She was learning *The Art of Cheating* at a crazy fast pace.

I *had* indeed only asked her if she had sex and so nothing else was told because it wasn't *asked*. But apparently – some other shit *did* go down.

*   *   *   *   *

169

So Shay and crew were spending the weekend with four other guys…all of 'em young Ques from the yard. She tells me that Maria and Angie were invited cuz they be having orgies with the Ques on the regular. While Tasha hadn't done the orgy thing…she does fukc one of the Ques named Tez from time to time, so basically it's a spring break trip with the Ques and their groupies. Sashé was the friend who they all wanted to fukc but they knew she was faithful to her boyfriend from another school. She knew when they invited her that they were all plotting on her…but her plan was to stick to her guns. The first night was where it all got the wildest. They all got sloppy drunk and started playing freaky games. Then Sashé and one of the Ques, Chad, sat off to the side smoking while the rest of the party played Truth or Dare.

*   *   *   *   *

"Oh, that's right," I interrupted. "I forgot Chad pledged Que."

Sashé followed up with, "Oh, you know the *Chad* I'm talking about?"

"Yeah…he was there the night of **KeLLy's Revenge**. The night I caught her tryna cheat."

"Oh, right. Right," she recalled. "Ok, well me and Chad were just smoking and watching them play."

I hung my head, "See? I thought you only smoked weed with me."

"Daddy…please," she pleaded. "I have to get this out of my system; please just let me finish. I wanna be transparent with you."

"Ok," I sighed again. "Go on."

*　　　*　　　*　　　*　　　*

By the time Chad and Shay was halfway done with the blunt, the other girls started making a big fuss about sucking dick. One thing leads to another…and they decide to have an oral sex contest between Maria and Angie. So, they move chairs to the middle of the floor and two of the Ques take a seat as contest volunteers. Angie wins the contest with flying colors…making the nigga bust in less than ten minutes…in front of the whole party.

*　　　*　　　*　　　*　　　*

I couldn't help but interrupt again, "Yeah, that's a sure bet. Big girls always suck dick better."

"Are you tryna say I don't give good head?" Shay challenged.

"No, I'm not saying that. But I mean…you've only sucked Keith and me – like *ever*. I wouldn't put you in no *dick-sucking contest*…especially not against a big girl."

"Oh, whatever," she smacked her lips.

"So, you didn't participate in the contest?" I wanted to know.

"Absolutely not. You know me better than that, Daddy."

"Ok, so what happened then?"

"Well, after that, 'Ria and Angie started putting the challenge out to the boys. They all started asking who eats the best pussy."

"Ok," I waited for her to finish.

"Well, you know how boys are. They all say they're the best."

"So, four of them…four of y'all," I started calculating. "You got ya pussy ate."

"Yes," she confessed.

"By who – *Chad?*"

"Yes, Daddy. We all got on the couches and tables and the boys started eating us, and then everybody started having sex."

"But you and Chad didn't?"

"No. I stopped him."

"Whatchu mean? He ain't finish eating it?"

"Oh, no. He ate it 'til the contest was over," she clarified. "We were off to the couch on the side. I mean…he didn't *win*. But everyone was horny after that, and it just started happening. Everybody started fukcing…and then Chad went to get a condom."

"And then you stopped him?"

"I stopped him when he came back with it and put it on. I'm not gonna lie – I was horny. I wanted to let him, and I was going to. But when he got on top of me…I started feeling guilty and I stopped him before he put it in."

"Wow," I was speechless.

"Please don't be mad," she said again apologetically. "I didn't lie! We didn't have sex. I stopped him, got dressed, and left the room. I didn't drink with them the rest of the weekend."

"So, when you left the room, he ain't follow you? He ain't keep trying to fukc?"

"Chad?!?! Heck no, he just walked over and started fukcing Angie while she was giving Tez head. I went in the bedroom by myself."

"Hmm," I paused. "But why, though? Why you ain't fukc him if you was horny like that? What's there to feel guilty about? You been cheating on Keith with me for a long time now."

"Right. But I stopped Chad because I felt guilty about cheating…on *you.*"

"On me?" I repeated her words, caught off guard.

"I told you I wouldn't have sex. Like…that's the thing. I wasn't even thinking about *Keith.* The whole time I was thinking about you. How I didn't wanna mess anything up with you. How mad I would be if you were having sex with somebody else. I wasn't thinking about Keith at all."

I was stuck, "I mean, I don't know how to take that. Like…so…why did you tell Keith then? You told him that? Like…you told him about the orgy?"

"Well, yeah…I was mad at how he was talking to me," she got louder. "So, I just told him outta anger! Like, he just acted like he was *so* convinced that I've been down there fukcing all the Ques on campus."

"But why would he think that, though?" I wondered. "Cuz all the chicks you hang with are set-outs?"

"I mean, he knows I just met all them when I got to *Central*. I didn't go to high school with any of them! I don't know them like I know *Kourt*…or *Kris*. They're just girls I go to school with."

"So, what was it, then? Why would he even think that?"

"I don't know. Well, Tez's cousin is one of y'all's bruhs from Keith's chapter," she speculated. "Maybe Tez exaggerates about things."

"What you mean *'one of y'all's bruhs'?*"

"Well, I'm just saying that Tez has a cousin that's a Nupe at Keith's school. I think it's Keith's LB, actually."

I let out another long sigh, thinking about the Nupes at Keith's school, "Yeah, but I told you I don't really fukc with that chapter."

"That's irrelevant, Daddy!" Shay snapped. "You asked me what would make Keith think I was down here cheating on him. Obviously, nobody on campus knows about you and I – except my small crew. So, Keith knows nothing about you. But maybe…just *maybe*…one of the Ques said something to *Keith's LB* to make him think one of them were doing me. The Ques."

That made sense. After a brief second, I said, "So, you went ahead and told him because that's what he's thinking anyway."

"I told him outta anger. But also because he just kept hounding me about it! And like you said, *'sometimes you have to give something small up to get away with something bigger'*…right?"

"You told him about the spring break head so that you could get away with cheating with *me*."

"Yes. Exactly. But the way I said it…I was trying to convince him that that was the most I had ever done with one of them boys. I was telling him how I stopped Chad and everything. I mean…I didn't say I was feeling guilty about you – I told Keith that I was thinking about him…blah blah blah. But I just wanted him to know that I didn't have sex with them like he was thinking. I'm not what he thinks I am."

"But you *are* a cheater," I kept it real.

"Only with *you*," she replied. "And that's what's weird. I didn't feel bad about Keith…I really stopped Chad because of *you.*"

"So, that's why you broke up with him?"

"No. So, then after I tell him…he goes on to tell me about how he's been cheating on *me!* He tells me about three girls that he's fukced and how he thought I was cheating a long time ago and so *he's* been cheating!"

"Oh damn," I shook my head again.

"I know!" she couldn't believe it herself. "And one of the girls he fukced *before* I even met you. Matter of fact…*two* of the girls. One of them was KeLLy's friend *Danni.*"

"DANNI?!?!" I yelled. "What? How?!?!"

"Apparently they met in St. Louis last year at the *Konklave.*"

Wow. This was crazy. I remembered Kells and *her* crew had road tripped to St. Louis last summer for the *Kappa Konklave*, our national meet. I also remembered KeLLy calling at the end of the night and telling me she was back in the hotel room with Danni and that they were going to *sleep*.

Now I'm hearing a different, more detailed version of the story.

Apparently, Sashé's boyfriend Keith (who was also a Kappa, but that's a whole other story) met Danni at the party and invited the whole crew back to the Nupes' room to hang. That's when Danni fukced Keith. Sashé couldn't confirm if *KeLLy* fukced anybody that night…although Keith said, *'they ALL fukced'*. And I couldn't be too sure myself, because that night…I was actually trying to shake KeLLy myself for some new pussy *I* came up on.

So, when Kells was supposedly back in the room calling it a night, I was out on my own mission anyway. But *now*…Sashé got me wondering if KeLLy cheated on *me* that night…with one of the Nupes from Keith's *Oklahoma* chapter.

It would be a strange type of poetic justice in this portrait of the *Art of Cheating* if that was true. I mean…I was on some real scandalous shit fukcing Sashé anyway…considering, if nothing else, the fact that her boyfriend was a Nupe. But like I told Shay when I met her – I wuttin' fukcing with that chapter like that.

"I don't even know what to say," I kept shaking my head.

"Well, I'll tell you what I said. I saw that as the perfect opportunity to get out. And I told him we were done."

"Just like *that?*" I asked. "Like……*just like that?*"

"He's been cheating on me for the last *two years* almost! Hell no. I'm done," Shay had her mind made up. "You know I fell outta love with him long ago anyway, Daddy. I love *you.* You're perfect for me."

I couldn't believe my ears, "But…"

"Let me finish," she cut me off again. "Before me and Keith fought, all I could think about was how to tell *you.* How to tell you what happened and praying you wouldn't get mad at me and want to cut me off. But then…there's more."

"What more?" I tried to brace myself again. This conversation just kept getting deeper.

Shay continued opening up, "Like…that night…the whole *scene.* The orgy…all the sex…the drunken fukcing. That shit turned me on. Like…*seriously.* I went in the bedroom and masturbated. Wishing you were there. If you were there…I woulda participated.

"It was like the ultimate rush Daddy. I wouldn't have fukced any of the boys except you…but I woulda most definitely got down. Now I can't stop thinking about it. It just made me want to do a threesome even more. Or even a foursome. I don't know."

My eyes got big, "Damn. You serious."

"I'm dead serious, Daddy. We like…we *have* to have a *threesome.* I mean, I wouldn't even mind two other chicks and making it a foursome because I really *really* wanna have sex with girls. Like now…more than ever after *that.* Oh my God, baby – Angie was eating Tasha out…and it just looked like it was feeling so damn *good* for Tash. I got wet just off of seeing that."

"Wait a minute…I thought Tash wuttin' down for girl on girl??"

"Well, yeah…that's what she told me when I asked!" Shay cried out. "But I *saw* it. Apparently, it's a different story when the liquor flows."

Apparently! Damn!

Now I'm wondering if I coulda really set some shit off last night with Lil Rico!!! I dropped the ball for real!

We dropped the ball, nigga! These hoes go!!!

"Damn! So…we coulda had a ménage with Tasha the other night? You saying she woulda been down?!?!"

"No," she shot my hopes down. "I mean, really – at this point – I don't even *wanna* do it with Tash anymore. I don't understand why she would tell me *'no'* on the threesome, but then in the same breath tell me that she would fukc you. Then I see her letting another girl *eat her pussy???* No. Something about Tash, I don't know if I trust."

Shit!!!!

Stay cool, Rod…

"Uhm…ok," I winced.

"What? Why you say that like that?" Shay wondered. Did she say something to you? Is there something you wanna tell me???"

"I mean…I'm just saying. We was just all in the bed together."

"Yeah, I know. I mean we were drunk…nothing happened. I didn't really *expect* anything to happen. But that's why I didn't even press the issue that night, I'm just not feeling Tash like that anymore. I'd rather wait on Kourt."

"Oh. Ok. The missing BFF," I teased.

"Shut up, silly. That's what else I wanted to talk about. Kourtney is coming home in a month," she switched gears again. "Like…literally 4 weeks to be exact. She's gonna be here for the weekend before summer classes…like she said. And I told her she can stay with us."

"Us??"

She giggled, "Well – you. We're going to stay with you at your place for the weekend."

"Hmmmm…is that right?" I licked my lips. "Ok, sooooo…"

"She's down. We've already talked. And neither of us will be on our monthly either…before you even ask."

"Cuz you *know* I was gonna ask," I said with grin. "Ok. So, she's down."

"Yes. But…if we are gonna do this – like seriously bring another woman in the bedroom – we need to talk about some ground rules."

"Uhm…ok. Like?"

Shay took a deep breath, "First…I need you to know I don't lie to you about anything. I'm not sleeping around with anybody else and I'm honest about *everything* with you. I've never really felt like I had to be honest with anybody else like this…but there's something about you. Maybe it's the fact that you're so good at cheating and lying that I'm scared you're gonna catch me in a lie."

"Man, shut up," I waved her last comment off.

"No, I'm serious. The point is: I don't lie, and I'm not sleeping with anyone else. I want you to be honest with me the same way."

"Ok," I thought that was fair enough.

"So, have you?"

"Have I what?"

"Lied to me? Or slept with anyone else? Lied to me about sleeping with anyone else? Did anything behind my back that would be considered cheating?"

"Damn…you really asking me all'at?"

"I'm giving you a chance to be honest. If there's anything you wanna tell me or something you've done with somebody else and didn't know how to tell me…then now is the time. I'm not going to be mad – I just want you to be honest with me if this is going to work."

This was my chance. My chance to come clean and be open about everything. But only a fool would think I would take this chance…after all the bullshit I went through telling KeLLy about Cookie. I had learned my lesson…wuttin' no way I was telling on myself again.

But then again…I ain't want nothing to come back and bite me in the ass with Sashé. I started thinking about how wild I got when my car engine went out. I thought about all the random chicks off *MySpace*, one in *particular* who I really did need to tell Shay about, eventually.

Then I thought about the one-night stands from the club scene I came up on while hanging out with Ricky Rhymes and his VIP section access. The groupies he introduced me to at the studio and during the promo last month.

I had cut my creeping down a helluva lot, but nowhere near completely. Then, of course, there was the Tasha incident last night – which, *as far as I could tell*, Sashé didn't know about. I mean, it was a long shot, but she wuttin' giving me no hints or indication that she knew what happened right under her nose in the bed with us.

And you ain't bout to tell her ass, either!

Shut up, nigga – I know. I can't try to act like a angel, though. I gotta give something up.

I exhaled and closed my eyes, "Ok. So, I'm not perfect."

"This is true," Shay agreed. "So, tell me."

"Ok, the night you and Kourt left…when you was on your period."

"Right…."

"Well…I was horny as hell. So I called – "

"Wait, don't tell me," she cut me off. "You called KeLLy and y'all had sex."

"No. Close. Actually…I sent a drunk text to *Cookie.*"

"COOKIE?!?!" she couldn't believe what I said. "Oh wow. You had sex with Cookie again, Daddy?!?!"

"Yes," I admitted. "Just that night. I was drunk, horny, frustrated. Apparently, she was just getting off work and came right over."

"Work?!?" she gasped, shocked yet again. "It was like the middle of the night – what the hell does she do? Is she a stripper now or something?!!?"

"Actually, yeah. She work at the little club off 350 not far from where I just moved from."

"Oh, wow! I was just joking."

I laughed, "Well, nah…yeah, I'm for real. So, we had sex that night…but I ain't fukced her since."

At least that's my **story**. *I done actually fukced Cookie twice since then.*

Yeah, nigga, but Shay don't need to know that.

"Hmm. I shoulda known you would have sex with her again. I don't even think I'm mad. If you woulda said *KeLLy…then* I woulda been pissed."

"Why *KeLLy*?" I was curious.

"Well, just because…that would be like me sneaking to fukc Keith and not telling you," she explained. "KeLLy is different."

"Good point," I was impressed.

"So, is that it?? Just that one time?" she kept probing. "Be honest, Daddy."

I sighed one more time, "Aight. It was one other time a few weeks ago."

"With Cookie?!?!"

"Nah. I fukced this white girl I met off *MySpace*."

"Oh, really? A white girl…hmmm," she took it in.

"Yeah…she had fake tits. It was weird, I had never felt no fake tits."

"I'm just surprised you had sex with a white girl. I didn't know you liked white girls."

"I don't discriminate. I fukc with you, right?"

"That's not funny, Rodney!" she snapped sharply. "You know how I feel about that!"

"Ok, I'm sorry. I'm just playing," I immediately apologized. "But I told you, baby…we should be able to tease each other about shit like that. You know you got some white girl in you."

"Ok, but I'm not white and you know I hate when people make fun of me like that! You know how much I…"

"Ok, lil baby," I cut her off. "I'll stop. I'm sorry. But yeah…I did a white girl; just that once."

"So, you only did it that one time – you wouldn't do a white girl again?" Shay was eager to know.

"Nah, I ain't say that. She wuttin' my *first* white girl, I was just telling you about the *MySpace* situation. Shiiit, hell yeah I 'a fukc a white bitch again! Damn right."

Shay giggled at my energy, "Well, I'm just asking because…you know my other best friend is white."

"She is?"

"Yes…I told you this. *Kris* – she was the one recording me and Kourtney when she ate me out."

"Aww, yeah that's right. The white Russian chick. I ain't never met her, though."

"No, you haven't," she affirmed. "But she's a sexy bitch."

"Is she down???"

"Me and Kris haven't talked in forever. But one of our other mutual friends is getting married this summer. So I may run into Kristina there."

"Yeah, but is she down?" I asked again anxiously. "Does she like black guys?"

"She *only* fukcs with black guys," Sashé emphasized. "But…that's not what I'm worried about. I don't know that she's into chicks."

"Aww, ok. Gotcha."

"What about Cookie?"

"What about her?"

"Is she down? Why can't you ask her?"

I shook my head, "Nah, Cookie strictly-dickly. I know that much. But I thought you was only comfortable with Kourtney anyway?"

"Well yeah, but Cookie is cute from the pics you showed me. I'm trying to step outside of my zone a little for you, Daddy," she told me. "But I mean, if she's not into chicks then she's off-limits. Just like Tasha."

"Ok."

"I'm serious, Rodney. I don't want to hear about you fukcing Cookie again. You have no reason to," she ranted passionately. "If you wanna have sex with another girl…I'm ok with it. I'm *telling* you I'm ok with it – but she's gotta fukc me, too. *Fukc cheating*. We can do her together. But bi-chicks only. That's the second ground rule. First, we keep it honest. Second, bi girls only. If you play…I play."

"Aight…I'm with it. I won't. I promise. What else?"

The rest of the ground rules were simple: I couldn't have any contact with any girl we played with unless Shay knew about it. And of course, no unprotected sex with the other chick – I had to strap up. Everything else was a go.

Sashé felt like I was helping her unleash a **beast** of her own and the plan was to stay on the same page so we could tame and feed our **beasts** together. And our first shot at enjoying a meal together was coming up soon.

Like Shay said…Kourtney was coming back home in just a few weeks.

*　　*　　*　　*　　*

185

May 2006

The week before Kourtney was coming home was *Finals Week*, the last week of classes down on the yard. Though I had graduated almost four years earlier…I had a final test of my own that week.

Finals Week also meant that KeLLy was finally going to walk the stage and graduate.

Like I said at the beginning of this episode…when KeLLy and I finally broke it off for the last time, it was awkward. All'at awkwardness came to a head the weekend she graduated. We had been on our *'break'* since late December and had all but moved on. The more time I'd been spending without KeLLy, the more time I had invested in a relationship with Sashé.

But Kells didn't know about Shay, not exactly, anyway. She knew Sashé from campus, of course, but not personally. But I had a close call in November of last year, where KeLLy read a text from Sashé while she was using my phone. I was almost caught red-handed. I mean, I *was* caught, but the way me and Shay played it off and stuck to the story we came up with was BRILLIANT.

KeLLy never brought up Sashé again after that so as far as she was concerned, I was just doing me during our break. She had no reason to think I was fukcing with Shay or *anybody* from campus, but it was safe to assume that Kells assumed I would at least go back to Cookie. But because Kells knew the history of me and Cookie, I knew that was the last person that she wanted to see me fukcing with after her.

Since KeLLy and I had taken our break, I felt it was best that she ain't have no details on what I was doing or how I was living. So, just like with my sister, Ronnie, I went through similar great lengths to keep my shit on the low from Kells, even though we wuttin' together or even on regular speaking terms. But most of all, I wanted to keep Sashé a secret at all costs. That was one conversation that I ain't think I'd ever be ready to have.

But if Kells was graduating, I was expected to be there. Although we were no longer talking daily, KeLLy and I still had a mutual amount of respect for each other, and our history together wouldn't allow us to act like strangers. Her family all expected me there. Her friends, my friends…all they'd known for the last four years was *'Rodney and KeLLy'*. We hadn't been seen together in months, but it would be even *more* awkward if I *wasn't* at her graduation.

We both agreed on this. And even if none of that was the case, *KeLLy* still expected me to be there. I already hadn't granted her request to stay together until after this graduation was over. So, the least I could do was be there to support and cheer her on. After all, it had been a long time coming for her.

I picked up Lil Rico early that morning and we hit the highway to head to the Burg. We sat with her family at the commencement, and everything was cool with no drama. But then…

There was this guy at the ceremony with Kells' family who I didn't recognize. After putting two and two together…I realized that this nigga was the guy KeLLy had been *dating* for about a month.

This made me feel some type of way.

In all the pictures we took after the ceremony, you could see it in my face. Even Lil Rico could tell something was bothering me as we left the graduation and stopped by Sashé's crib before we headed back to KC. It was hard to even hide it from Shay, as she could tell something was bothering me that I ain't wanna talk about. She even tried to make me smile by reminding me that whatever was wrong – once we had this ménage with Kourt next weekend, I would forget about it.

Still, I couldn't sleep that night. I needed to know what the fukc was going on. I needed answers.

Why you tripping, though, Rod?

Whatchu mean? I might be falling for Sashé and on my own streak of HoLLy BeLLigerence, but I still got love for KeLLy.

You mean 'you got a weak spot for KeLLy', nigga.

Whatever, nigga. Just let me do what I do. It's time to bring closure.

*   *   *   *   *

The morning after the graduation, I texted Kells and told her we needed to talk. She responded with a callback, and as soon as I asked her who that nigga was, she already had her response ready.

"I knew you was gonna ask me that," she said calmly.

"I'm sure you did. So, who is he?"

"His name is *Douglas*. We've been dating for almost a month."

My heart skipped a beat, "Damn. So…"

"Rodney," Kells lowered her voice. "Remember, we're not together anymore."

"I know but…damn. I ain't know he was gon' be at the graduation. The nigga was sitting with yo parents n'shit."

"Well…"

"Well, what???" I snapped back.

"*You* didn't want me anymore! What am I supposed to do? Keep waiting on you? You don't even call me anymore, Rodney."

"Man, I know but…I'm just saying, Kells. I wuttin' ready. I'm not ready to see that."

"Why, Rodney? I mean, you out here doing you!"

"I know. But still…"

"But *still what?*" she sounded agitated. "Why? What is it?"

"I don't know," I sighed, not able to put my finger on it.

"You miss me?"

I smacked my lips, "Maaaan."

"I miss you. I'm not scared to say it. I've never been afraid to admit that."

"I didn't say I didn't, though."

"But you didn't say you did, *either*," she quickly pointed out. "Look, Rodney. I love you…I still do. But I'm not gon' wait on you forever and you obviously are moving on. Let's be adults about this. We grown. You might prefer them little young, childish bitches – but me and you are grown."

"You taking shots???" I frowned. "Wow. Same old KeLLy."

"That wasn't a shot. You know you like 'em younger than me. It's ok. I'm accepting it now."

"Whatever."

"It was nice to see you, though," she suddenly switched moods. "I'm glad you came. You looked really nice."

"Thank you. I'm proud of you," I told her.

"Like…*really* nice," she repeated flirtatiously.

"You did, too," I tried not to blush.

"Thank you. So, I heard you got a new place in Overland Park now."

"Yeah, that's right."

"So, why haven't you invited me over yet? I don't get to see the new spot???" she shot back aggressively, catching me off-guard.

"Uhm," I mumbled.

"Don't bite ya tongue, baby."

"I'm not."

"I mean…you don't miss me, Rodney?" she asked again, this time with more intent.

"Man, why you keep asking me that?"

"Because I wanna hear you say it. Or *not* say it. I wanna know if I'm the only one that still holds on to this."

"I mean," I took a deep breath, softening up. "I miss you when I talk to you, ok? When I see you, I miss you. If I keep you outta sight…I can handle this better. It's when I see you again – that's when it gets bad."

Kells paused before asking, "So, is it bad now? Now that you're talking to me again?"

"It's not helping," I admitted, feeling my heart beating faster.

"Well, I apologize. But I mean…I *did* just graduate," she giggled. "And speaking of which – where is my graduation gift???"

"Oh, damn," I was caught off-guard again. "What do you want?"

"I wanna see the new place," she responded without hesitation.

"KeLLy," I started shaking my head, feeling pressure in multiple places.

"No, I'm serious. That can be my graduation gift from you," she continued. "I want dinner. We can have dinner at ya new place. Or wherever. And then you can show me the apartment."

"Man, I don't know."

"What are you scared of? That's the least you can do Rodney…after all of this. Take me to dinner, and then let me see ya new place. I know we not together; I know you moving on. We grown. I'm trying to move on, too. This is just a graduation gift."

I bit my lip, thinking about her suggestion. It was tempting. But that wuttin' necessarily a good thing. After a brief second, I asked, "So, just dinner…and then you see my spot…and that's it, right?"

"More like…dinner…and then we go back to yo spot for dessert," she clarified with mischief.

"Kells…"

"Rodney. It's my graduation," she cut me off again, taking command. "I'm not taking no for an answer."

I was at a loss for words and didn't know how to respond. Knowing she had me backed into the corner she wanted me in, me ex-girlfriend then went in for the kill shot, whispering seductively, "So, what time should I be there? I'm free after 6 today."

*   *   *   *   *

12

That cute little dimple on the left side of KeLLy's face gives me goosebumps instantly. I tried to keep my composure. I did a great job of keeping my cool, for as long as I could.

But after dinner, KeLLy stood in my living room, just looking at me with them soft brown eyes, and asked me why I hadn't shown her the bedroom yet. She was always witty with her flirting, and I took it as a joke, but deep down I knew she what she wanted. I wanted it, too.

We hadn't seen each other in months…hadn't been alone even longer. She was moving on with *Douglas*…but ole Dougie Doug couldn't touch her the way I could. I knew her body; every sleek curve, every sensitive spot, every inch of her frame was still my playground.

Her feet were still soft, toes on point. KeLLy never missed a nail appointment. That was one of the things I loved about her – she was so feminine. So *womanly*.

As I sat at the end of the bed and caressed her at heel and ankle, Kells looked down at me, biting her lip. Her front teeth were gapped, but somehow, she always pulled off the sexiest looks. Tonight was no different.

She licked her full, juicy lips as she watched me massage her. *Avant's* new album, *'Director'*, had been playing from the computer in the other room for about 15 minutes now.

"You know I miss how you used to rub my feet every day, Rodney," her voice was soft, yet commanding against the music. She's had a little to drink. Well, we *both* had a few drinks at dinner, but KeLLy wuttin' the type to get *white-girl-wasted*. She took a sip of her red wine as she watched me closely, looking away ever so often to check out my bedroom setup.

"You know you shouldn't have to miss this," I whispered lowly. The buzz had taken over now, there was no turning back.

"What you mean?" KeLLy cut her eyes at me. "You rub *her* feet everyday now – not mine."

"Who is *'her'?* I asked what she meant by that.

"Oh, I'm not playing that game with you, Rodney. I don't know *'who'*, but whoever it is…she ain't *me."*

I licked my lips, admiring her smooth, chocolate skin, "No, she's not."

And indeed she wasn't. Sashé was as opposite of Kelly as she could be…right down to the simple routine of regular pedicures. Shay's feet were soft and in great shape, too – but *KeLLy?* KeLLy took pride in the things that made her a woman. Her hair, her nails, her style of dress. The way she carried herself…her dedication to staying reserved and tasteful. She had Sashé beat by a landslide in her womanhood.

So, why am I leaving KeLLy behind for Shay again? What was it that drove me away from Kells in the first place?

Tonight, I couldn't put my finger on it. All I could see in front of me was the woman I had given so much of myself to. The woman who had seen me at my most vulnerable moments; the one who held me down through the roughest times.

Tonight – my *ménage* was between KeLLy and my past. Tonight was the last dance with my former lifestyle…my last chance to be normal again.

And I wanted to take full advantage. Somehow, I knew this was a graduation ceremony for *me* as well. After tonight, I was stepping into a whole new world. This last dance had to be enjoyed.

"Stand up," I demanded suddenly.

"Now??? You just gon' stop my foot massage like that?"

"I wanna look at you," I told her nonchalantly. "I ain't seen you in forever."

"Whose fault is that?" she lowered her eyes.

"Don't start," I warned her. "Stand up. Come on."

She bit her lip before complying softly, "Ok."

It was just me and KeLLy. No drunk roommates or freaky friends. Kells didn't have bi-curious best friends. I couldn't stand her homegirls – the way it *normally* is with relationships and friends. There were no ropes or handcuffs. No surprise candle-wax attacks; no bite marks to nurse afterwards.

Tonight, it's just plain and simple.

It felt like old times. KeLLy ignored calls from *Douglas* – the same way she would ignore calls from her campus boyfriend, *Jamal*, when we first hooked up so many years ago. KeLLy had started off as my little secret, helping me fine tune my techniques in *The Art* before I was truly addicted. She helped me creep on Cookie in the beginning, and I helped her get over on and lie to her guy. We made a great team back then…two cheaters in perfect sync. Tonight was our reality of a reunion.

KeLLy looked at me with a certain look in her eyes, as if she was accepting our fate. She knew that this was it for us. And in typical KeLLy-form…she made sure she left me with something to remember.

I didn't get that *good look* at her standing up, not like I wanted. Before I could spin her around…KeLLy took matters in her own hands.

She pushed me down to the bed…not playfully, but still sexy and seductive. As I fell on my back, she started unbuckling her belt buckle, pulling her jean shorts down to her ankles and whispering, "You knew what you wanted from me, Rodney. You knew what you were doing."

"What you talking abo…"

"You knew what you wanted to do with me from the very beginning," she looked down at me with fire in her eyes.

I was both moved and surprised at her aggression, lowering my eyes and biting my lip. She flexed her thick legs fiercely, enticing me. Her pink panties stood out in the dim, candlelit room, and I coulda sworn I saw a damp spot in the crotch. But then again, it was kinda dark and I was tipsy from my new drink of choice, *Henny*.

It had been so long since I'd seen KeLLy's body, I couldn't hide my excitement, "Dammit, KeLLy…baby."

"This is what you wanna walk away from?" she gave me that good look I was after, spinning around slowly with her hands on her hips and turning her neck to look me in the eye from every angle. It was then that I noticed that her panties were actually a g-string thong.

FUKC!!!

Has her ass gotten bigger?

KeLLy always had a nice, thick, and round ass. After months without being behind it…my mouth was watering at the view. She knew I loved her ass; she could tell I was salivating at it.

She smacked her left cheek, grabbing and cuffing her own meat as she made contact. When KeLLy's ass shook…it had waves in that muthafukca. I missed seeing those ripples.

She then quickly turned back around to face me, trying not to blush, and doing her best to keep a straight face. I always knew this freaky, promiscuous side of KeLLy wuttin' for everyone to see. KeLLy was raised to be old-fashioned – carrying herself like a lady in the streets and a real freak only in the sheets. She was nowhere near as open as Sashé.

KeLLy was the *church girl* turned *schoolteacher* and kept her freaky side behind exclusive closed doors. Remember, she was with Jamal for 7 years before cheating with me. KeLLy took pride in her mystique, and it was what made the sex with her intriguing. With KeLLy, I always felt like I was getting her to do things she normally wouldn't do. It was my pleasure to have another chance to do so tonight.

"Damn, that's how you feel?" I wiped the drool from my bottom lip.

"Hmmm…you tell me," she moaned. "How do I feel?" She took a step closer and turned around to poke her ass out, grabbing her left cheek again in front of me before following up with, "Feels soft to me."

"Damn. Me, too," my jaw dropped in awe as I started squeezing eagerly. "Damn, it's so soft, baby."

"Oh, I'm *'baby'* again now?"

"I'm just saying."

"What are you saying, Rodney??" she twirled back around ever so gracefully and then leaned in and over me. Her 34C's hung in my face through her blouse, and now she was close enough for me to see the beads of sweat forming on her brow.

Wiping her sweat away gently with my right thumb, I held her face with my palm before I spoke, "Don't act like that, Kells."

Before I could get the words completely outta my mouth, Kells dove in and pressed her lips up against my mine…sticking her wet tongue in.

I felt the tingling all the way down to my toes. KeLLy rarely kissed me – this was no secret. She made up for all the missed kisses within those few hot, passionate seconds, apologetically sucking my lips into unspoken forgiveness.

She straddled me and my back hit the bed again, chasing me with her tongue out as she grabbed the back of my head. I could feel her hips swirling and grinding on me to the music. Her rhythm was perfect…as always. Her formal dance training was her strength in the bedroom…as she knew how to move without effort. Her entire body was in perfect harmony with each movement as she continued to kiss me.

I was tingling…everywhere. Our moans seemed to be just as in tune, in between the lips smacking and heavy breathing.

My hands couldn't stay still. One second I'm squeezing her ass and guiding her grind, and then the next I'm gripping her shoulders, reaching underneath her armpits.

She pushes me away and starts tugging at her shirt, pulling it over her head and tossing it to my right towards the closet. She's got this smirk on her face, and all I can stare at is that damn *dimple* again.

My dick started trying to break free from my shorts as she sat on top of me in her bra and panties. I was sure she was sitting on a damp spot now; I could feel her warm juices seeping through on my leg.

"I shouldn't be kissing you, anyway," she rolled her eyes. "I know what you like to do with that mouth."

"Damn, for real??" I bit my lip, pulling my shirt over my head.

"I'm just saying," she mocked me.

"Saying what?" I leaned forward to grab her face.

"Hmmmm…you know I like that rough shit."

"You just saying what, girl?" I asked again, this time more forcibly.

"You…nasty," she panted and our lips met again with another uncharacteristic sloppy kiss…as KeLLy dug her nails into my shoulders. This made me thrust into the air, and I wrapped my arms around her tightly, using my legs to flip us over.

She was now on her back, looking up at me with eagerness mixed with shock, "Hold on now! Not that damn rough, boy!"

She brought me back to our reality, where the *beast* had to play nice. But there she laid…legs propped open, mine for the taking.

"My bad," I apologized gently. "It's just been so long."

"Be gentle, baby," she urged. "It's been a while for me, too, like *literally*."

My eyes got big, "Like…what? You saying you haven't…"

"Not since you," she finished my thought. "Not since we broke up."

She was touching herself…tracing her fingers down her breasts and into her panties, looking me dead in the eye.

"Are you…"

"Yes, I'm serious," she read my mind again. "Not too rough."

I agreed without hesitation, caught up in the notion that no one had touched my KeLLy since me. That shit was a real ego-stroker…whether it was intentional or not. I ain't know if Kells was *'waiting'* on me or if she was just hesitant to let her guard down and go there with somebody else. Either way, it indirectly had to do with me, so I had a moment of being full of myself when she said that. Now I was just as motivated to give her something to remember *me* by.

I reached for her waistline and started yanking at her panties…almost ripping 'em. She gives me a side eye, but in the same breath, lifts up so I can pull her underwear down. I could see the film of wetness as they started to peel away from her pussy, and she sees me looking and bites her lip. I then started kissing her legs as her panties reached her ankles, my eyes still focused on her pussy while she rubbed her clit with her index finger.

"You nasty," I whispered.

"No, I'm n…"

Before she could finish her words….I dove in at her, taking her clit and finger in my mouth, sucking and licking, jerking my head back and forth as her juices splashed on my chin.

*She tastes sooooo…**nostalgic**.*

KeLLy then grabbed the back of my head and pushed me in deeper. I responded by sticking my tongue inside of her…trying to force it in to stretch her tight walls apart. But only the tip of my tongue is successful; she was much tighter than I remembered. Her sweet moans got louder as she locked her legs around my head, lifting up to meet my face.

I planted one hand on the mattress and the other around the small of her back, and started giving her pussy lips long, wide tongue strokes as she grinded against my mouth in perfect rhythm.

Damn, I miss the way she moves. It's always so fluid.

Her legs started shaking and she collapsed down to the mattress in submission. Once her legs fell to the side and freed my neck…I pulled away and stood up to rip away at my shorts.

"Don't move," I commanded mannishly.

"O…ok," she stammered. She kept playing with her pussy as I got undressed. I smiled at her head twisting and turning, turned on at her being lost in the moment. My dick popped out and up as I tossed my shorts and underwear to the side quickly. I stood there for a second…jacking my dick, watching her.

There's something about watching from a slight distance, not quite close enough to touch. I can hear her finger squishing around; every breath and sound she lets out is right there in front of me. KeLLy has always been familiar with her body…she *loves* to play with herself. As I stood there to enjoy the show, she made sure to give me a good one.

I watched in lustful silence…squeezing and stroking my **wooD** as she took her finger away from her wet lips and into her mouth, sucking the juices off slowly.

I looked at her lustfully, "That shit taste good, don't it???"

KeLLy didn't speak, instead she just nodded her head in agreement.

"Can I eat some more??"

I had no intentions on waiting on her reply. I quickly tossed her legs to the side and jumped back in the bed face-first in between her legs. Her pussy was so wet. I put my face in it and wiggled it from side to side, tongue swinging the opposite direction of my head.

KeLLy gasped…holding her breath momentarily. I could see her hands gripping my bedspread; I had her where I wanted her now.

Then, without warning, she jumped away from me — slamming her hand on the bed as she stared down at me with lowered eyes, "Boy, what are you trying to do to me?!?"

I wiped my face, crawling up towards her, "Stop running."

"I'm…*hmmmmm*…not," her voice faded off again as I started rubbing her clit rapidly with two fingers. Her body arched into the air, and just as quickly I took my fingers away, sitting up on my knees now. The look on her face was a mixture of surprise and desperation, as she watched me taste her off of my fingers.

My taste test involved more licking than sucking…as I ran my tongue down my index and middle fingers slowly. We stared each other down the whole time.

Abruptly, my dick jumped up towards my stomach, taking Kells' eyes with it. She bit her lip again and hopped up, lunging at me. She stopped at my fingers in front of my face, stuck her tongue out, and helped me lick them clean. Then she leaned closer and took my tongue in with hers…kissing me again with deep passion.

Damn.

We both embraced each other tightly…kissing and scratching, scratching and kissing. My hands found her bra band on her back, and I started to unsnap it. But KeLLy suddenly pulled away and gave me this look, and I immediately let my left hand fall to her waist, my right hand still on the fastener. We chuckled…reminded of days when I could only unsnap a bra with *two* hands. KeLLy used to fukc with me about it, telling me how I had to be smooth to *get that unsnap moment just right.*

I had come a long way since those days, as her bra was in our laps a half second later. She reached down with her right hand to toss it away and grabbed my **wooD** with her other hand, "Hmmm…there he is."

I closed my eyes and bit my lip, head leaning back in pleasure, in a trance. Her tongue tracing above my goatee brought me back, and we started kissing again.

We never kissed so much before. I knew we'd never kiss again.

KeLLy started laying back toward the bed…pulling me down with her with our tongues still tied in a wet tangle. This shit was driving the *beast* into a horny rage; I could feel the hairs on the back of my neck standing up.

She then took my dick in her hand and started rubbing her wet pussy lips with the head…grinding her clit up against it. I grabbed a fistful of her hair with my left hand, squeezing her left tit with my other.

"Roddd…neeeey! Staaah…ppp! D…don't puulll my hair…liiike…tha that! Stoppp!" she squealed in reaction and tried to pull her head away, but the *beast* wouldn't let go.

"*Shut* up," he grunted behind my voice.

KeLLy stared me in the eyes again…this time as if she's asking me something or like she was trying to read me. I'm trying to figure out what she's thinking as the *beast* made his next move…slapping her hand away from my dick.

And then…it happened.

I entered her slowly as her eyes rolled into the back of her head. She licked her lips – bottom one first – moaning while her tongue traced her top lip, in sync with my full penetration.

KeLLy's pussy was so tight, much tighter than I remembered. I had every inch inside of her as I held her legs up in the air, watching her squirm. Her muscles started clenching against my throbbing dick and she let out a long exhale of a moan. Her pussy pulsated, clenching in a call-and-response with my **wooD.**

"Fuuuuuuuuuck," I groaned.

"I know," Kells nodded at me. "Mmmm hmmmm…"

"Why…yo pussy so tight?" I pulled out and looked down at her juices glistening on my shaft. My heart was racing.

"I told you," she whined. "Come ohhh…onnnn."

I thrusted back inside as her voice drifted off into a gasp for air and the *beast* grabbed her hair again. This time KeLLy let the *beast* have his way; this time she just goes with the flow. The *beast* loves the submission. As he let her hair go, he then pushed her right leg back towards her against the bed.

KeLLy was still flexible…even after all these years.

We both found our eyes looking down at the thrusts while I humped her slowly, letting her pussy muscles grip me so I couldn't pull out. Our breathing patterns quickened almost simultaneously, and she started grinding up at me.

'Grown Ass Man' suddenly comes on out the speaker, as if these next few minutes were made for a movie.

It's like she's dancing to the music as I fukc her. Her timing to the beat is so perfect it forces me to fall on beat with my strokes. I leaned in closer, holding my weight up with my right elbow on the mattress, other hand still pinning KeLLy's right wrist down.

She moaned loudly, "Hmm…yes! Deeper!" Her pussy was splashing as the *beast* got more aggressive. "Shit…yes…hmmm! Yes, Rodney!"

I can't remember it ever being this wet. I can't recall the last time she said my name like this.

The *beast* takes complete control again…grabbing at KeLLy's neck with force. To my surprise, she immediately shifted her body to the side so he could get a better grip.

Wow…

Kells bit her lip, moaning, "Come on, *Daddy.*"

"Hmm, hell ye…"

Wait. What did she just call me???

"It's…yours…bay…bee. Cum come…cum on, Daddy."

I can't believe my ears. But the *beast* doesn't let me miss a beat. I started putting my hips into it…grinding against her walls in a circular motion, stretching my back inward so I could feel her clit. I remembered KeLLy's clit swells up when she gets fully aroused, and I was eager to watch it as it enlarged.

"Damn, Kells."

"Don't stop...don't..."

"I'm not."

"Hmmmm, baby! Damn...I missed...you."

"It's still mine???"

"You in it."

"Hmmmm...fukcin right, I am," I moaned back. "Hold ya leg up. Hold that muhfukca up, KeLLy."

"Ok...oh," she gasped. "Ok, Daddy."

I couldn't believe she was calling me that shit. It had the *beast* giving her a looooong stroke – lifting up in the air as I pulled out, and then slamming down with all my weight and force as I thrusted back deep. KeLLy was holding her legs up in the air by her ankles now...squeezing her tits and pinching her nipples as I hit it.

"You better quit calling me that," I warned her in between breaths.

"I...can't. I..."

"Hmmm. You better..."

"Baby...hmmm!" she yelped. "What...are...you?! What are you...doing to? To...to me???"

I grabbed her by the waist and started really digging in, pausing so she could feel my dick jump inside her. The sweat off my forehead and chest dripped down on top of KeLLy's dark torso…and she wiped it in with hers. We was making a hot, sweaty mess, with the bedspread now drenched in her juices as they ran down her ass crack onto the mattress.

She kept squirming, "Yes…*yessss!* Right…*ther…*"

I put both my hands around her neck and started pounding.

"Oh my God, Rodney! I'm 'bout to cum…don't stop! Oh my…hmmm…fukc!!!"

I felt her pussy start tightening up and had to put my back into it to keep her from pushing me out.

"Hmmmmmmmm…shiiiiiiiit…fuuuuuck me! Fukc me, Rodney! Come…onnnn…hmmmm!!!"

I looked down at my shaft, which was now completely covered in Kells' creamy release, and it made me start fukcing her harder. All my feelings and emotions poured out with each thrust, and KeLLy began shaking and twitching, screaming louder each time I went back in deep. She started slapping her clit with her hand and then rubbing it furiously, cummin' all over me.

I wait 'til she's done shaking before I pull out again, with her letting out a deep breath as my dick popped loose from her tightness.

"I ain't done with yo ass yet," I told her. "Turn over."

Before she could even let my words sink in, I was flipping her over and flexing my strength, expressing my dominance physically. KeLLy moaned and groaned as she complied…putting the perfect arch in her back while she laid her face on the bed. Her hands grabbed the comforter in anticipation.

Kelly's ass is soooooo…throwback.

I just stared at that round and juicy apple-bottom for a minute. Her dark and smooth skin gave the greatest contrast to her pink insides as I spread her lips apart and leaned in to get another taste.

"Got…dammit, Rodney. Shit."

I'm sucking her lips, tongue kissing her pussy with deep, circular waves.

"You clowning now."

"Not yet," I slurped.

"Oh yeah???"

I got a firm grip on her left cheek and used it for balance as I shoved my **wooD** back in her hard. She lifted her head up from the bed and put her right hand against the wall where I should have a headboard.

Now she was throwing it back at me…so I grabbed her waist with both hands again and started matching her intensity.

"Come on…do it, baby" she cried out. "Do it."

Reading her mind, my right hand slammed down on her cheek. HARD. And then again…HARDER.

"YES!!! Do it aga……OH!!!" she yelped. *"SHIT!"*

I started giving her stinging slaps, smacking her ass with rage, fukcing her from behind like an animal while I watched her cheeks ripple and welt up. My dick started to swell.

"Hmmm, get it! Get…it mmm…hmmm yes! Oh SHIT, not so HMMMM!!! Dammit, NIGGA!"

I'm showing her ass no mercy…tossing her arm back to the bed as she tried to reach back to stop me. The *beast* was drooling now, sweating like a pig and growling with the back shots.

"O…k. Ok," she was out of breath as her body went limp. I gripped her waist again to hold her ass in the air and she propped it up to keep taking my dick-down. Her juices were splashing, making that squishy sound again. She then turned her face to the left and started watching our reflection in the mirror next to my closet door.

"Say it, baby," she whispered as I kept humping hard and forcefully.

"Come on…say it," she repeated.

Say what? What is she talking about?

"You know what I'm talking…about. Just…say it."

"Say…hmmmm…what?" I growled. "What you want me to…say????"

"Hmmmm! You…know! OUCH!!" she started stuttering, bracing herself. "Hmmm you you you…know!"

Yeah, you know, nigga!

"Do I, *bitch?!?!?*"

Damn, I can't believe I just…called her…that!!!

Kells starts going crazy, *"Hmmmm…YESSSS! Say it again!"*

"You my *BITCH?!?!*"

"Yes…oh my gaw…what the…fukc!"

"Huh, bitch?!?!" I yelled furiously. "You hear me?!?!"

She started running her words together fast and frantically, *"OhMyGodRodneyI'mBoutToCumAgain!!!"*

"Cum all on my dick again! Yeah…like that! Just like that!"

Slapping the mattress with her right hand and holding herself up with her left, she started throwing her ass back at me again – this time pushing me backwards, making me hold on tighter.

Fukc.

I FEEL IT, TOO.

"Hmmmm yeah…cum with me, baby! I feel it…I feel it, too," she sped up her humping, making her ass cheeks clap.

DAMN…FUKC!!!

"You…you do? You…fa feel dat sh…shit, Kells??? Hmmmm shit! OH…SHIT!!!"

I was thrusting with newfound purpose as the nut started shooting out of me, deep into KeLLy's loins. Her pussy started gripping me again uncontrollably…making it ooze out from the bottom of my sack. My heart was thumping.

I ain't even think about pulling out. But KeLLy wouldn't have let me anyway, as she grinded her ass up against me, keeping me inside until I collapsed on top of her. We laid there in silence for a few seconds, genitals still mutually throbbing, the both of us panting and gasping for air.

Kells spoke first, smiling and giggling, "You done with my ass now?"

"Shut up," I mumbled, shaking my head.

"I'm just saying... *Daddy'.*"

"You tryna be funny," I pulled out and rolled over to my right.

"No, but for real," she flips over, laying her head on my chest. "That was some good shit."

"It was," I couldn't agree more.

"Like...for real."

"I know."

"That's how you giving my shit away now???" she pinched my chest.

"Come on, don't start," I flinched, biting my lip.

"I'm not...I'm not," she insisted, kissing the spot she just pinched. "I'm just saying."

"Why you let me cum in you?" I stared at the ceiling, processing what just happened.

"Why you ain't pull out?" she shot back sarcastically.

"Hmmm. I just…couldn't," I admitted, shaking my head. "You still on the pill?"

"Nope," she replied with the quickness.

"Damn."

"Damn," she echoed mockingly.

"So, now what?"

"What you mean???"

"What happens next?" I wanted to know.

"I'm not trying to get pregnant if that's what you're thinking."

"I didn't say that."

"But I know how you think," she reminded me. "Nothing happens next, I know we're not together."

"But what if you…"

"I'm not, I doubt it," she answered before I could ask. "I'm not even ovulating. Just stop thinking about it for now, baby."

"Ok," I sighed, letting it go.

"Just lay here. Fall asleep with me one last time."

"Ok."

"Can I just have *that?*" she looked up at me, sweet and innocently. "That's my last request…I promise."

I lowered my eyes and squeezed her ass cheeks again, "Mmm hmmm. For graduation, right?"

Kells laid her head back on my chest, whispering softly, "That's right. You get it now."

*   *   *   *   *

When I woke up in the middle of the night, the music was off and most of the candles were out. The bed was still wet, and now that I had cooled off from the sweating earlier, I had goosebumps and the shivers. And, as expected, KeLLy was gone.

I knew when I started to doze off that she wouldn't be there when I woke up. When KeLLy and I started off all those years before, the both of us were creeping and I got used to her always sneaking out like a thief in the night when I fell asleep after we got it in. The closer we got over the months, the less she would leave. Tonight, however, the tables returned to where they began…and it was the final touch to our final rendezvous.

In all likelihood, I had seen the last of KeLLy.

The clock on my nightstand read **4:17am** as I pulled my naked body underneath the covers. Quickly in my head, I reminded myself of my alibi for Sashé that evening.

I had told Shay I was out with Lonnie and Tre clubbing, and even stepped away from KeLLy to call her *'when I got home'*. My bases were pretty covered there. Shay was still in the Burg and would never think that I was doing the shit I had done tonight with KeLLy. As far as she was concerned…KeLLy and I were long done. And as far as

Kells, she still didn't have a clue who I was truly moving on with.

I knew as I laid there in the afterthoughts that my run-in with KeLLy was risky. But this **beast** of mine was harder to keep in check than I thought. Lately it seemed like the more sexual activity I had, the more I wanted. My dick was hard and throbbing again now. Even after that huge nut I shared with KeLLy earlier, I was still in need of some more action. I'd always had a high sex drive…but this was ridiculous.

I rolled over on my stomach, grabbing my rock hard dick and pointing it downward…hoping that it would eventually go soft. It wasn't working.

As I rolled back over, I threw the covers off of me, grabbing my dick with my left hand. Then I closed my eyes and imagined them all.

KeLLy…Sashé…Tasha…Kourtney…Cookie.

I pictured them all in the room with me, kissing and sucking all over…pussy juices everywhere.

With each stroke I got closer…and CLOSER…and closer…to realizing what was starting to become a real reality for me and my **beast**: my *ménage* obsession was turning into a far-fetched fantasy again.

Don't give up just yet, bro. Stay focused.

Focused on what, though? Nigga, I just came in KeLLy!

So, you got yo rocks off one last time — so what?

So, what if that come back and bite me in the ass with Shay? You heard her say 'anybody but Kells'!

Man chill out, bro! The shit ain't gon' get back.

Here you go with that shit!

Just hold on one more week, Rod. The shit is right in the palm of our fukcin' hands. You can't give up now. Let it play out...

Deep down, I knew my inner *beast* was right. I was still closer than I'd ever been, there was no denying that. I had to find a way to shake my anxiety and do whatever it would take to pull this shit off.

Now, more than ever.

*   *   *   *   *

13

The next week was rough. I found myself in a horny state of hypnosis – all day, every day. All I could think about was sex.

At work, it was the worst. It's about a year after *Sassy* now, and even though her fine ass never came back to work after that shit, I still worked with a bunch of bad bitches in this call center.

Remember *Chelle*, Sassy's friend? Well – I mean, of course, I never fukced with Chelle cuz once she found out I was a Nupe, she had me hook her up with *Ricky Rhymes*. But she was still around and important to mention here for good reason. Chelle had been hanging with this little skinny white chick at the gig who was extra flirty with me lately.

Let's call her *Laura*.

Laura was mostly skin and bones with no curves. But now that it was warming up outside, she was always walking past my desk with her toes out – and this little bitch had some gorgeous ass feet. And y'all know ever since Tianna, I been on this low-key foot fetish. So, now I'm paying more attention to Laura's hints at work all of a sudden.

I wuttin' 100% sure if Chelle had put a bug in Laura's ear about my ways. Remember – Sassy pretty much told Chelle everything about our fling and Chelle swore she would never run her mouth. But the way I think, since

Chelle and Laura are work buddies now, it's highly likely that Laura knows what I'm capable of.

Well anyway, I started getting these urges for Laura at work this week. Suddenly I got vivid images in my head of me taking her in one of the meeting rooms and fukcing her brains out.

There's this *white-girl aspect* to my fantasy about her. When I think of white girls, I think of that carefree, down-to-go-with-the-flow, wherever, whenever type shit. Kinda like how Sashé is. Shay has all the swag and personality of a white girl; maybe that's why she's so open. It's super rare that you find a sista like that.

But shit, this Laura chick was a *real* white girl, and I started having these twisted images of fukcing her all through the halls and on top of desks n'shit.

Of course, they're just *HoLLy Thoughts* – nothing I expressed or would act out on in real life. But then *this* week, the *beast* started making me believe that Laura would actually be down for the shit if I just put it out there.

By midweek it was taking everything in me not to just tell this chick how bad I wanted to fukc her. To make matters worse, Laura usually stops at my desk every day.

Well, on Wednesday, she ironically stops at my desk and starts talking to me about how she's getting her toes done again later that day. Then Laura does something she'd *never* done. She asks me what color I preferred to see her toes painted.

"I mean…it's not up to me," I tried to play it cool, hoping she'd change the subject.

"Well, I just figured since you look at my toes everyday anyway," she grinned. "I might as well ask you how you want 'em."

"Girl, stop playing. You not tripping off me sneaking a peek at ya toes like that."

"Hey! Maybe I am. Maybe I'm not. Maybe I like the attention," she winked at me.

"Mmm hmm," I squinted. "If that was the case, you wouldn't hide 'em when you know I'm looking."

"Hey, you gotta admit…it's kinda creepy with you always looking down at my feet and all," she giggled. "But I'm used to it now. It is kinda cute."

"I'm just looking."

"I know!" Laura exclaimed. "So, call this a truce. I'll stop hiding them…and even let you pick the color I get 'em painted tonight."

"Yeah, right," I shook my head. "You just fukcin' wit…"

"No, I'm not!" she cut me short. "Pinky swear! Whatever color you want. I'll even send you a pic after I get them done."

"Ok, yeah you playing," I leaned back, waving her off.

"I'm not! What's your number? Or do I have to get it from Chelle? I know she has it."

I cut my eyes at her, "Mmmm. Nah, I'll email it to you. You ain't gotta ask her."

"Ok!" Laura bit her lip. "Email the color you want, too, ok???"

I wanted to just tell her whatever she needed to hear to get her away from my desk before I said something inappropriate. I knew she had no clue how much I'd been fantasizing about her lately, but at the same time, she was clearly flirting.

Just let it play out, Rod. It's ain't that big a deal.

You saying that now, but you know what shit like this leads to!

Yeah, and we both know that's where we wanna be led to, nigga!

What happened to us holding on for a week? Kourtney gon' be here this weekend, nigga!

So what? We need the extra practice, anyway. Look at it as strength and conditioning training.

FUKC!!!!!!

So, of course I ended up telling Laura the color I wanted. And of course, she sends me a picture of her toes as soon as she walked out the salon that night. And of course, that made me wanna text her and tell her to come put 'em on my chest so I could fukc her life away.

Gotdammit, man! I can't keep fukcing around on Sashé if I wanna have this ménage. Why is this shit so hard?!?!

Yet another night without the answer to that question led to hours of watching white-girl porn on my computer. It's the only thing I could think of to keep from sexting Laura. So, I went online to visit my favorite free porn sites.

Blackgirlonline.com was #1 on my list, but I mean – the name itself went against my pink-toe craving at the moment. The best part about *BGOL* was the *Forum Section,* though. This is where I stayed up on all the current shit happening in the world. Before the blogs, *TMZ, ShadeRoom,* and *WorldStar* sites, BGOL was the one-stop shop for everything back then. One of the things the usual posters stayed on top of was referring folks to the best sites or download links for all types of music, software, and movies – including, of course, *porn.*

I started searching the BGOL threads for *white girl* clips, and I found a post with a bunch of download links within seconds. But as I waited for the downloads, I caught a sponsor ad at the bottom of the *Forum* page for another site – *AdultFriendFinder.com.*

Well, this should be interesting.

The ad had this bad ass white chick on the banner, advertising their site as the *#1 Sex Personals Site.* There was even a message about meeting locals in your area strictly looking for sex.

This shit gotta be a joke, right?

My horny curiosity eventually got the best of me and I took a peep. The shit was unlike anything I'd ever seen in life.

It was like *MySpace* or *BlackPlanet* on sexual steroids. This *Adult Friend Finder* site had everything you could think of for a muhfukca strictly looking for sex buddies – whether you were looking for singles, couples, or even groups. It took you through a series of sexual preference-oriented questions n'shit, and then let you search for other members who you match with. A real live dating site…but with much more emphasis on *'hooking up'.* The webcam section was the craziest – everything from solo to couple and group fukc sessions were all happening live.

I quickly discovered that the free membership was limited. If you wanted to send multiple messages to your matches or watch the live cams for more than a few minutes…you had to sign up for the paid *silver* or *gold* member levels. That's how they got you.

Withing minutes of scrolling, I was seconds away from pulling the trigger. I mean, they had tons of profiles pulling up right in my *Overland Park* zip code, but I couldn't click on 'em unless I paid. I sat there staring at my monitor in awe, my curiosity getting the best of me.

Man, like who woulda knew this shit was even out here?!?!? Fukc!!!

But the way my debit card was set up, wuttin' no way the paid member fee was going down tonight. So, instead, I settled for the free member level, uploaded a picture of me in a towel, and sent a few winks out to some locals. You could at least do that as a free member…and it was worth a shot to see what happened.

After that, I switched browser tabs to check back on my porn downloads and noticed the *megaUpload* links were moving slow as fukc. This wasn't good. Especially since *Adult Friend Finder* had me harder than steel at the moment. I needed to bust a nut so I could go to bed soon.

I decided to visit my go-to backup 'free' porn site, *Rude* dot com. So, *Rude* was this site with pics and vids submitted by members on some *homemade* porn shit. Homegrown porn was starting to become yet another fascination for me. There's just something about the intrigue of regular people fukcing like porn stars on camera. *Rude* had plenty of these types of clips, so I found this interracial orgy joint that was broken down into 5 clips, about 6 minutes each.

The first clip was some bullshit. It started with these two white chicks playing cards with a quartet of black dudes, talking shit and drinking. The chicks was all touchy-feely, of course, and I almost thought it mighta been some scripted shit. The lighting and quality wuttin' professional though, and you could tell they was in a real house and not on some set. Looked more like a vacation spot. The chicks seemed older than all the guys, but the brown-haired one appeared younger than the other chick.

After a couple of minutes, I figured out there was a white guy behind the camera, recording as he walked around to the side of the table to focus on the older looking chick, a brunette slimmie with some nice tits. She started unbuckling the pants of this black, bald dude and pulled his dick out to give him a hand job. The camera guy then pulled *his* out and shoved it in the brunette's mouth while she worked. He was talking to her like she was his *wife*.

The second and third clips were more *hand jobs* and *head* but by the end of the third one…the two chicks were bent over in the living room, sucking black dicks and getting fukced from behind. Just as I started rubbing my girth through my underwear and getting into it…the short clip ended.

The thing about *Rude* that was annoying – you could only watch 3 video clips a day for free unless you created a profile. *Rude* was free to join and free members got access to about 90% of the site, while paid members could access the full movies that played on subscriber channels, as well as unlimited video clips. Still, the free profile got *6* clips a day vs the 3 for *non-members*…so I decided to create a profile.

Shoulda thought about all this before I started clicking on the clips, but hell — I'm horny.

Aight, so I'm about halfway through the *Rude* profile setup screens when I get this pop-up window from *Adult Friend Finder*. I scanned it over, quickly realizing that it was a *private chat window* from one of my *Matches*.

Oh shit, bro! It's somebody online right now, tryna chat wit a nigga!

See what she talmbout then, nigga!

I couldn't click on her profile because remember — you gotta be *silver* or *gold* to view profiles. But this chick sending me a chat message had a gold member banner next to her avi…so I'm assuming *she* could initiate things with members that I couldn't. I could at least see her profile pic…but it only showed this shot of her waist and ass in some boy shorts. And she was a black chick — a little darker than Sashé, with an ass-to-waist ratio outta this world. That was enough to make me hit pause on the *white-girl craving* for a few.

So, I opened the chat window to read her first message with anxious curiosity.

FoXXXyBiNaTure: "Hey there. Nice pic…"

It wasn't until then that I noticed her clever screen name. Now I'm wondering if *mine* sounded corny.

FREAKY816PLAYBOY: "Thanks baby girl. How are you?"

FoXXXyBiNaTure: "Horny. Lol u?"

"FREAKY816PLAYBOY: "Haha...the   same actually. That kind of night..."

FoXXXyBiNaTure: "Tell me about it. So are you from KS?"

FREAKY816PLAYBOY: "Missouri but I stay out in Overland Park. You? Ya profile says Lee's Summit..."

FoXXXyBiNaTure: "Yep...I work out in OP sometimes. So what r u looking for? U single?"

Hmmm…good questions. I really ain't know what I was on this site looking for. It was just one of those horny nights where I was caught up in fantasyland…and up until then, I really hadn't thought about what to do if I actually *made contact* with somebody. Meeting chicks off *BlackPlanet* and *MySpace* was way different than this. *Adult Friend Finder* was actually *set up* to meet people to *fukc* – without the fronting and beating around the bush.

*This was more **new territory** for me.*

FREAKY816PLAYBOY: "Lol...to be honest, I don't know yet! I kinda stumbled on this shit by accident and started browsing. It's wild..."

FoXXXyBiNaTure: "I know right! I'm still kind of new myself, I just joined last week. Still just looking."

FREAKY816PLAYBOY: "So u like what u see so far?"

FoXXXyBiNaTure: "Hmmm...that depends."

FREAKY816PLAYBOY: "On what...?"

FoXXXyBiNaTure: "You didn't answer my other question boo lol..."

FREAKY816PLAYBOY: "What question???"

"FoXXXyBiNaTure: "Scroll up..."

I really ain't have to scroll up to look again. I mean, I avoided that question intentionally...duh.

Man, just answer her question, Rod!

Bro, how am I supposed to answer that shit?!?

Just tell her wassup! Tell her the damn truth, nigga!

I mean, what's the truth? I'm **technically** *single. Me and Shay ain't together.*

Dawg, she ain't gotta know shit about Shay!

Man, see there you go! So what about our 'agreement'?

Man, what?

You heard what Shay said: 'First we keep it honest. Second, bi girls only. If you play...I play.'

Nigga, I know you see this FoXXXy chick's username! You want her to spell it out in a different language, nigga?

Man, fukc you, nigga! So I should tell her about Shay, then!

Unless you shouldn't. Just feel her out first, brodie. It's just chatting.

What he said made sense, but I still wuttin' sure if he was right. This was all new territory for the both of us. Reluctantly, though, I decided on taking my inner *beast's* advice and typed out my next response.

FREAKY816PLAYBOY: "Lol ohhhhh...THAT question. Yeah. I'm single..."

FoXXXyBiNaTure: "Hmmm."

FREAKY816PLAYBOY: "Hmmm...what? Is that a good or bad hmmm?"

FoXXXyBiNaTure: "That's just a shocker. I'm licking my lips at ya pic..."

FREAKY816PLAYBOY: "Oh yeah? Hmmm...so what you looking for Ms. Bi-Nature???"

FoXXXyBiNaTure: "It's on my profile..."

FREAKY816PLAYBOY: "Yeah but I can't see that..."

FoXXXyBiNaTure: "Oh that's right lol..."

"FREAKY816PLAYBOY: "Damn you paid that fee huh??? Baller!!!"

FoXXXyBiNaTure: "LOL!!! No...it ain't like that! I wish..."

FREAKY816PLAYBOY: "I'm just saying...I can't see ya profile. I'm a freebie..."

FoXXXyBiNaTure: "Lol mmm hmm. Well...I'm really looking for a couple. But...I kinda like what I see, so I guess it's cool that you're single."

FREAKY816PLAYBOY: "Damn...for real?!?! So you like 3somes n'shit???"

FoXXXyBiNaTure: "I've never done it, but I wouldn't mind having one. That's what I wanna explore...it's something about sex with a woman but then again, I just imagine it would be that much better if we had some dick in the picture lol..."

"FREAKY816PLAYBOY: "Damn...straight up huh? So you've had female sex before?"

FoXXXyBiNaTure: "Yes...omg I love it! Is that bad? Don't judge me lol..."

FREAKY816PLAYBOY: "It's not bad at all...that shit turns me on..."

FoXXXyBiNaTure: "Hmmm...hell yeah! Too bad you don't have a woman..."

FREAKY816PLAYBOY: "...Yeah. Too bad huh??"

I had a chance right there…to just come out with it and tell Foxxxy that I had a chick I was fukcing with. Sashé was down for the ménage; all I had to do was make the trio happen. But…*how?*

The cheater in me couldn't figure that part out. I ain't know how to just *tell* a chick that I had another chick who was down. And one of the hardest things for any man to do was turn down new pussy. If nothing else, this Foxxxy chick was a potential piece of brand-new cat. And my greedy, untamed **beast** wuttin' making this no easier.

Man, don't do that, Rod! What if her and Sashé don't click? What if they ain't each other's type? Just let it play out, nigga!

This was new territory for me…

Still, Foxxxy and I kept chatting. We got on the subject of favorite positions and freaky thoughts. We talked about masturbating and favorite porn stars. Foxxxy was really into oral sex; she said it was the only way that she could cum. I started talking shit about how I could make her cum on this dick harder than this tongue, and she responded by telling me how she cums the hardest *when she gives head.*

FUKC.

Yea, this some wild shit, HoLLyRod.

After a while, she said she had to get up early and needed to call it a night, but she wanted to talk to me again. She tells me to hit her on *Yahoo Messenger* tomorrow, since it was free to talk there. She also promises to send me more pics through there. I was tempted to try to keep her online…but right as she was trying to say goodnight, one of my porn download links completed.

Perfect time for some shooting practice. So, I tell Foxxxy goodnight and log off of *Adult Friend Finder,* opening up *Windows Media Player* to watch the porn clip.

It was titled: '*2 White Girls BBC Threesome*', but when I opened it, it wuttin' a interracial joint *at all* – the two females are both black. A classic bait-n-switch. The scene was one from the *Booty Talk* series. I couldn't think of the guy's name, but the females I recognized fa sho. Caramel-colored *Lacy Duvalle* and *Obsession,* the redbone. I mean, I guess Obsession maybe *coulda* been mistaken for a white girl under the right light – but not *really.*

Obsession was a legendary HEAD MONSTA, though. The nearly 11-minute clip opened up with her giving some mean suck and throat action, complete with sound effects and all. But watching this clip presented me with a new dilemma. Obsession immediately made me think of *Cookie.*

Not only were they both built similarly with the small tits and fat ass cheeks, but their head techniques were damn near a splitting image of each other. Obsession was always so sloppy and wet with it, and you could tell she loved sucking dick – especially with how she looked up at the nigga with those big ass eyes.

Man, I miss how Cookie used to suck me up like that.

Who you telling, nigga? We need some of dat shit!

Like right now!

My horny rage was outta control. It was much worse than the night I sent Cookie that drunk text after Sashé and Kourtney left me. But tonight, I wuttin' gon' fall asleep waiting on a reply text, so I took my hand off my dick and reached for my phone.

She answered without hesitation…before the second ring was done, "Oh my God! I was just thinking about calling you!!"

"Oh for real?" I bit my lip, feeling the early signs of checkmate.

"Like, no lie! What are you doing up???" she was full of energy. "It's almost 4 o'clock."

"I mean…what *you* doing up?!?!" I asked, hoping she was up doing the same thing as me.

"I just got off work," she explained. "I'm on my way home."

"You should be on your way to me."

"Rodney!" she yelled in shock.

"What?!? I wanna see you."

"At 4 in the morning, Rodney?! Oh my God, is that the only reason you called me??!?!" she gasped. "No…cuz all you wanna do is have sex! I'm not 'bout to come over there!"

"Don't act like that," I replied calmly. "I just wanna go to sleep with you."

"Whatever, nigga!" she snapped back. "I'm already downtown, anyway, bought to cross the bridge. No."

"That's fukced up, Cookie," I shook my head.

"No, it's not. It's messed up that you only call me when you want sex."

"That's not true cuz I want sex a lot and I don't always call you."

Cookie smacked her lips, "Yeah, well whatever. It's 'cause you got all them other lil hoes! Why won't you call them to get some pussy???"

"Cookie," I whispered, trying to entice her.

"For real! I can't stand you."

"You don't mean that."

"Yes, I do! You so full of it!"

"So, why was you 'bout to call me at 4 in the morning, then?"

She paused, stopping dead in her tracks, "Uhm. Don't worry about it."

"Nah, fukc that!" I smirked in the darkness. "Tell me."

"No," she refused softly.

"You wanted to see me."

"Hmmm. Maybe," she confessed, obviously being coy about it. Her voice made my dick jump in my lap.

"Come see me, Cookie."

"Noooo! I can't," she whined. "I'm already up North, anyway."

"Maaaan…that's dat bullshit!" I frowned up. "So??!?! Turn around. I need to see you."

"I would, but not tonight."

"When, then???"

"I don't know. Soon. This weekend?" she asked. "What you got going on this weekend?"

"Hmmm…when you talking? Friday? Saturday?"

"Friday," she thought it over. "Or Saturday. I'm off Saturday."

"Shit – Friday *or* Saturday," I told her either day worked. "Or *both*. I ain't doing shit."

"Don't play, Rodney. I'm for real."

"Me, too. I need some of that."

"Whatever," she smacked her lips again. "You get pussy all the time!"

"No, I don't. Not like yours," I stroked her ego, laying it on thick. "You know what I'm talking about."

"No, I don't," she lied. "Tell me."

"You just wanna hear me say it."

"Yup. Say it."

"I just want you to…"

"You want me to what?" she cut me off, lowering her voice.

"Suck this dick how you do," I matched her tone.

"How you want me to suck it? Say it."

"Slow. Nasty. Sloppy. You know how you like to do, Cookie."

"Hmmm…I only suck *your* dick like that."

"Whatever," I refused to believe that.

"I'm serious," she claimed. "It's how you be moaning and talking through it. That turns me on; makes me wanna keep going. I'm so serious! I don't even like sucking dick like that. You make me wanna do it."

"Cuz you be doing that shit so right," I licked my lips again, reminiscing. "You gotta gimme dat shit when you see me this weekend."

"I am."

"Don't play."

"*You* don't play," she shot back. "You gotta give it to me good, too. I ain't been having sex. I'm so horny."

"You know I'ma give it to you."

"Promise me," she wanted reassurance.

"I promise."

"Ok. So I'ma see you Friday?"

"Definitely," I confirmed one last time.

"Ok…I'ma call you. I just got home; I'm 'bout to get in the shower."

"Can I watch?"

"What? Boy, how???" Cookie giggled. "Shut up!"

"Take some pictures for me," I requested, horny and desperate.

"Boy, you know I do *not* do that! Bye, Rodney! I'ma see you in a couple of days."

"Ok, I gotta get up for work, anyway," I told her, looking at how late it was. "Goodnight."

"Bye!" she hung up, ending the postponed booty call.

I knew it was wrong – setting up another rendezvous with Cookie. Just the same as it was wrong to be talking to chicks over the internet after I had *just* fukced *KeLLy* again. But like I said…this **beast** of mine had one helluva hunger and I was just moving without thinking. I needed to get some Cookie again; there was a good chance that I wouldn't have this opportunity again. I knew it was greedy. I knew I was tripping.

*   *   *   *   *

It wuttin' until Friday morning that I realized just *how much* I was tripping. The *good morning* text from Sashé brought me back to my new world of reality, and I suddenly remembered that I *did* have plans that weekend.

How the fukc you let me forget dat quick?????

Nigga, I thought you just wanted to get belligerent again one time for the one time! Don't put that on me!

SASHÉ: "Good morning Daddy! I know you have to be at work at 11 but what time do you think Kourt and I can come over??? We wanna go swimming later on today..."

Fukc me, man! I gotta get my head in the muhfukcin' game, bro.

*   *   *   *   *

14

This journey is a real trip. But this wuttin' the first time I overbooked. In my early days of pussy chasing…I used to set *hooKup* times with multiple parties, just in case any of 'em cancelled, or I wanted to pick and choose at the end of the night.

This *was* a bit different, though.

I had already planned on Sashé and Kourtney spending the weekend with me…in hopes of finally completing my journey into the world of *ménages*. I couldn't remember this during my horny rage, however, and now I had *Cookie* trying to come through and gimme some on Friday. Cookie was talking like she wanted to spend the night, and I even told her I was available both Friday *and* Saturday nights. Somehow, I had to figure out how to pull this shit off.

The easiest thing to do woulda been to just cancel with Cookie, *right?* These text messages made shit a lot easier these days in *The Art of Cheating,* giving me extra time to think about my approach.

So before I replied to Shay, I touched base with Cookie again, sending her our code phrase.

ME: "U busy right now?"

COOKIE: "I'm ALWAYS busy…"

ME: "Ok so...about tonight..."

COOKIE: "I knew you was gonna play me. Smh."

ME: "No that's not it. What time were you trying to come?"

COOKIE: "I don't know. I have to work tonight."

Yeah, see wuttin' no way that was gon' work. Cookie don't leave the club 'til after 3, and Shay and Kourt are tryna spend the night. Cookie might as well just wait 'til *Saturday*.

ME: "Yeah I'll probably be knocked out by then."

COOKIE: "Oh for real?!?! You can't wait up on me???"

ME: "No...I said probably. Stop tripping...I'm just saying. I gotta work Saturday morning..."

COOKIE: "Ughhhh...you get on my nerves! So why u just didn't say that the other night?!?!"

ME: "I was half sleep...and horny. Just come Saturday..."

COOKIE: "What time??"

ME: "I don't know, sometime after I get off. I'll txt u..."

COOKIE: "Whatever."

ME: "I'm serious. Tomorrow."

Cookie ain't believe I was serious…and even *I* couldn't say I was with a straight face. It had been almost two months since I had some Cookie, and she still was ranked #1 overall in the bed. It was definitely worth the risk, but still way too close for comfort. If Sashé and Kourtney were ready to start our weekend *right now*, at *8 in the morning*, there was a pretty good chance that I wouldn't have time for any extra visitors today. Postponing 'til tomorrow at least bought me some time to stall.

Now that the coast with Cookie was clear, I finally sent Shay my reply.

ME: "Y'all tryna go swimming NOW? It's 8 o'clock lol."

SASHÉ: "Lol no silly! We were thinking after noon or whatever. Can we get your key when u leave for work?"

ME: "Ok. I'm leaving at 10:40."

SASHÉ: "See you at 1030 Daddy."

*   *   *   *   *

The last time I had to work with a *ménage* set up for later that night was a short, half day that went by quickly. Today felt like a déjà vü of that *Sassy* debacle, as I was haunted by flashbacks of how shit didn't go as planned. But last time, it was a Saturday. This time around being Friday, that meant I would have to sit through a *full* day of outgoing calls and anxiety.

I mean, I ain't have no real reason to think it wuttin' going down this time around – Shay and Kourtney showed up right when they said they would, before I left for work, with overnight bags and excitement. But still, that anticipation was torture and for most of my shift, I just had that funny feeling.

It was hard to stay busy and keep my mind off of later. Laura stopped by my desk, as usual, and asked if I enjoyed my pics from last week.

"I was surprised you didn't ask for more," she teased.

"Shit…I almost did, quiet as kept."

Laura smiled, "Well…you know closed mouths don't get fed around here in Kansas."

"So what if I keep my mouth open?" I flirted back. "What you gonna feed me then?"

Laura paused and bit her lip, turning red, "Talk to you later, Rodney."

The look on her face as she turned to walk away was priceless. I wanted to just get explicit with her; she was lucky we were at work. There was now no doubt in my mind that she wanted to gimme some pussy, and it just enhanced the recent feeling I was having of being overwhelmed. It suddenly seemed like I had more on my plate than I could fit in my mouth, but I was determined to somehow make it all happen.

I spent the next few hours at work chatting with *Foxxxy* on my phone through *Yahoo*. I couldn't open the pictures she sent from my cell, but the way she talked was a turn-on in itself. Maybe it was the intrigue of talking to somebody with a freaky mind that was so close, yet so far away. Whatever it was, it had me on edge.

Conversations over the net were always informal and direct. I had been chatting with chicks online since freshman year in college nearly a decade ago, and most conversations turned to a sexual nature on the first contact. But this chick I met on *Adult Friend Finder* was a different breed – it was apparent that everyone from this site was looking to fukc. No smoke screens…no bullshitting.

FoXXXy was open about her freakiness and wanted to know my preferences in detail. But when it came down to it, she wuttin' as anxious about actually *meeting*. She was looking for a couple, after all. She made it clear that she was definitely attracted to me, but since I told her I was single…she ain't want to start fukcing and get attached, because she had a guy she was seeing occasionally. *'Too bad you're single,'* she kept saying. And I just kept going along with it, knowing that Sashé was down, but at the same time unsure about how to make it all connect after telling white lies and being sneaky in my discovery.

Somehow, I had to start figuring out a way to bring balance to all this shit and keep this inner *beast* of mine fed. One way or another, I was gon' take advantage of all this shit.

*   *   *   *   *

Around 5:30pm Shay sends me a text that makes my heart skip a couple of beats.

SASHÉ: "Hey Daddy! The Kappas are having a stepshow and party in Lawrence tonight, we're thinking about going."

Damn. Here we go.

ME: "Oh ok, that's cool boo…"

SASHÉ: "It's kinda last minute, I know. We'll have to leave in a cpl of hrs to try to catch some of the show…u know I hate rushing…"

ME: "What time does the show start?"

SASHÉ: "At 7! U wanna go???"

ME: "Hmmm….no, not really. I'ma be tired when I get off. Plus I don't get off til 8, y'all would have to wait on me…"

SASHÉ: "We'll wait if u want us to Daddy…"

ME: "No, that's cool…go have fun. I'll be home when y'all get back…"

SASHÉ: "Why u don't wanna go with us? U got somebody else coming over?"

ME: "Yup, my other pair of freaky friends coming to hang with me tonight..."

SASHÉ: "Don't play with me! Tell them hoes to back up!"

ME: "I'm just playing baby...."

SASHÉ: "I know you are. You ain't crazy..."

ME: "So y'all gonna be gone when I get off?"

SASHÉ: "Hmmm yeah, more than likely. Kourtney is getting in the shower again now..."

ME: "Again...?"

SASHÉ: "We took one earlier after the pool..."

ME: "Damn and y'all ain't wait on me?!?! How was swimming?"

SASHÉ: "It was fun! Omg I love your pool! Can you go swimming with us tomorrow?!?!"

My apartment complex did have a nice pool. It definitely had potential to lure some panties off over the upcoming summer.

ME: "U know I will boo..."

SASHÉ: "Yay!!! Ok, we'll bring u the key in a little while Daddy..."

ME: "Ok, txt me when y'all outside..."

Great. So, now my night was back in a status of uncertainty. Everything was always so spontaneous with Sashé. Maybe that's why I kept holding on to Cookie and the lifestyle of cheating because things were always so calculated and planned out when I was doing my thing. With Shay, it was always spur of the moment, go-with-the-flow type shit. It was throwing me completely off my square.

This wuttin' the first time I *overbooked*, but this was without a doubt, the first time I overbooked only to end up *by myself* at the end of the night.

*   *   *   *   *

Sashé and Kourtney stayed out late, to the point where I fell asleep waiting on them to come back. Another drunk and horny night with no pussy. When Shay finally called me around 5 in the morning to let me know they was almost home, I cursed at myself for canceling my sure-pussy date with Cookie.

I had to be up for work in a couple of hours, and Sashé sounded worn out on the phone. Frustrated as all outdoors, I hopped up out of my sleep for a minute and start talking shit with nobody else in my room, once again feeling defeated.

*"Now see, I'd 'a been wrong if I woulda got some pussy tonight, up in here waiting on yo ass! This some bullshit – I coulda fukced Laura **and** Cookie by now!!!!"*

And, as crazy as the notion was, I really *believed* I coulda pulled it off. Why not? I mean…my skills in this *Art* were undeniable. I might be still learning the ropes on getting *two of 'em* at once but sneaking to get pussy on the side was my *specialty*. By now I had learned enough to get away with some shit like that. The greed in me was sure of it.

Still, I got up out of bed to unlock the door for Shay and Kourt, dragging my feet on the carpet as I stumbled back into my room. I heard them barging in a few minutes later, heels tapping against the tile by the front door.

They came in whispering, trying to be quiet, but I couldn't make out what they were saying. They stayed in the front room for a little while…long enough for me to doze off again. By the time Sashé cuddled up in the bed next to me, I was too tired to even roll over; couldn't tell if Kourtney was in the bed or not.

To say I was cranky when I left a couple of hours later for work would be a big misuse of words…and niggaz know how serious I am about these words.

I was pissed…

*   *   *   *   *

And then to top it off, I had to sit through *another* boring shift at work. It wuttin' as bad as the day before, since I was only doing a half day. But that morning went by hella slow. Eight in the morning on a Saturday was too early for anybody to message me back, so for the better half of the day my phone stayed dry.

This whole *ménages* journey was becoming way too long and drawn out. One minute it's right there within arm's reach and the next minute I'm ready to just forget about the fantasy and stick to what I know.

Don't start bitching up again, bro.

Dawg. I can always get a bunch of pussy…this is SCIENCE. Maybe the thought of having it all go down at once is really just jack-off material.

So, you just ready to give up?

I mean, that shit happens in the movies and for big stars with money! Why am I expecting it to be reality for a regular nigga like me?

You doing it again, Rod…

I work in the corporate cotton field 40 hours a week, and I'm playing with money to pay the bills.

Man, for crying out loud!

Yeah, I'm hanging with Big Ricky Rhymes from the radio station, and he got me recording music with Jaz now, but that shit might not ever take off. Who the hell am I to think that I'm entitled to rock star life??? I've had it good enough as it is.

Just stay focused, HoLLyRod…

I already had it good before Sashé. I had it real good…with KeLLy.

Let it play out, brodie…

Look at me now! Stuck and chasing fantasies!

We right there, nigga!

I mean, even the word 'ménages' — the sound of it, the way it's spelled and misspelled, the whole eroticism behind it is nothing but bait. It draws you in; it puts you in a state of thirst. It's almost a trick within itself. A never-ending riddle.

Dawg, all we gotta do is just hold on 'til tonight, nigga! Just a few more hours, Rod!

Yeah, I had it real good before. I know I told KeLLy I wanted more…but this morning I'm feeling like I don't even know what 'more' means anymore.

And now you thinking about KeLLy at a time like this! What a surprise!

I wonder if she's up. She's only texted me once since our *hooKup* last weekend, to let me know she made it home. I tried texting her on Monday and never got a reply. Now's a good time to try again.

ME: "Hey you..."

If I know Kells, I know she's up this early, anyway.

But then 7 minutes go by. Then 8…

What's taking her so long to reply????

Cuz KeLLy ain't tripping off us, nigga! That's why!

She finally hits me back after almost *11 minutes*. At **10:03am**, I get a text that reads:

KELLY: "Hi. Sorry. I almost texted u last night."

This made me smile. Hearing from KeLLy again made me feel normal; it put me back on the other side of that anxiety fence.

ME: "Oh yeah? Lol what stopped u??? Wassup..."

KELLY: "I needed your address."

ME: "Lol like that huh? You was tryna stop through??"

KELLY: "No. I needed to send u something."

ME: "Lol what u mean?!? Send me what???"

KELLY: "Nvm now. I decided not to."

Huh??? What is she talking about???

ME: "Uhm....ok. What was it??"

That's strange. Suddenly I felt weird about this exchange. It just didn't...*feel* right. The disadvantage to texting was the lack of voice tone and body language. I couldn't tell if Kells was joking or serious. And all of a sudden, it sounded serious.

And she was taking her time again to text me back.

What the fukc man?

"ME: "?????"

I'm rocking in my chair now...trying to focus on the call in my headset, rubbing the back of my neck with my left hand. The customer's voice started to fade away as he rambled, and I reached back for my desk drawer with my right hand – taking another peek at my cell phone to see if KeLLy replied yet.

It's been another 8 minutes. And nothing. What the hell is going on here???

Ok. What the hell could it be? The first thing I thought about is how I came inside of her. But I mean, she *can't* be pregnant – it's been too soon for her to know that...*right?* Maybe I'm just tripping out. I don't know what else it could be, but maybe it's nothing at all.

But why she still ain't texted me back?????

I started to shut the drawer again in frustration, but then the screen lights up as I receive an incoming text.

Finally.

But it's not from *KeLLy*.

COOKIE: "U busy right now?"

ME: "I'm ALWAYS busy..."

COOKIE: "Hey big head...question: why do we have to keep doing the cheat code if u and KeLLy broke up???"

Ughhhhhh...I don't feel like dealing with this!!!

ME: "Oh my God Cookie...it's too fukcin early!!!"

COOKIE: "Lololol!!!! It's almost 11 boy, shut up! I'm just kidding...stop being a grouch."

ME: "Whatever."

COOKIE: "Listen...do you still want to see me today??? Because I want to go swimming."

I slammed the drawer shut, now highly frustrated. I ain't feel like hearing that shit right now!! I needed to know what the hell was going on with KeLLy; what the hell her text was about.

I started texting Kells again...I ain't heard back from her in 15 minutes now.

"ME: "Hello???"

This time she texts right back.

KELLY: "Yes??"

ME: "What are u talking about? What were u gonna send me?"

KELLY: "I said nvm Rodney. It doesn't even matter anymore."

ME: "Maaaan......what the hell?? Can u tell me what it was please?!?!?"

This shit was really working my nerves now. I needed answers. But then the next incoming text was yet another *non-Kells* message.

SASHÉ: "Good morning Daddy! How's work??"

Are you kidding me???? It's like everybody is up all of a sudden!

ME: "Hey boo. Work is fine. How are u feeling?"

SASHÉ: "My head is pounding! Oh my goodness...we partied too hard last night lol..."

ME: "No shit..."

SASHÉ: "Are u mad baby? Kourt thinks you're mad at us...please don't be mad!"

ME: "I'm not mad..."

SASHÉ: "Are u sure Daddy?"

ME: "I'm sure..."

SASHÉ: "Ok good. Because we need to ask something else..."

Oh wow. I can't win for losing.

But before I can respond to Shay's text…I get another text from *Cookie*.

COOKIE: "Hello?!?!?! Are u ignoring me Rodney???"

And then…*finally*…KeLLy again.

KELLY: "Never mind Rodney. It's not even worth it. It's just best we let it go."

ME: "What is that supposed to mean Kells??? What the hell is going on???"

I've never typed so fast with one finger in my life. There I was — sneak texting on the floor with a little over an hour to go in my shift, hiding my frustration and true thoughts from both my co-workers and clients on the phone, and ready to snap out. Saturdays were always chill though; we only had to work one weekend a month in this department and less than half of my team was here today. Good thing my manager wasn't around, because she woulda definitely seen me going back and forth between my computer screen and desk like I was, and I hated any two words that bitch ever said to me.

And my continuous incoming texts weren't helping my attitude.

SASHÉ: "...Daddy? U there...?"

What the hell was she trying to ask me? What now? What next???

ME: "Yes. My bad babe. Wassup...?"

SASHÉ: "Lol almost thought u were ignoring me...u said u weren't mad tho. Tonight we're gonna make it up, I promise Daddy..."

ME: "What did y'all wanna ask me Shay???"

SASHÉ: "Oh. Lol. Right. Well......my mom gave us coupons for free massages so we're gonna go to the spa here soon. Kourt wants to know if we can smoke a blunt of your GG before we go..."

Ain't this a...

ME: "Ok. Sure. It's where it was last time. So y'all leaving again???"

SASHÉ: "Yeah, we're gonna go to the Plaza and then out for drinks with Kris before she goes to work. We should be back around 6 or 7."

ME: "Ok that's cool I guess."

SASHÉ: "Are u sure? U said 'I guess'..."

ME: "Yes I'm sure boo. I'm getting off soon so just leave the door unlocked."

SASHÉ: "Ok. Can we still go swimming when we come back?"

ME: "Yeah. Of course."

SASHÉ: "Oh my god you're the greatest! Ok! Talk to you soon babe..."

I started shaking my head at how easily Sashé could switch my mood up; how she forced me out of my funk simply by acting like everything was always a-ok. It wuttin' even some shit she did on purpose. Things with Sashé are just...*different*.

But I was still irked at KeLLy's lack of response and clarity, and now I was back at square one again with my doubts about this *ménage*. This weekend was supposed to be filled with me being smothered in pussy, but now it just seems like Shay and Kourt was just staying at my apartment to avoid staying at home with their parents. The whole shit was starting to take a different form.

Now I'm an hour away from clocking out, with nothing to come home to after my greedy overbooking turned against me the night before. From too much…to too little…to not enough…*again.*

KeLLy still ain't texted me back.

Cookie won't stop.

COOKIE: "Smh I can't believe u!!! Are u really not gonna text me back?!?! Can we go swimming today or not?!?"

You know what?

ME: "Yeah. I'm 'bout to get off work in a min. Can you be at my spot in like an hr?"

COOKIE: "Dang! So now you wanna rush me??"

ME: "I'm not rushing u. I told u I wanna see you…I just gotta be somewhere at 6. So can you come now or not?"

COOKIE: "Yeah I can. Lemme hop in the shower and I'll text u when I'm on my way…"

Wait. We really doing this, my guy?

Man, *fukc* it. Time to take the gloves off. Ain't nothing like a risky day of cheating to balance everything out again.

*   *   *   *   *

15

Let's describe **Cookie**. The memory I have of her on this day is a great visual.

I'm sitting on the west side of the pool, watching her as she walks in the water with her chest and head above the surface.

Cookie had a round and brown face, big brown slanted eyes, juicy and full lips. She was small up top; *really* small. The sun was beaming down on her neck and shoulder blades, and you could see the definition in her arms as she untied the bow on her hair, letting her micros hang down. She turned and headed towards the pool stairs, her back now facing me as I took another sip from my drink.

She stepped out of the water slowly, wearing a white two-piece. Her ass was so big…it literally looked too heavy, as if it was weighing her down as she climbed up the stairs. She turns to her left and starts walking down the poolside, watching me watch her from the opposite side. Her legs were toned up nicely…calf and thigh muscles flexing as she walked. She looked great in that swimsuit. Her abs were starting to come in nicely.

Cookie was the only one of my chicks who worked out on the regular; she was the athlete of the bunch. Her high school basketball and track experience made her a health buff…so she stayed in shape. It also made her naturally a tomboy…and a constant competitor. She stormed toward me with that look of challenge in her eyes, and I knew what was coming.

"You really not gonna get in the pool with me???" she frowned at me.

"I'm at the pool with you," I replied sarcastically.

"You know what I mean, stop playing!" she snapped. "Come on!!! You not just gon' sit there the whole time! What is wrong with you?!?!"

"Get in for what? I'm chilling."

"Get in so you can swim with me, butt-head!!!" she whined. "Come on…so we can race."

"Race??" I turned my nose up. "Girl…you thew."

"Come on!!! What – you scared I'ma beat you???"

"Yeah right," I thought that was comical at best.

"Well, come on then, old man!" she shot back. "I bet you get smoked!!!"

Her voice was somewhat raspy, opposite of the soft spoken Sashé or commanding tone of KeLLy. She stood there looking down at me, holding her hand against her forehead to block the sun. Cookie had a big ass forehead, and them braids pulling her hair back made it look even bigger.

"You can't get ya hair wet anyway," I reminded her with a smirk.

"I told you I'm taking these out tonight anyway," she grabbed her braids, stretching. "Quit making excuses! You just know you gon' lose! Come on! You better get in this pool with me, Rodney Lee!!!"

"Aye man, don't be saying my name like that!" I scowled at her.

"What?!?!" Cookie looked to her left and right. "Don't nobody know you; don't nobody care!"

"Girl I'm hot out here," I dusted my shoulders off with arrogance.

"Yea right – in your dreams!" she started laughing hysterically. "Come on, Rodney! I'm 'bout to get you wet if you don't get in this pool with me!"

"I ain't gotta get in the pool for you to get me wet."

"Rodney!" she blushed and glanced to the far end of the pool, at the Indian man holding his young son up in the deep end of the water. Then she whispered, "Stop being nasty!"

"Fukc them," I shrugged.

"You are something else! You get on my nerves!!!" she spun around and stomped back towards the pool, fussing and pouting.

I had planned on not getting in the pool because I ain't wanna get my trunks wet before my swimming date with *Sashé and Kourtney* later. I was on some real ***HoLLy BeLLigerence*** again right now. Playing with fire…yet determined not to get burned.

See, when I got home from work, my weekend guests were already gone. But there was evidence of their sleepover scattered everywhere. The bathroom was the worst – hair in the sink, flat iron and combs, toiletries all over the counter. Both their duffle bags were in my bedroom, and they brought enough shoes to last them a week. Heels and *Air Jordan's* – typical *young bitch* swag.

My apartment was about a 5-minute drive from the call center, so I got home around **12:15pm**. I had the place camouflaged within a half-hour. Before I moved anything, I took pictures of the spectacle…to put everything back in place later. After hiding all the bathroom mess under the sink and tossing the bedroom clues in my walk-in closet, I pulled the comforter and sheets off my bed and threw 'em on top of the bags and shoes. I only had one spare set of sheets so I would have to get 'em washed and dried before Shay and Kourt came back later.

I had *5 hours* 'til they were due back…which meant I had 4 hours to *play*. As long as I had Cookie out by 5pm…there was no way I could get caught.

Right now, it was just after **2pm**, and I was just starting to feel my buzz. Getting my trunks wet wuttin' a big deal, I finally decided, so as Cookie stepped back into the pool – I got up and started walking behind her. The way her cheeks bounced in that bikini, I could figure out something later on the trunks.

*   *   *   *   *

"Man, why is your ass so *fat?!?* Like…*look* at this shit," I shook my head at Cookie's naked body in front of me.

"I can't see it! Shut up! It's not even that big for real," she was full of modesty.

"You can't see it from *my* angle," I clarified lustfully.

We were in my bed now, fresh out the shower from our hour-long swim. We didn't shower together. Cookie was in and out before me and she was lying on her stomach now, sprawled out naked across the bed.

She was so petite that it just ain't seem like this ass belonged on her. Yet, there it was. She had this same fatty when I met her as a college freshman four years earlier. And even though she had grown into a much more womanly shape since then…this ass was still mutant. It wuttin' no catching up or growing into that muhfukca.

I walked up behind her, blue towel covering my lower body. My dick was semi hard as I grabbed her right calf, "For real. The shit almost look fake."

"Nigga, my ass ain't fake!!!" she cried out, offended at the notion before looking back at me over her left shoulder. "And it don't even look that big like y'all be making it out to be!"

She sat up…bending over on all fours, looking behind me at her reflection in the wall mirror.

"Who is *y'all*???" my jaws tightened.

"Just y'all; niggaz in general. Everybody," she explained. "All them niggaz at the club that just go crazy over it. All that money they throw at me. I just don't get it."

"You complaining like they throw it away!" I stepped to the side to watch her in the mirror as she bounced it lightly, making my bed squeak.

"Oh, I'm not complaining! Them tips helped me finish paying for school. And helped my mama pay her debt off! I ain't complaining at all. I'm just *saying*…I don't get it. It's just an *ass*."

"You can't see it from the angle we see, though," I tried to convince her. "I'm telling you."

I was standing at the foot of the bed and to her right as she was bent over, still watching her ass jiggle in the mirror. Without warning I smacked her right side with my right hand…hard and with sting.

"Stop! I'ma kick you!" she sunk her body into the bed as the smacks sounded off.

"No, stay like that – for real!" I wanted her to keep her back arched. "You gotta see this shit."

She looked at me with curiosity, "How???"

I started walking back into the bathroom to get my phone. Cookie followed me with her eyes, "What are you doing?"

She was sitting Indian-style on the bed, facing me as I walked out with my phone in hand, getting the camera ready.

These camera phones were really changing the game. And my Motorola flip was killing shit. Not only could my shit record 30-second video clips – but it also had a cold ass 2-megapixel camera that got some pretty good shots.

"Man, bend back over," I demanded. "Come on."

"What?!? No, Rodney! You not 'bout to take pictures of my naked ass!" she shook her head. "Hell no! So you can put them on the internet?? Hell no!!! Put that camera down!"

"Come on; your face won't be in 'em! And I'm not tryna put you on the internet, I just need you to see what I see."

"No, Rodney!"

"Come on," I pleaded. "Why you acting like that?"

"Ughhh! I hate when you say that!" she rolled her eyes. "You always say that."

"Come onnnnnn." I climbed in the bed…still in my towel as I nudged her with my leg.

She reluctantly started turning over…looking at me the whole time, "I'ma eff you up if you show this to anybody. I'm not playing, Rodney."

"I'm not," I promised. "I just wanna show you. Here…scoot over."

She sprawled back across the bed on her stomach – giving me her backside view, but without much active participation. I grabbed her left leg, spreading it away from her right. Her meaty pussy lips poked out at me.

Gotdamn, her pussy is so meaty!

Cookie had one of those rosebud snatches. Her lips were fat and hung out; you could spread them and lay 'em to the side and it looked like a flower. I started snapping away, getting as many pics as I could.

Her ass is so round…it looks like it's literally sitting on top of her!

And the cuff between cheeks and legs is so…detailed.

I reached in and spread her lips apart…and she was sticky wet on the pink inside. She let out a soft moan. I'm stuck – still not used to how fat and meaty her pussy is, even after all these years. But she's gotta see this shit…so I kept snapping away.

"Damn, how many pictures you gon' take???" her voice was lowered, and as I touched her pussy trying to position the lips just right, she was starting to squirm.

"Let me do what I do," I mumbled.

Her pussy was thumping now…starting to run down my fingers as she moaned, "Hmmmm…Rodney! Stop!"

"I'm not doing anything," I played innocent.

"Mmmm…yes you are…sta," she lost her voice and her back arched in the air as my thumb found her clit. My phone hit the bed as her ass came toward my face.

I then cuffed her left cheek tightly, right thumb entering her slowly as I massaged her pelvis with my other fingers, pulling her towards me, "I'm not."

I leaned my face in as she propped up on the bed with her elbows. Sucking her pussy was like sinking my face in a big piece of watermelon…her juices started gushing out at me immediately. My towel came loose as I shifted my body…my still semi-hard dick flopping free.

Cookie kept moaning lustfully, "Dammit. Shit. Hmmmmm…ok. Don't stop."

I could see us out the corner of my eye in one of the mirrors at the head of the bed. It looked like I was lifting her in the air with my right hand, as I continued to thumb-stroke her pussy with double penetration from my tongue. Cookie started desperately grabbing the bed sheets — pulling them away from the mattress.

Just that quick…she was cummin'.

Cookie was a cummer…a quick one. Unlike KeLLy, who would be lucky to have one orgasm in a session, Cookie was a *multi-cummer*. She came fast and plentiful, sort of different from Sashé, who took a while to cum, although Shay could cum more than once after she got going.

Cookie was ranked #1 for a reason. It was almost like she could cum at will. She'd proved this one time after I talked shit about controlling when I could cum. She took on the challenge and we had a session to see who could cum within a minute of the demand. She won that shit without a question…and from then on, I knew she had complete control of her pussy. She could make it grip at will. Keeping it in as we switched positions was never clumsy with Cookie – she really knew how to position her legs and torso with every shift and movement in the bed. She was a real *beast* when it came down to the get-down. Always had been.

Cookie started grinding against my chin…burying my face in her ass as I grabbed her with both hands by the waist, sticking my tongue deep in her from behind. She was now in the air, on her hands and toes, and I stretched my legs out underneath her.

"Fuuuuck! You are so…nasty," she grabbed at my ankles as her juices ran down to my neck.

"I know," I slurped.

She hopped away from me…falling forward and on her right arm. It left a stream of drool and pussy juice hanging from my face…and it dripped down to my stomach.

My dick was standing up straight in my lap and caught her eyes. She sat up to lean toward me…coming close to my face as she whispered, "Can I do you???"

"Don't ask dumb questions."

My head fell back as she put her right hand against my chest and started kissing my stomach…licking the drool up and grabbing my balls with her left hand. She pulled them downwards…making my wooD stand up, throbbing repeatedly.

"Hmmmm. You know I love sucking it," she put her lips around the bottom of my shaft…slurping softly as she massaged my balls. Her right hand found its way to my dick head, and she started rubbing the mushroom with two fingers…sending sensations up my spine and making me cringe.

"You like that?" she looked up at me momentarily and then pushed me backwards, climbing closer. My back hit the bed…but I kept looking down at her as she worked. She put her right hand on her pussy and then wiped the juices on my dick…stroking it up and down slowly, letting spit hang from her tongue as she opened her mouth wide, looking down at it.

I humped up in the air at her face and she took me in and out with a loud slurping sound…making me groan almost as loudly, "Shit…fukc yeah."

She swallowed my dick again…her mouth wet and tight with each suction, still massaging my balls with her right hand. She was moaning as she sucked…squirming in the bed with me, both our bodies steady pulling the sheets out of place.

I was breathing hard, "Yeah…hmmm. Suck dat shit, Cookie. Got…damn! That shit feel…"

"Hmmmm," She lifted her head up to look me in the eyes. "Feel like what??"

"It feel…like," I drifted off as she took me back in her mouth…looking up at me.

Dammit, this bitch looks like Obsession sucking my dick!

I started reaching for the back of her head unsuccessfully. She was really showing out now.

"Feel like what?" she asked again with a whisper. "Mmmm…*sluuuuuuuurp*. What it feel like?"

"Mmmm…like. Shit, it's so *warm*. Wet."

"Yeah? You like that?"

I closed my eyes, biting my lip again, "Hell…yeah. That…shit feel like…like ya pussy."

This made her stop sucking me…sliding her face away as she continued to jack my sloppy wet dick off, "Oh, whatever! It can't feel *that* good."

"Why you stop?!?!" I cried out in agony.

"This pussy feels better," she cut her eyes.

"Baby, that mouth is amazing," I licked my lips at her.

"Hmmmm," she squeezes my dick tightly with her hand and starts sucking me again. This time I leaned my upper body forward and grabbed the back of her head…thrusting up at her and pushing her head down with each bob. She's got her mouth and throat open wide now…letting me hit her tonsils with ease.

My toes start curling. Nobody can suck my dick like Cookie. She really takes ownership in this shit.

"Shit, Cookie! There…you…go…fukc! You so nasty."

She's sucking and slurping away…pulling me closer as she grips my thighs, making me suck my stomach in at her gobbling. My dick started swelling in her mouth…and she could feel me getting close.

"Hmmm," she kept slurping loudly, mouth full of dick. "You gon'…cuhm…in…mah mouf???"

She ain't gotta ask me twice. By the time I make out what she's saying…I'm squirting and shooting down her throat as she grabs my dick and starts pumping it out of me, never taking her me out of her mouth. She sucked and puckered on the head with her lips…drinking every drop.

"Hmmmmmmmmmmm…damn! Damn, Cookie."

She keeps stroking my dick…even faster now, as she sat up on her butt, pinching her left nipple in lust. Her big areola takes up most of her tiny tit, but her nipple is huge between her fingers. She's turned on to the max.

"I ain't done with yo ass…you owe me," she said aggressively. "Come on."

"I do?? Damn, you cussing n'shit," I was shocked at seeing this side of her.

"I'm horny now. Come on. Give it to me," she bent back over on hands and knees in front of me…and I backed up off the bed, standing up behind her to look at her posture.

I'm 'bout to fukc the shit outta this girl.

"Reach in that nightstand," I instructed firmly. "Hand me a condom."

"Where…in here???" she stretched out for the door handle. "Oh, you don't keep 'em under ya mattress no more???"

"You don't know me," I rolled my eyes.

"Yeah, I do, nigga! This the same nightstand you had in the *Kappa House* when you met me."

She had me there. And she knew which corner I kept my condoms in, too…as she handed me a rubber without changing her position. I took the package out of her hand and noticed my cell phone laying to the side as I strapped up.

Hmmm…

"Come onnnn! What are you doing??" she looked back at me and eyeballed me eyeballing my phone. "Oh no…don't even think about it!!!"

"Come on…ya face ain't even in it. Bend over," I picked the phone up off the bed, hitting the camera button. My dick was jumping in the lens as I looked down at it.

"Ok…come on, before I change my mind," she spread her ass cheeks for me and I slid my **wooD** inside with my left hand, trying to hold my phone steady with my right. Her pussy welcomed me with a strong snug, and she slammed her ass back at me. I had to hold on with both hands as I started thrusting…and it took me a split second to realize the camera was pressed up against her ass.

When I pulled it away and pointed it down at my penetration…the clip stopped, forcing me to start a new one. Right then…I noticed the time on my cell.

It was now **4:44pm**. This was cutting it really close.

But this pussy was too good for me to care. I started pounding away at it as she met my strokes…ass smacking against my thighs, sounding off like applause. Her pussy lips were so fat around my dick…and the condom was now drenched.

"How…it…look???" she asked in between breaths.

I couldn't respond to her…so I kept thrusting away, lifting up into it as I stroked. The clip stopped again…and I started a third one, biting my lips as I looked down at it.

I ain't realize my stroke game looked so mean…

"Ba…by? Fukc. Get it," her ass slammed into my stomach, catching my sweat falling from my forehead. My dick was harder than before now…and I could feel her pussy clenching on me, challenging me to go deeper.

And then…it happened.

The camera image gets replaced by the caller ID with an incoming call:

--------—SASHÉ --------

Without blinking, I dropped the phone…and it bounced to my right side. I slapped Cookie's ass cheek and keep pounding away.

"Shit. I'm 'bout to cum again," she shuddered.

"Come on…cum…all…over this…dick," I grunted in between thrusts.

"Well, come on then…give it to me!" she moaned anxiously. "Quit…hmmmmm…*playing!!* COME ON!!!"

Her voice screamed with lustful provocation, making me start humping her with hard, long strokes. I can see her juices splashing – actually *splashing* – on my shaft, and she started ripping at the sheets again.

"Yeah! Cum'ere," I turned it up a notch. "Bring yo ass…here…come…hmmmmm…come on."

Cookie keeps taking my penetration…moaning and cursing at me even louder now. I felt the calm before the eruption again…as my dick swelled up.

"I feel it," she panted. "Hmmm…I'm cum…min! Cum wit me. Cum wit me, baby. I…feeeel…it…hmmm."

We started nutting in sync as I stood up like a frog and grabbed her by the waist again. She was shaking beneath me…gyrating and moving her hips as she let it all out. She kept her ass poked up high in the air and laid on her neck and chest, breathing hard.

The nut was still running out of me as I humped and pumped away harder and harder. "Hmmmmmmm…fukc," I cursed as I slowed down, dick throbbing.

I pushed her forward and watched as my dick came free…still jumping and hopping around as I pulled the condom off. The nut splashed and dripped onto the bed as the rubber peeled away from my flesh.

Cookie bounced her ass, "You still cummin???"

My knees buckled and I fell to my right…laying my head to the side, up against her sweaty back, "Dammit, Cookie."

"Now tell me my mouth feel as good as that did. Don't lie."

"Shit…damn near," I told her, trying to catch my breath.

My phone started ringing again…lost and vibrating in the sheets. It felt like it was next to my left foot.

"Damn…somebody really tryna get in touch with you, huh?" Cookie asked, full of sarcasm.

I sat up to reach for it so I could see who was calling, "I told you I gotta be somewhere at 6."

"What time is it???"

I heard her asking about the time. But seeing ------- **KELLY** ------- on the caller ID screen startled the fukc outta me.

Damn.

I then was reminded of our exchange earlier…and how she left me hanging.

Now she's calling???

What the hell????

"Rodney??" Cookie's voice snapped me outta my thoughts.

"Oh, my bad. It's 5:01."

WAIT………5:01?!?!?!?!?!

I hopped up suddenly, looking both ways like I was seeking direction. I needed to get this show on the road!!

"Lemme see the pictures," Cookie wanted to see the footage. "And did the videos come out good? I wanna see."

"Uhm…yeah…ok," I couldn't focus. "Hold up."

My phone started ringing again. This time it was *Sashé* calling a *second* time.

Cookie sat up and turned around to face me, "Come on – you ain't in that big of a rush. Tell whoever it is you gon' call 'em back. Lemme see what you were talking about."

"I gotta go, Cookie."

"Well, you better come on, then!!! I'm not getting dressed until you show me!" she threatened. "I'm supposed to be spending the night anyway!!"

OH MY GOD!!!!! She can't be serious!

Unless she IS, nigga!

*   *   *   *   *

16

Cookie wuttin' joking, and as she walked into the bathroom, she was fussing the whole time about me rushing her. Meanwhile, Sashé was calling *again*, a third time now. Back-to-back-to-back…

Me not answering her calls was a huge violation in *The Art*. Every unanswered ring was digging me deeper into a damage control hole. Not to mention the likelihood of Sashé *actually showing up*.

Bro, what if she calling like crazy cuz she ain't far away???

Fuuuuuuuuck!!!

I gotta get this bitch outta here…like now!

"You not about to put me out like I'm some two-dollar hooker, Rodney," Cookie kept fussing. "I don't care how late you are."

I'm pacing around my room in my gym shorts as she yells from the bathroom. Then I hear her turn on the shower and my heart skips two or three beats.

"What are you doing?!?!" I shouted.

"I'm hopping in the shower!"

I started to stomp towards the bathroom, but then noticed the sheets all over the bed, which stopped me dead in my tracks.

It's wet spots all over, nigga!

Gotdamn, bro! And we barely got time to wash deez muhfukcaz!

"Nah, man I gotta get in there!" I screamed at Cookie again. "I gotta get ready!"

I started tearing the bed sheets away…balling them up as I glanced around the room. My eyes then locked on the condom on the floor next to my foot.

Where is that wrapper?

"Well, get in here with me, then," Cookie yelled from the shower. "I'm already in."

I dashed through the bathroom and tossed the sheets on the floor, opening up the washing machine. There was a wet load in there already, and my heart skipped yet another beat when I saw what it was.

Towels and bikini swimsuits.

Shay and Kourtney's laundry from the day before.

*Oh…shit! **SHAY!** I gotta call her back! Where my phone at?*

"What are you doing? Are you washing the sheets? You must got somebody coming over," Cookie accused as the room steamed up. She could see me through the shower glass door…but at this point it barely mattered.

I swiftly threw the wet load in the empty dryer…and tossed the sheets in, starting the quick wash cycle. Time was ticking.

"Did you see these sheets, girl?" I asked rhetorically. "I ain't sleeping on them muhfukcaz after that…shut up!"

"Whatever," she smacked her lips. "It ain't like you ain't never kicked me out before to get some other ass. Let's not even go there."

She was referring to college days, and she was right. Remember, I was a senior when Cookie was a freshman, and that being my last year, I went out with a bang. One time in particular – which was probably the night she's talking about – I kicked her out because I *'didn't feel right with her spending the night'*. But the truth was that night I had another chick coming through and wanted to record us fukcing *after* I had *secretly* taped Cookie. Worst part about it…it was Cookie's *birthday*.

"Let's *not* go there! Why you bringing up old shit???" I rolled my eyes, irritated.

"I still can't believe you did that! You used to do me so wrong!" she started flashing back. "Ugh…I can't stand you!"

"See? I shoulda never told you."

"*Bullshit* you shoulda never told me! I wanna see *that* tape, too. I know you ain't record over it, even though you said you did!"

"Girl, I don't know what you talking about; I erased that shit after I told you," I lied with a straight face. "Hurry the fukc up! I gotta go."

"You showing me that tape, Rodney," Cookie waved me off. "I don't care what you say."

Unless I AIN'T!!!

Wuttin' no way I was showing Cookie *that* old tape. She lucky she even knew the truth now about me secretly recording us. I been done told her I kicked her out cuz I had somebody else coming over that night. But I ain't never gon' tell her how I kept the tape running and recorded both her *and **Ebony***, this other freshman at the time who Cookie couldn't stand.

That was some HoLLy BeLLigerent shit I was on back in college…but if all these chicks woulda got along in the first place, I coulda *been* had my ménage fantasy fulfilled.

This was low-key all Cookie's fault to begin with. She had been around the longest…even before KeLLy. She knew how to please me best, and would pretty much do anything I asked, but her otherwise competitive spirit was shot down when it came to serious relationships. Cookie resented the fact that other bitches stayed on my heels, so rather than make herself stand out and outdo what the next bitch was willing to do – she fell back.

KeLLy was domestic…raised to cook, clean, and take care of home. She showed me from the jump that she was down for her man from that angle. Overall, KeLLy was the same type of old-fashioned woman that my grandma was. She had that foundation, ya dig? I wuttin' even looking for that wifey-type, but when me and KeLLy started kicking it, she stood out like that. Kells was made to be somebody's wife, whether I was ready for that or not.

Cookie had watched her moms be that type of woman for her gambling and alcoholic father, and she wuttin' having it for herself.

'A woman will do all that for a man and he'll still cheat just like my daddy cheated on my mama,' she used to tell me all the time.

Cookie held on to that shit and looked at me in that same light. But if Cookie wouldn't have let KeLLy outshine her on all'at other shit that mattered outside of sex…she woulda never became my main *side* bitch. Cookie coulda been my main, *period.*

Once Kells came in the picture that last year on campus…Cookie stopped acting right. Cookie had too many niggas chasing her; she was still young and free. So, she did her thing and I did mine. But our sex – that was always undeniable. Without her putting in extra effort, sex with Cookie was always the way it should be…and we both knew that was the case.

After my **beast** came uncaged with Tianna, Cookie even took my new *aggression* in stride. We was just compatible like that, I guess. The same way Cookie could fukc the shit outta me…I fukced her in ways that no other measured up to, and it kept us coming back. That bomb ass sex was the only edge Cookie kept over KeLLy. As slight of an edge as it was, Cookie always had that spot.

When KeLLy and I first made it official that summer after I graduated, I was faithful in the beginning. If Cookie ain't have that real good nookie, I might've never cheated on KeLLy in the first place.

Is that where it all started?

Cookie could very well be the reason I mastered *The Art of Cheating*. She knew she could eventually get me to cheat on KeLLy; she knew she had that power over me.

But then she let *Sashé* creep into that spot with her bi-sex ways. If Cookie was bisexual and on this *ménage* shit…that #1 spot would never be up for grabs like it is now. That was yet something else that she wuttin' willing to compete with as far as a man. Cookie wuttin' gon' change her sexual preferences for me. She had real confidence in her sex game, and with good reason. But Cookie also had limits, and until I met Sashé, breaking those barriers were only fantasy.

I've gotta take my shot at making this shit really happen, though, so I can't let Cookie fukc this up right now. At the same time…I gotta keep her in my back pocket. She don't know that she being replaced (again) and I don't know if I really wanna cut off contact with her completely (again).

I gotta somehow get her outta here without incident.

"Look…I'll show you the tape later, I gotta find that shit!" I yelled from the bedroom, spraying down the mattress. "But hurry up out the shower so I can show you the pictures, girl."

Cookie yelled back, "And the movies you just recor…"

"And the movie clips, too!" I finished her sentence. "Hurry up, man, so I can get in!"

"I'm getting out now, shut up! I need a towel!"

"Where is the towel you had outside?!"

"We shared your towel – remember?!?!" she reminded me. "Damn, you getting old!"

"Oh yeah, it's by my trunks in there…on the floor."

MY TRUNKS!!!!!!

I suddenly remembered that Shay and Kourtney were coming over to go swimming, and I wuttin' supposed to get my shorts wet. The washer was already started…

SHIT!

Think, Rod. Just think.

Where is my phone??? How much time do I have???

Yo cell is sitting on top of the tv, bro. The time now reads 5:10pm.

I need to call Sashé back!

"I'm going on a diet," Cookie's voice startled me again. She was standing in the doorway now, looking down at her body as she dried off. She didn't need to go on a diet.

"Why you ain't leave the water running???" I barked at her impatiently.

"You ain't tell me to," she replied with an attitude. "Lemme see them pictures."

The phone screen lit up in my hand with an incoming text from Shay:

SASHÉ: "Why are you not answering? Are u at home?"

Gotdammit…gotdammit, Rod!

I stepped away as Cookie moved towards me…but in such a way that she ain't notice. Even when my phone started ringing with *another incoming call*…I didn't so much as flinch. The caller *this time* was a breath of fresh air…the perfect interference.

"Wassup, cousin," I spoke into the phone, watching Cookie get dressed.

Lil Rico was hype on the other end, "Yoooo, what up, cuzz! Are…are you at home???"

"Yeah, I'm 'bout to leave in a minute," I told him. "Getting ready."

"Yeah, I was gonna see if it was cool I came over tonight."

This was my chance to walk away and into the other room, out of Cookie's sight. I stepped into the office and opened the door to the balcony. The humidity outside made me start sweating again almost instantly as I pulled the door towards me…leaving it cracked.

"Nah bro, not tonight. I got some action later on," I whispered, trying to keep my voice down.

"Nigga, yo ass always got action!" Lil Rico laughed. "Come on, cuzz, I just don't feel like going home when I get off work."

"Tonight is no good, cuzz. Come next weekend. I got a lot going on right now."

Rico started to say something but was cut off with that call-waiting beep. Sashé was calling me back…*again*.

"Aye, but lemme hit you back, Lil Rico. I gotta get this call," I glanced over my left shoulder to make sure Cookie wasn't coming to find me before I clicked over.

"Hello?"

"Oh my God, what are you doing??" Shay sounded flustered. "I been calling you like crazy!"

"I know, I just picked up my phone," I lied. "My bad."

"What the heck were you doing??" she asked again. "Are you at home? We're almost in Overland Park…"

"I'm almost home. Coming back from the park with Tre."

"You went to play ball???" Shay was surprised. "Is Tre coming over to swim with us, too???"

"No, I just dropped him off," I lied again, so I could get to the details I really needed to hear. "How far are y'all away?"

"Maybe 15 minutes, I don't know," Shay responded casually. "We're getting on *435* now."

"Ok, I'll see y'all in a minute."

"Wait!" she stopped me from hanging up. "I was calling to see if you can get us some liquor."

"I got some Hennessy."

"We want vodka, Daddy!"

Dammit Shay. I'll be glad when this girl turns 21.

"Ok," I shook my head, holding my sigh in. "Ok. I'ma have to go back out."

"Why? You said you're not home yet."

My eyes got big, and I replied quickly, "I'm pulling in the lot now."

"Aww, man," she sounded disappointed. "Baaaby!"

She then started talking to Kourtney, who I heard fussing in the background.

"I thought y'all was out drinking with Kris," I probed, trying to halfway change the subject.

"Yeah, but we only had a couple of shots!" she told me. "Well, you're just gonna have to take us to get liquor when we get there, Daddy."

CHUUUUUCH!!!

Bingo! Just what we needed, nigga!

"Ok boo. I need blunts anyway, I smiled at the new window of opportunity. "So, ok. Lemme get in the shower, babe. I'll see you in a minute."

"No, wait, Daddy," she stopped me again. "Can we just use the bong?"

Gotdammit, this girl will not let me get off the phone!

I took the phone away from my ear and stared at it in the palm of my hand. It was **5:20** now; we had been on the phone for almost 5 minutes. With Cookie still in my apartment, and the sun beaming down at me…my body temperature was nearly boiling.

"Yeah, of course," I bit my tongue, concealing my frustration. "I'm just saying I can get blunts for *me* when I go to the store. Just hurry up and get here."

"Ok, and leave the door unlocked if you're getting in the shower," Shay made one last request.

"Aight, I got y'all," I promised.

"Ok, Daddy. Bye," she finally hung up.

I moved swiftly back inside and headed straight to the bathroom to turn the shower back on, sitting the phone down on the counter. Then I yelled out to Cookie, "Where my towel at?"

"It's in here," she was fully dressed and sitting on my bare mattress with her legs crossed when I walked back into the room.

"Man, I gotta hurry up."

"Can I see the pictures so I can go??" Cookie asked, sounding hasty.

"Why I can't show you later??"

"Cuz you can show me now," she replied quickly.

"Man…where my phone at? You 'bout to piss me off, girl.

Cookie followed me back into the bathroom, "Aww baby…stop acting like that. I'm 'bout to go; I gotta take my hair down."

We then leaned against the sink and started looking through the pics…each one causing Cookie to have an outburst, "Oh my Gosh! That's not me!"

"Girl, you tripping," I shook my head in amazement.

"Rodney, look at my ass," she gasped again. "Oh my Gosh…"

"I told you."

"Lemme see what you recorded," she requested.

"The clips real short," I gave a warning.

"Ok, *and?* You better not show nobody, Rodney."

"This the one I fukced up on," I scrolled through the footage. "I forgot I was recording, just that quick."

"I told you, this nookie too good," she giggled. "See, look at you."

"Shut up."

"Damn. I do look good right there. Rewind it," she bit her lip, mesmerized at the playback. "Wow."

"That's what I'm saying."

"Yeah," she nodded her head. "That's why they go crazy."

"Man, look at that shit," I stared in awe at her ass on the screen.

"See? You shoulda went to Vegas with me," Cookie cut her eyes, referring to our conversation last year about making a stripping road trip. "We could be rich by now!

"Man, shut the fukc up, dude," I didn't need the reminder. "Aye, I gotta get in the shower, for real."

"Oh for real? You kicking me out cause I brought up Vegas?!?"

"No…Cookie! I gotta go!" I snapped, raising my voice. "You gotta go – for real."

"Ok, I'm just playing, dang. You gonna walk me to the door?"

"Come on."

After I closed the door behind her, I went into *pledge* mode – dashing across the apartment back to the bedroom and into the closet. I had the original sheets and cover on the bed within seconds and checked around on the floor thoroughly to make sure it was clear.

I then stood there for another few seconds, scanning the pics in my phone before pulling Shay and Kourt's shoes and bags back out of the closet. I was moving quickly…and wasn't sure if I put their shoes exactly back where they were…but that ain't matter. It just needed to be as close as possible.

After I unzipped both bags, I pulled a bottle of body spray out of Sashé's…and let out a light mist in the air.

5:33pm

The sheets were done and needed to be dried. Shay and Kourt's load was still wet in the dryer so I tossed a couple of softener sheets in, along with my swim trunks. Then there were the things under the sink. I spent a few more seconds making sure I got the sink counter mess more replicated and had to step out into the doorway to look at my phone again because of the steam filling up the air.

Now all I gotta do is make sure they stay away from the dryer.

At this point, I'm standing in my living room in my gym shorts doing one last scan. My phone vibrated in my hand again, and I noticed that I had 2 unread texts from KeLLy. This threw me off for another split second, but I realized wuttin' no time to read or reply. Plus the shower water was loud enough that when I thought I heard voices coming up the stairs outside…I second-guessed reading the messages and had to check to be sure.

So I ran to the window by the office…and looked outside at the parking lot. Sashé's car was parked where Cookie's was before.

Shit. They here.

I took off back towards the bathroom, running across the couch. I damn near fell on my face once I reached the bathroom floor, but I kept my balance and tossed my shorts to the floor as I heard the unlocked door opening.

Sashé headed straight for the bathroom…but by the time she turned the corner, I was already in the shower.

"Baby, you're *still* in the shower???"

Close fukcin' call, Rod! Now let's get ready for the big game!

*   *   *   *   *

The real coverup and damage control started about 20 minutes later, as I rode in the backseat of Sashé's blue '98 *Chevy Caprice*, going back and forth in my texts with Kells.

Some weird shit was starting to unravel, so I asked Shay to drive. She ain't think much of it; her and Kourt had been riding around like that all day. As they chattered up front excitedly, I was in the back text-cheating with my ex.

ME: "My bad, I can text tho."

KELLY: "Yeah I figured you're probably with her now."

ME: "Who are you talking about Kells?"

KELLY: "Your new girlfriend Rodney."

What???

ME: "I don't have a girlfriend tho Kelly.

KELLY: "I'm not gonna go back and forth and be technical with you. U know how u are with words. We both know who I'm referring to."

I stared at the screen as we pulled onto *119th* and headed west. It's easy for me to assume she was talking about Shay…but not so easy for me to tell her what I'm thinking that's she's thinking. *The Art* won't let me do it.

Kells sends another text while I'm contemplating how to reply.

KELLY: "I knew that bullshit u came up with about the reason she had your # was a lie. I just couldn't prove it at the time but I knew it was bull. Why would u be buying them lil girls liquor during homecoming anyway? I knew there was more to it…"

Yeah. She definitely talking about Sashé.

But what do she know? She can't know…everything.

Nah, not everything. Be cool, Rod.

KELLY: "…but I just played along with it because I didn't want to believe it. I just…looked the other way. When she approached me on campus and said she sent you that text on accident, she just had this look in her eyes."

ME: "What look KeLLy?"

KELLY: "That look…she was focused. Like…the story she was telling was a movie. I've told stories for you before. You're a good teacher Rodney."

Damn, man.

ME: "I don't know what you talking about Kelly. I told u I knew she didn't mean to send me that, but I never told her to talk to u! She did that on her own…."

"KELLY: "Yea that's what y'all made it seem like. I couldn't prove it then, but I know now. Just know that I know."

ME: "What do u think u know Kelly?"

KELLY: "I'm sitting here laughing at you still trying to play it off. Laughing...and looking at this box I was going to mail you."

Wait...what?!?!?

ME: "Uhm...what? What box? What's in it?"

KELLY: "Don't worry about it. It's not even worth sending."

ME: "What are u talking about Kelly?!?! What are u on? Like wtf are u saying?"

KELLY: "Nothing. I told u. I know."

Ok. Now I'm bugging.

Chill out, Rod.

Dawg, if she knows, like — if she knows EVERYTHING that I been on with Sashé. Dude!

She don't, bro. Ain't no way she could know.

All those times I was sneaking in and out the Burg to see her, when Kelly was right across campus? If she knows THAT…

Bruh, she don't!

Fukc bro! What does she KNOW?!?!?!

KELLY: "I know you didn't just meet her at homecoming and bought liquor for her friends cuz they asked. That's what you told me, but I know that was a lie. I know she and her little friends hung with y'all at the hotel room…that's what you didn't tell me."

My head dropped, and I started rubbing my eyelids. This was getting ugly.

KELLY: "I know you and her been fukcing since before homecoming last year. I know she's the real reason we broke up. I know more than u can imagine. And I have proof."

ME: "Proof?"

KELLY: "Pictures. Things she's said out of her own mouth. U forget we were at the same school Rodney? You don't think them little girls talk? Why would one of her friends post on Facebook about 'HoLLyRod the Kappa'? That's a coincidence too?? Is it another Kappa named HoLLyRod??"

Man, what the fukc is FACEBOOK???

Like, what is she talking about?

I mean, I have been around a lot of Shay's friends. From the jump I've been on some hot shit around her friends; I knew that shit would bite me in the ass one day.

Yeah, but what the fukc is Facebook???

ME: "What the hell is Facebook Kelly??? I really don't know what you're talking about!"

KELLY: "Oh that's right...u can't get on Facebook because you're not in college lol! Yeah. Check ya hoes boah. U didn't cover all ya bases this time HoLLyRod. Are u not HoLLyRod the Kappa?"

ME: "I'm a Nupe."

KELLY: "Lol right."

My heart was racing now. Kells obviously knew some shit…and not knowing exactly what or how she knew was killing me. Clearly the evidence was coming from Shay's circle of friends, though. All these freaky, little hot-tailed bitches Shay had me hanging around; all this new territory I was in was getting the best of me.

Fukc!!!

It was bad enough keeping Sashé on her toes so it ain't get back to her boyfriend, Keith. It really wuttin' no way to ensure her friends would play by the same rules in *The Art*. In any other situation…I woulda considered them a liability. What was I really thinking???

I mean…some of the creeping I've done in the past was even hidden from my family or closest Nupes. You never truly know how shit will accidentally get leaked, so it's always best to play it safe.

And this *'Facebook'* shit KeLLy was talking about was for real some shit I wuttin' looking out for.

What the fukc are Shay's friends posting on about me?

Ain't no telling, bro! But it gotta be some internet site they posting to…right? What the hell is 'facebook'?

KELLY: "That's the best u can come up with huh? I'm not surprised. You're probably sweating bullets right now wondering what all I know and how I found out."

This is throwing me off my square. So much so that I ain't realize the car had stopped and Sashé was in the front seat yelling my name.

"Rodney! You don't hear me?!?!" she was staring at me in the rearview mirror.

"Oh my bad, I'm tripping."

"Who are you texting?!?!" she exclaimed.

"Yeah, tell that hoe you got two bad bitches ready to get crunk tonight! She can wait," Kourtney chimed in.

Shay laughed, "Right. Come on, Daddy. We wanna go swimming."

"How y'all tryna get drunk and get in the pool???" I wanted to know.

"We big girls!" Kourtney yelled in response. "It's not like we're gonna get drunk and drown!!!"

"Yeah, we're not getting in the deep end!" Shay turned to face Kourt. "Are you getting in the deep end???"

"I'm not getting in the deep end," Kourtney turned around to look at me. "Are you getting in the deep end, HoLLyRod?"

"I'm getting in some deep end," I paused so they could appreciate my wit. "But I'll be back."

Kourtney laughed as I get out the car, "Aww yeah, nigga??? His slick talking ass!!!"

"I know…don't you just love it?!?!" Shay gleamed with joy.

The whole time I'm standing in line for the liquor, I'm texting KeLLy…who's sent me a streamline of messages since I left the girls in the parking lot.

KELLY: "I mean I know she's younger and a pretty girl and all, but seriously Rodney…I wouldn't expect you to make somebody like her your girl. She has zero personality…she's not even your type…

"…but I guess she IS your type huh? I knew it was someone else. I knew when u said u wanted space. You don't just disappear like that…there had to be someone else. But HER??!?! I can handle you moving on…but this is the same bitch you swore up and down you wasn't fukcing with!!! When she's been around all along…

"…this shit HURTS Rodney. She has a key to your house. She's the one who put ya kitchen together…I knew u had to have some new bitch when I came over there, but HER?!?! It's like you're moving on as if nothing we had mattered. You wouldn't even give me a key when we didn't live together!!! How is she NOT your girl?!?!

"...I would never do you like this Rodney...never disrespect you or embarrass you for all your friends to see. You really thought that none of this would get back to me?!?! You wanted it to. You wanted me to know. Got me looking like a fool in front of everybody. I've always been a fool for you. Why her Rodney?!?! You think she's prettier than me???"

ME: "...Kelly. Stop. It's really not like that."

KELLY: "Spare me that shit Rodney. You're lucky I love you how I do, like really fukcin' lucky! Cuz if I didn't I would've just sent you this shit and not even ever talked to u again after. You're lucky I have a heart...

"...but karma is real Rodney. Karma will come for you. The next bitch won't be so nice when you fukc her over in the end. Your day will come. Remember that. Just leave me alone."

I paused to pay for the drinks, and I could almost hear Kells' voice in my ear. There's a specific tone I can just feel through her texts. It was eerie as fukc.

ME: "KeLLy...stop, please. I don't like how you're talking..."

This wuttin' part of the plan. There wuttin' supposed to be drama...

I walked to the car slowly, putting my phone away as I started across the lot. Sashé and Kourtney were in the car grooving to music, not paying me any attention. They were completely oblivious to the emotional exchange I had gotten myself into and just ready to get the party started.

I need to get my head back in the game.

Yeah, nigga! And fast.

*   *   *   *   *

"What does it look like I'm doing??" Kourtney stared at me with her light brown eyes, "I'm pulling your shorts off."

"We should all get naked," Shay suggested with a smirk.

"I agree," Kourt rolled her eyes. "This nigga pulled that *steam room* trick again, bitch…"

They both busted out laughing…rolling around in the bed. The three of us were lying on our backs in our pajamas, with me in the middle, cover and sheets pulled down. Kourtney was on my right side in a oversized t-shirt and booty shorts, tugging at *my* gym shorts. Sashé had on the least clothing…curled up against me in her panties and bra. The beam from my walk-in closet was the only light shining in from my right and behind Kourtney.

"I'm used to it by now; I just try to stay naked," Shay told her.

"Come on, HoLLyRod…don't be shy now," Kourt kept tugging at my clothes.

"Shut that shit up," I helped her pull my shorts to my ankles, and Shay kicked them off with her feet as she rubbed my chest through my tank top. Kourtney put her right leg across mine and brought her knee up to my crotch. She eyed my bulge as she started mimicking Shay's chest rub on my opposite side.

This shit is really happening.

"What happened to the blunt???" Kourt asked suddenly.

"Shay had it," I snitched.

"Nuh uhn," Sashé denied my accusation. "I never took a hit from it."

"So where is it?" Kourt raised her eyebrow.

"I passed it to one of y'all," I looked at the nightstand. "I coulda sworn I handed it to you Shay."

"I don't have it," Shay confirmed.

"Y'all done lost the blunt?!?!" Kourtney couldn't believe it.

I sat up slightly, looking to either side, "I know it's gotta be somewhere, for real, dude."

"Maybe y'all finished it," Shay shifted to the side.

"I only hit it twice," Kourtney shook her head.

"So, where is it at, Kourt?!?" I eyeballed her.

"Baby!" Shay snapped, shaking me by the shoulder. "Fukc that blunt."

"That's *yo* friend that lost it," I shot back, confused about where it could have gone that quick.

"Baby," Shay lowered her voice sternly. "It's gone."

"We need to do a strip search," Kourtney smiled, curling her tongue.

"No, he needs to eat my pussy," Shay had other plans in the works. "Like right now."

Damn. Like that???

"Aww yeah? Like that?" Kourt echoed my thoughts and shot me a look. "You heard her, shawty. Do what you need to do."

"Damn, baby."

"It's so wet right now," Shay closed her legs tightly, squirming. "It's like…leaking."

Kourtney reached across me for Shay, "Lemme see."

I nudged Kourt with my forearm and she willingly fell back and grabbed my right thigh, running her nails up the side.

"Watch out. Lemme see first."

Shay lifted up and started to pull her panties down with my help. Looking me in the eye the whole time, her once unblemished eyes were now bloodshot red and sitting low. These last few months seemed like they moved so fast…the both of us shedding layers of innocence otherwise untouched. This was all new territory for *us*. But a natural fantasy just the same…so without hesitation, instinct took over.

Sashé licked her top lip…watching me as I sat up and faced her, slowly moving her silk underwear down her legs. I bit my lip, stopping at her kneecaps…glancing down at her soaking wet pussy lips, and then back into her eyes.

"How I want you, baby?" I asked, almost whispering.

"Dripping wet," she lowered her voice even more. "Hmmm…and ready to *fukc*."

I licked my lips, pulling her panties down, "You how I want you now?"

"Yes, Daddy," she bent her knees upward, and I moved down to the end of the bed to pull her feet through, tossing her panties to her left. She scooted up and Kourtney reached over again, this time rolling her whole body towards Shay and leaning in for a kiss. Her hand fell on top of Shay's clit…and she started rubbing her pussy as they licked each other's lips.

I pulled my wife-beater off and threw it behind me, then took Shay's left ankle in my hand and tossed her leg to my right, trying to get a better look. Kourtney's hand was moving in a circular motion against Sashé's labia…slowly, fingers on the outside. Kourtney's dark skin was barely visible…like *KeLLy's* blackness. The way she had half her body laid across Shay – how her thick, chocolate ass poked out to my left – her whole *posture* reminded me of KeLLy.

The *beast* slapped at Kourtney's cuff hanging out the bottom of her skimpy shorts. She responded by pulling away from Shay, and quickly pulling her bottoms off, kicking them to her left before she started kissing on Shay again. This time, she sat on her knees, rubbing Shay's quivering stomach.

I started puckering on Sashé's feet…kissing her from her ankle to her upper thigh, each kiss barely inches apart.

"Hmmmm," she moaned sensually. "Fuuuck."

Shay's head squirmed as my lips moved to her inner thighs. Kourtney then helped her sit up straight, reaching around to get her bra off. Sashé's huge breasts came free…and Kourtney immediately took her right one in both hands, squeezing and kissing as Shay fell back against the bed.

Using Kourt's naked ass for balance, I dove in at Shay's pussy, taking her hood and lips in my mouth, sucking slowly. Her juices immediately drenched my face and started running like water down to my chin. She draped her leg across my right shoulder, pulling me in closer.

I continued to suck away, gripping Kourt's soft, juicy cheeks with my left hand. Kourtney fell back to the bed, grabbing my head with her right hand, poking her ass out more for me to keep caressing as she kept sucking on Shay's nipple. Her body shifted again…she was trying to get my crawling fingers to touch her pussy. I couldn't quite reach it, but the more she twirled her hips…the more I could feel the warm air, as if her pussy was letting out deep breaths.

The noise of heavy panting from our lungs was unmistakable, though, as the three of us filled the room with gasping sounds, mixed in with loud sucking and kissing.

Sashé had right hand on top of Kourtney's head…left hand on top of mine, as she twisted her body to meet our mouths. Her moans were turning into light squeals, blending in with the squeaking bed rocking back and forth, "Mmmm…yea…hmmmm. Dammit, y'all. Shit…"

Kourtney saw this as motivation…scooting her body downward toward me, licking and kissing all over as she made her way. Sashé pushed her head down in anticipation, grabbing my ear with her other hand. I then took my face away, moving to the right to make room for Kourtney.

We both laid our head against Shay's inner thighs…helping her spread her legs apart as she looked down at us. She was clasping her own titties now, squeezing her left nipple passionately.

Kourtney and I locked eyes…and she smiled at me as our legs intertwined. Kourtney had some real thick thighs; they were borderline chunky now that she was laying half naked with me. She reached at my chest – clawing at it as she looked down at my stomach. My dick was poking through the waistline of my boxer briefs…twitching.

"Hi," Kourtney whispered, breathing in my face.

"Hey," I bit my lip and smiled.

Kourt brushed her nose against my mouth, "Whatchu doing down here??"

"The same thing you tryna do."

"Oh, so you reading my mind now?" she asked, voice filled with sass.

We both leaned into each other with our tongues out…and flickered them at the tip. Sashé started rubbing her clit and stuck a finger in her wet opening…then me and Kourt attacked her fingers and pussy lips with our tongues, mixing our drool with Shay's sweet juice.

Kourtney started rubbing the top of my dick with her thumb…gripping the head and tugging, causing me to groan, "Hmmm…"

I can't believe this is happening!!!

Kourt moved in closer to me, pushing me out of tongue's reach of Shay's pussy…and started hogging it to herself, ferociously smacking and sucking like she was trying to drain her. She then pulled my dick free with her hand as she turned on her stomach and jacked me while she ate. I lifted Shay up with my right hand by her left cheek and pushed Kourtney's head in with my left…grabbing at her hair and directing her head.

Kourtney started humping and grinding against the mattress and letting out high pitched moans. It was driving me nuts. Her movements were fluid, arching her back and rolling like a snake. It's so…*fluid.*

*Like…**KeLLy**. Dark, fat ass. Just like KeLLy…*

But this thick, chocolate sista with the ghetto booty and hand on my dick was *not* KeLLy. She was far from it. KeLLy would *never* be eating pussy with me – let alone *Sashé's* pussy. Sashé was my little secret that KeLLy was *never* supposed to find out about…this path I was on was so taboo.

*Kells would never understand this **beast** inside. I always knew the truth about me would hurt her…*

But how did KeLLy put everything together, bro? Like seriously?

Yo guess is as good as mine. It ain't like I planned to be this close to Sashé. I never thought any of it out. All of this just kind of…happened!

My thoughts were interrupted by Kourtney lifting up to crawl up Sashé's body for another kiss…this time taking her face in hands and giving it to her long and deep, French style. I rolled over and did the same to Shay's sloppy kitty…taking her clit hood in my lips and sucking as I stuck the tip of my tongue in her.

Sashé's pussy was so *tight*. Always so TIGHT.

My tongue could barely open her up…as her walls spread only momentarily before clamping down firmly on it. It forced me to start digging in by pushing my head into her…and she started moaning and screaming, moving away from Kourt's kiss, "Hmmmmm ohhhh…oh my. Daddy! Hmmmm…damn. I can't take it!"

"Damn bitch….is he that dope?" Kourt's eyes got wide as I slurped away.

"Girl," Shay panted. "He knows exactly what he's doing."

"Better than me???" Kourt wondered, reaching down at Shay's pussy as I kept licking.

Shay struggled trying to judge our skills. "Hmmm…I don't…I can't say…hmmmm. *Both* of you are good. Hmmm…*so good.*"

"Damn, I need to see how good he is," Kourtney looked hella intrigued.

"Yes," Shay agreed. "Hmmm. Yes, you do."

"I don't know," Kourt thought about it for a second, watching in amazement. "He must like how you taste, girl."

"Oh, he's not selfish…hmmmm," Shay moaned again, responding to my feasting. "Are you, Daddy?"

I started licking Kourt's fingers with Shay's pussy and mumbled calmly, "Nope."

"Can you make her cum, baby??" Shay twitched in place.

"You know I can," I slurped loudly.

"Can you???" Kourtney asked curiously.

"Lay back," I sat up as Kourtney laid in the middle of the bed on her back.

Shay moved to where I was laying before, reaching under Kourt's shirt to grab at her breasts. They started kissing again and I moved to my left, spreading Kourt's legs apart. Her pussy was as bare as Shay's…but with fatter, longer lips, and a pierced clit. She locked legs with Shay and started playing with her pussy, grinding against her *own* fingers now.

I grabbed her right ankle and started kissing her at the heel of her foot…grazing my teeth along the base and taking two toes in my mouth. Her foot was soft and smooth in my palm…and she wiggled her toes back and forth in a frenzy. I chuckled at her ticklishness, she writhed like KeLLy used to when I sucked her toes.

Bruh, why you keep thinking about KeLLy??

It's just spooky how she talked to me earlier, threatening to send a package to me on some revenge shit.

I mean – what the hell was she gon' send, though?

I can't figure that out, but I've known KeLLy long enough to know she can act a fool at times. She was so…mad at me.

Something is up, nigga. Cuz even when you told her the truth about Cookie, she ain't take it THIS hard.

Yeah. I guess the truth about Sashé is just that much harder to come to grips with…

"Come here, Shay," I demanded.

"Yeah, baby?" she looked down at me between Kourt's legs "What you want me to do??"

"Learn how to eat pussy."

"Really?!?" she responded in shock. "You're gonna teach me???"

"I can help, too," Kourtney stretched her left leg out, holding on by the ankle.

"Yeah. You got the best teachers right here, right now," I told Shay. "You gotta take advantage of this."

I scooted to my left and made way for Sashé…and now she and I were positioned in between Kourt's legs. Shay started rubbing her friend's clit with her thumb. Kourtney's large, engorged clit was poking out, pink head throbbing.

"Ok, what do I do?" Shay was eager for her lessons.

"Watch me first," I instructed.

Kourtney grabbed my head and lifted up to meet my face, as I stuck my tongue out wide…running it up her slit. I pointed the tip of my tongue out like an arrow as I found her clit head. Giving it a couple of jabs before I ran my tongue back down her slit, I then stopped at her opening. I curled my tongue upward before I stuck it inside, using my fingers to spread her lips.

Kourtney's pussy started immediately leaking on my face. I took Sashé's left hand and put it where my fingers were separating Kourt's lips before and had Shay hold 'em open as I fukced Kourtney slowly with my tongue.

"Damn, Daddy…is that how you do me??" Sashé watched my technique up close. "Hmmmm…shit."

Kourtney started losing her cool, "Girl…what. The. FUKC!!! Hmmmmmmm…"

Shay grabbed Kourt's hand, "I told you."

"You *did!!!*" she whined.

I started shaking my head back and forth and circling my tongue around Kourt's hood and Shay's fingers. Kourtney started humping upwards at my face…and then I pulled Sashé closer to me with my right arm. Our legs tangled up, and Shay's oversized D-cups rested against my chest, damp with sweat.

And then…*it happened.*

Sashé leaned in and started licking at Kourtney's wetness…teaming up with my tongue to taste every drop. She had never performed oral sex on a female…but she knew what felt good to her. She was moving her tongue and skull in sync as Kourt grabbed her by the head and threw her own back…bumping against the wall behind her.

"Dammit, Shay! Girl…SHIT!" Kourtney cursed. "Hmmmmmm…right there!"

I watched Shay closely as she licked away, and I started coaching her, pinching her nipple as I spoke, "Hmmm…yeah. Slow down. Slow down, babe…suck on it."

Shay had a mouthful, and her words were muffled, "Lie tis???"

Kourtney squirmed, "Yeah…hmmmm. Like that…"

I put my face down in it again, taking Kourt's lips in with Shay's, drooling and slurping away. Her clit ring started clanging against my teeth and both of the girls broke into a synchronized moan…all of our bodies twisting and turning.

Kourtney's body jerked a little more aggressively and she jumped away from my wet mouth…panting and looking down at me, "Dammit, boy! What are you…trying to do to me???"

Her voice, especially with the panting, sounded like some shit KeLLy said to me the last time I tasted her sweet chocolate.

Man, this shit 'a never go down with KeLLy and any of her friends!

Hell nah! I mean, for one, I can't stand most of Kells' friends like that, especially Danni's uppity ass!

Danni was damn near the complete opposite of KeLLy with her redbone, petite ass frame. But she was always one of our worst critics, forever keeping some shit going between us. Sashé and her friends were never like that when we were together. Besides *Maria*, we all got along.

And look at us now! I'm helping Shay eat her chocolate friend, showing her how to eat it.

This woulda never happened before. The very thought of Danni's pussy in my face almost disgusts me.

Like…who would wanna fukc with her little boney ass anywa…

WAIT!!!! KEITH! Sashé's ex-boyfriend!!

What you saying, brodie?

That lil nigga cheated on Shay…with KeLLy's friend Danni!!!

So, you thinking that's how word got back to Kells?

Come on, dawg. That's gotta be how KeLLy knows!!!! If Danni and Keith still in contact with each other and fukcing around – THAT'S IT!

It all makes sense! Danni would be more than willing to prove to Keith and KeLLy that Shay and I been creeping around for these last few months. Danni would give her life to help piece that puzzle together. Why I ain't think of this shit before???

I mean…but the problem with that is, Shay said she never told Keith about you, Rod. Right?

Nah, fukc that! I'm on to something.

Danni would be the one to snoop around in all the right places. Especially with her being an AKA…she was still connected to campus affairs. Danni was the type to be KeLLy's eyes and ears when Kells wuttin' seeing clearly. KeLLy *did* say that she saw something on that *Facebook* site from one of Shay's friends. More than likely, it was *Danni* who pointed it out in the first place.

Why the fukc couldn't she just stay out of our fukcing business?!?!? Kells and I done been through enough to not have to end up as enemies. The thought of KeLLy hating me forever behind all this feels like a ton of bricks on my shoulder.

But in my *reality* at the moment…it was the weight of *Kourtney's* thick thigh resting on my shoulder. She was spreading her lips with two fingers now….and Sashé was fingering her while she flickered her tongue quickly against Kourt's clit. Shay then sat up on all fours, her ass popping in the air. Sashé ain't have a round, fat ass like Cookie or

Kourtney…and she definitely ain't have that thickness to her physique like her predecessor KeLLy.

Sashé's backside was just right, though…extra toned up with a small cuff. And her legs were long and smooth – hairless like her pussy. She kept eating away at Kourtney's puddle…reaching down to play with her own pussy with her right hand.

"Hmmm…Shay…damn!" Kourtney was in heaven. "Hmmmm…fuuuuuuck. Stick ya finger ba…ck oh my Gawd…yesss."

Sashé was instantly becoming an honor student at this shit….and I could tell by the way she was rubbing herself that it turned her on to the max. She was finally living out her fantasy…having the best of both worlds in her face and at her fingertips.

I stepped back to the foot of the bed…just watching now. Shay spread her knees apart…laying her titties against the bed as she leaned into Kourtney's snatch. Kourt almost instantly locked her legs around Shay's head, thrusting up at her face…and Shay doesn't miss a beat.

I started rubbing my dick through my briefs. Gripping it at the base…tugging it and stretching it, trying to make it harder. All this pussy-eating and lack of attention had my **wooD** on standby.

What the fukc is this about???

I don't know what's going on, bro. But we need to wake this nigga the fukc up!

"Give it to me, Daddy," Shay urged in agony. "I want it."

"Yeah, come on," Kourt added her two cents. "I wanna see you fukc her."

Bruh, this can't be happening. It's only semi-hard! What are you doing, nigga?

Don't put this on me! I'm just a voice in yo head, remember?

Aww, nigga, don't even try it! This is yo area! You usually done took over by now! What's the problem?

Just relax and focus, Rod. We got this.

Sashé was still dripping with anxiousness, "Come on, baby!"

I hung my head in embarrassment, "You gotta help me get hard."

"What?!?!" Shay turned around quickly. "You're not hard???"

"He went down, lil baby," I confessed, trying to sound unbothered.

"Girl, you better suck dat nigga's dick so I can watch y'all!" Kourtney had the perfect remedy in mind.

Shay was already moving towards the foot of the bed before Kourt got the words out. Still bent over, but now facing me with her ass towards our chocolate third party. Kourtney gave her a nice smack on her left cheek as she sat forward.

"Ouch!" Shay yelped.

"You like it," Kourt fired back. "Shut up."

Shay proceeded to knock my hand away from my boxer briefs and snatched 'em off. Then she pulled me closer by grabbing my legs as she greedily took my head in her mouth. She started sucking – just the head – and massaging my balls gently. Her hands were sloppy wet…a mixture of her saliva and Kourtney's pussy juice. As it started to grow in her jaws…she began stroking it…getting it sloppy wet and lubed up. Her wrist flicked back and forth as she stroked…and I started humping her warm mouth.

"Hmmmm, hell yeah," I felt my mojo coming back as my **wooD** hardened on her tongue. "Suck that shit."

"Damn, bitch…you just a head monsta tonight!!!!" Kourtney cheered her on. "Hmmm…suck it, Shay. Get it."

Taking a fistful of hair, she started guiding Shay's head up and down on my shaft, squeezing her left tit from behind. My **wooD** started hitting the back of Shay's throat…filling her jaws up as my erection took full form again.

That's what the fukc I'm talking about!!!

I told you we got this, Rod.

Ain't nothing like some good head to get it popping. The only other thing besides head that was sure to get my dick rock-hard was kissing, something KeLLy always hated to do. I mean, yeah – she kissed me more in our last days. But overall, I had to get my kissing fix elsewhere the whole time we was together. Cookie knew KeLLy wouldn't kiss me like I wanted. That's how she lured me in the first time we cheated. It all started with a kiss.

Why couldn't KeLLy kiss me like she did last week? If she woulda just kissed me like that when we was together, Cookie woulda never had the chance to tempt me like she did so many time over the years.

Lack of kisses helped make cheating my favorite adult habit…and now the way Sashé was kissing and licking on my dick right now was all KeLLy's fault.

Man. If Kells could read my thoughts or see what I had in front of me right now…maybe she would finally understand my choices.

Then again…maybe not. Even *I* don't fully understand when it all boils down to it…but I gotta blame somebody other than myself.

I can't believe this shit is happening…but…is this too much to ask for?

Sashé didn't think so…as she pulled my dick outta her mouth with that popping sound, a big stream of spit dripping down to her tits. Kourtney started rubbing it in as Shay turned back around to bend over in front of me and they licked each other's face.

I moved in closer as Kourt nudged Shay in my direction, then spread her ass cheeks apart, watching me stroke my dick before I buried it in her friend.

"Yeah…he's hard as a muhfukca now, girl," she told Shay. "Hmmm…put that shit in, HoLLyRod!"

My dick slid in slowly…as Shay always wanted the first stroke to be *extra slow*. Her pussy was so tight, it immediately started throbbing and gripping me involuntarily, tying to adjust to the penetration.

"Ugh…ho-ly…shit. Hmmmm," Shay gasped, bracing herself.

Kourtney ran her tongue down Shay's back as I settled in deep, and then up my stomach and chest…stopping at my chin, tongue hanging out. I started thrusting, turned on by Kourtney's freakiness. She stands up on the bed…and pushes Shay's face in between her legs…grinding her pussy as I stroked back and forth.

Kourt's eyes were lit up, "Oh yeah? That's how you laying that dick, boy? Cum'ere."

She then leaned in and stuck her tongue down my throat…and we started kissing like animals. Her drool dripped off my bottom lip and on top of my thumb resting in Shay's ass crack. I started rubbing her hole with my thumb while I fukced her…and she moaned loudly, sucking Kourtney's pussy in front of her, while Kourt kept licking and sucking my lips.

"Hmmmm," I grunted. "You nasty."

Sashé suddenly started throwing it back at me. She never does that, though…and the way her ass was bouncing back on it was totally surprising. I ain't know Shay could move like that. Kourtney grabbed her ass cheeks and started helping her throw it on my dick…encouraging her with lustful outbursts.

I can't believe this shit is happening…

Shay was putting her back into it…and the way Kourt had her cheeks spread, it made Shay's ass look more round than usual, almost in the shape of KeLLy's backside.

There you go again, nigga…thinking about yo ex!!!

And there my **wooD** *goes again…getting soft and weak!!! Fukc, man! Not again, bro!*

Stop thinking about KeLLy, Rod!!!

Shay ain't notice it softening up. She and Kourt were going crazy now…both of them moaning like they was almost at climax. My **wooD** stiffened up again briefly and I grabbed Shay's waist with both hands…penetrating her hard and deep.

As long as I just keep it in deep…it should harden back up enough for me to get back focused.

Sashé started grinding against my stomach…helping me keep it deep inside her.

Does she notice now?

Nah, bro…she can't. And it's just about fully erect again, nigga. I know she feel that shit.

"Yeah, baby!" Shay's pussy starts clenching up. "Don't stop…I'm cummin'! Don't stop!!!"

I couldn't stop if I wanted to. I was almost sure that if I pulled out, my **wooD** 'a go down again.

"Damn…hmmmm…hell yeah, girl!" Kourtney kept talking her through it. "You cummin' on that thick dick, girl…yes. Let that shit out!"

"Yeeeah…let it out, lil baby," I bit my lip, concentrating.

"Don't…pssst…stahp…YES!!!! HMMMMMMM!!! DADDY!!!! SHIIIIIIIIT!!!! OH MY GAWD!"

She started nutting hard as fukc. So hard that she fell to the bed…abruptly pulling her face away from Kourt and pussy away from my dick.

DAMMIT! I wuttin' ready!!!

Neither of them could see my dick go limp, as Kourtney threw her head back and started fingering her pussy with two fingers…seconds away from exploding, "Dammit, bitch – I was 'bout to cum, too!!!"

Sashé was breathing hard…twitching underneath her friend, "I'm…sorry. I couldn't…help it. Daddy can make you cum. Make her cum, Daddy."

"Yeah, come on. Gimme dat good dick, too," Kourt collapsed to her knees and turned around, bending over to the left of Shay, spreading her ass cheeks apart. She started bouncing and jiggling in the air…pussy juice dripping.

And there I stood, going softer by the second…shaking my head, as I…*shook my head.*

Wake up, HoLLyWooD!!! Wake the fukc up!!!!!

I cannot believe this shit is happening!!!

*   *   *   *   *

Wake up, HoLLyWooD!!! Wake the fukc up!!!!!

17

After all the shit I had put myself through to get to this moment…there I was, with two willing and able, sexy ass females – straight muthafuKCin' *limp-biscuit!!!*

I'll go to the grave before I ever tell Lil Rico this story. With the way I talked down to him when he couldn't get it up with Shay and her friends…Lil Rico would never let me hear the end of this if he knew!!!

This is what they really mean when they say, *'you get caught with ya pants down'.* I mean, it's happened to the best of us. Niggaz are lying if they say they ain't never had that moment when they couldn't perform up to par. The experts say it can come from stress or anxiety; even drinking too much can keep you from getting hard. I think I even read somewhere that fatigue can be a trigger.

Blah, blah, blah, nigga! This is dat bullshit!

I CAN'T BELIEVE THIS SHIT IS HAPPENING.

Sure, I'd had a helluva weekend…a helluva journey up until this point. All day long I had this feeling of being overwhelmed, like I was doing too much. Mentally and emotionally…I was drained. It only made sense that my body was giving out on me – there was no *Sunny D* in my system, no ginseng in my blood. I hadn't had time to just sit down and plan any of this out; it was all over the place. And it ain't help that I couldn't stop thinking about KeLLy's ass all of a sudden.

But still…this wuttin' supposed to be happening; this shit is unacceptable in a ménage.

Yet, I'm a man of many xxxperiences, so even when I'm in new territory…part of me has been here before. This ain't the first time my dick done gone down. Whenever this happened before, I'd just go to the *smash-technique*.

What's the smash-technique, though, Rod???

Nigga, you know — the smash! Where you smash ya limp dick inside her with ya thumb and hump her like y'all clothes-burning — hoping it gets hard.

Plenty of men have resorted to this…and plenty of women have looked the other way in times of desperate measures.

There's only one major issue with using the smash-technique right now, though. The success rate of the smash is next to ZERO *in a condom* – you can almost forget about it. I mean…I could see if I already had the rubber on, then *maybe*. But ain't no way in hell I'll be able to put a condom on a *soft* dick…and *then* get my *smash* on.

And I can't hit Kourtney *without* one – that's against the ground rules Sashé and I agreed on. The situation called for some quick thinking…and like y'all know by now, it's *The Art* that guides me.

There's maybe 5 seconds that have passed in silence…and Kourtney was still bent over, playing with her pussy as she waited for me to give it to her. Sashé, knowing that I wuttin' gon' hit it raw, started crawling to the right of the bed toward my nightstand…going for my emergency stash of condoms.

Shit, Rod! The condom stash!

It's at this point I suddenly remembered that I had one missing, from when I fukced Cookie just hours ago. I reacted quickly…grabbing Shay by the ankles, and then reaching for her calf.

"I wuttin done making you cum Shay," I pulled her back towards me. "Hold on."

Shay was used to my aggression…and didn't resist. Within a split second she was bent back over in front of me, waiting for me to give her some more D.

But it just wuttin' happening. I was squeezing the life outta my dick and stroking furiously now…praying to the *cheat gawds* that neither of the girls called me out on my temporary impotence.

Even though they were both oblivious, Kourtney couldn't hide her frustration and collapsed to the mattress, furiously finger-banging herself. She was lying on her stomach now, grinding against the bed and looking Sashé in the eye as they flicked their tongues at each other. I tried my best to play it cool and started to rub Shay's pussy with two fingers from my right hand…still jacking my soft dick with my left.

No matter what I tried though, my dick just wouldn't get hard.

Shay was sloppy wet…and Kourtney's pussy juices were splashing as she started to smack her pussy lips with her hand. Even *this* couldn't get my **wooD** to come to life.

The girls still paid me little attention, even as I grabbed Shay by her waist to pull her an inch or two closer and stepped onto the bed with my left foot. Squeezing my semi-hard dick in the middle of my shaft…I watched as all the blood rushed to the head, swelling it up like an oversized mushroom. That was all I needed for the *smash-technique*.

So now I've got my left hand on Shay's cheek…and poking her pussy with my thumb. With a quick half thrust, I eased the tip inside her alongside my thumb. Her walls barely divided, quickly clamping back down on my head, before I could pull my thumb completely out.

"Ouch, baby!" Shay yelled. "Not so rough!!"

If only she knew…

See, here's where the *smash* gets tricky; I'm not home free just yet. The hardest part about getting ya smash on is keeping the limp dick in for the first few pumps without it sliding out. Sometimes you get lucky and can put dick in while sliding ya finger or thumb out…executing a true, even switch.

Tonight I wuttin' so lucky, and I stood as still as a statue for a couple of seconds…looking down at the tangled web I had weaved, shaking my head in disgrace. My thrusts (if you could even call 'em that) were weak and without force. Still though – my semi-erection was holding steady. If I could pull my thumb out, I might be fine.

Slowly…I released my right hand grip from my shaft and pushed in deeper. Shay's pussy had a firm hold on my head and I felt her muscles start pumping as she slammed her ass backwards again. She was anxious…and still sensitive from cummin' only moments ago. I can tell because she started *moaning* from my weak, barely-hard **wooD** – and soft dick wouldn't feel good to any chick unless she was in a serious horny rage. Judging by the sultry, seductive moans in the air – *horny* was an understatement.

Both Shay and Kourt were ready to get fukced…and not now, but *right now*. This shit was crazy.

I *was* finally starting to feel some sensations, though. Shay's pussy was gripping relentlessly – contracting on my near flaccid meat and right thumb as I held her still. If she moved too much more, I knew I would slip out. So, holding her in place with my left forearm – I pulled my other hand away from my shaft and outta her snatch.

OH SHIT – IT WORKED!!!

A smile started to form on my otherwise nervous face. I should finally be home-free now. Sashé felt me move my hand away and almost instantly started grinding back against me again…this time much slower. Perhaps she could tell I was having some trouble. Whatever the case was…it took little time for her to be in sync with me again, and my **wooD** grew bigger and stronger with each stroke.

As we started rocking the mattress, Kourtney curled her right leg up, still playing with herself. She then crawled up under Shay to start sucking her huge tits. She smacked and slurped as she sucked…making Shay grip even tighter with her pussy muscles.

Gotdammit, her pussy is so tight, bro!

The sensations were getting stronger. I could feel the hairs on the back of my neck standing up; goosebumps on my arms.

Kourtney had managed to crawl completely up under Shay, and had her legs spread out as they kissed…one hand still playing with herself.

Shay's pussy wrapped around my head tighter. I was almost hard enough to pull back and start stroking.

"Yeah, Daddy," Shay whispered, cheering me on.

Kourt followed suit, continuing with being Shay's "Hmmm…get that shit, girl."

Their voices sent chills up my spine…and a rush down to my loins. And then…*it happened.*

There are many feelings in the bedroom that can be considered bad. But there's no feeling worse than *cummin' before you're ready.* Except…*cummin' before you're completely HARD.*

The squirts and shots are more like spurts and drops…and whatever erection you had forming goes away sooner than instantly.

My heart skipped a beat, and I tried to hold my breath in hopes of holding back – but there was no use. Within a couple of seconds, my limp meat slid outta Sashé and flopped against my right thigh as I stepped back, panting hard.

"What's wrong, babe?" Shay cried out in frustration.

I knew there was no point in playing it off at this point, but pride is a muthafukca. So, instead of answering Shay and coming clean, I dropped to my knees and spread her cheeks wide…going in tongue first. Chicks tend to not ask too many questions with their pussy in ya mouth.

Her knees buckled and she fell on top of her best friend…who immediately wrapped her legs around Shay's waist and started swirling her hips. Their kitties were stacked on top of each other now. My hands still on Shay's ass…I leaned in closer, ran my tongue downwards toward her clit, and started sucking away. I could hear Kourtney playing in her pussy again…and I gave her a hand while I devoured Shay.

Kourtney started squirming and shaking, "Shit, I'm 'bout to cum!"

Before she could finish her announcement, my face was in *her* pussy…licking and sucking her fingers and lips. Almost immediately, Shay frantically scooted up towards the top of the bed and sat on Kourtney's face, screaming, "Oh my God…me, too!!!"

"Hmmmm…mmmmmm hmmmmm," Kourtney moaned and groaned loudly.

Shay's voice almost drowned Kourt's out, as she yelled even louder, "Yessss…oh hmmmmm. My…aaaaaaaargh…SHIT!!!"

Their screams were mixed with agony and pleasure…and even as Kourtney leaked all on my face and started shaking uncontrollably – I still felt like a loser. Even as Shay rolled over to the side and cursed at the heavens, I still felt like *I blew it.*

"Daddy, I never came so hard," Shay tried to catch her breath. Even as she said that…I felt like I hadn't accomplished anything worth talking about.

I never came so SOFT…

"Girl, my pussy still throbbing," Kourtney shook her head. "I can't even move."

"Me, too! I'm still shaking! Feel how fast my heart is beating!"

"Oh my God, girl – feel mines!"

"Oh my God!!!"

My head fell into the bed, feeling defeated and inadequate. I coulda went to sleep right then, right there on my knees. I just wanted to forget about this night. And honestly, at this point, I was ready to forget about *all* my threesome fantasies and put this bullshit about **ménages** behind me. Maybe I had finally bitten off more than I could chew.

"Did you cum, Daddy???" Shay looked over at me as I laid still, playing possum.

"Girl, dat nigga out for the count," Kourtney giggled.

"Awww, Daddy, I wanna watch you fukc her!" Shay whined like a brat.

"Bitch, he ain't used to all this chocolate," Kourtney teased.

"Girl, please – his ex was blacker than black like you!!! He loves dark girls!!! Right, baby??"

Damn, that's fukced up, brodie.

Bruh, just let it go. I don't even wanna think about it. We fukcin' blew it.

*　　　*　　　*　　　*　　　*

NYE 2007

It's almost time to start heading out. But a few moments ago, something strange came over me and I got lost in an unexplainable trance. So, I'm standing in the bathroom mirror now – reminiscing about my **ménages**...

"It's crazy how the tables can turn so fast," I mutter under my breath, slightly shaking my head as my memories start to wander into the not-so-distant past.

Before I get too deep in thought, Sashé yells from the bedroom on the other side of our apartment, "Babe have you seen my pink lip gloss?!?!?!"

Why would her lip gloss be in here??

I don't understand why she leaves shit in this bathroom anyway...that was the point of me letting her have the main bedroom one.

We've gotten a lot closer. But it still irks me when she leaves shit on this side of the apartment. This *'officially living together'* thing is a bitch at times.

"BA-BY!!! You can't hear me???"

And *still*...she can't be away from me for more than a few seconds before hysteria.

"Yea, babe," I answered her gently. "I don't see it in here."

"I don't know where else it could be!" she whined, stomping around the apartment. "Dang it!"

"Is that the only lip gloss you got?!?!"

"No," Shay replied, sounding like she was in the kitchen now. "But I like the glitter."

GLITTER???

Sashé is such a girly girl. And I know she just being particular cuz she wanna look a certain way tonight, but I really hate going out on New Year's Eve, anyway…so I'm getting even more irked at her femme energy right now. But I guess I love her for that type of shit in the end.

This journey though…

So much has happened since that night we met…so much has happened since that smash night with *Kourtney* a year and a half ago. We've become something different altogether – our vibe is on a space age level. I never thought Sashé would last this long, honestly. I damn sure never planned out for it. But then again, a lot of my sexcapades never have any forecasting attached to 'em. And let's be honest – that's exactly what this started off as – a sexcapade.

That's what they *all* start off as in *HoLLyWorld* …even with *KeLLy*.

Kells and I ain't seen each other since that last sexcapade we ended on. We've maybe spoken twice in the last 18 months. Sashé did one helluva job in the process of elimination with my former lovers…and KeLLy was main priority on her list. But I don't wanna get away from the point I need to make here. The point is – even though we had some drama in our closing moments…Kells and I ended on pretty much the same note we *started* on.

*It always starts with **sex**.*

And now, with Sashé, what started off as sex has completely turned into something else altogether.

Well, wait. I won't say *completely*. What we got is still *very much* sexually oriented. I guess a better way to explain it would be to say that after a crazy unexpected turn, my relationship with Shay became something much more *deeper*.

It's crazy how what starts off as sex can grow into a real relationship. But believe me when I put y'all on game – *most* relationships are like this with men. All it takes is the right set of circumstances when you're having fun. And after I met Shay, I was having *way* too much fun.

I was having so much fun that week we played with Kourtney that I couldn't even show up to perform for the big stage. I don't think I ever beat myself up over something like I did with that incident. I literally couldn't sleep for weeks after that shit. I started working out again on the regular...getting my body in tip-top shape. And when you training for sexcapades – the workout routine involves more than just running and lifting. For the first time in a long time...I was practicing *edging* again – trying to build up my stamina and take my lasting power to different plateaus.

Did it help me perform better? Naturally...of course. But it did nothing to calm the *beast* down. That was something that I was gon' have to finally learn how to tame on my own, using my own self-motivation and will power. My *limp-biscuit* night was all the motivation I ever needed though. I quickly realized that if I hadn't been so damn *'HoLLy'* leading up to that ménage...then I woulda been aight. I mean, it's not rocket science. But I had to fight with myself for the longest before I really came to grips about it.

I'm getting off track again here. But it's all related to what me and Shay have become, so I'll keep going. Try to keep up.

So, before I met Shay, I had never even considered a lifestyle where I wuttin' fukcing multiple chicks on the side regularly. In order to achieve that playboy life I had for so long...I had to become a master at *The Art of Cheating*. I mean...cuz ain't no chicks out there that's cool with their guy banging a bunch of other pussy, *right?*

Well...remember I said in the beginning and all throughout this story...things with Sashé were *different*. And I had to realize that this chick was serious about being okay with me fukcing other chicks...as long as she was involved. See...that's where I was getting the biggest mind-fukc of my life – that *'as long as she was involved'* bit. It was crazy enough that I found a chick that was cool with sharing...but even crazier that she wanted to participate.

All this new territory took some adjustment. Some *major* adjusting.

On average...at any given time, I kept about 4 or 5 chicks locally who I could call on for fun times. Some of 'em ain't give a fukc that I had a chick; some of them didn't need to know. But with the roster rules in the *Art*, I was used to having options and then having to choose which option to exercise for the night.

To transition from this lifestyle would be a challenge for any man...especially when he's knee deep in the habit. Hell – I'm not even talking about all the long-distance pussy I kept on deck; all the chicks I had constant cyber foreplay with to pass time at work or set up a future session. After that night with Kourtney, I realized I had serious issues when it came to the concept of being alone – and the word *'overcompensating'* was understating.

I mean, I had a chick who was into chicks, yet I was still tryna meet chicks online and still fukcing around with my old flames like Cookie and KeLLy. Still tryna bang strictly-dickly chicks who wuttin' down for the ménage. Just cuz it was new pussy. Just cuz it was what I was used to doing. But why couldn't I just fukcing stop?!?!

This was becoming more and more of an unanswered question the more that I asked myself over….and over….and over again.

Remembering the journey is crucial…these moments of staring in the mirror are necessary. Especially on nights like these.

It's always about the *sex*. In the beginning…and in the end…it's *always* about the sex.

During the relationship…it's the sex that leads to *The Art of Cheating*. Whether it's not enough sex or not the right *type* of sex – all cheating (or lack thereof) is sexually influenced.

Fukc a title. Whether it's wifey, BM, girlfriend, or side chick…the main bitch you fukcing *is* your main chick when it comes to *The Art*. The one you have sex with the *most* – *that's* yo main bitch.

Sashé had become that bitch.

That night was the last night I ever seen Kourtney. I never brought up a ménage again to Shay…and for a while it never came up. But Shay and I had some wild, animalistic sex and there was never any holding back between us. She wanted to do all the same shit I wanted to do. We watched porn and masturbated…*together*. She couldn't ignore her attraction to women. It turned her on to a different type of wetness and she badly yearned for a female's touch. My embarrassment from that night with Kourtney forced me to take a backseat. Whatever Sashé wanted to express or explore in that area…I told her I was good with it. I knew if I stayed patient and got my act together in the meantime…the opportunity could come back up. Next time…I would be prepared.

Shay wanted some pussy…and she wanted it bad. Her thing was, though, as attracted as she was to women –

she was still a shy girl at heart and couldn't break that
barrier with somebody she wuttin' familiar with. Her vibe
with Kourtney was a long time in the making; they had
years between them as friends. She wuttin' close to any
other chick like she was with Kourt, and Shay felt she had
to make a connection with any potential third before she
was ready to get down like she got down with Kourtney.

Torn and bursting with curiosity…she turned to me
for help. She started asking me all sorts of questions about
my sexcapades. She wanted to know the who, what, when,
and where…but most of all – the *how*. Sashé wanted to
know how I had so much sex and what I did to pull it off.
She already had her own testimony about how drawn *she*
was to me sexually…but she needed more. What do I say
to these chicks to turn them on? How do I learn a
female's body the way I learned hers? She knew it was
different for a guy but she ain't care. She needed to know
how it all happens for me.

I found myself telling her stories; *episodes* if you will.
Stories and episodes of my most devious acts that led to
ultimate sexual experiences in the end. It almost became
like a confessional for me, in a strange way.

We'd talk out all the steamy details…and then fukc
like porn stars. My pussy-chasing habits were fascinating
and erotic to Shay. In a crazy way, the shit made her want
me even more. And it made the sex between us *amazing*.
Just between the two of us it was *xxxtra orgasmiK*…and
Shay decided she wanted me involved with anything
sexual she participated in. And even though I wuttin'
pushing for the threesome like before…Shay wanted me
there whenever she finally did find another girl she was
comfortable enough to explore with, so it was bound to
be a ménage by default.

That shit made it easier for me to start fading out my
habit in spurts. And it took me a minute, but I calmed

all'at shit down…right at the right time. It made the night of my first *true* ménage both possible and nearly *impossible* at the same time.

There was yet and still a journey before that first one, though. Shay and I went on the hunt together. And I mean, I took this girl on the same hunt that I was on alone or with my niggaz before. This shit was unheard of. We met a lot of bitches along the way, but none of them seemed to be that *'one'*. She had to be the right *everything* for Shay – shape, size, even skin tone. We spent all year after that night in 2006 with Kourtney looking for a girl. The shit was almost a lost cause.

For the first time ever…I was actually almost *tired* of looking for new pussy. And when we finally found her – the one that was perfect for Shay – it was by *accident*. A perfect situation that was right under our fukcin' noses the whole time!!!!

But then *that* bitch eventually went and got a boyfriend and left me and Shay right back where we started.

So right now, me standing in this mirror, reflecting – it's my way of getting ready for the game. Shay's back on the hunt. And tonight…she has to look perfect. Of course she's fretting out about her lip gloss – Shay was a girlie girl.

Tonight we were going to a club called **Ménages** for a New Year's Eve party.

"Babe, what are you doing?" Shay asked anxiously. "Are you ready??" I can hear her heels on the floor as she walks across the apartment into my bathroom.

"Did you find ya lip gloss??"

"I did," she updated me, looking me up and down. "Hey. You look nice."

"I know," I replied smoothly. "You, too, lil baby."

"Did you look up the directions?"

"No, I tried to put *'Club Ménages'* in *MapQuest* and it ain't come up."

Shay's eyes got big and she started yelling, *"Baby!!!!!* It's called **Ménages KC!!!** And the address is on the *C4P* site!!!"

I chuckled and pulled her close to me, "Hey…calm down. I'm just playing. You are so slow."

"I'm just making sure," she whined. "Stop teasing me!"

"I know you wanna get there on time. I know how to get there, babe."

"Hmmmm…you smell good, too," she melted in my arms, changing the subject just that quick.

"Are you high, babe?"

"I am…but you smell good."

"Girl, are you ready to go?" I shook my head.

She started posing in the mirror, "*We* look ready to go."

We stand there for a few seconds, hugged up and watching each other in the mirror. Shay is definitely ready to step out, her cleavage is screaming for attention out of her silver glittery skirt, and she's got a damn matching crown on her head.

"So, wait," I raised my eyebrow. "What's the plan?"

"Same as always, boo. We go to have a good time, and if we find the right one, we bring her home."

"Really?" I wasn't expecting that answer. "We tryna take something home *tonight???*"

"Uhm, yeah," Shay gave me a confused look. "It's New Year's Eve!!!"

"Ok, but you said the same as always and we never just bring somebody home," I reminded my partner-in-crime.

"Ok…right. But it's New Year's," she reiterated. "And if it's the right one – why not? Babe, come on, the name of the club is *Ménages KC*. It's a *New Year's Eve* party, invite only, at a place we found on a *swinger's* site. You know what that means."

"I mean, I'm just making sure we on the same page," I explained. "And it's a New Year's Eve party…at a club. Like a *real* club. So, I'm just saying – it could be like any other night where we just trying to *meet* people. You not usually on the one-night-stan…"

"I know…I know," she cut me off. "And I'm with you, babe. I'm just saying…it's New Year's."

"I know it's New Year's," I rolled my eyes. "That's why we should just be kicking it with family n'shit, anyway."

Shay lowered her voice, "I know you don't wanna go out, babe."

"No…I'm cool. I'm not tripping."

"You not? Promise?"

"I'm not. I promise. I know you just wanna find a girl. I know you wanna party."

"And you know I wouldn't be out looking for somebody if *Kris* was still down, right?" she looked at me with puppy eyes.

"I know, babe," I smirked. "You high, babe."

"I am…so what?" she shot back. "Shut up! You are, too!"

"You can't *tell* I am, though."

"Take them shades off and I bet you can!" she waved me off playfully.

"You know I can't do that," I retorted calmly.

"Babe, lemme wear 'em," she whined again.

"No. You look sexy when you high."

"You're teasing me again," she pouted.

"No, for real, Shay," I was being serious. "You know you got them big eyes."

"See!!" she squealed.

"No," I grabbed her hand. "Babe, you look cute when they get low."

"I look cute all the time," she corrected me.

"You know what I'm saying."

"I do," she admitted with a big grin. "Babe, come on, it's after 10. Let's go."

"Girl, I'm waiting on *you,*" I stepped outta the bathroom and into the hallway. "Come on. I'm ready."

*　　*　　*　　*　　*

18

We're walking out to the car now, and I'm still in deep reflection, feeling on top of the world.

Ok, so it's **December '07**…and even though the ménage snafu was way back in the *Summer of '06*, no matter what, on nights like these…I always mentally go back to that moment.

I mean…it's when everything…*changed.*

That pivotal night mighta never even happened if KeLLy and I ain't fall out so bad on the way back from my aunt's funeral in 2005. Looking back on it now, it's easy to see how that became the window to this journey into ménages. It wuttin' the first time things got heated like that with me and Kells, but it was only two weeks after meeting Sashé.

She was bound to be my getaway.

I was on an exit mission from the moment we met, subconsciously trying to leave my entire past behind me. Hell…I didn't talk to my sister Ronnie for months after that funeral, and when we finally did reconnect at the end of the *Summer of '06*…I couldn't even remember what we really fought about before.

See, by ***Labor Day 2006*** – just a few months after my *smash-technique* night with Shay and Kourtney – my sister was being flashed on every Kansas City news segment damn near every *hour*...as the prime suspect in a gas station shooting.

I was vacationing in Cali when I first got the call, or should I say *slew* of calls. Everyone...I mean, damn near everyone I knew in KC had flooded me with calls that day...telling me what they saw on the news report. I ain't know *what* to think; Ronnie and I hadn't talked in damn near a year. Hell, I was talking to *all* of my hood folks less, since moving outta the city and into upscale Overland Park on the Kansas side.

Sashé had never met my sister, didn't even know I *had* a sister until that day. I was dreading even calling her to tell her that *that girl on the news* was my family. I remember being nervous as fukc when Shay answered the phone in her usual vibrant mood that day, unsure about how to tell her that our adventures may have to get put on chill so I could buckle down and handle business.

But Sashé understood *family was family* and surprisingly hopped on board, damn near immediately. Dealing with the police and media frenzy was a lot less stressful than it coulda been otherwise. Shay's bubbly, square attitude had rubbed off on me at the right time.

What's even more strange was the fact that her and Ronnie actually *got along*. Even though Sashé had never been around any of the type of shit she would see during those eight months my sister was on the run from the Feds...she fell into her new role as my main chick with flying colors, and ironically clicked with my folks when I needed support and unity in my circle now more than ever.

Without me going into too much detail here, it's important to note how my sister's situation made it nearly impossible for me to continue on with my *HoLLy BeLLigerent* ways when it came to cheating. Suddenly, I

had to be far more careful about who I could trust –
especially with bitches from the town. My habits, my way
of doing things had to be switched up. It was during that
time that I had new incentives *not to cheat*, and Shay being
who she was helped continue to still feed the **beast**
throughout it all.

She had a **beast** of her own at this point, with its own
cravings for taboo sexual fun. Her appetite for sex had
grown; the more I let her explore, the more she wanted to
experiment with. And the more she let me experiment
with her…the less I did anything behind Shay's back.

Things are different for us now, heading into the
New Year. Circumstances sealed our bond; the journey
has been a long and productive one.

Still though – even tonight, eight months after
Ronnie was *finally captured* and while she sat awaiting
trial…we gotta move a certain way. Ronnie had more
enemies out here besides the media and police, and Shay
now knew how to move in the shadows. The crowds we
now partied with respected having discretion with
identities.

But tonight would be our first time with *this*
particular bunch, a new swingers group Shay had found
online.

"Do they have hotel rooms available?" Shay
wondered. "Do you know, babe?"

"This ain't like the last one we went to. It's not even
at a hotel – that's what I been saying."

"I know it's not like the *last* one, I wasn't saying
that," she shut the car door, putting her seatbelt on. "Are
you sure you're okay, babe? You seem fussy."

Given the circumstances…I'd rather be at home tonight. That was obvious. I mean, we hadn't been to a swingers' function in a minute, and it was NYE. I was used to bringing in the New Year with family.

I put the key in the ignition, starting up the car, "I'm fine. I'm just saying…it's not at a hotel; it's at a *club*. So how much *'playing'* can they *really* be doing at the party? If you find somebody…we gon' have to bring her all the way back out here…to our place."

"How do you know they don't have rooms close?" she asked again.

"Because I know where the club is – I told you. It's the spot that used to be *Club 151*; they must've rented it out or some shit."

"I mean, it's a bunch of swingers partying at a club; I'm sure they probably have a hotel they usually go to afterwards. Even if they don't – "

"Even if they don't, what?" I cut her off aggressively. "You know how I feel about muhfukcaz knowing where we live. We ain't never had nobody we don't know at this spot!"

"I do know how you feel, babe," Shay said softly. "That's why I'm talking about hotels – duh!! Turn the heat, up babe!"

"It's warming up now. Here, gimme ya hands."

As I rubbed her hands to help warm her up, Sashé looked at me with those eyes, still innocent at first glance. The way she stared at me was the same after all this time, with sheer trust and admiration.

"Why you acting like that???" she almost sounded like me.

"Acting like what, babe?"

"Like I don't know how we move these days! You acting like I'm all clueless, Daddy."

"I know you not clueless...shut up," I shook my head. "You just never know who might be at these things. And you never know who knows who we are."

"Babe – you realize I've been around over two years now? I might be still learning...but I'm not so innocent anymore. I got your back."

"You help keep me on my toes, I'll give you that," I had to admit.

"So, trust me like I trust you so much. We've come a long way, Daddy. Relax. Loosen up. I just wanna have sexy fun with some sexy people like us!"

"Shit...I just hope it ain't a bunch of fat, old people," I turned my nose up at the thought.

"I'm pretty sure that it won't be," Shay replied confidently. "The girl I been chatting with from the site isn't old or fat – and she's part of the staff, I think."

"What girl? I thought you said this was the spot that couple you were partying with owned."

I can never keep up with all of our *friends'* in the lifestyle. These days Sashé does most of the chatting and connecting, as I've taken a back seat to the hunt.

"Couple??" she thought about what I said. "Ohhh you mean **Shima** and her boyfriend? No, babe. Well,

Shima's boyfriend, **Chris**, is like a promoter or something; he helps out with the events. But they don't *own* the club, that's another couple."

"Who? What couple owns the club, then?" I wanted to know. "I'm confused."

I was backing the car out now, looking over my shoulder in vain. The parking lot to our building was nearly empty...and traffic would probably be just as light by now.

"Turn your lights on, Daddy. I've never met the couple who owns the club, love. I only met Shima's boyfriend once, remember?"

Shima was the Asian chick who Sashé met off *MySpace* and befriended last summer during the hunt. She was bisexual and a sexy, little petite young tender – but she had ground rules with her boyfriend, Chris. They never *'played'* without each other.

Oh, the irony.

Since Shay only wanted to play with other females, and not involve any other men in our sexcapades, Shima was off-limits sexually. Still, the young couple had become good contacts for other folks in the sharing lifestyle. They were the ones who put Sashé on the swingers' website – *C4P.com*, a place where couples and singles could meet and get acquainted. Shay made us a *'couples'* profile on there a few months back and had finally convinced me to go to a live event.

"Right...ok. I'm with you," I nodded at her. "So, who is the girl you talking about? You said you were chatting with a chick on *C4P*."

"Oh...right," Shay sat up in her seat. "Daddy, she is sexy; you'd like her! She has a nice ass and she's kind of darker than me. She lives in Lee's Summit, but she works out here in OP I think. Anyway, I'm pretty sure she said she was going to be working here tonight. At the club."

"She a single? On C4P?!?!" I was intrigued. "Black chick??"

I hadn't been online chatting for a while; I let Sashé handle that now. I'm just burnt out – still agitated that we had to get back on the hunt, and the last time I was internet searching, I was up to no good. I'm cool on all'at now.

"Yes! She's single. And black," Shay's voice was filled with excitement. "But I met her on *Adult Friend Finder*; she's not on *C4P*, Daddy. You know it's not many sexy singles on there."

"Right, I know. Ok, I'm with you. But what she talking about? Sound like you already got something set up."

"No, I just know she's going, and she's nice looking. Shima says this is the place where the sexiest party; she's been trying to get us to come out forever, babe."

"Well yeah, but by the time you knew Shima was in at the club – we already had a playmate – remember?? We didn't need to be out on the prowl."

"Baaaabe," she cried out in her signature whiny voice.

I looked over at her as I changed lanes to hit the highway. She was pouring *New Amsterdam* gin into a big red cup that all seemed to come outta nowhere.

"What??" I pouted.

"You're still upset about Kris."

"Nah…I'm not upset; you know that. I'm just saying…that shit was all we – "

"I know…it was all good," she interrupted my rant. "You're right. Perfect situation."

"Perfect playmate," I added.

"But now she's got a man, Daddy."

"Fukc him."

"Babe," she whispered in a pleading tone.

"Ok…ok. I know," I let it go. "I'll stop."

"I'm sure there's another 'Kris-like' situation out there, Daddy. We just gotta find her."

"And so, off we go," I rolled my eyes again.

"Don't act like that."

She could feel the sarcasm in my voice, but I could feel her vibe and how we felt was mutual. Neither of us wanted to be on the hunt again after having so much fun with Kris – Shay's Russian friend from high school. They had reconnected last year, not long after that night with Kourtney.

Kris was a bad white bitch, with niiiiice perky tits and a curvy shape. Though her and Shay went back as far as high school…they had a much different relationship than her and Kourtney.

Sure, Kris was a witness and camerawoman to Sashé's freaky taboo side in that drunken night with

Kourtney that started it all...but that's where the freaky shit had stopped. As far as Kris knew after high school, Shay was only into guys. After my sister went on the run, Sashé shortened her circle, too, and didn't hang with her campus crew as much over the last year and some change. Kris became her 'new' partner in wild drunken partying, but Kris didn't do girls.

Or, so we thought.

On nights like these...it's hard not to reflect on my journey into ménages; hard not to go over all the fine details, the mishaps, the close calls, the frustrations.

All'at shit felt like it was worth it on the night it finally happened the way it should...the way I had always fantasized about for so long.

"Act like what? You know you feel the same way," I reminded Shay that my feelings had validity.

"Oh, I wouldn't mind fukcing Kris again. You're right."

"So why can't we???" I proposed.

"We're on our way to *Ménages*," Shay deflected, trying to ease my frustration. "To find something better."

"Babe, it's nothing like that first time, or the right one. Think about the few ménages we had besides Kris. Nobody compares."

"There hasn't been *that* many others."

"There's been enough," I pointed out.

"Not really," she disagreed. "We haven't really had many options, love."

"Cause you so picky!" I blamed Shay.

"I can't help it!" she blurted out. "It's different with girls; you know how I get."

"Right! But that's why the 'Kris' situation so hard to replace," I countered, going back to my original point. "Man, fukc that – gimme yo phone! Let's call her!"

"Babe, you're high. We're not turning around; we're almost there."

"I'm always high," I mumbled dismissively.

"And I tried to get her to come already," Shay continued. "She's out at some place with *Jeezy*."

"Her new dude," I shook my head in disgust. "See, what kind of lame ass name?"

"Be nice, Daddy."

I sighed, "Whatever. You know she's the perfect match."

"Baby – it almost didn't even happen!" she shot back. "All of that was by accident! Have you forgotten??"

"Are you serious right now?" I snapped. "You're drunk. Of course, I ain't forgot. I can tell the story like a movie."

"That *was* like a movie," Shay started reminiscing. "Crazy. I came so much."

"Me, too," I licked my lips.

"Maybe I *should* call her."

"You should!" I couldn't agree more.

Sashé started laughing as she leaned on my shoulder, "Daddy, stop it – I'm not! Listen...I promise tonight will be better, ok?"

How the fukc can she promise that?

Yeah man. I don't think she understands.

The first night with Kris was beyond epic.

Yeah, Sashé just a little tipsy right now and feeling confident about tonight. But let me paint this picture one more time to myself before we pull up to this party.

Every journey has a climax. And since we're bringing in a New Year anyway, it's only right to end our reflections with recapping the last year. Let's go back to that crazy summer night with Kris.

* * * * *

June 2007

Aight, tonight is my last time...I swear.

So, another thing I've learned in *The Art of Cheating* is how much luck plays a part in becoming a legend. As luck would have it, it's not easy finding a chick to bring into the bedroom when you got a lady that's down. At this point we've tried everything – and I'm about ready to just give all of this shit up.

Sex with Shay is almost enough to keep me at bay...and now that my sister is locked up and our hood is in the middle of this turf war – a nigga can't move around freely in a lot of the places I used to anyway.

Lately it's been more about *her* than satisfying my cravings for other pussy...but Sashé is so *particular!*

It seemed like most of the online chicks I suggested all had something going on that turned her off. They're either too chubby or not cute enough in the face. The ones who do fit Shay's standards are all too far away...and I don't even wanna begin to think about spending money to take our sexcapades on the road. It can't be that serious. At least for me, it's not. I think I'm just about over finding a perfect playmate online...and right now that's my safest route to search through with all this street drama popping off.

I mean, why can't Sashé just take over this searching thing anyway? I'm so sick of *Adult Friend Finder* – 90 percent of the freaks on there are couples and we ain't tryna kick it with couples; we want a single female. And the few singles that we've found local to the area are only looking to play with the *female half* of couples. It's just rare to find a female looking for a couple in this lifestyle.

I really fukced up with the first chick I met on *Adult Friend Finder* – **FoXXXyBiNaTure** – leading her to believe I was single. She was looking for a couple from that first night last spring, when I was so used to cheating. I didn't know how to just be upfront. She might've been perfect for Sashé's preference...but it was too much of a risk to bring them together. If FoXXXy and Shay got too close...they would end up talking about our relationship casually and they would casually find out I had lied in the beginning. I couldn't chance it...things were too on point with Shay now, it just wasn't worth it.

I knew I had to cut off my chatting with FoXXXy at some point. I had already cut off 99 percent of all the other side shit I had going on, and even though we hadn't met in the flesh, I still got on and instant messaged her on the side while I was searching for playmates for Shay. Usually when FoXXXy saw me online at *Adult Friend Finder*, she would hit me on *Yahoo Messenger* to talk some shit.

This particular, hot ass summer night didn't start off any other way.

FoXXXyBiNaTure: "Wassup stranger..."

Freaky816Playboy: "Lol wassup lil mama...how u been?"

FoXXXyBiNaTure: "Horny as usual. I see u on AFF lurking around again..."

Freaky816Playboy: "I see you. Look who's talking..."

FoXXXyBiNaTure: "Hey! Don't judge me! Lol!"

Freaky816Playboy: "Don't judge me! I'm just looking...like you..."

FoXXXyBiNaTure: "Right. But not looking for the same things..."

Freaky816Playboy: "Don't remind me..."

FoXXXyBiNaTure: "Lol! Don't sound so disappointed. You're not the only one not having any luck..."

Freaky816Playboy: "I'm bout ready to give up...it ain't no real freaks on there tryna meet up..."

FoXXXyBiNaTure: "You ain't tryna meet up boy! You scared anyway..."

Freaky816Playboy: "Scared? Girl shut up – that's you! You aint ready..."

FoXXXyBiNaTure: "What if I said I am though?"

See, I should stop right here. FoXXXy had been a tease for a little over a year now; she knew how to get me started. But anytime I tried to take it offline...she hesitated and said she wanted a couple. I just couldn't take the risk.

Freaky816Playboy: "I know this routine lol..."

FoXXXyBiNaTure: "LOLOL!!! No...for real Mr Playboy. You're not the only one ready to give up on what you thought you could find..."

Freaky816Playboy: "What does that mean???"

FoXXXyBiNaTure: "Scroll up. Ask me again how I've been..."

Freaky816Playboy: "Haha....hmmmm. So are you saying you wanna meet up? Just me...even though I'm single..."

FoXXXyBiNaTure: "Maybe. What you doing tonight?"

I hadn't quite put together a plan for tonight just yet. Sashé had been out with Kris all day doing what they do...and I knew she was coming home late. After graduating last month, Shay immediately told me she didn't wanna move back in with her parents....and that she wanted to move in with me. She had it all figured out, too. She had a little money coming in from her internet modeling, and though she couldn't really afford to put in on rent, she could take care of all the food and household expenses until she found a job in her field of study.

So far, it had worked...not only keeping me *fed* and *fukced*...but also keeping me *focused* on not cheating. It's always harder when you got in-house.

Still...this FoXXXy chick was like that one last fantasy...that one deal I couldn't close, and it was tempting.

Freaky816Playboy: "Hmmm...Idk...what should I be doing?"

FoXXXyBiNaTure: "You should be heading to Lee's Summit...to get this wet ass pussy..."

Freaky816Playboy: "Damn...like that?? Right now??"

FoXXXyBiNaTure: "You not coming for real..."

Freaky816Playboy: "Cuz you not being for real lol..."

FoXXXyBiNaTure: "No...I'm serious. Why not? I know you not a psycho at this point lol..."

Freaky816Playboy: "Lol...do you?"

FoXXXyBiNaTure: "We've chatted long enough. I have a good feeling you're not. Lol"

Freaky816Playboy: "Damn...you for real wanna meet?"

FoXXXyBiNaTure: "I do. Cum on before I change my mind..."

Freaky816Playboy: "Oh you rushing me?? I told you – I run this shit..."

FoXXXyBiNaTure: "Lol shut up boy. No I'm not rushing...I need a minute anyway."

Freaky816Playboy: "Mmmm hmmm. See you playing..."

FoXXXyBiNaTure: "No, I'm not baby...I really am horny. Just gimme like an hr to get home and get ready. Ok? I'm for real..."

Freaky816Playboy: "Ok...we'll see...

FoXXXyBiNaTure: "Ok. Stay logged on, I'll let you know when to head out."

Freaky816Playboy: "Aight, I'ma hop in the shower too."

With about six hours to spare before Shay came home...pulling this off and getting this last bit of cheating off my chest should be a cakewalk.

But I swear, though — tonight is my last time. I promise it is…

*   *   *   *   *

19

The **Summer of 2007** was indeed a hot one.

You woulda thought I learned my lesson by now, but yet here I am – on *Highway 435* again headed to *the Missouri side* for some new pussy. Having Sashé living at the spot didn't take much getting used to...we had spent the majority of last year together anyway. It's just this *other* new territory that was a struggle – this being faithful for the greater good shit. Sometimes I still get weak.

For the most part, like I said, lately I been good. Meeting up with FoXXXy tonight is risky and I can already feel the guilt sinking in. But then, at the same time, I ain't had no other pussy on the side in a minute and it's been even *longer* since I had some *new* pussy. You never really miss the chase...it's clear to see that now.

I was most comfortable when I was calling all the shots. It's frustrating when you spend all day hunting and ya eating partner don't approve of the catch. The shit had become more of a chore since that night with Kourtney. I don't even think Sashé understands how hard it's been for a nigga like me to start doing better. I mean I literally had to give her my *BlackPlanet* and *MySpace* passwords in hopes to keep me in check. That shit was unheard of. But what a helluva start.

I mean, but I had to keep *some* dignity – she couldn't have the *Yahoo* password. She never asked to see the instant messages, and even if she did –they all got deleted daily anyway. But still, it's the *principle.*

Yahoo was where I had learned how to be the sneakiest since the early days of technology and its effect on *The Art of Cheating.* A good portion of communication with Shay happened on *Yahoo* when KeLLy was too suspicious of my phone...and with all Shay had learned from me about cheating up until this point – it was a wonder she hadn't ever thought to check behind me there. Sashé knew I was a cheater; she knew I was good at it. She's been exposed to the stories now; she knows most of my tactics. Literally.

Could this be a setup??

If so, why is it that we can still get away with sneaking around on Yahoo?

Well – the more I thought about it, Sashé just trusted me, in a way that I'd never been trusted before. She knew the things that tempted me, and she did a helluva job to keep me focused on her. She didn't mind me being attracted to other chicks; she got turned on just knowing what turned *me* on.

She wanted me to fukc other chicks, she just wanted to be included. The thought process still fukcs me up; it's not what they teach little project boys about life and relationships. She even tells me how she believes in me...that she knows I don't have to sneak around, and I'll get better one day.

So maybe she *does* know it's been a process with me fading out cheating. It's crazy how even though we have yet to have a ménage...she's helping me through my sexual cravings. She's such a slut when we fukc, a real fukcin' primal animal.

But as much as she was in tune with what kept me satisfied...she ain't have a complete understanding of my *beast*...and how greedy *he* had become while in captivity for so many years.

I had gone months now playing by the rules. *Cookie* was even a thing of the past...after finding out that I skipped over her *again* and picked Sashé – Cookie fell for some guy she met on the internet and moved away to New York. My biggest temptation and main side chick was on the other side of the country now…and therefore no longer a threat.

All that was left were the randoms and long-distance freaks...and that was all a matter of controlling urges and habits. Over the last year...I've slowed it down tremendously. Other than the online sex chatting that Sashé knows about and sometimes participates in, I really don't communicate with other females at all these days. Most of the time that I do – I'm trying to make a connection for *Shay*. Shit really feels like a *chore*. It's more work than I thought it would be, and I deserve a treat for my efforts. FoXXXy will soon be that treat. She's the last of my 'side' chances.

I'm pulling in the driveway of my aunt Shirley's house when I get a text from Shay.

See? You done thought her ass up, nigga!

SASHÉ: "Hey Daddy. We're on our way home. Have you ate yet? Want food?"

This is what I was afraid of – that Shay may come home sooner than she said earlier. That's why I left not long after I showered – just to already be outta the house.

ME: "No babe, I'm in the city leaving the studio. Gonna stop at my aunt's for a minute, I can eat there."

SASHÉ: "Ok, well we'll probably be drunk by the time you get home. Be safe love."

ME: "Wait...who is 'we'?"

SASHÉ: "Me and Kris! She's gonna stay the night."

ME: "Oh. Ok."

There was really no reason for me to get excited here. Kris had stayed the night plenty of times...and we all know she don't do girls.

SASHÉ: "See you soon Daddy!"

So now I'm walking down into *Aunt Shirley's* basement...ready to get my buzz on. The cloud of smoke was as thick as I expected – my cousin *Benny* was posted up playing video games with one of his homeboys. There was this thick chick in the corner of the room and I wuttin' sure if I recognized her but she seemed to know who I was when I walked in.

Benny's face lit up, "Aye shit, there go HoLLyRod – fukc it, you ain't gotta roll up. My cuzzin got me!"

He seemed to be talking to the chick, and I ain't even need to clarify. This nigga always needed somebody to roll a blunt cause he couldn't twist up to save his kids' life. Damn shame. But I wuttin' tripping – that's what I was there for.

The rushed plan was to hang out Aunt Shirley's until FoXXXy was ready for me. It was just now **8:30pm**, about 45 minutes since we chatted, and my phone was fully charged. I was logged into *Yahoo* and had a pint of *Hennessy* to go with the fifth my cousins had on the table. Shit was 'bout to be lit.

I was finishing up my second glass of cognac when I got the instant message from FoXXXy.

FoXXXyBiNaTure: "U there??"

Freaky816Playboy: "Yup...waiting on you..."

FoXXXyBiNaTure: "Ok, I just got home. Getting in shower now."

Freaky816Playboy: "Ok cool, I'm on the MO side already...not far."

The Hennessy was kicking in a bit, and Benny was passing me another blunt. The best feeling in the world when you tipsy, got a bad bitch at the crib, and ain't cheated in a while was knowing that you 'bout to get away with creeping one more day. I had only seen a few pics of FoXXXy; this was '06-'07 and digital pics were still few and far in between. But the shots I had seen were nice. She was short and on the thicker side, with commanding hips. I was almost sure she ain't no kids, but again...my thoughts at this point were blurry. What I really started tripping off was how little I knew about her.

I've been chatting with this chick online for a solid year and I only know her by her screen name. In the real world, she's probably a whole other person...but when she's logged in, her *beast* comes out through cyberspace. The internet is really turning into a monster out here...it's giving folks a new way to express themselves and act on their desires. If I met this FoXXXy girl in the real world, I probably wouldn't be prepping to fukc her tonight, with so little personal information shared. I'll never not be amazed at little facts like that.

After drifting off in my thoughts for a minute, I noticed I was really feeling the GG and *Henny* now...and Cousin Benny had found his way to the other side of the room, in the chick's ear. She was being ironically quiet and low-key as fukc. I know I knew her from somewhere but there was never no telling with Benny. He's made her stand up and come closer to where I was sitting at the table in the middle of the basement. It's here that I noticed how *juicy* this chick's *ass* was...and I think to myself aloud, "Gotdamn, that ass is fat."

"Cuzz, you fukced up!" Benny started cackling.

Oh damn. I couldn't believe I said that shit in front of ole girl like that. It had been a while since I'd been belligerent to a bitch; I almost felt rusty. But I couldn't help myself. It had also been a while since I been around a juicy ass, and this chick Benny was preying on had a super fatty. I could feel my **wooD** responding to the scenery.

I need FoXXXy to hurry up and shoot that address.

I looked down at my phone and realized that I had two missed *'Hey'* messages from FoXXXy; she's been trying to hit me for the last half hour.

Wait — *half hour???*

Bro, it's been 30 minutes since we last IM'd???

FUKC!!!!

Ok, I'm most definitely getting rusty. My fingers were dashing now, trying to respond.

Freaky816Playboy: "Hey wassup, my bad. I put my phone down. U ready??"

Hopefully she's not far away from her computer.

Shit, hopefully she's on her phone and ready to get it popping like I am!

I rarely drove to the MO side unless I was headed to the studio or work. It'd be a shame to waste a trip this way. A real shame.

My phone started to light up and vibrate on the table, but I sat there stuck and Benny noticed before I did, "CUZZ! Snap outta it! Get yo phone!"

I jerked outta my trance and reached for my cell, "Damn, bro. I'm tripping."

"I know you ain't bout to drive all the way back to Kansas, nigga," Benny had a look of concern on his face.

"Nah, I'm good, cuzz. On errthang."

Benny handed me the blunt, "Yeah ok, nigga! We gon' see."

So, I'm trying to keep talking shit, but my eyes felt heavy. I opened up *Yahoo*...and there were no reply messages from FoXXXy yet.

Damn — what the fukc, yo! I coulda sworn I just got a message! I'm tripping.

Benny was all in the juicy-assed chick's ear...they both was whispering low n'shit. I could tell this nigga was gon' fukc. It was honestly pissing me off — as it always did when my younger folks were more on point with the action than myself.

This nigga don't know what to do with all'at. Get the fukc outta here.

I was still scrolling through my phone, trying to figure out where FoXXXy's messages disappeared to. At that moment, I get a pop-up text from *Sashé*.

SASHÉ: "Rodney??? Are you ignoring me???"

*Ignoring her? Wait…did I miss a text from **her?***

Then, before I could blink again...Shay was *calling* me.

Oh shit. I'm getting sloppy. Strangely, this feels like déjà vü.

"Hello?" I answered calmly. "Hey, boo."

"Baby! Why didn't you text me back?" she sounded fed up. "Where are you??"

"I just saw you texted me again; I didn't see the first one, baby," I was telling the truth.

"Are you ok?!? When are you coming home??" she inquired frantically.

"I'm good, babe; just hanging out with Benny. What did the text say?"

"It said you need to hurry up, we need you!"

"We??"

"Babe, I told you Kris was spending the night!" she exclaimed. "We need your help right about now."

"Y'all drunk."

Shay laughed, "We *definitely* are. When are you coming home?? We need you, Daddy."

"I'm drunk too, man," I confessed, trying hard to stay alert. "What do y'all need me to do? Is it going down??"

"Babe, I told you," she whispered into the phone. "She's not like that."

Right.

"Right. So, what's the emergency?"

"We just need an honest opinion and you're the most blunt person we know," she started to explain.

"Oh, so everything is *'we'* now??" I chuckled at the irony. "Kris knows me like you do??"

"Kristina knows you because *I* know you. She's my right hand."

"See, I thought *I* was ya right hand," I pretended to be offended.

"Or she's my left and you're my...hey, you know what I mean, Daddy!" she regathered herself. "When are you coming??"

What's the rush? They old enough to buy liquor now! I don't get it.

"What do y'all need, babe??"

"Don't laugh!!" she warned me.

"Babe, I'm not laffin'..."

"Ok," she paused momentarily. "So, we need you to check our moves out, tell us if we'd be good strippers."

"Say what?" I was confused as ever now. "Girl, what??"

"We wanna know if we have what it takes to be strippers! I think we can do it. Kris isn't so sure."

Ok....they've been drinking something serious. About as serious as myself. I'm fukced up right now...so buzzed that it's taking longer than usual for me to actually register what Shay is saying to me right now. She wants me to hurry home...to watch them...pretend to be strippers.

What the fukc?!? We ain't even got a pole...let alone a stage at the apartment!

It's always some ole crazy shit. I'm telling you!

"Shay...are you serious??" I straightened up, giving her my stern tone. I could hear Kris in the background slurring her words.

"Don lissen to her, Rod...she's wasted!"

"I am not!" she barked at Kris. "We are some *bad bitches* – all we have to do is get some rhythm! Daddy, can you just hurry home??"

"Ok, babe...I'll be there in a little bit."

"You leaving now?"

"No. Gimme a second," I lied, knowing damn well I needed way longer than that. "I'll be there. I promise, boo."

"Ok...ok," she calmed down, her voice soft again. "I'll talk to you soon, Daddy."

She hung up the phone screaming something at Kris. I couldn't make out what it was, but she sounded excited as hell.

The things that happen in my world...it's always a wild ride.

Now that I was off the phone, I noticed Benny had disappeared...and his homeboy was nowhere in sight. The juicy booty chick was still sitting off to the side, quiet as fukc.

"You good?" I asked her.

She mumbled a reply, but I'd already tuned her out as I suddenly remembered what I was supposed to doing. I need to hit FoXXXy before she changes her mind!

SHIT!

Snatching my phone up off the table again...I'm in *Yahoo Messenger* within the blink of an eye. There were several messages from FoXXXy...and she ain't sound too happy. She think I stood her up and got into some other shit.

Dammit, man! Fukcing around with them drunk muhfukcaz....

I could tell FoXXXy wanted to get down and was indeed serious about meeting up. She had left her address and phone number for me to call if I saw the message within the next 10 minutes. But her last message was sent *17 minutes* prior. Just my damn luck. Still...like the true cheater I was, I wuttin' 'bout to give up.

I done made it this far...put this much effort into shaking my main – I gotta seal the deal.

It's only right, nigga!

So now I'm dialing FoXXXy's line...hoping she was still waiting around for me. It was after **10pm** now.

Where the fukc did the time go?!?!? This is crazy.

And she ain't picking up, bro.

Fukc me, man!

I stood up quickly...trying to get myself together. Bad idea. As soon as I got to my feet...I was falling into the table just as quickly. Luckily, Benny caught me before I fell on my ass, "You cool to drive, cuzz??"

Where did my cousin come from that quick? Damn — the room is spinning.

"I'm good, bro," I lied again, this time to my first cousin. "I'm' bout to go to Lee's Summit. I'm straight."

"Nigga, what's in Lee's Summit? You might as well crash here...Momma ain't upstairs anyway. You know they ain't coming home 'til in the morning."

"What you 'bout to do, nigga? You leaving??"

"Nah, I'm chilling," he told me. "I'm saying you can sleep up in Momma's room, cuzz. You don't need to be driving."

Fukc all'at. This nigga bout to get some pussy and tryna get rid of me. I know what time it is. I'm on the same shit. Fukc that.

"Nah, fukc that. I'm 'bout to get outta here, bro."

Benny was no longer paying me any attention that quick and was all in ole girl's face again...looking like they 'bout to kiss. I walked over towards the couch on my right...where Benny was sitting earlier playing PlayStation with his homie.

But I have no idea *why*.

What was I walking toward the couch for? I just remember it looking like it was the softest place on earth at the moment...and I just needed to touch it for a split second with my back.

*　　　*　　　*　　　*　　　*

The vibrations from my phone woke me. Sashé was blowing me the fukc...*up*. But all *text messages*. And more notifications from *Yahoo*.

I read Shay's last message first.

SASHÉ: "Lolol ignore that Daddy. I'll see you soon."

And then FoXXXy's.

FOXXXY: "I can't lie, I still want you to cum over. The door is unlocked, just don't be too late papi...."

Then I looked at the time. It was **2:07am.** FoXXXy sent her message 23 minutes ago...about 10 minutes after Sashé's.

Hopping up without hesitation and grabbing my keys off the floor in front of me...I dashed up the stairs and out the front door, not even stopping to make sure I turned the lock on the knob. I've come way too far to turn back now.

*   *   *   *   *

20

The intoxication had worn off just enough for me to not see double-vision as I was driving...but I was still pretty lit. I was more motivated than ever though, flying like a mad man, dick hard as titanium. I'm sure the liquor had a lot to do with my stiffness...but my anxiousness was the biggest driving force. I was on a real mission...the mission of all missions – with what I was planning.

I just hope it's not too late.

Man, I can't believe I fukcing passed out on Aunt Shirley's couch like that, though! And my cousin Benny ain't shit for leaving me there – with all this action I had on deck tonight.

That nigga somewhere fukcing while he left us to spend the night in a coma sexless!

I can't let him outdo me, I taught him everything he knows.

Yeah, fukc all'at!!!

It still ain't no stronger feeling than the thought of some new pussy, my nigga.

And knowing you gon' get away with it. Let's go, Rod!

The door to the apartment is unlocked, as I expected. I walked in through the front room slowly. The lights were all out so I was trying real hard not to bump into anything. The light shining from underneath the bedroom door was all I needed to keep moving towards.

There's music playing from the computer, and one of the speakers had been moved to the bedroom from the desk. *'I Wanna F*ck You'* by *Snoop Dogg* and *Akon* is apparently on repeat – the last few seconds were playing as I walked in but when I got to the bedroom door, it started up again.

As I opened the door, she was standing in front of one of the wall mirrors on the left side of the bed – in pink thong panties and red stilettos, grabbing her bare titties and squeezing. I immediately kicked my shoes off and walked to the nightstand to turn the lamp on.

"Why you got the big light on?" I wondered.

Before she could answer – I darted back to the doorway and hit the light switch, dimming the room as I pulled my shirt over my head, "It's hot as fukc in here, too, man."

She started rocking to the music as she spoke, never taking her eyes off the mirror, "Just get naked like us, Daddy! Join the party!"

Kris was spread out across the bed on her back...ass naked. Her tan was amazing. She had the perfect shade of creamy skin...with detailed tan lines around her tits and crotch. I stared at her for a few seconds, as she watched Sashé dance, her head hanging off the bed slightly.

Kris was a dirty blonde, and her pussy had the sexiest landing strip I had ever seen. The fact that it was the *first* landing strip I had ever seen was way beside the point. The immediate thought that came to mind was how I was gon' try to stick my whole face in her pussy...a thought that caught me off guard. I'd never eaten a white girl's pussy before. I mean – yeah, I've hit a few white chicks but never got fully into it. Sucking pussy had never even crossed my mind. That landing strip was crucial.

Her 36D's looked perfect. I mean boob-job type perfect. But I'd asked her in the several times she'd lately been hanging around if they was real. The third time I'd inquired, Sashé just told me to grab 'em so I could have proof for myself. Tonight I was actually seeing them bare for the first time, and her small nipples were a darker pink than her huge areolas. Now I ain't know whether to stick my face in her pussy or her cleavage first.

But it was definitely going down. I was being fully controlled by the *beast* now, and he was out for blood. Three seconds had passed before I was in my boxer briefs, sitting on the edge of the bed where Sashé was dancing. Kris's head was now next to my left thigh.

"Oh, you ain't gotta tell me twice! What the hell y'all up in here doing still up? Y'all still drinking?"

"Hell, we sobered up now, Daddy. We just can't sleep," Shay updated me.

"Yeah – waiting on you, sir," Kris chimed in with her faint accent. "Took you long enough."

"I know!!" Shay cosigned her. "Some good you are, babe!"

Dammit! Ok...I admittedly was not prepared for them to no longer be drunk. This may make it a bit harder. But I can't be deterred. I gotta kill' em with the laidback charm now and keep paying attention to every detail. I got this.

"Oh, I can be of some good...*don't play,*" I arrogantly spoke up in my own defense. "So, wait – y'all not even drunk no more? Y'all just up dancing in mirrors n'shit?!?"

Shay spun around and kept gyrating, "Oh, I think we have it down now!"

"Shay's been in that mirror all dang night!" Kris shook her head.

"You been practicing, too, Kris? Lemme see what you got."

"I'm tired now," she whined. "I just wanna lay here."

"That bitch doesn't even need practice, Daddy! She's a natural!!" Shay kept moving to the music...touching herself as she danced. She looked sexy as fukc admiring herself...focused on her own groove. Though she wuttin' halfway as fluid as ole KeLLy was in her movement, Sashé had a seductive nature about herself that was hard to deny. Both Kris and I stared at her for a couple of moments in awe.

"You not that bad yoself, babe," I bit my lip.

"I keep telling her!" Kris agreed with me. "Maybe she'll listen to you, Rod."

"I always listen to Daddy."

Kris rolled over to her side, scooting closer to me, "See? There ya go."

Sashé spun around and faced us now, twirling her hips. She was humming along to the song...which was playing for a third time now. Her nipples were erect, and I could feel throbbing in my briefs. The scenery was starting to get to me.

If I ain't know no better, I would say that Shay could sense my arousal, too. Hell...it felt like I could sense hers. Without her saying a word, I could tell she was loving this moment. The vibe was just right, there was some real chemistry in the air between us.

The *three* of us.

None of this was planned. We had never even had the discussion. Sure, Shay and I had brought up Kris in our ménage talks, but because Kris wuttin' into girls...she was always out of the question. Tonight felt different, almost as if it was meant to happen this way all along.

It's kinda hard to explain, because on one end it felt like we was all just going with the flow...like we was just gon' let whatever happened happen. But, deep down inside – from the deepest, most passionate place in my loins to the most complex part of my mental senses – I felt like this was a situation that was entirely under my control. And maybe it always had been. Maybe it always had been about *me*, making the right moves at the right time...getting a real feel for things before I reacted, and choosing the right window of opportunity when that small split-second chance presented itself.

I was gonna fukc Kris, whether she was down to fukc Shay or not. And I knew Sashé would be ok with it. Somehow, I just knew trusting my inner **beast** on this one was the right move.

This **beast** of mine was the real issue. Learning how to *tame* him versus knowing when to *let him loose* was the challenge I was determined to overcome on that night. There was a thin line between *forcing* a situation versus *making a situation happen*. Tonight, I wouldn't make the same mistakes I made with Kourt – doing too much...not focused on the main course in front of me. There was no need to sneak around like I tried to do with Tasha...no logic in trying to get off without Shay being involved. If I was gon' force my hand in this, it had to all be out in the open.

And I was sure if I played my hand the right way with Kris, she would be willing to do whatever she said she wouldn't do before. Sexual chemistry in the air was a powerful aide…I learned that during this long journey. Even when you *not* just going with the flow, and you plotted the shit out in your mind…it's gotta still *feel* like it's just going with the flow. The possibilities have no limit…when everything just feels right. Especially when you're around pretty girls with wet temptations.

"So, I mean, what – y'all was having a competition?" I asked Kris.

"Well…not exactly," she giggled. "Your girl just has this crazy idea."

"It's not so crazy!" Shay quipped. She's dancing directly in front of me now.

"Oh, right. Y'all wanna be strippers now."

"I just think that we'd be good at it!" Shay was overly excited. "And make a lot of money!"

"Wait. Y'all serious for real," I finally realized this wasn't a joke. "I do like the money part, though."

"See?" Shay shot Kris a look. "Told you he wouldn't care if the money was worth it."

"I ain't say I didn't *care*," I corrected her. "I'm just saying…I like *that* part of it."

"I know what you mean, babe. Same page."

"I'm saying, though. Y'all not 'bout to do that *for real*. Stripping ain't no easy hustle."

"Daddy, you don't know any strippers!" Shay yelled, totally forgetting about Cookie being a dancer before she moved away to New York. "We can do this!"

"I am *not* dancing naked anywhere around *here!*" Kris declared. "Hell no!"

"We can find somewhere far but not too, too far...seriously! It's just dancing!" Shay kept trying to sell us on the possibilities. "And Daddy, we can use the extra money until I find a better gig."

There was some strategic planning necessary...but I had to admit it wuttin' a bad idea. The only problem was: none of us were in the right mind to do any strategic brainstorming tonight.

"Can we talk about this in the morning or something?" I suggested, ready to call it a night.

Shay didn't respond, but instead straddled me. I fell back onto the bed smoothly, holding her in place on top of me. She kissed the top of my head as her titties covered my face. She smelled like cocoa butter; her skin was soft as usual. I started to kiss on the top of her breasts, but she hopped up almost as soon as we fell on the bed...and started walking to the other side of the room.

What the hell?

I sat halfway up, resting on my elbows...watching her. My right hand brushed against Kris's stomach. Since she was lying with her head on the opposite end from mine, my hand was right below her tits as she laid on her side. I had the notion to reach for her, but then she sat up herself. First on all fours, with her ass tooted up for like a half second, and then on her knees, stretching her arms up in the air. Kris's titties sat so right. She caught me looking and gave my head a quick rub...smiling at me before getting up off the bed.

"Ok, but we *will* talk about this." Shay mumbled firmly. She walked over by the door, picking up the speaker off the floor and then headed to the computer in the other room...turning off the music.

Kris was standing in one of the other wall mirrors now, checking her frame out. She was curvy as fukc...specifically for a white girl. She wuttin' skin and bones at all. I mean, she ain't have the fattest ass – but neither did Shay. Her hips was a little wider than Shay's, though...so it made her ass look nicer. She was definitely the nicest white chick that had been naked in front of me before.

I was drooling with anticipation...but with my mouth closed. That way...no one knew how anxious I was. It was important to play it cool...and not move too fast.

I sat up straight now and shifted around so I could lay on the bed the right way – with my head on the pillows up top. Almost as soon as I laid down again, I sat back up to throw the covers back...pulling the sheets down to my calves and keeping my feet covered.

Sashé was back in the room now...with a lighter in hand, lighting candles in the windowsill. I reached over to turn the lamp off and the room was now dimmed to perfection. Kris was the first to get back in bed, crawling in from the bottom and laying on my right side. Shay soon followed suit and got in on the left. Nearly at the same time...their feet found their way under the covers touching mine. Sashé then laid her left leg on me, scooting closer as Kris got comfortable, laying her head on my chest.

All of this made my dick start stretching my boxer briefs.

We all laid quietly for about 90 seconds, a silence that couldn't quite be defined as awkward. Few words needed to be spoken here. Ironically enough...the words I chose to break the ice were not as smooth as one would think, "Man. *Ain't y'all horny?!?*"

Yeah...I know – the *beast* had no chill.

Kris was the first to speak, lifting her head up and looking at Sashé before locking eyes with me, "My thoughts exactly. Yessss."

"Ditto," Shay whispered seductively.

I mean...like I said before, sexual chemistry in the air is a powerful thing. I didn't need to be as smooth or calculated here. Nor did I need to say another word.

My right hand was already at the small of Kris's back where her tattoo was, and instead of continuing to rub – I started squeezing...bringing her closer into me. She put her right leg across mine, so now her and Shay's legs were touching as we all played footsies under the sheets at the bottom of the bed.

Shay started kissing my left shoulder blade as I turned in towards Kris. I bit my lip in anticipation, and Kris rose up with her tongue out. Before I could blink or prepare myself, she licked my front teeth resting on my bottom lip and started rubbing my stomach...then Shay's leg.

"You have perfect teeth," Kris lowered her eyes at me.

"Damn...like *that?*" my voice sounded deeper, almost as deep as the *beast's.*

Shay was circling her tongue in my left ear now, her body up against my back as she reached around to grab my dick through my underwear. Her nipples were rock hard...and my dick felt like it was gonna explode trying to expand. Kris stuck her tongue in my mouth and pulled me closer as we started to kiss. I felt Shay's grip get firmer, and she moaned...licking the side of my face as I kissed her friend with lust.

The kiss lasted a few seconds before Kris came up for air. Sashé then climbed on me even more, licking my lips with her own tongue...and I stuck mine out. Kris and Shay both started flickering their tongues on mine...and then they lunged at each other for a kiss. I fell back against the bed, and their heads were at my chest as they locked lips...the *both* of them now reaching into my boxer briefs. I put a hand on each of their ass cheeks and gripped firmly.

By the time I got adjusted...Shay started kissing my chest, and then down to my stomach...her left hand at the top of my dick, thumb rubbing the head. Kris started kissing me again, with her right hand at the base of my **wooD**. I started scooting up...trying to come out of my underwear.

We were all in sync...as they used their feet to kick my briefs down to my ankles, and we wiggled them away. So, now I'm sitting up slightly, and Shay's head is at my stomach with my left hand on top of it, massaging her scalp. Kris holds my dick up by the balls and Shay takes it in her mouth. Her initial sucking starts off in a pool of spit...as it almost immediately starts running down my shaft and onto Kris's hand.

Kris scoots up and takes her hand away, letting Shay go to work. Her hand still wet with Shay's mouth juice, Kris then puts her hand between her own legs...grinding against me as we kept kissing. She starts moaning and moving in rhythm with our tongue dance. Kris is a great kisser...and the way Shay is slurping on me right now...it's taking my kissing skills up a notch of their own.

I took my left hand away from guiding Shay's head for deep sucking...and started rubbing Kris's titties. Her nipples are small...but just the right size when hardened. This was also a sensitive spot for her, as she let out a series of heavy breaths and low hums. Sashé responded with some moans as my dick stiffened in her mouth, and Kris curled her leg up on me...rubbing her soft feet on my skin.

My breathing starts to quicken now, and I scoot to my left to make more room for Kris. She sits up on her knees now, tongue still in my mouth...and starts to rub on my chest and head while I squeeze her ass cheeks. Her ass is actually softer than Shay's, which shocks me.

"Hmmm...yes," Kris whimpers. "Grab it."

Shay is bent over at the foot of the bed, bobbing up and down on my wooD...not paying me or Kris much attention. Her ass up in the air catches my eye though...and I started to sit up to try to lean forward – all while keeping my dick in Shay's mouth and tongue still twisted with Kris's. Shay doesn't miss a beat...chasing my dick as I shift...putting a hand on my thigh for support while I sit up on my knees, humping her throat with instinct.

Kris has joined me and is up on her knees now. I've got my right hand aggressively palming her ass and my left hand gives Shay a nice hard slap on hers...making her suck my dick harder. Kris had her hands on my head now as we kissed. She's more aggressive with it at this point – slobbing me down and swirling her tongue in and out of my mouth, licking my face by default.

I looked down, and Sashé had her left arm around Kris's right leg...pulling us all in closer together. We all adjusted accordingly, and Kris spreads her legs to let Shay rub near her landing strip. The candlelit room was filled with our shadows on the walls. These were the types of moments that would be the best if captured on camera — this whole scene was orgasmic and erotic. Hidden cameras and posing for footage were old habits though. This was too spontaneous for that kind of shit. It's all in the moment now.

So, when I started drooling mid-kiss and pulled away to watch it run down to Kris's left titty...I did so without thinking. She moved back and held it up for me...eager for me to put my mouth on it. The sweat beads on my forehead got mixed in with the ones on her chest...and I started sucking and licking all over...grazing her nipples and areola with my *'perfect'* teeth. Kris started to shiver and I could see Shay fingering her now, while she kept sucking my **wooD**. My dick was sloppy wet...and spit was running down my leg and all over the bed.

Kris is really shaking now...and starts to collapse on the mattress, as if she can't take the way Shay is touching her. Shay doesn't let up, though. My dick pops out of her mouth with the same type of sound...and she crawls towards Kris...both hands running up her friend's legs. I mimicked the chase...falling down on my right side, mouth still on Kris's chest. My left hand was reaching down where Shay's face was...trying to feel that landing strip. I felt Shay start sucking on my fingers as I touched Kris's meaty clit, which was now dripping with a blend of creamy wetness and Shay's saliva.

Dammit. My dick is jumping.

"Oh my God," Kris whispers under her breath. "Y'all so nasty."

Neither Shay nor I responded with words...instead we both moaned in agreement as I started kissing on Kris's stomach...watching her squirm from Shay's clit kisses. Her legs were moving...stretching out and then bending her knees back and forth. Her toes are fukcing perfect...with her French tips curling up. I take one in my hand and start massaging as my head moves further down. Before I bump into Shay's head...she stops sucking on Kris to let me taste her friend's juices off her tongue. Shay was breathing hard, moaning with nearly every little move. I can tell she's turned on to the max, so I take my left hand and start touching Shay – from her huge breasts, down to her tight stomach, and then down to her tight pussy...which was leaking when I make contact.

"Hmmm...yea, Daddy."

She knows I love it. She keeps kissing me passionately, while rubbing on Kris's clit with her right thumb. I can taste the pussy on her lips, and we scoot in closer to kiss deeper. Our hands locked up for a split second as we both played with Kris...who was shaking her head back and forth at the top of the bed while being the willing victim of torturous pleasure. She's got her right hand on Shay's head...caressing it like she's in pure bliss – fukcing up Shay's otherwise perfect wrap.

"Uhhhhmmmmm....don't stop. Yes. Suck it," Kris was squirming even more now as Shay and I took our kissing to her pussy lips. We're both doing tongue flickers...taking turns to swap sucks on her clit hood. Kris had a meaty pussy...almost as meaty as Cookie's – but no pussy was meatier than Cookie's. At any rate, Kris has a nice, fat pussy...and the labia didn't hang outward. Her clit was much smaller than Shay's, however, which was a weird exchange cause Shay had a smaller pussy.

I wondered whose was tighter? Knowing I would soon find out, I got chills up my spine.

Sashé could feel the goosebumps as she rubbed on my back, and she started digging her nails in me...letting me know how much she knew how much I was enjoying this shit, "Mmmmm, baby...I know. She tastes good."

I slurped and smacked, "Mmmm hmmm."

Kris sat up so she could look down at us feasting. I glanced up and made eye contact; her eyes were lowered and she was biting her lip. The look on her face was priceless...sexy as ever. She then grabbed her ankles and spread her legs more...and her pussy started throbbing in our face. It's at this point that I noticed how tight it appeared to be. It looked like a finger would barely fit in.

Shit.

I started sucking her hood harder...touching her hole with my finger as Sashé tongue fukced her. The juices increased and started running down our faces. Shay starts licking my face...trying to taste every drop. She's so nasty; I love this shit.

"I can't believe y'all got me doing this," Kris moans in agony.

Shay tried talking with a mouthful of Russian pussy, "Hmmm...don't mmmm say y'all hmmmmm..."

"Oh, for real?" I mumbled. "It's like that??"

"Daddy, you make us bad."

I was jacking my dick now...hands wet with Kris's juices, "I didn't do anything!! I came home and y'all was naked in *my* bed!"

"He has a point there, Shay," Kris agreed with me.

"Oh, but I ain't made my point just yet."

"Well, damn," Kris sounded genuinely shocked. "What comes next?"

I sat up to get closer to her face...licking my lips, "You."

Kris threw her head back in pleasure at my reply...and Sashé kept licking away as I kissed Kris on her neck, near her ear. She reached for my head and pulled me in yet closer...pinching her nipples to the natural beat our heavy panting and slurping created. My dick was jumping outta control now near Shay's face...and she grabbed my balls…pulling them slightly and tracing 'em with her fingertips. It felt amazing...making my dick stand up taller.

No *smash-technique* was necessary tonight. Tonight I'm focused and fully loaded. I pulled away to my left, reaching for the nightstand. It's time to make this official.

Sashé started to move up towards Kris's face, licking and kissing her torso along the way. She was lying on her left side now...and as soon as they were at the same eye level, Kris reached for Shay's titties...and they started kissing like crazy. It's like they've been waiting years for this kiss...waiting on the right circumstances or man to influence their desires to explore. They shifted towards the middle of the bed as I slid a condom on...and now they were both reaching for each other's kitties – their fingers doing damn near the same rubbing motion as their lips smacked. The two of them were in total sync with few words being spoken. Everything is just on the same vibe.

It's crazy how it's all happening.

I'm moving back towards them, dick full and on hard now. I reached for Kris's left leg, and kind of ducked under and around it, positioning myself to where I could slap her clit with my dick.

"Damn!" Kris gasped. "It's so hard!"

Sashé is still kissing away as Kris looked down at it...trying to prepare for the initial penetration. Her hands were touching Shay all over now...the closer I got to giving her this dick — the hornier she became right before our eyes.

"You ready??" I asked her, my voice barely above a whisper.

Kris nodded her head, opening her mouth to let Shay's tongue in again. It's something so sexy about watching women kiss. I swear this is what set me off at this moment...it made my *beast* temporarily lose regard for others — and in the next split second, I'm shoving my entire dick in Kris. Not gently. Not slowly. She got the whole whammy in one forceful push.

"OH...shit!!" her eyes widened and she scooted away...causing Shay's tongue to end up on her shoulder and arm. There's no running from the *beast* anymore, though...so just as soon as she's scooting away and up the wall, I'm chasing her ass with this hard ass dick — making her take it balls deep again. Her pussy started gripping immediately...and she was shaking underneath me. Shay was playing with Kris's clit again — but this time tracing my dick as I started to get full strokes in.

"Give it to her, baby. Make her take it," Shay was scooting up with us and being the ultimate team player...holding Kris in place and whispering things in her ear that I couldn't make out.

I'm grabbing at Kris's tits when Shay suddenly hops up and straddles her body across Kris's — in front of me as I thrusted. Shay's back was to me...and she was scooting up to sit on Kris's face. Kris then put her hands on Shay's waist, bringing her in closer. I'm in total awe.

Kris done went from 'strictly-dickly' to the biggest bi-freak we've had in this journey. This is fukcing epic.

Shay held Kris's legs up, and I reached around to grab her left nipple – holding myself up with the right side of my body. I'm digging deep in Kris...and she's lifting up as much as she can to meet my strokes. I could hear her smacking away at Shay's pussy, but I couldn't get a good enough view while still giving her legendary *HoLLyStrokes*. Shay then put both her hands on the wall at the head of the bed in front of us...and started grinding on Kris's face. Their moans started getting super loud and more frequent.

Kris's moans almost sound like she's whining. I've heard that whine plenty of times...it's a mixture of agonizing pleasure with slight pain that hurts so good. I kind of had a similar feeling with how tight Kris's pussy lips were wrapping around my **wooD** – and how I had to seemingly reopen her up with each stroke. It's almost so tight that it hurts my dick – this same shit used to happen when I first started fukcing Shay...although I don't notice it as much anymore these days. The fact was, though, I was in the bed with two of the baddest bitches the Midwest had to offer....and each of 'em had pussy that was the next-best thing to virgin-tight.

How could I be so lucky?

I was mentally drifting...searching for the answer to a question I would likely never get when Sashé starting jerking...slapping the wall with her right hand, "Oh my GOSH...dammit, Kris!!"

Kris gave her a cocky moan of a response, "Mmmmm hmmm."

"She a natural, baby??" I asked for confirmation.

"Daddy, yes!!! I'm 'bout to...I'm...'bout to cum."

Kris tried to mumble a muffled '*Me too*' but you could barely hear her behind Shay's orgasmic screams. But I could feel it just the same...as her pussy started throbbing on my dick. She starts reaching up for me, slapping the bed with her other hand. I couldn't tell if she was trying to push me away or pull me closer or just touch me period to calm me down – but I ain't need to know the answer as much as I needed to get my nut off.

I planted my right hand on Kris's leg behind her kneecap and held her in place as Shay fell off to the side…exhausted from her release on Kris's chin.

Now I'm really going to work, as Kris grabs me on my cheeks with both hands...pulling me in, trying to get every inch without running. I'm slamming down into it...the dark skin of my **wooD** looked crazy dope against Kris's light ass complexion...and her pussy pink was showing as I pulled out and went back in.

Sashé, still trying to be as involved as much as possible, finds the strength to somehow sit up on her knees and face me...helping me hold Kris's legs up, "That's right, Daddy. Fukc her. Hmmm...oh man, that looks so sexy!"

She's staring at my dick disappearing inside of her friend...and it made her start playing with her tits again. She then lunged at me with her tongue out, and we started kissing once more – this time, drooling on Kris as we panted like dogs with it.

"Yesss...hmmmm...fukc me, Rod!" Kris yelled at me. "Give it to me!"

Between Sashé's wet kisses and Kris's wet grip on me...I couldn't take it anymore. My dick swelled up...and I started thrusting harder. Kris's head was banging up against the wall now...and Shay reached down to put her hand in the way. Kris kept taking it, her left hand on her clit...rubbing it fast as if she gon' cum *again*. Her pussy looked swollen when I glanced down...but I coulda been tripping and lost in the moment.

"Hmmmm...ohhhh fukc...I'm cummin!" I closed one eye, feeling sensations all over. "I'm fukcing...cummin!!"

"Let it out, Daddy! Hmmm...yes...mmm hmmm."

I'm following Shay's instructions to a tee…letting out each drop with more and more force...letting out all of my frustrations from the journey along the way. It felt so good to finally let off in some new pussy like this...and Kris was the perfect playmate for the occasion.

She looked defeated as I finally pulled out, and I could tell she hadn't been fukced like that in ages...if ever *at all*. She's gon' get fukced like that again and again…the longer she stays around me and Shay. I could definitely get used to this.

My dick was still throbbing when I pulled the condom off...and some of my semen splashed down on Kris's stomach. She immediately started rubbing it in with her pussy juices...with Sashé lending a helping hand.

Ok....so now I'm hard as steel again – just that quick.

"Bend over, Shay, baby. Lemme get it."

"Yes, Daddy!" She doesn't hesitate...and puts her ass up in the air in front of me...reaching back to spread her right cheek...and using her left hand to finger her pussy. Then...right before I put it in, she turned around and looked at me smiling, "You're not gonna be trying to *'smash'* it in, though – right?

I'ma just act like I ain't hear that.

Don't worry about it, I heard her ass!

Suddenly I'm focused on making sure Shay forgets about that limp-biscuit bullshit and never brings it up again. I slide my bare dick in slowly...making her tense up as I go deeper.

"Shit! Ok, ok, Daddy! Go slow."

"Nah, fukc that! You wanna talk shit? Come here...bring it back. Y'all getting fukced all night. Fukc the dumb shit."

They both giggled...but Shay's laughter ended awkwardly as she tried to handle the stiffness I filled her up with. Kris, still with the look of exhaustion on her face...grabbed Shay's right hand and squeezed it as tight as Shay was gripping the sheets with her other hand.

"Girl, that's why you call him *Daddy'*, huh???"

"Yes...hmmmmm...*yes!!!* Ok, Daddy...*ok!!!*"

*   *   *   *   *

We fukced that night 'til the sun came up, then had a few more rounds the next day. Kris ended up being a regular sleepover buddy, and we got to the point where it was just a normal thing for any of the three of us to be in the spot butt ass naked at any given time.

It became the perfect harmony for a few months. I thought it would last forever with the way we became regular sex buddies, and I literally stopped fukcing outside of our trio. Kris was an ideal prize for a journey well-traveled, but alas, all good things must come to an end.

*   *   *   *   *

NYE 2007

Like I said earlier...Kris now has a boyfriend of 5 weeks...and she's officially off-limits again.

Shay and I are at it again – back on the hunt. But this time, the both of us are more prepared for what comes next. We've learned so much since all this shit started. We got enough trial and error to know how these things go with other folks and that also gave us the chance to learn plenty about ourselves.

Nights like these, I always get deep in my thoughts and reflect. From the way KeLLy and I ended to how the Kris ménage fell in my lap...it's all relative. I had chased ménages for years, trying to live out my fantasies and bumped my head plenty of times along the way. On the actual night all the dots finally connected, I was one greedy choice away from not even making it home to take advantage.

What if I had ended up at FoXXXy's instead? The whole hypothetical thought was chilling. That was one of the first times in my history with *The Art of Cheating* that I had made such a *conscious* choice...and just decided to go home to my girl. This is always where I ended my reflection – on how making a choice in the *opposite* direction of cheating got me what I was trying so hard to get this whole time.

I never hit FoXXXy up again after that...even deleted her off my contact list on *Yahoo*. Though we never fukced (hell, I never even met her) she was the last of my skeletons. In a way, that's my biggest takeaway lesson from all of this.

Knowing when it's worth it to be open and honest with your partner goes a very long way.

"Come on, baby, are you ready??" Shay asked eagerly after we finally parked outside of *Ménages*.

"Yea...just trying to get my thoughts together," I stepped out the car and walked around to open her door.

She steps one foot out, and her legs are fukcing killing shit. I'm staring at her skin...waiting on her to get out the car completely. After a couple of seconds, I notice she's distracted and looking down in her phone.

"What's wrong, boo?"

She stepped her other foot out, still locked in her phone, "Oh nothing, love. I'm just trying to check this – "

"Come on, lil baby," I cut her off anxiously. "It's after 11 already! Let's get in here. Tryna check what?"

She finally steps out the car, pulling her long coat around her shoulders, bundling up, "I just got this text from FoXXXy. She was trying to see if we were still coming."

Wait...what? Who???

My heart skipped a beat, "You say what, babe? Who?"

Shay started scurrying up the sidewalk, walking ahead of me towards the club, "FoXXXy, babe! Come on, let's get to the door...it's cold!!!!"

Man hold up...what the fuke???

"Babe, who is FoXXXy??"

"Oh, I didn't tell you her *name*, Daddy!" Shay stopped in her tracks. "The single girl I met online I was telling you about earlier – the thick, black chick who's working here tonight? Her name is FoXXXy."

*   *   *   *   *

21

Club Ménages KC was a three- story, full-blown nightclub located near downtown Kansas City. The crazy thing was – the building used to be *Club 151* for a while, not long ago. I would frequent the spot with *Ricky Rhymes'* entourage when he did radio station sponsored events at *151* – which was quite often between **2004-2006**. By **New Year's Eve 2007**, the club had apparently been sold to new management.

The hunt is what led us here tonight. Our path was like many first-timers' in the lifestyle. You start off as a couple looking to add another female to spice up your relationship. Back in those days, there wuttin' a lot of open female bisexuality everywhere you looked. Most women who were into other women were discreet about it, as was the case with Sashé. Not only would her family likely not approve...she had her own future to think about if her true sexual appetite ever was exposed.

So, we had to learn to be careful in how we moved. Not even close family knew how we got down. And since we were keeping it so hush-hush, that meant that nearly all of the potential third parties we met back then were essentially *strangers*.

Before long, we found ourselves in the swinger circuit, where we learned the ins-and-outs of the 'lifestyle'. There were rules. Rules that we had to *establish* and rules we had to *abide by*, to get close to what we were ultimately looking for.

C4P.com had become a virtual lifestyle tool for us in 2007, and we chatted with a bunch of folks online, getting to know the ropes. There were lots of bi chicks out there in the cyberworld...but very few that were looking to get with a *couple*. The couples in the scene were looking for other couples more than anything. But Sashé wuttin' gon' have sex with another man; she was in it for the *women*. Certain couples wanted a straight male to double team the wife – but Shay wuttin' having that either. If I played, she played, and vice-versa – period.

Which brings me to another necessary flashback: the first **C4P** event that Shay and I attended *prior* to this NYE party.

*　　　*　　　*　　　*　　　*

April 2007

There was a meet and greet at a hotel back in the spring...a couple of months before hooking up with Kris. The event was in the hotel's basement hall...and there were *'play on site'* after-parties in select guest rooms.

The scenery was wack as fukc – and it was a BYOB, beer cooler type of crowd. But there was this one chick, a Hispanic slim bitch who we vibed with most of the night.

Let's call her *Mami*.

Mami was with a crowd of folks at the basement party but was technically there as a *single*. So, we kicked it for a little while, had drinks and laughs with her crew. Shay and I were newbies with this being our first event like this. Most of the rest of the crowd knew each other from previous events.

None of them really attracted us sexually, but they were some cool people to hang with, so it was just kind of whatever. Mami was fukcable, though...and so when she invited us up to one of the after-sets in a private room – I left it up to Shay as far as if it was a go. Shay ended up being down; she had made a rare connection with the chick while we kicked it in the basement.

So, when we get upstairs to the room...there's a big ass *orgy* going on. I mean, there's people fukcing on the queen beds, and there's a bunch of other folks just sitting around and chilling. Watching. There were maybe 20 or 30 people in the double-queen-bed room and this was a situation that neither me nor Shay had ever been around.

After a minute, we noticed that Mami was hugged up with one of the black dudes from the basement party earlier. They seemed to have known each other most of the night, but again – Mami told us she was there as a single, so we didn't think much of them caked up at the after-party upstairs. Well anyway...me and Shay were over in our own corner, and Mami eventually made her way to us, and it kicked off.

Mami strips me down naked and starts sucking me off as Shay undresses her. She had great mouth – and my shit was standing up and ready to cum within a few minutes. Mami senses it and reaches down for her jeans, looking for a condom as her and Shay shared a brief kiss. I strapped up, and Mami bends over so I can start banging it out. Shay was getting super turned on.

Now remember – we're in our own little corner while a room full of fukcing is going on. This is a first time for us – the environment, the idea in general. You never really think about this type of shit until you get in the situation but whether you're into group sex, threesomes, or whatever – it's hard not to be highly aroused in a room full of sexual activity. Shay had mentioned the rush she felt during the spring break orgy last year, but the two of us were now finally in that moment for the first time together. It's almost an unexplainable type of feeling – but I can tell you it's strong as fukc.

I say all'at to say *this* – as strong as that arousal is and can be – all it ever takes is one split second of being uncomfortable to snap you outta it.

So as Mami is bent over and taking these backshots – she's helping Shay get undressed, hands down in her panties. Without warning...this older black guy walks up to Shay's right side and starts rubbing on her now bare shoulders. Before I can blink – Shay turns around abruptly and stops dude, putting her hand on his chest...pushing him away.

Mami stands up, my dick falls out and goes limp within a split second, and now I'm in dude's face telling him to fall back. This is when I noticed it was the *same* cat that was hugged up with Mami when we first walked in the after-party. Mami is talking to Shay, explaining that this is her ex and they still play together often. Shay is listening but getting dressed...and not saying a word. Dude is in my way, apologizing...and now I'm suddenly uneasy and paranoid about the whole ordeal, so I tell him to back up so I can put my clothes on. Four minutes later, we were out the building and on our way home.

*　　*　　*　　*　　*

We kept our profiles on the *C4P* site, but that was the last time we ever planned to go to an actual event with multiple people and all'at *extra* shit. Shay then met this Asian chick, Shima, off *MySpace* and even though Shima had a boyfriend and came as a couple package – Shay still liked to hang out and go to regular clubs with her. No sex ever went down, and she had only met the boyfriend,

Chris, once or twice at clubs out partying. Chris was a promoter of some sort.

Well, anyway, Shima just became a cool buddy for Shay – a bisexual chick who she could be herself around. I never hung with them or any of the few friends Shay had connected with during this hunt. I wasn't interested in new friends – I was only down for the *sex* part of it. I had too much going on with getting ready for my sister's court case and other family shit on the side. So, because the lifestyle was my escape away from more serious realities – I didn't need the extra shit that came along with it.

Come to find out, Shima and Chris were also on the **C4P** site and part of an exclusive subgroup within **C4P**. Shima started telling Shay about how the admins of this subgroup had their own *nightclub* for people trying to meet others in the lifestyle. Her boyfriend Chris was one of the promoters and knew the club owners pretty well. Well, like I said before, our last experience had us both hesitant to go to another public event.

Shima was an exotic looking, bad ass Asian bitch who only partied with upscale crowds. She tells us that we should accept her invite to join the swingers subgroup on **C4P** so we could have access to the **Ménages KC** nightclub parties. Shima promised that the *subgroup* crowd was a completely different bunch than the one we experienced before. It was immediately tempting from the jump.

First off, the group was a private, *invite-only* group – and they never had events open to the general public. The general public couldn't afford to be a part of this group if they wanted to, if I'm being honest. They had an annual membership fee of $250 per couple and $350 for singles – which got you into their events for *regular admission fees*, like $15 per couple and $30 for singles. Single females had certain exceptions. For instance, they could join *or* be invited as a third party to a couple and pay super discounted rates to attend events.

To become a member, you went through a screening process that required you to be of a certain 'quality' as far as sexiness and cleanliness. Once approved, the group admins then (and only then) allowed you to come to their events. It was your choice whether to pay the one-time annual fee or pay the admission fee for non-paid members at the door of each event. This was definitely a more upscale, elite type of crowd; doctors, attorneys, business owners with the money to play the way they preferred to play.

Two of the group admins were also in the nightclub industry – and owned some club space all over the country. In early 2007, they came across what used to be *Club 151* in Kansas City and decided to renovate it for their private swinger group events. Their goal was to create a Vegas-like, erotic environment for upscale professionals in the lifestyle to meet and have a good time. The group had grown now that they had a nice place to party at, and since their events weren't open to the general public – they could party how they wanted to, whenever they wanted to.

So anyway, even with all this intel and backstory, Shay and I had *still* been skeptical about getting out or joining this private, upscale group officially. But then we saw an ad for the **New Year's Eve** party on the **C4P** website, and the post had links for an official website for **Ménages KC** – with pics and images. The shit looked so dope, so decked out – it seemed unreal. When they set out to make this shit feel and look like some shit out of a movie – from the pictures, that's exactly what it was. That's what finally broke us down...*seeing* that shit via the C4P social site we were already a part of. Even this early in the era, the power of social media's influence was strong as fuck.

So, we agreed to check out the NYE event...and started the subgroup screening process at the beginning of December, shortly after Kris became off-limits. I won't get into the process here...but in the end, we were accepted and given the choice to pay the annual fee or attend our first party and pay the *non-paid member fee* at the door. The NYE party was $100 per couple for non-paid members. Seemed reasonable for an upscale NYE event...so we decided to check it out.

The thing was though – we still didn't really know what to expect. The goal was to potentially meet the right female who was down to play with a couple, one who was on Shay's level. *Ménages* seemed like the perfect place to find that one, but still – we had little clue what to really expect.

At least we would know *some* of the people at *this* event. Shima and Chris were familiar faces, and we had chatted with a few members recently – mainly the group admins during the member approval process. So, getting ready for this event tonight...I had found myself in this deep train of recollection – remembering the journey so I would be focused and ready for whatever the night might bring.

*   *   *   *   *

NYE 2007

There we were – seconds before we finally walked in **Ménages KC** for the first time...and Sashé was telling me that some bitch I almost cheated on her with was 'bout to be *upstairs*.

Now I'm nervous and leery about this shit all over again. It's like I'm right back where I started.

We gotta buckle down, bro.

Real talk. I can't let this night end fukced up, no matter what.

"Babe, wait up. I feel like I'm forgetting something," I thought about going back to the car, just to buy some time.

"Daddy, come on! You have everything, I'm sure. I'm ready to party!!"

Fukc!

Let's just get up in here, brodie. We here now.

When we got to the sidewalk leading to the door, I started tripping off how they had the shit set up just like a *regular* club. There's bouncers and police security at the door checking ID's. Once they confirm you're over 21, they then check to see if your name is on the exclusive member list. You don't even get in the first set of doors if they weren't expecting you.

So they pat us down, we get past the security checkpoint, and then get escorted to coat check. Here, they check your ID again, make sure you're on the list, and then collect any money owed. I paid the $100 and we checked our coats with the older redbone chick working the post. She's actually fine – which throws me off initially. Now I'm wondering if the *staff* goes through the subgroup member screening process.

"Babe...it's so nice in here!" Sashé was in heaven.

She wasn't exaggerating. Walking from the coat check area to the main bar, I was in a familiar place...but the club looked much different from the way it was set up during those hip-hop nights and concerts in *151* days.

First off – the light scheme was way more sexy than before. They had the shit laid out with black light, really giving it this crazy neon effect everywhere you looked. *151* only had *some* areas with black light, but these folks at **Ménages** had gone all out. There were mirrors all over...and the whole bar was lit up. I wanna say it was *flashing*. They had flat screen tv's above the main bar and they all had pornographic images on them.

The three bartenders I first noticed were in lingerie – fishnets and panties, ass hanging out. Two Black chicks, one Latin girl – and they all looked no older than 25. That threw me even more off – most of the folks in the lifestyle we met were much *older*. I think to myself, maybe the staff isn't really part of the 'group' – but they're just dressed for the occasion. I mean, it is New Year's Eve.

I ordered Shay a *Long Island Iced Tea* and a *Corona* for myself. The plan was for me to not get *too* fukced up. With me being the driver and male half, I've gotta stay alert and pace myself. Sitting at the bar waiting on our drinks – we noticed they had a kitchen area to the side taking full orders. The Latina bartender tells us that we missed the free food they had out earlier, but we can order from the kitchen until 1:30am.

"I'm not hungry right now, baby," Shay tells me. "Can we go look around and check it all out?"

"Yeah, babe, soon as she come with these drinks," I'm high as a space shuttle right now and my thoughts were racing as I peeped the scene.

There's a white couple sitting down at the other end of the bar, talking to two black chicks. One of the black girls appears to be a bartender or waitress – she has on the fishnet with the panties outfit. The couple looks like they are no older than 40. They were on the slim side of the weight scale, too – *another* shocker. Most of the folks at the hotel event were heavier, if not older than air.

The black chicks both looked fukcable from a distance. The one in regular clothes was short and healthy. She almost looked familiar, but I knew it wuttin' FoXXXy. I couldn't make out her face, but her tits were huuuuge. They looked like they was gon' rip her skirt apart. Observing this was when I noticed that she wuttin' exactly dressed 'regular' after all. This wuttin' a skirt I would see in a regular club – this was some shit outta a sex store, not meant to stay on long.

The bartender comes back with our drinks and she winks at Shay as she hands them over, "Enjoy your night, sexy. Thanks."

"Thank you, gorgeous!" Shay responded with a big grin. "I plan to!"

Women flirting was still weird to me. Times have really changed from when I grew up.

"Well, have some fun for me! I'm not off 'til 2!" the bartender tells Shay. "My damn feet already hurting."

"Awwww girl, I know what you mean. You want me to have my Daddy give you a foot rub when you get off??"

The Latina bartender looked at me and smiled, "I definitely wouldn't mind. But my boyfriend might."

Shay giggled, "Oh, well, never mind – we don't wanna get you in trouble!"

The bartender kept her eyes on me, still checking me out, "All trouble ain't bad trouble!" She licked her lips and looked away. "Whew! Nah, lemme take care of my customers before I start something! Come back and see me before y'all leave, though."

Damn.

The Art of Cheating is real, nigga.

Shay and I took this as our cue to start our tour of the place. She had never been to *Club 151*, so for her this was *all* completely new. For myself it was more of a remix, but the scenery and setup still had me beyond impressed.

The building was already a good facility to begin with. But now that it was strictly for swinger events, some of the features had been upgraded. The sound system was much better, and as we walked through one of the short halls to the main dance floor, we got to see even more special lighting effects. There were a few folks dancing on the floor to the 80s music – and they were grinding like they were ready to start fukcing. They were barely dressed – the guys were all shirtless and the chicks were in skimpy teddies with straps. Although there was no way they could have come out in this freezing weather like that, I started to feel like maybe Shay and I were a little overdressed.

Damn, bro, maybe we shoulda brought a change of clothes to party in.

We were looking like movie stars. I was in full blown 'HoLLy' mode – complete with button down, jeans, and shades. Shay's skirt stopped just below her crotch, but she still had on some shit she would wear to a regular spot and it was nothing like the lingerie we was seeing on some of the other girls.

The east end of the dance floor still had the stage area famous for concerts back in the day, but now they had a *stripper pole* installed. This area used to be packed back in *151* days with club twerkers showing out. But now there was just one white chick on stage…working that pole like it was more than a hobby. She had on a long, fitted dress when we first walked into the area. She came out of that muhfukca within seconds and started spinning around the pole in her underwear. Instinctively, I looked around for security, thinking this chick was 'bout to get thrown out. But no one even *shrugged* at her getting undressed – they just let her do her thing.

To the right of the stage was what used to be the VIP area...with tables and booths that spread the length of the club in a roped-off section. On the opposite end was a door to a patio area with another bar. The section was still there in a similar setup...but the tables now looked like they were glowing. Now it felt like some *real* VIP shit – sparkling bottles, candles, and flowers. I never seen shit like this at *151*. New territory...for me and Shay both.

"So, how do we get upstairs?" Shay screamed in my ear over the music, "Looks like there got tables up there, too."

"If it's still like it used to be, it should be some stairs over there before you get back to that main bar," I pointed to the left across the dance floor.

"Well, can we see if we can find a table upstairs? So we can see the whole dance floor?"

I took her by the hand, "Come on, boo. I got it."

We started walking from the stage and VIP area, crossing the dance floor and moving through the crowd. There was way more folks here than we expected, but then again, we ain't really know what to expect. From the way Shay was smiling, she was just as happy as I was to finally be around a more upscale group – and it didn't hurt that we hadn't seen any uglies yet.

We get halfway across the floor when the DJ changes the song to *'Sensual Seduction'* by *Snoop Dogg*. This stopped Shay and I dead in our tracks. Even though we preferred the explicit version *(Sexual Eruption)*, we listened to this song repeatedly whenever we kicked it and vibed together. It was always like an instant mood changer and the timing here seemed like something outta a movie.

Shay turned to face me and we started doing our thing. She's twisting her body, swirling side to side in front of me as I grooved with a cool ass two-step. The GG was really kicking in now, and I could tell Shay was feeling her iced tea. She's biting her lip at me, something she only does when she wants to fukc. The way she looks in this short ass skirt, I wouldn't mind taking her off in a corner somewhere. Knowing I couldn't do that is what made this moment beautiful. Our dancing was a silent expression of what we were both feeling...an exchange of signals that our audience may pick up on, but only us two truly knew how deep the message behind this moment really was.

The way the beat builds up is so perfect. Our strength was built upon seduction...and how we expressed it the way we did was hard to come by. We both knew this. It's as easy for anyone else to see as we groove.

Sashé started singing along, "I'm gonna take my tiiiiime..."

And I chimed in, "She gon' get hers before I..."

"I'm gonna take it slooooow ooo ooo oooooooh," Shay was feeling it.

"I'm not gonna rush the stroooke...so she can get a..."

We moved closer and started grinding, really getting into it. Shay's come a long way the last few months on this dancing thing. Practice makes perfect, and her and Kris's new stripping hustle was paying off in multiple ways. Our shared rhythm right now was just flawless.

But what was really on my mind as I started to spin her around and show out a little – was what to do if or when we run into this *FoXXXy* chick. I've gotta get ready for this shit...it could all blow up in my face here tonight.

The odds of it being the same chick I was 'online creeping' with were both slim and large at the same time. And if she's here, the likelihood that we run into her is super high. I don't know how the hell I ain't realize Shay had been chatting with some chick with the same name *anyway*.

It's like – since I stopped cheating n'shit, I pay less attention to what Shay is on! I'm missing details I woulda picked up on otherwise.

Did she say this chick lived in Lee's Summit in the car??

I don't know, bro. But I'm almost sure my FoXXXy lives in Lee's Summit – that's why I was parlaying at my aunt's that night we was supposed to hook-up. Awwww...fukc, bro!!!

That's when it hit me. That night I fukcing passed out. That night FoXXXy left the door open for me and I decided to go home instead. Chances are she was mad about that shit!!!

You know bitches hold on to shit like that!!! Hell, for all I know — she coulda been talking to Shay since then!!!

Yeah, but it's been like half a year, bro.

And that's more than enough time to be on some plotting shit!

Ok, but still. The chances of Shay being in on it are next to zero — come on, dawg.

Nah, that ain't something I'm even remotely worried about right now. Shay woulda been said something to me.

But this FoXXXy bitch? Man...wuttin' no telling how she felt about me shaking her that night, and the thought of her and Shay ever getting casually close was what I was always afraid of. The truth about me being part of a couple was something FoXXXy wuttin' never supposed to find out.

I gotta be quick on my toes...much quicker than the way I'm gliding across this floor right now with the now infamous Sashé.

Just relax, bro. If this is the same FoXXXy chick, we can use the fact that we never met up to our advantage.

Yeah, she might not even recognize me, or it could all be a coincidence.

Or — you can always play the 'mistaking me for somebody else' card.

Nah, cuz that bitch seen my pictures, bro. If she HoLLyDigital like me, she 'fukc around and know where they saved at.

Yeah, that's right. That might not fly, after all, bro.

Shit, man! I gotta figure this shit out, dawg.

So, when the song ends, I finally lead Shay up the stairway to the second floor. I still know my way around the club well. I had many cheating episodes that featured this building during my heydays with KeLLy. This used to be me and Tre's spot, and whenever the radio station was in on events, I was part of Ricky Rhymes' entourage. We even talked about me performing here, before I ever got serious about the music. Shit used to get real live in this muhfukca. It felt crazy to be walking through the spot now – in a completely different era...a completely different mindset.

The second floor was open with a full view of the stage and dance floor. The tables and booth couches were set up like the VIP on the first floor. There was a VIP section up here, too, but we could choose wherever we wanted to sit.

There were less people on this floor. The bar was empty except for an old couple sitting on the stools. From a distance, they had to be in their sixties, though the lady half appeared to be shaped fairly well. Either that, or the old bitch had a boob job.

Shay and I chose a table opposite of the VIP, and we could pretty much see everything at this point. By now I'm really high as fukc, and I got my 'HoLLy Shades' on so my view of things are a little darker to begin with. But as I'm looking down on the first-floor VIP, I swear I see this guy on the couch getting domed up.

Damn, I know I ain't tripping.

There's a bunch of people still out on the dance floor and the downstairs VIP looked way more crowded than initially. So, I'm thinking:

Man, ain't no way they don't see this chick bent over on the couch. She bobbing her head to the music on this nigga's dick in front of everybody.

I reached over the table to grab Shay's attention, and she reached back almost simultaneously, "Babe, do you see that man getting head?!?!?!"

"Man!! That's what I'm saying!!! This shit is crazy!"

"Do they think nobody can see them??" Shay was in total shock.

"Man, fukc nah!" I yelled out. "They know errbody can see that shit. They like 'fukc it' – it's New Year's."

Shay laughed, "Is that how you wanna bring the New Year in, Daddy???"

"Shiiiiiit...not if it's gon' get us put out!! Fukc that – they gotta know the club owners or something! Shit...they 'fukc around and *be* the club owners to be on that type shit!"

"I don't know, babe! You see anybody else getting it on?"

I put my shades on the table and started to do a quick scan with Shay, looking around for other belligerent acts of lewdness. She points out the girl on stage with her ass out. A few others had joined her – but they was still in dey skimpy clothes. Then I spot a couple across from us in the middle of a serious make-out session, but I ain't see no *dicks* out getting sucked.

The two of us shared a brief laugh as we sipped on our drinks, overall still in culture shock. This was a wild bunch regardless, and I still couldn't believe we were in a place like this...enjoying the moment on some worry-free shit. I could never have been here with KeLLy; she wouldn't have been caught dead in this club. If Cookie was here with us right now, *she* wouldn't believe it was real, as square and naive as her ass was. Sashé had grown to somehow just 'fit' me...we were true partners in crime at this point. Literally.

"Man, this shit is craaaazy, yo," I shook my head at the couple downstairs. "They gon' put them out, I promise!"

"Like you said, babe," Shay tried to reason. "Maybe those are the owners."

"I guess," I took another sip of my *Corona*. "What time is it, boo? Is it almost midnight yet?"

She pulled her phone out of her small handbag, "It's 11:40 now. Almost."

"We need some more drinks! They ain't got no champagne??"

"I don't know, babe! This is my first time here, too!" she reminded me excitedly.

"Wassup with Shima and Chris? Are they here? She ain't texted you?? I don't recognize none of these people from the site!"

"Well, you know some of these people probably not even on *C4P*," she pointed out. "I think they advertised this event to the public cause it's New Year's."

"Oh, right...right," I nodded. "But shit, some of them gotta be new members like us, right?"

"I guess. My phone isn't getting service in here, babe; I can't see if I'm getting texts from Shima."

The music seemed to slow down when she said that. If she wuttin' getting service, there was a slight chance we could miss that FoXXXy chick all together. I crossed my toes for good luck down in my *Kenneth Cole* shoes, hoping that was indeed the case. I just wanted this night to go smoothly...and being in completely new territory was already a challenge in itself.

It was hard to prepare for whatever came next; wuttin' no telling what we might come across with each passing second. I was nervous as fukc...but with all the times I had been nervous in this long journey, I had definitely learned how to hide it.

Never let 'em see you sweat.

"Well, we need some damn champagne or something!" I glanced around, looking for the bar. "It's almost 2008!"

"I know!!!" Shay agreed. "Oh wait, here comes the bartender, babe."

"Good! See? They right on time around this muhfukca! I love this place already!"

The bar was to my right, towards the stairs and west end of the club. Shay was sitting on my left side, across from me at the table but we wuttin' facing each other. It's like we was sitting side by side with the table in between us, so we could see the whole scene. So, I'm leaning in to talk to her over the music, and even though the bar was to my right – for a split second, it was actually *behind* me so I ain't see the bartender approaching us.

Shay's face lights up as she looks past me to greet her, "Hey!! I thought that was you!"

I spun my chair around slightly to my right and seen her walking past me and around the table to Shay's side. Shay gets up and they share a hug. The only thing I could see was her fat ass cheeks, hanging out of the boy shorts. Her legs were thick and defined in the fishnets and she had on open-toe heels. She's about a half inch taller than Shay, and her hair was in a bob cut. I ain't see her face until the hug ended and they both turned around to face me.

It's *her*. I've seen enough pictures to recognize FoXXXy's round brown face; she looks exactly as I remembered her.

"Soooo...this is my boo! Boyfriend, babe – whatever we call it these days! I just mostly call him *Daddy!*"

FoXXXy laughed, "Girl...you wasn't lying – he is cuuuuute! So, should I call him *Daddy* too? Just kidding! Nice to meet you, finally. I've heard so much." She stared me up and down with a smirk before leaning in for a hug.

Play it cool, Rod. Maybe she don't recognize you.

Ain't no way she don't, though. Fukc!

Just let it play out.

Ok, ok. Stay cool.

FoXXXy smelled lovely...like some sort of vanilla mist. She hugged me tight – super tight. Her leg brushed against my dick in my jeans...and as she pulls away, she nudged it with her thigh, smiling at me with bad intentions. I almost forgot about staying focused as that tempted the *beast*.

I licked my lips instinctively as she leaned against Shay in the chair. Then Shay scooted over so FoXXXy could scoot in.

"See Daddy, I told you you'd like her! She's a sexy bitch, right?"

I tried not to stare, "That she is."

"No, really...what should I call him?" FoXXXy kept smiling. "Mr. Playboy???"

My heart skips...

"He's most definitely a playboy!" Shay exclaimed. "Clearly!"

FoXXXy echoed her, full of slick wit, "Clearly..."

Don't flinch, nigga...

"No, but he goes by *Rod*," Sashé tells her.

I shot a mean look at my girlfriend. She know better.

"Oh, I mean...wait," Shay immediately tried to correct herself, realizing what she'd done.

"Girl, it's okay," FoXXXy cut her off, putting her hand on Shay's leg. "I know how we get about our 'governments' around here. Ok, well, my real name is *Tiffany* if that makes you feel any better, papi."

"It's cool. I ain't tripping," I remained calm, smirking. "Can we get some drinks, though? Bring the New Year in right?"

"I got y'all. What you want, girl?"

"I'll take another one of these," Shay motioned to her glass. "Wait – what is this again, babe?"

"Long Island."

"Got it," FoXXXy winked. "And another *Corona* for you?"

"Yeah, but I need a double shot of *Henny*, too."

"Grown man, huh?" she lowered her eyes.

"No question."

FoXXXy smirked, "We'll see."

She walked away quickly, but with a strut that made my knees weak. Shay must've felt me start to lose my balance because no sooner than my knee buckled...I felt her behind me, embracing me tightly. The kiss on the back of my neck sent chills down my spine.

And that's when it hit me.

The power in what we shared was centered around our openness. If FoXXXy ended up being on some plotting shit...I could always just *admit* to her being an online chick I was *'sex chatting'* with on the side. I could even tell Shay that we talked about meeting up...and since we never actually *did* – Shay gon' easily look at it like I was just *being me* online. The night we were supposed to 'meet up' I was having ménages with Shay and Kris – I ain't even need no alibi. If it came down to it – I could just tell Shay most of the truth...and she won't hold on to it or let it break us.

Things with Sashé are different like that. She'd helped me nourish my cravings; I'd helped her become herself. What happened with FoXXXy ain't even shit to trip on...especially because what happened is that *nothing ever happened.*

The Art of Cheating is a complex game...but once you've mastered it, it's always in you.

I turned around and hugged Shay tightly. Her cleavage was in my chest and I caught myself staring as we stood still.

I wanna touch her all over right now.

"Babe," Shay called out to me softly.

"Yeah?"

"You forgot to tell her we need champagne…"

"Damn!" I snapped my finger. "Ok…I'll go get some."

"No, don't leave me," she gripped my arm.

"I'll be right back. Chill," I walked her around to her side of the table and pulled out the seat. As I turned around to catch FoXXXy, the older couple from the bar had walked up on us.

I'm caught off guard, and almost bumped into the wife. She put her hand on my chest as I grasped her left arm, preventing the collision. Her heavier-set husband was on the opposite side, and gently put his hand in her lower back, helping her stay balanced.

"Oh, excuse me," I apologized quickly. "Didn't see you coming."

Stepping towards me, the full-bearded, round-shaped man replied calmly, with his hand extended, "No, excuse *us*. We did kind of creep over unannounced."

His grip was firm, like a businessman. His style of dress was smooth – all black suit, top button open on his grey collared shirt, cufflinks beaming. His watch caught my eye, though. The diamonds seemed to match his wife's ankle bracelet; them muhfukcaz was sparkling something way too serious.

"*George Copeland*," he smiled at me. "This is the lovely Mrs. Copeland."

Before I could speak, the wife hugged me like she missed me...and before she gave me a peck on the cheek, she said, "You can call me *Carol*, honey."

"Nice to meet you," I responded politely. "I'm Rod...this is Shay."

"Yes we know; we met earlier," Carol told us. "We're *LifestyleCouple69*, your group admins."

George took Sashé by the hand and greeted it with a kiss while Carol waited to get touchy-feely.

"Ohhh...right...okay!" I nodded my head, glancing at Shay. "Right on, right on."

"Yeah, well we saw you guys made it – wanted to thank you for coming out and partying with us!" George explained. "Welcome to **Ménages!"**

"Yes, thanks for having us," Shay was gleaming. "This place is gorgeous!"

"Oh, dear – the pleasure is all ours!" Carol gave Shay a kiss on the cheek. "You two are the beauties!"

"Well, you look like you're having a good time so far," George observed. "Mind if we join you for a bit?"

"Oh, not at all! Sure," I motioned for them to have a seat. "Yeah, we just getting a feel for everything. It's uhm...*different.*"

George and I started to pull out seats for the ladies, almost at the same time. Carol pushed hers away and took Sashé's hands as she started rocking to the music, telling her husband, "Oh, honey, I don't wanna sit down now, it's almost the New Year! Let's dance!"

George chuckled, "Well, there you have it! That's the Mrs. for ya – she's a dancing soul at heart!"

I licked my lips at Carol, "Well, that's a beautiful thing."

Shay's eyes widened with joy, "Oh, I love to dance! Me, too!!"

The ladies started grooving together as George and I made conversation. Carol didn't look close to his age...and I could only conclude that she's older than me in the face. She was in tip-top shape otherwise – and I'm not ruling out plastic surgery, but I mean, damn – this old lady had some appeal to herself. She moved far better than any older white woman I had seen in my time, and her body was amazing. This old lucky bastard was a lucky one indeed.

Turns out, they *were* the club owners and group founders – in the lifestyle together going on 30 years. They had traveled all over the country, lived in various cities with larger swinger networks, and had some good times with good people. George was in real estate, and investing was more of a side thing. **Club Ménages KC** was something they had started this past year, and they were excited to see it growing in their hometown of Kansas City.

FoXXXy comes back with our drinks, and George sends her back to the bar for a bottle of *Rosé*. She scurries off again without a word.

"We appreciate the invite," I told George humbly.

"And you guys are the type of couples we wanna see at *Ménages*," he continued. "Only the hottest; the most sexiest crowd! We've been together 30 years – we can spot a good vibe when we see one."

Carol was rubbing Shay down as they danced next to us, "And great dancers! Did you ask him yet, honey?"

George smiled at me and leaned in, "The Mrs. really liked the way you moved down on the floor. She wants to get a dance with you before the night is up. Of course, if your lady wouldn't mind?"

"Just one dance, sweetie," Carol told Shay. "I promise not to eat him alive!"

"Oh, I don't mind! Go for it!" Sashé replied before looking to me for approval. "Babe?"

"No doubt, I can dig it," I grinned. "You got that coming."

The DJ hopped on the mic to start the countdown, and I coulda sworn it was the radio station jockey *KC Swift*, but shit was moving too fast for me to be sure. FoXXXy came back with glasses and a bottle on ice, just in time, and George started pouring us all a glass, even his half-naked bartender. Sashé comes to stand by my side, glowing with excitement as we all toast to the New Year.

After all the hugs and kisses, the Copelands dash off to the dance floor...but not without me promising to catch up with them before we called it a night.

"The night is always young", they said as they pranced off, telling FoXXXy to take good care of us.

"You know I will," FoXXXy blew George a kiss.

"Oh, I know it, baby," George responded smoothly. "Happy New Year!"

Shay rubbed my leg under the table, "Well, they were nice!"

"They're good people," FoXXXy agreed. "But they definitely like y'all."

I bobbed my head to the loud music, "That's wassup."

FoXXXy sat one leg on my lap, "I can't blame them either."

My dick started growing in my jeans, and Shay's hand brushed against it. She smiled at me from the other side of the table, with the same devilish grin I see when I look in the mirror.

"You having fun, Daddy?"

"I am," I confirmed. "You good?"

"Fabulous," she took another sip of champagne.

I found myself subconsciously grabbing on FoXXXy's ass, "So, what you doing when you get off?"

"I'm wondering the same question," she bit her lip.

"You working 'til the club closes?" Shay wondered.

"Yeah. All night."

Sashé stood up and walked around to the other side of the table. She wasted no time in rubbing her hands on both me and FoXXXy, "Well, that sucks!!!"

"It is what it is," FoXXXy shrugged. "Have y'all been upstairs yet?"

"Upstairs?" Shay looked at me curiously.

"Oh, they got the third floor open?" I glanced at FoXXXy. "I ain't never been on that floor."

"Oh, y'all gotta check it out," our freaky bartender's eyes lit up. "Come on."

"What's upstairs?" Shay anxiously wanted to know.

"Come on, girl! You'll see!" FoXXXy stood up, leading the way. "Grab y'all drinks. Come on!"

*   *   *   *   *

It's dark. Almost pitch-black dark...but they had these shelves along the walls with candles lit all over. The room was just one big open space, with long leather couches on the walls...circling the room. There were three larger sectional couches in the middle of the floor, in case you wanted a center view of the action. Or better yet — maybe it was in case you wanted to *be* the *central focus* of the action.

Either way, the third floor was full of action. This shit is where it was live.

FoXXXy had escorted us to the middle of the room, and we were sitting on a couch to ourselves on the wall. It was so dark when we first came up, that I thought I still had my *HoLLy's* on, and then realized I had left them downstairs on the table with our champagne. It took a second for both our eyes to adjust to the darkness, though, and it wuttin' until we sat down that Shay and I realized exactly what the third floor was.

We had to scoot to the right on our couch, to see around the couches in the middle of the floor. Directly across from us on the other side of the room, this white dude leaning up against the wall had his pants down to his ankles. His hand was firmly planted on this chick's head, as she was on her knees sucking away. She was ass-naked, spreading her ass cheeks and fingering herself.

As our jaws dropped at that — two short chicks stumbled across our view, and the white one pushed the short black chick onto the sectional floor couch. The black chick starts pulling her skirt up, and the white girl immediately drops down and starts sucking away, as the black chick wuttin' wearing underwear. Almost immediately as she tosses her head back in delight, she pulls the top end of her skirt down, and her huge tits come free.

This was the *open playroom*. This room was the length and size of the building...so we couldn't see every corner just sitting down where we were. But everywhere we looked, there was *fukcing* going on.

Sounds of slurping and moaning filled the air, and you could barely hear the club music downstairs. There were mirrors on some of the walls, and I now noticed a candlelit fountain in the middle of the sectional floor couches. This was a room and space meant for fukcing...and even though it was all out in the open, it still had a private effect to it. There was plenty of space to not feel crowded or uncomfortable. In fact, there were couples and singles sitting at some of the couches not being sexual at all. Just in the laid-back environment vibing as we were...drinks in hand, watching.

"Daddy," Shay whispered, in total disbelief.

"I know," I shook my head at the scene. "I see...I see."

There was so much going on, you didn't know where to turn. On the floor, a few feet to our left, this black guy had a chick with a fat, dark ass bent over. She had her face in between this other chick's legs, who was laying on her back...sucking a dick while she jacked off another. On the couches to our right, past the stairway leading back down to the club – there was a couple fukcing missionary, with the female's legs up on his shoulders...and he was giving her long, deep, slow strokes. Another chick sat next to them, playing with herself as she watched. The whole environment felt sexy; it was hard not to be aroused.

I sat back and put my arms up on the couch, *Henny* in right hand. Shay kicked her shoes off and curled up under me...slowly so I didn't spill my drink. To my left, FoXXXy got comfortable and laid her head on my lap...but propped up so she could see the action. She still had her champagne glass and sat it on the floor in front of us, easily within reach. Shay followed suit and propped up on the other side of my lap...and now their faces were close enough to hear each other's whispers.

"I've never seen anything like this," Shay drooled in amazement.

"Girl, that's what I was like my first time! They get wild around here," FoXXXy explained. "CEO's n'shit — these people got money, too...I'm telling you."

"I can believe it," Shay replied softly.

My left hand was palming FoXXXy's soft ass now...and she was squirming with each touch. Shay started to undo my belt, licking her lips at my bulge.

"So, this is how you get down, huh?" I whispered to FoXXXy.

"Nah, I never participated up here; I just like to watch. I been trying to find a couple that's down for a minute...you know that."

"I do???" I smiled, raising my eyebrow.

FoXXXy licked her full lips, "Yeah, you should know."

Before I could think of a witty reply, Shay stuck her tongue out and helped FoXXXy lick her lips. They scooted up closer towards each other in my lap, FoXXXy putting her ass up in the air. My dick was so hard now it hurt.

Still, I laid back and played it cool...sipping my drink nonchalantly, as if this wuttin' the first time I had two beautiful women kissing in my lap, in the middle of the club. All that was missing was a fat ass blunt to puff on...and I hadn't brought any GG in the club. Not that I *would* have tonight, though.

Yeah, sure I had sparked a few times in *151* in VIP with Ricky – but this wasn't *151* type of partying. And not Ricky, or any of my Nupe family – or even my childhood homies or blood family for that matter – had seen me in *this* fantasy of a reality. I had to act like I'd been here before. Because deep down inside...it's where I knew I'd always *belonged.*

I leaned down and sat my empty cup on the floor, eager to reach under Shay's skirt. She shifted and scooted even closer to FoXXXy...as another couple sat on the couch besides us, to my right. The small, petite chick looked Latino or Asian in the darkness...and was in panties only. Her small chest came along with the prettiest, long nipples, and her guy was flickering his tongue back and forth on 'em as she straddled him, unzipping his pants. She stretched her legs slightly to get a better grip as she reached down to pull his dick out...and now her right foot was on top of Shay's curled-up left leg and next to my right hand.

Shay doesn't move away. Instead, she reaches her left hand down towards mine. I reached out to grab her hand, but she missed me and touched the other chick's foot by mistake. I felt around in the darkness to find Shay's hand squeezing on the chick's foot, and she started tracing my fingers with hers, moaning as FoXXXy reached for her breasts.

My left hand was in between FoXXXy's legs now, and she moved closer to me so I could feel how wet she was. As soon as my hand touched her pussy through her panties, she pulled away from kissing Shay to tongue *me* down...kissing me with sloppy tongue swirls and wetting my face up. Instinctively, I grabbed Shay's hand and the chick's foot next to me, gripping tightly in lust and anxiousness.

I felt FoXXXy helping Shay unbuckle my pants...as we continued to kiss and my finger rubbed on her clit. She had fat pussy lips, but a small hole underneath her slightly trimmed hair. Shay was licking up and down FoXXXy's arm as she helped tug at my jeans. I then lifted up to help Shay pull 'em down, and my underwear dropped to the floor...dick standing straight up as I fell back to the couch.

FoXXXy was the first to start sucking...dropping to my lap with her tongue out, circling it around the head as Shay held it at the base, rubbing my balls. FoXXXy's mouth was cold on my dick, and I jumped slightly.

Did she slip ice in her mouth?

It felt good as fukc, though, and I started to make it jump in her mouth to let her know I'm wit it. Sashé was sitting up now, standing with one leg off the couch, her ass in the air. I pulled her skirt up to start playing with her pussy from behind...and as I looked to my right I noticed the chick next to us was now riding her boyfriend passionately, head on his shoulder as she bounced...watching us.

Now I can see that she's definitely Asian...and when I licked my lips at her, she licked hers back. Then she closed her eyes as her white boyfriend lifted her up and slammed into her. My eyes rolled back as I felt Shay's mouth sucking my shaft sideways...with FoXXXy slurping on my head, her drool running down to Shay's face. Shay was slurping on my shaft with the juices from FoXXXy's wet mouth...and my right leg started to shake, toes curling.

FoXXXy then grabbed my back with her right hand and dug her nails in as she got off the couch, taking more of me in her mouth before she dropped to her knees. She takes my dick out her mouth briefly, and her and Shay share another sloppy kiss as Shay gets off the couch and onto the floor, the two of them rubbing on each other's titties. I started unbuttoning my shirt...breathing hard and breaking a sweat when I felt FoXXXy's hand on my back again...nudging me to stand up.

Planting my right hand in the couch, I start to get my balance, and the Asian chick rubs her toes on my fingers as I stand. She reached out for my hand as I reached for Shay's head, guiding it to my **wooD**. My left hand then finds FoXXXy's head with ease as she starts to suck on my balls from underneath and Shay takes me deep in her throat, gagging. She comes up for air quickly, and FoXXXy starts sucking on me slowly...slobbering everywhere.

I look down and see that Shay is looking up at me....and this makes my dick jump in FoXXXy's mouth. She responds with a long moan, "Hmmmmm...you nasssy."

"Look at y'all, though," I mumbled, my mouth watering.

"Hmmmm....yesssss," Shay murmured. "I'm so wet."

Damn this shit got me so ready to fukc.

As I ripped my shirt away and pulled my wife-beater up to expose my stomach, I bit my lip as my two head doctors started clawing at my stomach. In front of us on the center couches, there's another ménage going on with three chicks, as another black girl had now joined the duo from earlier. The black chick with the huge tits was standing up on the couch with the white girl sucking away, her hands spreading the black chick's legs as she licked upward. Black chick was crouched over as she stood, kissing the other black girl while she fingered the white girl roughly. There was a black guy standing near them, jacking his dick off in the shadows as he watched.

The Asian chick to my right was now on the floor, bent over closer to Sashé as her boyfriend fukced her from the back. She braced herself on Shay's leg...causing Shay to turn and face her momentarily. They immediately recognized each other, and it was safe for me to assume this was *Shima* and her guy *Chris*, next to us fukcing the whole time.

This shit is wild.

Shay and Shima kissed briefly, and then Shay bent back over to suck me off, her ass in Shima's face. Shima doesn't hesitate, spreading Shay's cheeks and running her tongue through...moaning as she tastes Shay's juices from behind while taking dick.

FoXXXy was grabbing my balls now as Shay sucked away, and she was licking Shay's lips as she bobbed up and down. I could see Shay had her hands between FoXXXy's legs...and FoXXXy was grinding against her touch.

"Hmmmmm...fukc, I'm so wet," she moaned and lifted up to start kissing my stomach, reaching up for my chest under my tank top.

"Yeah???" I looked down at my former sexting buddy.

"Hell yeah," FoXXXy replied passionately. "I need some dick."

Sashé started mumbling in between slurps, "Da…Daddy, hmmm cum…on. Fukc her."

Things couldn't be more *'HoLLy'* right now. This was sure to be a classic story, another legendary episode in the chronicles. A tale that was a long time in the making, for both myself and those that I'd live to tell the story to one day.

On this night I made history. A standard was raised yet again – on an already upper echelon of satisfaction. This was the beginning of a new way of life for me…a turn down a road I'd never come back from. For the *beast*, it was a coming out party – an environment where he could finally be himself and take his time doing it. This night was everything coming together…all of the trials and failures along the way had led up to this moment of clarity, this moment of truth. I had learned so much more about myself in the last two years…and what it would truly take for a woman to keep my sex drive in order.

Tonight was about finding sexual freedom – and realizing that lots of normal people have not-so-normal cravings and desires. Tonight, I found a true place to express instead of suppressing that feeling…and with a person that I've grown to love and have deep feelings for. There's no need to sneak around, when I'm with someone who wants what I want. Tonight is the night…that I finally get it.

But tonight wouldn't be one to remember without another classic fukc-up…*right???*

"Damn," I hung my head in letdown. "I ain't bring no condoms in, babe."

Shay had a look of desperation on her face, "You're kidding, right?"

"You can't be serious," FoXXXy chimed in. "Stop playing."

"For real, I…I didn't *know*."

"Baby!!" Shay squealed loudly.

I started stuttering, "I'm saying…how was I…man — I ain't expect – well, I mean…*come on*. Y'all ain't got rubbers at the bar?"

FoXXXy stood up, kissing my chest, "No, everybody just kinda…brings their own."

Shay turned around to Shima, "Does Chris have condoms?? Oh my gosh…babe!"

"We don't use 'em," Shima told her. "Sorry, boo."

"It's cool," I shook my head, feeling defeated. "It's all good."

"I gotta get back to work anyway, y'all," FoXXXy realized. "We'll talk later."

Shay stood up, fixing her skirt, "I can't believe you, babe!"

She started helping FoXXXy straighten up and looked at me with disappointment. She was really let down; I almost felt bad. But it wuttin' really a big deal. I mean, how was I to know they'd be fukcing right in the club? It had never crossed my mind that it would be going down *on-site;* I thought that type of shit happened at the after-set only. But shit…I guess you never know with these crowds – and Shay and I were still learning. The good thing was, we were both far better prepared than we would have been…had we not bumped our heads so much previously in this **ménages** chase. This was gonna be a lovely new year.

"Sweet Shay, baby…it's cool. I know now for next time," I tried to ease her frustration, looking at the bright side. "Relax, we'll be back. And I still owe Carol a dance, anyway. Let's head back downstairs. Where yo shoes at?"

FoXXXy helped me get dressed and made sure we had everything before we headed back down to the club area. Once we got to the table, FoXXXy showed us where the restrooms were on this floor and her and Shay went to freshen up before she went back to work. I was pouring more *Rosé* when Shima and Chris came down from the Playroom and stopped at the table.

"Well, you finally made it out – I see," Chris said to me. "What do you think? Having fun yet?"

"Man," I shook my head, still in a state of shock. "This is crazy up in here!"

Shima stepped closer so she didn't have to yell, "I hear you met the bosses."

"Yeah…I guess we did."

"Keep it up, whatever you did to impress them," Chris advised. "But hey man, good seeing you guys! We're headed downstairs for a while. Have fun!"

"Cool man, we'll be down soon. Right on."

Shay and FoXXXy came out of the ladies' room to the far right together and kissed one last time before the freaky bartender hurried back to work. Her 15-minute break had lasted a half hour too long…and she promised to hit us up later.

When Shay came over to the table, she had this look of fury in her eyes, "Babe! I am so mad at you..."

"Don't be like that. Cum'ere."

"No, don't touch me," she pulled back. "I'm horny...and I just wanna have sex right now!"

"Well, come on!!" I stood up, reaching for my belt.

"No. You owe Carol a dance and I'm dripping wet...ready to fukc. So come on, let's go downstairs. We can dance for a couple of songs...and then you need to take me home and fukc me."

"Damn, babe...you drunk," my jaw dropped. "Listen to you!"

Shay fell into my arms, whining like a baby, "So what!!! I can't believe you!"

"I just didn't know what to expect," I explained myself. "Come on, baby. You know I would've."

"Ok, ok. Next time, bring condoms, Daddy. This is **Ménages**. It goes down up in here."

I nodded my head in agreement, but at the time, even I didn't fully understand the floodgates we had just opened tonight. My journey to ménages had finally come into fruition and was now complete. But the dark path that this lustful journey would ultimately send me down...had only just begun...

FIN.
(Until We Cheat Again)

ABOUT THE AUTHOR

"HoLLyRod" – the author and creator of the highly
controversial and raunchy storyline, *The Art of Cheating* –
is the alter-ego and pseudonym for established writer
Rodney L. Henderson Jr.

Since graduating with a Business Administration degree in
Computer Information Systems from the *University of Central
Missouri*, Henderson has showcased his writing skills in various
forms of art – including radio commercials and music, as well as
poetry and promo spots for fashion companies such as
DymeWear Inc and *Ridikulus Kouture LLC*.

HoLLyRod's short story mini-series titled ***The Art of Cheating
Episodes*** introduces readers to the many characters and mystery
behind **HoLLyWorld** and *The Art of Cheating*, while chronicling
the ups and downs of infidelity through experiences based on
real life. The ongoing series has been re-released in a special
Extended Author's Cut Edition.

AVAILABLE IN eBOOK and PAPERBACK FORMATS!!!
AUDIO BOOKS COMING SOON!!!

Henderson currently resides in his home state of Missouri
and spends most of his time managing and writing for *Angela
Marie Publishing, LLC* – a company named after his late mother.

The Art of Cheating Episodes is published under *Lurodica
Stories*, an erotica division of the publishing company.

*"I just want to continue to be inspired at the notion of
making her proud and keep my promise to share my talents with
the world."*

www.HoLLyRods.com
www.facebook.com/TheArtOfCheating
www.twitter.com/TheCheatGods

Next up on
The Art of Cheating...

SEASON 2 – EPISODE 1:
Cyber Pimpin'

HoLLy seemingly learned his lessons from the **Ménages** journey and cut off ties with any & all remaining distractions. But *Tracy* is one online temptation HoLLy can't seem to break things off with, especially since she's sending gifts & wiring money on the regular. It's *technically* not cheating – after all, they mostly only communicate via texts. But how will he keep this cyber affair from *Sashé*, now that Tracy wants to start meeting in person?

Cyber Pimpin' kicks off another season of **The Art of Cheating Episodes**, full of new characters & twists...digging deeper into TAOC universe with more shocking reveals.

EXTENDED AUTHOR'S CUT EDITION
AVAILABLE SIDE CHICK DAY 2/15/2023

© 2023 Lurodica Stories
by Angela Marie Publishing, LLC

<u>Also by HoLLyRod</u>

The Art of Cheating Episodes
(Extended Author's Cut Edition)

SEASON 1
Episode 1 –Sassy
Episode 2 – Hangover
Episode 3 –HoLLy BeLLigerence
Episode 4 –KeLLy's Revenge
Episode 5 –The HooKup
Episode 6 – Ménages

SEASON 2
(2/15/23)
Episode 1 - Cyber Pimpin'
Episode 2 - Campus Record
Episode 3 – A Date with Karma
Episode 4 – The Wedding Party
Episode 5 – HoLLy & Sug

SEASON 3
(Coming Soon)

Angela Marie Publishing, LLC. All rights reserved.

Angela Marie Publishing
Presents

WDFFIL EP1: Facing the Music

The OFFICIAL Soundtrack to The Art of Cheating Episodes

AVAILABLE ON ALL MUSIC PLATFORMS

DOWNLOAD OR STREAM NOW!!!!

www.angelamariepublishing.com/WDFFIL

Angela Marie Publishing, LLC. All rights reserved.

www.ingramcontent.com/pod-product-compliance
Lightning Source LLC
Chambersburg PA
CBHW070732120726
47910CB00001B/74